Dark Season

JOANNA LOWELL

Crimson Romance
New York London Toronto Sydney New Delhi

CRIMSON
ROMANCE

Crimson Romance
An Imprint of Simon & Schuster, Inc.
1230 Avenue of the Americas
New York, NY 10020

ISBN 978-1-4405-9938-5
ISBN 978-1-4405-9939-2 (ebook)

For Minnie

Chapter One

The room went dark. Chairs creaked and silks rustled as the audience members shifted in their seats. The air was cold, colder than it had been but a moment before. Ella shivered. The woman beside her was twisting her gloved hands.

"That chill … " she murmured. "Do you feel it?"

Ella did feel it, the stroking cold. The hairs on the nape of her neck were rising.

"No more heat from the lamps," she whispered. A dozen wall brackets had been burning when she had paid her admission and made her way to her chair. Of course, she'd focused her attention on the enormous cabinet with the heavy wine-red curtains in the front of the room—how could she not?—but she *had* noted the lights. Bright, warm globes. A cheering sight in an otherwise dingy space. Then the men who'd formed a gauntlet near the entrance, each waving a pamphlet or newsletter—"Are you a member, madam? Sir, would you take a paper? Proves human immortality is a scientific fact, page seven, absolutely free, and one shilling sixpence per quarter will get you a subscription."—had abruptly ceased their proselytizing, fanned their literature out on the table, and turned all the lights off.

Without the flames of gaslights, rooms grew colder. That, at least, was a scientific fact. But could extinguishing the lamps really have produced that sudden icy breeze? Once she allowed the doubt to take shape, the chill seemed to worm its way deeper inside her. She would like to claim it was a draft, the dank wet air of the spring night seeping between the sash and sill of a poorly made window. But the room had no windows. And only one door. The skin on Ella's face seemed to be tightening. Only one door. It was shut now.

A man called out in the darkness. "'Hymn to the Night,'" he said. As he began to sing, a wavering chorus picked up the tune. In the front of the room, between the cabinet and the first row of chairs, a candle flared, and another. Shadows wheeled wildly on the walls and ceiling. Ella craned her neck, trying to peer between shoulders. The woman beside her was breathing shallow, excited breaths. The man on her right bumped her with his elbow as he shifted. He'd dressed his hair with too much oil. The smell was cloying. Ella pressed her spine against the hard back of the chair. She squeezed her knees together. Cold sweat tickled under her arms. Too many people, and all of them far, far too close together. She was hemmed in. How many pairs of legs would she have to climb over to get to either end of the row? A dozen?

She shouldn't have come. But that morning the girls in the boardinghouse had spoken of nothing else. One of them had spread a newspaper on the deal table in the sitting room.

"This won't be a common spirit-rapping," she'd said, pointing at the advertisement. "You've never heard of Miss Seymour? She manifested the Egyptian princess? And levitated Lady Cumberland's baby clear out of her arms?"

Ella had been forced to admit that she'd never heard of Miss Seymour, of Egyptian princesses appearing in cabinets, or of babies floating on ethereal tides of harmonized energy. She'd never heard of Mr. Hawkins, Master of Magnetic Healing, or of Mr. Colville, Professor of the Astral Arts, or of the half dozen other clairvoyants, phrenologists, mediums, and mesmerists the girls mentioned or their affiliated circles, institutions, associations, and schools.

"I should think you'd be interested." The girl with the newspaper had looked at her meaningfully. "Considering … "

Ella had looked down into the black folds of her skirt. The girl had meant, of course, that Ella was in mourning. That she should jump at the chance to speak with the dead.

Surely you don't believe all that? Ella had wanted to ask but didn't. Instead, she'd imagined Miss Seymour rapping out a message from her father.

I'm here to help you, my little one. I'm listening.

She'd tell him what had happened.

Papa, I ran away from cousin Alfred. You were wrong to trust him. He was going to have me locked up. I ran away to London, but I've no work and no references, and I don't know what to do. Papa, tell me. Tell me what to do.

And then Miss Seymour would rap out his answer. If only it worked like that. She'd had to leave the sitting room before the girls could see the tears in her eyes.

Spirit-rapping—it was nonsense. She knew that. But here she was, at a séance, surrounded by the credulous, or were some in the audience merely curious? Which was she?

The figures with the candles stopped moving on either side of the cabinet, the flames held up to their faces. They were young girls, their white foreheads illuminated, shadows making pits of their eyes. Another light bloomed, this one between the cabinet's curtains, and the singing dwindled, died on a long, low note, as the curtains parted. A woman stepped out from between them. She was tall, slender, her silhouette natural. No crinoline. No flounces. Her mass of unbound hair glinted in the candlelight. The profound hush that greeted her appearance was the hush of the tomb. She stood like a living statue, frozen in time before the onlookers, head tipped back, the arm with candle upraised. Suddenly, she howled, staggered. She swung her arm so wildly that the candle went out.

Ella realized she was leaning forward; the entire audience was leaning forward, straining to follow the moves of Miss Seymour's strange dance. It was as though Miss Seymour waged a battle with an invisible beast in the air, batting it away as it lashed back at her, twirled her so her body moved without her volition, limbs describing sharp angles. The only sounds in the room were sounds of the struggle: Miss Seymour's feet sliding and banging on the floor, her guttural breathing. Just as suddenly as it had begun, the battle was over. Again, silence reigned. Again, Miss Seymour stood motionless. More figures with candles were appearing beside her, filing out from within the cabinet—or from behind it—Ella couldn't be sure.

"A spirit is with us." Miss Seymour's voice was low as a man's, deep and husky. Somehow it carried to every corner of the room.

"She is unquiet, poor soul," said Miss Seymour. She looked up, jerking her head from side to side. Watching something only she could see.

"She is afraid to come nearer," said Miss Seymour. "She is one with the shadows. She is flickering around us." The candle-bearers thrust up their candles, and again, flames twisted. Shadows danced. Tiny specks of light gathered at the corners of Ella's vision. She shook her head to clear them. Her mouth felt dry, her tongue thick. Fragrant smoke drifted through the crowd, sickly sweet. What was burning? Who was burning it?

"We greet you with perfect love." Miss Seymour's voice rose to a shout. "Be not afraid!" Then she pitched forward and spoke in hoarse, rapid tones, addressing the crowd: "She wants to join us. She has something to tell us. Someone in this room knows her name. Call it out. Call her name. She will come if you call. Summon her from the shadows. They frighten her. She died so young. I can almost see her … black hair, black eyes … or is it the shadow that makes them so?"

A moan came from the crowd, and a woman stood. She'd been sitting in the first row, and Miss Seymour was at her side in an instant.

"Phillipa?" The woman leaned against Miss Seymour. "Phillipa? Is it you?"

"Yes," said Miss Seymour. "Yes. Phillipa. Call to her."

"Phillipa!" The woman's voice was so broken, so filled with longing that tears pricked Ella's eyes.

This is wrong, she thought dazedly. *This is wrong, ghoulish, and cruel.* Credulity fled. Curiosity fled. She felt emptied. Sickened by the spectacle, by every part of it. She had been sold a ticket to witness another woman's grief. As though it were merely an evening's entertainment.

The tiny specks of light were floating now, floating across her field of vision.

"Phillipa." The woman was chanting it. "Phillipa, Phillipa." And Miss Seymour chanted along with her.

The smoke had grown thicker. Ella clenched her teeth and gagged. The specks of light multiplied. Her body was shuddering. She could no longer deny what was happening. She went rigid, trying to lock her limbs, to hold herself still, to fight back, but she couldn't. She never could. She was going to lose control, have one of her fits. She was going to convulse in front of all these people, knock over chairs, kick, and froth. *Oh God, no.* She shut her eyes, but the lights were still there. Lacework. Snowflakes. Broken glass. Jagged teeth beneath her eyelids. *Oh God, oh God.* The pain had started. Those teeth were burrowing into her eyes. Rats scrabbled in her sockets, wiggled into her brain. Yellow teeth. Red claws. Hot, blinding flashes. *Oh God, no, not now, not this, no, no, no, no.* She wanted to scream, but her face was gone. Her body was gone. There was only the hard, hot pain in the center of her being, and the violent light shooting out in all directions. Voices wavered in and out all around her.

"Phillipa, come nearer! Speak, Phillipa!"

She wanted to block her ears, but she had no arms, no hands. Her head rang with Miss Seymour's voice, rang like a bell. The pitch was changing, rising higher and higher. The bell was cracking. Her head, splitting open. Miss Seymour's words bursting her skull.

"Come, sweet girl. Come as substance from the shadow. Come, Phillipa. *And I will bring thee where no shadow stays.*"

Then Ella heard nothing. Saw nothing. Felt nothing.

Chapter Two

Isidore Blackwood lurched through the hallway and out the back door of the public house. Even a sober man would find himself lurching in that building, a heap of sagging, worm-eaten boards, every floor atilt, and every wall off plumb.

But it would be a strange place indeed, Isidore thought, for a sober man to find himself. Sober, he certainly wasn't. The gin burned in his stomach. His eyes felt hot. He did not want the night air to clear his head and had no reason to imagine he ran any risk—the public house was beside the river and the air surrounding it particularly foul—but an eyeful of cold mist would be just the thing.

He stood blinking up at the light rain. Inhaled deeply. Thick, clammy night. London's vile brew. A large sewer flowed nearby. The wind cut the fecal stench with the more caustic aroma belched from the leatherworks and dye works downriver. He took a step forward, stumbled over a broken paving stone, but caught himself before he slid down the steep bank. His muscles tightened, his whole body surging with that primitive imperative. *Stay alive.* He scrambled back up to the level of the street. Then he threw back his head and laughed. How fitting if he died on this night. Stumbled again, pitched headfirst into the river, and drowned. Of course, he couldn't guarantee that anyone would remark the significance of the date. His body might not be found for weeks. Bloated and battered, pushed to shore by some unhappy sculler's oar. That would detract from the romance of it.

Christ, but his mood was black.

The rain came down more heavily. He'd lost his hat somewhere in the course of the evening, and his hair hung wet on his forehead. He walked slowly away from the river, turning down one narrow street then another. It was late, and he passed almost no one. Even the thieves had gone home to warm their clever fingers by the fire. A few cabs rattled by, splashing his boots. He could be riding in a town coach with his coat of arms on the door. Instead, he was soaked and exposed, teeth beginning to chatter, on the kind of night that kept the rats in their holes and the drunks in the taprooms and the beggars under bridges. The thought cheered him.

Hang his title and his dynastic responsibilities. He'd rather be a Smith or a Baker than a Blackwood. He'd trade his coronet for a song. He'd told his father as much during their last interview. He'd wanted to see the old man's face grow livid, his wasted hands whiten around the gold-knobbed cane.

Now his father was stiff and cold in the churchyard, and Isidore carried that image with him—Lord Blackwood twitching with impotent fury as his heir spat upon the family name and spoke casually of dividing the ancestral lands, selling the parcels cheap to merchants or farmers or, hell, making a gift of them to Irish laborers, why not. He wasn't sorry, but the memory sickened him.

He wasn't drunk enough. He wasn't nearly drunk enough.

Another cab approached at a walk, and he hailed it. Muttered the address of his club in Belgravia. But when he climbed down again, he wasn't surprised at where he stood. Not in front of his club. He'd given the wrong address. The rattling bones he carried in his head—*her* bones—had spoken for him.

He was in front of the St. Aubyn house. Clement's house. Lovely and imposing. A massive portico projected from its stone façade. Invisible from the street, on the backside of the house, the second-floor balcony overlooked a marble courtyard. Five years of rainstorms had washed that marble, but it would never be clean.

He wanted to drop to his knees and howl. He had done so then, in that courtyard, five years ago tonight. He had rocked beside her, the cold of the marble seeping through the thin cloth of his trousers. He had lifted her head, straightened her neck.

He had smoothed her hair, which was wet with her blood, so much blood that his hands came away black in the moonlight. When he gathered her into his arms, her weight was awful in its indifference. It wasn't her in his arms. It wasn't Phillipa. It was just weight. Dead weight.

In front of the St. Aubyn house, he didn't kneel, or howl. He stared at the light that glowed in the arched library window. Before he could think better of it, he had climbed the stairs and was pounding on the door.

Jenkins, bald as an egg and as expressionless, opened in an instant. He might have been standing behind the door. As though it weren't near to midnight. As though he had been waiting for Isidore to arrive.

Isidore fought the urge to shake the water from his body like a dog. His ride in the cab had chilled him.

"A towel, Lord Blackwood?" Jenkins signaled to a maid who had crept into the hallway to investigate the commotion. She gaped, showing all the surprise at Isidore's disheveled appearance that Jenkins did not, but turned smartly through a doorway at Jenkins's signal.

"I will see if Lord St. Aubyn is able to receive you," said Jenkins.

"He's awake," said Isidore hoarsely.

"Yes, my lord," said Jenkins.

"He'll receive me." Isidore watched Jenkins's thin, straight figure drift away down the hall, the dim light of his tallow candle winking. He wondered for a moment if Clement *would* receive him. They'd been like brothers once, but that was before. Since he'd arrived back in London a month ago, too late for his father's funeral, he and Clement had barely exchanged words, just a few courtesies occasioned by the chance encounter. It was what remained of their friendship.

He shouldn't have come. He was turning to let himself out when the soft "My lord?" arrested him. The young maid, holding out a towel. He took it, nodding as she gave a brief curtsy, and rubbed it roughly over his hair and face. Jenkins's candle was floating back toward him.

"Follow me, my lord," said Jenkins, as though Isidore had not been in the house a hundred, a thousand times before. They ascended the carpeted stairs and passed the library—door slightly open, light spilling through the crack—and then Isidore was being shown into Clement's study. Clement was standing in the middle of the room in black trousers and shirtsleeves.

"Christ, Sid," he said. "You look like a water rat."

Isidore responded with a shrug. He stepped closer to the fireplace as Clement moved over to the desk to pour him a glass of brandy. He squatted and slid the wrought-iron fire screen to the side. He thrust his hands over the logs glowing red in the grate, as near as he could bear to the writhing flames.

"Here." Clement stood over him with the glass. As Isidore rose to take it, Clement's nostrils flared. His eyebrows shot up. "You smell like a gin palace."

Isidore tossed back the glass, emptying it. He handed it back to Clement. Clement didn't smell like roses himself. He smelled astringent. Isidore dropped into a chair.

"I feel like Ozymandias," he said.

Clement poured him another brandy and refilled his own glass. He sat in the chair adjacent to Isidore's, smiling quizzically. "How the mighty have fallen," he said.

Isidore leaned back in the chair, resting the glass on his shirtfront. He dipped his chin and tried to look into the fire through the brandy. It blazed ochre, like desert sand.

"The 'trunkless legs,'" he said. "I feel rather as though my head has tumbled from my body."

Silence. The fire popped. Isidore sighed. Drained the brandy and set the empty glass on the floor. He wouldn't have had to explain himself to Clement five years ago.

"I didn't mean to come here."

"You shouldn't have." Clement stood and stirred the fire. A violent movement. He turned to face Isidore, back lit, the firelight touching his hair with gold.

Black and white knights. That's what Phillipa used to call them. Isidore was so dark, and Clement was so fair. Women tended to prefer Clement. Isidore didn't blame them. Probably better to throw one's lot in with the white knight. Less likely to end up dead.

"I thought you might have left already," Clement said. "Daphne said you'd been engaged to dine with her and Bennington but never showed up. We all imagined … " He broke off to give the fire another vicious poke. "Frankly, I didn't think you'd stay in town this long." There was an implied question that Isidore chose to ignore. He shifted in the chair. His wet clothing had begun to itch. He realized he'd forgotten to scrape his boots outside the front door. He must have tracked mud all through the house.

There was a roll of thunder in the distance.

"It was so much warmer that night," he said, rising to pour himself another drink. "There wasn't a cloud in the sky."

Warm, clear, bright with moonlight. A beautiful night. Everyone was flushed with drinking, dancing. He'd gone over it so many times, every detail, trying to identify the exact moment when all of the possible outcomes of the evening converged on the one. He didn't believe in fate. Phillipa Trombly hadn't been born to die at twenty years old at a party at Clement St. Aubyn's. When had it occurred, the moment? Before their quarrel? During? Or was it not until the very moment she started to fall that it was finally too late?

His mouth had gone dry. He drank, poured again, and set the decanter on Clement's desk between ledgers and an ink-stained blotter. Why was Clement awake? He'd imagined him brooding, remembering, but maybe the date, what it meant, had slipped from his mind. Maybe he was simply up late, tending to business.

The idea that Clement had forgotten made him want to knock the ledgers to the floor. He turned, gripping the edge of the desk with his free hand. It restrained his arm from sweeping the desktop clean. It also helped him keep his feet.

"If it had been raining, like tonight," he said, "the balcony doors would have been closed. She wouldn't have run out there." He forced himself to sip the brandy and glanced at Clement. "What can you count on in London if you can't count on the rain?" He laughed harshly and tipped back the glass. The brandy didn't even burn his throat. He was beyond burning.

"You're torturing yourself," said Clement. "What does it serve?"

"*Whom* does it serve? Maybe that's the question."

"Is it?" Clement shook his head. His eyes, green, were invisible, dark hollows in their stead. "Whom, Sid? Phillipa? You? Me?"

At the sound of that name—*her* name—Isidore flinched. Then he shrugged.

"I don't know." He laughed again, a strangled sound. "The devil, most likely."

Clement swore, tossing back the last of his brandy.

"It was ghastly for all of us," he said. "I thought of selling this place. I didn't think I could stand to live here … after."

"But you did," said Isidore. "You do." It sounded bitter. But why? He couldn't have expected Clement to close up his house. Clement had become the head of the St. Aubyn family young, as a boy at Eton, when his parents had died in a carriage accident in Scotland. Clement had always felt the weight of his responsibilities. Was he to have moved his sisters into a hotel for the season? Made of the St. Aubyn house yet another crypt, another shrine to Phillipa's memory?

He was finally drunk. He was losing control. He couldn't channel his anger. His anger was spilling over.

Clement picked up the poker then threw it down. The thud was muffled by the carpet. Isidore wanted to cover his ears. His grip on reality, on sanity, was slipping. Five years ago, had anyone heard it? The scream? The thud? The band had been playing. Couples were dancing in the ballroom. They'd quarreled, and then, or before, or after, the moment had occurred. He was trying to chase after Phillipa, but he was as drunk then as he was now. Drunker. Angrier. In the hall, he'd stumbled across a plump young man, too young for the depravity of that late-night revelry; he was lying in his own vomit. Isidore had nearly fallen in the mess, staggered, then dropped to his knees. The weight of his sagging head tipped him over, and he'd stretched out on his stomach, pressing his flushed cheek to the cool oilcloth that lined the floor along the wall. Maybe it came then, the moment that turned into *too late*. When he was belly-down on the floor.

Clement was speaking, and he sounded angry too. Isidore realized he preferred this to restraint, to the wall that had grown up between them.

"I couldn't pack up and run away to Italy, to Egypt." Clement bit off the words. "I had sisters to bring out. The barony to run. I couldn't indulge my grief or make grand, futile gestures or throw away my life. Too many other people depend on me."

"Clem—" Isidore began, stepping toward him. Clement had balled his hands into fists, and Isidore realized that his hands too were in fists. His hands were in fists, but his fury had fled. What was he going to do? Beat Clement senseless? Hope that Clement beat him senseless? They'd never fought in earnest, only scrapped in fun. Isidore had always been a hairsbreadth quicker to evade and deal blows. He'd had more practice. This was madness. The horror he was reliving was making him mad. He had to stop it.

"I don't blame you," he said, relaxing his stance. "You're right. It would have been ludicrous … " He waved his hand vaguely. "To shut up the house. Futile, like you said. I'm not thinking clearly tonight." He wanted to ask Clement why, why he'd pulled back from their friendship five years ago, why they didn't talk anymore in that easy way that bespoke understanding and acceptance, but if he started, he knew he'd turn maudlin.

I needed you, Clem. You closed yourself off to me when I needed you. His mouth quirked, but it was nothing like a smile. He wasn't one for admitting need.

Maybe Clement felt guilty it had happened at his house. Maybe he had other reasons to feel guilty. A dark thought, one that Isidore refused to pursue. He had long ago tried to give up assigning blame. He'd taken it all on himself.

"It's not your fault," he said. He half expected Clement to say it back to him—*It's not your fault either, Sid.* Wasn't that what people did? Mouthed platitudes? Salved the conscience of whatever wretch stood in front of them?

But Clement didn't say it.

Isidore leaned back over the desk and picked up the decanter. The stopper fell from his nerveless fingers. He put the heavy crystal lip to his mouth and drank. He shut his eyes, felt the brandy running through him.

"Oh, hell." The muffled expletive sounded close to his ear. Clement had grabbed the decanter from his hands. He swayed. Clement braced him with an arm then pushed him into a chair. Isidore let his head drop then dragged it up again in time to watch Clement stowing the brandy decanter on a high shelf next to his collection of figurines. Terracotta horses. A gift from Malvina, the sister closest to him in age. It amused him—Clement putting the brandy on that shelf as though Isidore was a child who wouldn't be able to reach. As though he weren't a man who stood over six feet in height.

Well, maybe he was behaving more like a child than a man. And maybe he couldn't reach it. His vision was swimming. The pools of light and dark in the study were flattening out into a checkerboard pattern.

White knight. Black knight.

I'm going to pass out. The idea was not unwelcome.

"Will you go to Castle Blackwood?"

Isidore came back into his body with a start.

"What?" he muttered. Clement was one of the few people who knew something of why he might not want to return to Castle Blackwood. Even as a boy, he'd been observant. Isidore could never keep his face from tightening when he talked about his father. Nor could he hide every burn, bruise, cut, and scar. But Clement, whatever he suspected about Isidore's childhood, also believed in duty, in discharging one's responsibility to kith and kin no matter what. He really was a white knight. A staunch defender of the Protestant succession. The perfect scion. Isidore couldn't answer. Couldn't imagine getting out of the chair, let alone taking up his father's mantle at Castle Blackwood. He would worry about all of that ... tomorrow. Or the day after.

"I know you loved her."

Isidore tried to sneer, but his face had gone numb. His eyes didn't feel hot anymore but cold. Vitreous.

Clement had turned to lean over the fire, bracing himself with both hands on the mantle.

You don't know. You don't know anything about it.

Clement held that posture, contemplative or despairing, Isidore couldn't guess. Clement had become a mystery to him. There were so many things they didn't know about each other anymore. It occurred to Isidore that he didn't want to let this state of affairs continue. That maybe he could change it. He opened his mouth.

"Have you been painting?" The question surprised him as much as Clement. It came from that other life they'd shared, their life before. Dull days of summer parties in the country. Long, peaceful days. He, sketching the beauties by some babbling brook. Clement, with his easel and that high, eager step, trampling the heather.

"From time to time," said Clement slowly, straightening. "Actually, I've been working on a series."

"Watercolor?" Five years ago, Clement had been making small studies of kitchen gardens. Herbs. Flowers. Vegetables. Very controlled. Very precise. He had the eye, and the inclinations, of a taxonomer.

"Oils."

"Ah." Isidore couldn't get out more than a syllable, but things had clicked into place. That sharp scent. Turpentine. Clement must have spent the evening painting in the library. That's where he'd set up his easel years ago, in front of the tall, south-facing window. The room received excellent light. But not at night. Clement seemed to anticipate his thoughts.

"I hardly need to see to work on these canvases," he said. "I'm not painting from life. Not waking life anyway."

"Dreams." Isidore's clothing was still damp, but the fire had finally managed to warm his extremities. He felt a languor stealing over him. It was dark in the room, and it took him a moment to realize his eyes had drifted shut. He heard Clement sit down beside him.

"Nightmares." Clement's voice was low. "It's a kind of bestiary. No one's seen them of course."

"No," said Isidore, eyes still closed. "Of course not." Who would Clement show them to? He had always been Clement's audience. And Clement, his.

"And you?" asked Clement.

"I gave it up." Isidore stood abruptly but had to sit down again. *Damn.*

"You're not going to get to that brandy."

"I might." Isidore waited for his stomach to settle. "If I keep trying."

Clement chuckled. There was real mirth in it. Warmth. Friendship. All at once, the tension dissipated. The night seemed like it might wind down, it might end. And there'd be a new day.

"I took up woodworking," said Isidore after a moment. "How's that for an aristocratic pastime? I learned from a Neapolitan hunchback who slept in the same room as his donkey."

"And where did you sleep?" Isidore could hear the smile in Clement's voice.

"On the other side of the donkey." He stood and this time kept his feet. "I preferred it to any night I ever spent under my father's roof."

"It's not his roof anymore."

Isidore ignored this. He reached and took the bottle down from the shelf.

"Sid … " A warning note.

Isidore sank to his knees in front of Clement's chair.

"One toast," he whispered. "To Phillipa. Then I'll go." He lifted the decanter, swallowed, and passed the bottle to Clement.

Clement considered the bottle. "I've said goodbye to Phillipa," he said at last. "I won't toast her. I'll drink to the future." He drank and stood. Isidore squinted up at him, no longer caring that he must seem ridiculous.

"You're staying here, Sid," said Clement. "We'll get you into a spare bedchamber. You need dry clothes and a night's sleep."

"If it's all the same to you," Isidore murmured, stretching out on the carpet, "I'll sleep on the floor."

"Fine." Clement stepped over him and returned the brandy to the desk. "Five years," he said quietly, as though to himself.

Isidore opened his mouth, but this time no sound came out. The carpet was thin, but he felt that he was sinking into it. He was relieved. It was that or slide off the face of the earth.

I was meant to sleep here, he thought. In this house, the house where it happened. If I'm going to sink down into hell, let it happen tonight. Let the floor open.

"Shall I have Jenkins bring you dry clothes?"

Isidore managed to turn his head from side to side. He was done speaking. Just like that, his words for the night had run out.

"How about a donkey then?" Luckily Clement didn't expect an answer. He was already leaving, shutting the study door behind him with a soft click. Isidore listened to Clement's muffled footsteps fade down the hall. He rolled onto his side and let the fire warm his back. He would sleep alone with his sins. If he woke up in a pit of fire, so be it. The waiting at least would be over.

And if he didn't? If he woke and there was no pit of fire? Could he stop running? Stay in England. Attend to his estate. Rekindle old friendships. Say goodbye, as Clement had. After five years, say goodbye to Phillipa. Let her rest. Let himself live. Start again. He had no words left, but he felt his lips make the shape. *Goodbye.*

And suddenly the darkness in the room didn't press down as heavily, and he slept.

Chapter Three

Ella didn't dare open her eyes. The lids pulsed unpleasantly. The pain in her head had subsided to a dull ache. Her limbs felt heavy. She tried to move them, and they resisted. It was a coverlet, she realized. A heavy blanket weighing her down. The softness of the featherbed swallowing her up. She was in her bedroom. Papa's hand was smoothing her hair from her forehead. The dear rumble of his voice comforted her.

"Rest, my darling. The worst has passed. You're safe."

Until the next time.

She gathered her strength to force her swollen lips into a smile. She would never express her bitterness, her despair. Not to Papa. Papa always believed she was getting better.

"This was the last one," he would say. "The very last." She loved him for it, his stubborn, groundless optimism, even when it made her want to scream.

"I'm sorry." She pushed the air through her swollen lips. *I'm sorry, Papa. It happened again.*

She listened for his deep, assuring answer—*Sleep, little one. Sleep. We can do anything in dreams*—and felt the hand on her forehead turn over. Knuckles pressed her damp skin.

"You've haven't got a fever. Can you sit up? Are you thirsty?"

It was a woman speaking, not Papa. Never again Papa. Papa was dead.

Where was she? Memory came flooding back. Cousin Alfred calling her into Papa's study. But it wasn't Papa's study anymore. It was Alfred's study. He'd already taken down Papa's maps and mounted his loathsome hunting trophies on the walls.

"This can't come as a surprise. You must have known you couldn't stay here. I wrote to the head doctor of a colony in Zurich.

21

I had his response today. The regimen is almost shockingly liberal. It includes concerts and dancing. Sunday walks in the village. The air is very good. You'll be happy, he assures me. It's a happy place." Alfred shoved the letter across Papa's desk. She stared at it, and at his pudgy hands. Unimaginable, that a man such as he had brought down those proud, swift stags whose heads reared from their wooden plaques. What would he be without his guns? Without her papa's estate? What if he had to fight a stag to the death with just those fat fists against antlers and hooves? What if he had to use those hands to earn his own fortune?

He didn't like the way she was looking at him. She could see it in his face. He was nervous. She made him uncomfortable. It was not good of her to enjoy it. But she did not drop her eyes. He kept his face a polite mask only a moment longer. He held the letter out to her, and when she didn't take it, his lips turned down into the nasty sneer she remembered from her childhood.

"Or I could put you in an asylum," he said, throwing the letter carelessly over his shoulder. "It's more than within my rights. For your own sake, of course, Ella. You're a danger to yourself. Do you know a bad bite to the tongue can be fatal? The lingual artery runs through it. If you sever it, your life can pour out of your mouth." He clacked his teeth together then smiled with closed lips.

She refused to show any emotion. It was easier than she would have imagined. Her heart was in the coffin with Papa. This man couldn't hurt her. He'd always hated her, hated her because he feared her. Even that knowledge didn't hurt her anymore. So what if people feared her? There was nothing she could do. She couldn't cure her brain. Mr. Norton had explained it to her. Her "anatomical abnormalities," as he'd called them. Damaged brain. Epilepsy. And now—this last was her own diagnosis—a dead heart. Let her cousin do his worst. She was ready.

"I could also have you put in jail," he said. "You're a danger to yourself, but you're also a danger to others. I'm soon to bring a wife into this house. I need to think of my offspring, Ella. I've spoken with Mr. Norton about your condition. Fits are the least of it. In advanced stages, the afflicted experience periods of delirium. Mania. A fury comes upon them. They commit unspeakable acts. Physical violence. Even murder."

This was too much. "So you'll put me in prison for the murder of your unborn children?" The sound she made wasn't a laugh. It was the result of a joyless spasm of her diaphragm. "Have you found legal precedent for such an act?"

He considered a cufflink. It looked familiar. Were the letters *GA* engraved in its gold? Had he removed it from Papa's sleeve before the coffin lid closed? He sighed. "I would explain to the authorities that you'd attacked me. Mr. Norton would testify to the possibility. But I would prefer to send you on your happy way to Zurich. I don't want any scandal."

"I am sure you do not," she said. "Have you told your betrothed that your nearest living relation suffers from a hereditary disorder? Is she a gambling woman?"

"I haven't," he said, shortly. "But we both know your late mother was the carrier. The Arlington family tree is well pruned and has always produced flawless fruits. No murderesses. No imbeciles. Not even a clubbed foot. It's enough to make me wonder if your mother was entirely … devoted … to her husband."

A slap in the face would have been worse. Rage choked her. She rose from her chair. She wanted to throw something at him, but the books, the lamp, the letter opener, the sealing wax, they were all Papa's things. Even Papa's pot of ink would be sullied if it touched him.

"So you'll go to Zurich?" he said, rising. "I've hired Mr. Norton, and a nurse and a lady's maid, to escort you. It's for the best, Ella." He tried to gentle his voice. "I do want the best for you. I wish you hadn't been born into this family. And I wish your father hadn't brought you up with false expectations. But I do wish you well."

The mention of Papa had undone her. The heart she'd thought dead in her breast throbbed within her.

The morning light was streaming through the study window, lighting up the blond whiskers that curled away from his cheeks. With the whiskers, his round face seemed a foot wide. "Arlington Manor will blossom without you. You cast a pall on your father's life, and I won't let you cast one on mine. God knows it's not your fault you were born as you are." He rounded the desk and came near her. She did not flinch away. He walked softly—the hunter in him—and she realized he was approaching to deliver the deathblow. "But you are tainted. And you will not remain under this roof. Which, lest you forget, is my roof."

As if she could forget. As if she would ever forget.

But that wasn't the right memory. Something was missing—Days? Weeks?—between Papa's study and this bed where she found herself. What had happened? She squeezed her eyes shut, tried desperately to summon an image. Oh, yes. She'd ridden for the first time on the train. The landscape had rushed by. Green flashes, then gray and more gray.

Let me not have a fit. That's what she'd prayed the whole journey. For the past several years, they'd been coming less frequently. But if she had a fit on the train and the nurse and Mr. Norton attended her, undressed her, all would be lost. They would find the velvet pouch she'd sewn in her skirts, the pouch that contained a chatelaine watch, a gold necklace, a gold bracelet, two jeweled hair clips, two small silver spoons, a silver thimble, a pearl necklace and earrings, and a ring set with a tiny blue sapphire. Everything of value she'd had the good sense to hide before Alfred confiscated her possessions. *His* possessions, he'd called them. She needed them. They were all the security she had in the world.

As the train approached London, her courage almost failed her. It was a mad idea, running. She would be lost and alone. She would have to sell her last remaining tokens of home for room and board, and even her cache of treasures wouldn't last long. She would convulse on the mud of an alley, and rats would lick her cold bones. But it would be better than life as a prisoner in another country. It would be better than life in an asylum. In London, she could mingle with families, even if she couldn't have one of her own. She would survive until Mr. Norton's predictions came to pass and her disease progressed to the point where she felt herself going mad. Then she would throw herself into the Thames. She refused to be locked up, studied as she beat her heels on the floor and chewed through her cheeks, forced to live when she had decided she should die.

It was sin to destroy oneself. But not to let the river swallow what God had already destroyed.

She thrashed her head on the pillow. The knuckles pressed against her forehead again, succeeded by a cool washcloth.

"Be still, miss. Be easy. You're safe now." The woman's voice was kind. "Easy. Easy."

And with something like ease, Ella slipped into the shadows.

When next she woke, it was morning. She could smell the faint odor of freshly baked bread. Birds were making a small racket. She opened her eyes. She had a blurred impression of blue and gold, which, blinking, she resolved into flocked wallpaper with a bright floral motif. She was in a well-appointed bedchamber. A wardrobe stood against one wall. A tidy fire glowed in the fireplace. An empty writing desk was positioned near the window. And in the blue damask chair a young maid, round and neat, was watching her closely.

"You're awake?" The maid sounded uncertain. "Shall I fetch your breakfast? And send word to Mrs. Trombly?"

Ella nodded, unwilling to trust her voice. The maid was not inclined to linger. She almost leapt from the chair in her haste to leave the room.

I'm awake, Ella thought, *so don't fear, little rabbit, the monster is sleeping.* She couldn't blame the maid. Not really. She must have looked frightening enough last night, contorting or, at best, rigid on the bed. "Biting and knocking"—she'd once heard her episodes so described, by maids talking in the hall. Biting and knocking. Horrible. It was a small mercy that she couldn't see her own face when the seizures struck. Alfred had seen it. She'd had an attack one summer in the rose garden during his visit. She fell on the path right at his feet.

You didn't even look human. You looked like a beast.

She ran a finger over her teeth. Mercifully, they were all there, unchipped and firmly lodged in her gums. She touched the back of her head. The birds singing outside the window could find far worse lodgings than her hair. It had been burred into impossible knots, nests upon nests of snarls. She rolled her wrists and her ankles, articulating the joints. Every muscle in her body felt strained.

The maid was back with the tray. Tea and biscuits and hot slices of ham. The smell made Ella's mouth water, but she knew she had to eat sparingly. Even her organs felt tender. Ella pushed herself up, arranging the pillows behind her. She was dressed in bedclothes, she noticed. Bedclothes not her own. It was hardly worth blushing about, considering.

"Mrs. Trombly will be up to see you when you've finished," said the maid as she set the tray across Ella's lap. She hesitated by the bed. Her light eyebrows were knit and her lips pursed. Clearly, she wanted to mine Ella for information, some tidbit she could bring downstairs to share with the rest of the servants. The house must be in an uproar. It couldn't be every night that a young woman out of her senses was carried through the front door. Well, Ella wouldn't oblige her. She had nothing to add. She spread butter on a biscuit and took a cautious bite.

"It's heavenly, thank you," she said. Her throat was raw, but her voice was strong. The maid opened her mouth then shut it again, turned swiftly, and bounded into the hall. Like a jackrabbit, she was. A lively thing. The picture of health.

What must she think of me?

Ella ate slowly, washing down each mouthful with tea. She tried to focus on chewing. But she couldn't keep herself from casting back, struggling to recall the events that had led up to her waking in this house. Every time, she reached a yawning black gulf that frightened her.

Breathe, she told herself. *Stay calm.*

She would get them back—these missing moments—she always did. When the maid returned to take her tray, she was staring at the wall. Squares of brighter blue and gold alternated with faded strips. Traces of the pictures that had been removed.

"Are you finished, miss?" asked the maid, dubiously. Ella had managed only two biscuits. The ham lay untouched.

Ella nodded. Then she said, "Yes, thank you."

Emboldened, the maid rose onto her toes. "And are you quite all right, miss?"

"Quite all right," echoed Ella, an answer she could see afforded little satisfaction. The maid, taking up the tray and preparing to bounce off again, nearly crashed into the woman entering the room.

"I'm sorry, Mrs. Trombly," she gasped, bobbing her head, and more precariously, the tray, before launching herself through the doorway.

"Not at all," murmured Mrs. Trombly, smiling at Ella. She was a short woman, with graying chestnut hair swept away from a narrow face rendered lovely by large, wide-spaced hazel eyes. She came forward and sat lightly on the blue damask chair. Ella smiled too. She resisted the urge to play with the edges of the coverlet and met Mrs. Trombly's eyes.

"How do you feel?" asked Mrs. Trombly. She had a pleasant, cultured voice with a timbre that struck Ella as somehow familiar. She didn't wait for Ella to answer. This haste, and a certain breathlessness, betrayed her embarrassment. "I am Mrs.

Louisa Trombly," she said. "I want to welcome you into my house. I understand this introduction is most irregular. I took an unpardonable liberty bringing you here, but I hope you can pardon it. Your collapse was shocking. No one knew what to do. No one but Miss Seymour."

Ella dropped her gaze. The dizziness had returned. Her gorge was rising. Miss Seymour. The flickering lights, the cloying scent of the smoke, the shrill voices. Ella swallowed hard. The gulf into which her last hours, last days, had disappeared was filling in with sights and sounds. She rather wished it wouldn't.

She had convulsed in front of dozens of people. An audience had watched her writhe on the ground. Her blood ran cold as her thoughts took an even more dire turn. Surely Mrs. Trombly wasn't the sort of woman who would want to inquire into her identity? She was clearly a gently bred lady, a lady of the *ton*. She might very well move in the same circles as her cousin. But few people in London even knew of her existence, and Alfred would hardly have advertised the disappearance of a blight he wouldn't otherwise have had to mention: the one wormy apple shaken down from the Arlington tree. He probably counted her flight as a blessing. Unless he suspected she would resurface on her own, flaunting herself to damage his reputation. God knows it had occurred to her.

No, even if he were looking for her, he would be doing it discreetly. But perhaps Mrs. Trombly was a philanthropist, a woman who relieved herself of excess conscience and income by adopting causes. Had she been waiting for just such an opportunity, a madwoman delivered into her charge that she could use to furnish some brand new hospital for degraded females? Was it for that she'd been brought here?

Delusions. Wild, unfounded fears. Ella was too ready to see locks and keys at every turn. She should speak. She pried her eyes away from her fingers—they were plucking, she realized disgustedly, at the coverlet—and looked again at Mrs. Trombly. The woman's lips were parted. High spots of color flamed on her cheeks. There was something she was burning to say, Ella was certain. And she was also certain that she didn't want to hear it.

"I thank you, Mrs. Trombly," she said. "You shouldn't have put yourself through any trouble on my account. I feel much better."

"I didn't call for the doctor." Mrs. Trombly studied her with concern. "Miss Seymour said sleep was what you needed. There are some salves on the bedside table. For your lips, and whatever bruising … I can call a doctor now, if you wish."

"No!" Ella tried to soften this exclamation. "That won't be necessary. I feel immensely refreshed and won't impose on your household any longer. If the maid would help me dress … "

Return my gown, that is, she added silently. *With my whole fortune swaddled in its pleats.*

"I don't know how to address you," said Mrs. Trombly.

"Reed," said Ella, the name springing from nowhere. "Eleanor Reed. I'm lodging in Bloomsbury Square."

"You're lodging in Bloomsbury Square," repeated Mrs. Trombly. The faint question in her voice seemed to indicate not that she doubted this was Ella's situation but that she rather doubted it ought to be.

"I've only come recently to town," said Ella. "I'm seeking a position. As a governess or schoolteacher." She expected to see horror on Mrs. Trombly's face. *A governess or schoolteacher with fits? Who rolls on the ground like a mad dog?* But the woman's face did not change.

"I see," she said. Then, delicately: "You are recently widowed?"

Of course, Mrs. Trombly had noted her gown, matte black silk trimmed with black lace.

"No." Ella shut her eyes briefly. "My father."

"I'm very sorry," said Mrs. Trombly, and she did not press for more. She drew a breath as though collecting herself to return to the matter at hand and continued, "Miss Seymour felt you should be brought here, at once, to maximize and prolong the psychic contact. Miss Seymour explained everything." Mrs. Trombly rose and stood by the bed. Ella wanted to shrink from her, ashamed—this woman too had seen her like *that*—but instead she took a deep breath. What had Miss Seymour explained?

"I see," she said, though she saw nothing.

Mrs. Trombly reached out as though to brush a lock of hair from Ella's face then dropped her hand. She stepped away from the bed with visible effort, sinking back into the chair.

"Miss Seymour said you would be dazed today and would need a great deal of rest before you could share your experience. I do not intend to hurry you. I can't imagine how strange, how powerful … But I am beside myself, Miss Reed, wondering. Yearning. To know what you know. What it was like. Did she … speak to you, Miss Reed?" Mrs. Trombly was on her feet again. Her hands were clutched before her. "Do you sense that this was her chamber?

Ella had not sensed anything, but suddenly she knew. She must have known from the moment Mrs. Trombly opened her mouth. The ragged edge that crept into her voice. And now, the stark need in her eyes.

"Phillipa," she whispered. Mrs. Trombly was the woman who had cried out to Phillipa.

"I miss her," Mrs. Trombly said simply. "She died five years ago, five years as of yesterday. That's why I went to the séance. Every year on the anniversary of her death she feels so close I imagine I can hear her footsteps on the stairs. I can hear her voice. I am not a member of any spiritualist society. I don't know exactly what I believe." Her wandering gaze fixed on Ella. "But last night, she came to you. I saw it. We all saw it. You were … changed. Miss Seymour says it was a strong and complete possession. You merged with her. There might be some natural sympathy between you. A reason why she chose you for her vessel and not Miss Seymour.

But you are sensitive to the forces around us, Miss Seymour is certain. Have you ever worked as a medium?"

"No." Ella pressed her fingers hard into her cheeks.

"Has anything like … what happened last night happened to you before?"

"No!" Ella flinched. Then she continued, more composedly. "Of course not. And I hope it never does again." That, at least, was true.

"It was dangerous." Mrs. Trombly's eyes glittered. "It was a most dangerous connection. Miss Seymour sat with you for an hour until the worst had passed. But the first contact is always tormentous. And you aren't trained, like Miss Seymour, to handle your gift."

"Gift?" The bubble in Ella's chest threatened to burst. When it did, hysterical laughter would issue forth, a high, thin stream of it.

"I want to hire you as a private medium." Mrs. Trombly walked to the writing desk and opened a drawer. She lifted out a framed photograph and slid a finger gently across the glass. She looked up at Ella. "I don't expect you to perform miracles. I just want you to remain open to her, to Phillipa. To guide her. And to tell me what you sense from her. You will live here. I trust you'll find it closer to what you're accustomed to than a boardinghouse."

She was fishing, but Ella would not rise to the bait. The less she said about herself the better. Fewer words, fewer lies.

"You will receive wages," continued Mrs. Trombly. "I happen to know a few families in London who employ private mediums." She smiled, a sweet, sheepish smile. "It's not so outlandish. Though I do feel odd about it, and I can see you do too."

"Pardon me, Mrs. Trombly," said Ella hesitantly. "I am unknown to you. You have no character for me. I can give you no references. To invite me into your house seems … " She fumbled for the right word. "Rash. I have no inclination to embark on a career as a medium—"

"You want to be a governess," Mrs. Trombly interrupted. "So you said. And I can promise you a position as a governess. It would be easy for me to secure you one, and I'd be only too happy to do so. After one month's time, Miss Reed. Just one month." Her delicate, careworn face was illuminated by those tilted, shadowed eyes. "I can't give up hope. Even after all this time. If there is a chance, any chance at all, that I can have some message from her, a word or sign, something to let me know she's all right ... if you can help her find her way ... "

Ella heard Miss Seymour's voice again. *She is afraid. She is one with the shadows.* What had happened to Phillipa? Ella could not bring herself to ask, but the desire to know suddenly consumed her. Mrs. Trombly's eyes were fixed on her. She was waiting. Hoping. Yearning. It was hard to meet her gaze. Ella wanted to say something so that Mrs. Trombly would stop looking at her with that naked need.

I can't help Phillipa find her way. I can't find my own way.

She almost envied Phillipa. That woman was lost to the world because she was dead. Ella, on the other hand ... Ella was lost to the world because she was alive. Less than wholly human but alive. She would never marry. Never have children. Now that Papa was dead, she would never again know what it was like to be loved.

"I can't," Ella began and hid her face in her hands. She heard Mrs. Trombly cross the room and felt the bed dip as she sat down beside her.

"I am too familiar," said Mrs. Trombly. "Forgive me. It is because you are connected with my daughter." And her hand brushed Ella's forehead. Ella let her own hands fall.

"What if I am not connected with her?"

"You are." Mrs. Trombly stroked Ella's hair, tugging at the knots with gentle fingers. "How else would you explain what happened last night?"

The explanation had been drilled into Ella's head by Mr. Norton. She could repeat it now. Nothing could be easier.

I have a disorder of the brain. I suffer from epilepsy, somnambulism, vertigo, and migraines accompanied by scintillating scotoma. I am on the road to insanity, and along the way I may very well become a murderess.

And she could conclude with her vow, the one she had made to herself. *But I will not go mad. I will not become a murderess. I will not be locked up. I will die before I allow these things to happen.*

But how awful it would be to say these things. To say what was running through her mind. *Mrs. Trombly, I have been planning my own death since I first learned what I am. But I do not believe this qualifies me to speak with the dead.*

She remained silent. She let Mrs. Trombly untangle her hair. The motion was so practiced, so gentle. A mother's touch. But that was just it: Mrs. Trombly was not her mother. Ella was not Phillipa. She could not take advantage of Mrs. Trombly's grief, her willingness to construe mortal illness as supernatural ability. She must reject Mrs. Trombly's offer. It was on the tip of her tongue.

I cannot do as you wish, she would say, and she would walk out the door, catch a hansom cab to Pimlico, gather her belongings from her room, and find new lodgings in another neighborhood. She would inquire at schools, answer advertisements. It would be difficult to find a job without references and without connections, but she would keep trying.

But what if I can? What if I can do what Mrs. Trombly wishes?

She sagged against the older woman's shoulder. Would it be so terrible? She could bring Mrs. Trombly peace. Tell her that Phillipa had moved from the shadows to the light. Out of all the lies she had told and would tell, this lie would shine forth, an act of mercy. Of grace. She could live with Mrs. Trombly in her house. She could set Mrs. Trombly's heart at ease. And Mrs. Trombly would find her work as a governess.

"You will stay?" Mrs. Trombly's fingers never stopped, and as Ella lifted her head, she felt a sharp pain in her scalp as a few hairs broke.

"I will," she said before she could stop herself, exultant and ashamed. *May God forgive me.*

The picture Mrs. Trombly had taken from the drawer was facedown on the coverlet. Ella reached out and turned it over. The girl who had sat stock-still for the photographer had Mrs. Trombly's narrow face and pointed chin. There was something fierce about her. Foxlike. Skittish, wild, and quick. She looked more alive than Ella could ever remember feeling herself. She looked as though she knew she deserved life. It was a bauble she could play with, treat carelessly. A pretty golden bracelet. Not an iron shackle. Not a curse.

Why am I the one who still breathes?

She put the picture down carefully, aware that Mrs. Trombly was watching her closely.

"I think I need rest after all," she said.

"Of course you do," said Mrs. Trombly, rising. "Lizzie will fix you a tray whenever you wish. I don't expect you to come down to dine tonight. Recover your strength." She turned as though leaving then paused at the door and looked back. "Thank you," she said. "I really am so happy you're here. We have so much to talk about. You'll want to know things about Phillipa, and I … I do enjoy speaking of her." Those sad eyes were luminous. "You'll tell me things too," she continued. "My husband is away on business many months of the year. In South America. My son-in-law took an appointment in India, and he and my eldest daughter have been in Bombay for three years. I haven't met my youngest grandson." She smiled briefly, delight in the existence of this new grandson tempered by his absence. "My daughter Edwina married two summers ago and is mostly in Suffolk." She rested her hand on the doorframe. "Well," she said. "I've been very much alone. Only Phillipa is with me."

Ella leaned back against the pillows, unsure what to say. The birds were still singing. The room was clean and bright and should have been pleasant. But Mrs. Trombly's sadness was like a grain of musk, permeating everything.

"My mother died when I was a baby," Ella said at last, stammering slightly. She hadn't intended to trade confidences, but Mrs. Trombly's vulnerability struck a chord within her. "I don't remember what she was like. But if I can imagine that she loved me as you love Phillipa, I might be able to feel I have someone with me too."

Mrs. Trombly's smile was kind and knowing, and if possible, sadder than it had been before.

"She did," she said. "I promise you she did."

As soon as Mrs. Trombly had left the room, Ella curled herself into a ball and drew the blanket over her head. She heard a little crash. She didn't crawl out to investigate. She buried herself deeper under the covers. She knew what it was. Phillipa's photograph falling to the bedroom floor.

Chapter Four

How does a man stop running? How does a man pick up his old life? Start again?

Step One: He burns the ticket he already purchased for the steamship back to Cairo. (*Don't tell Clement. Pretend the ticket never was.*)

Step Two: He plans—no, *vows*—to come out from hiding in Pimlico, to turn over the lease on his dreary apartments to a deserving, down-at-heel clerk (there were many such clerks in Pimlico), free of charge. Meanwhile, he re-opens Blackwood House (horror of horrors) in Piccadilly.

Step Three: He moves into Blackwood House in Piccadilly. He repeats to himself, "It's my house now, not my father's." Aloud, if need be. He allows himself to get rid of all the furnishings. To order his father's Sheraton desk chopped for firewood. This will ease the transition.

Step Four: He reads his estate manager's reports. He reads letters from tenants. He responds. He learns to associate "Viscount Blackwood" with himself. No more visions of the old man. Of those uncanny eyes—pale blue, almost white—alight in that gray wolf's face. Banish them.

Step Five: He accepts invitations to dine. Then he shows up.

Step Six: At balls, he refrains from scowling at marriageable young ladies. Is bland, polite, a bit dull. Does nothing to encourage the sentimental rumors his reappearance has brought anew to the lips of every scandalmonger in the *ton*. He bores the more inquisitive girls to tears.

Step Seven: He seeks out his friends, those friends he has ignored for a month in London and, from abroad, for five years before that. He makes amends. He rebuilds bridges.

Step Eight: He sweeps his mind free of cobwebs. He forgets he has secrets. He forgets. He forgets. He forgets.

. . .

Step one was easy enough. Sitting in the wingback chair in his bedchamber, holding up the steamship ticket, he decided burning was too high-pitched. Histrionic. No more of that. He ripped the ticket neatly into fourths.

Everything else would be harder. Would take time and effort.

Three days had passed since his midnight interview with Clement. He felt—still—that something had changed. Changed for the better. When he left his apartments that afternoon, the clouds had blown off. The air didn't bite at him as he walked along the narrow streets of Pimlico toward Mayfair. The faint foulness of the London air smelled sweet. It smelled like home.

Isidore Blackwood, the *ton's* most tragic Romeo, or most black-hearted Lothario, depending on who wrote the gossip column, had returned, not only to London, but to society. He was out in the light of day. And—heaven above—could it be? He was paying social calls.

His first visit was to Louisa Trombly. He had been avoiding Louisa. He knew it was unforgiveable, his neglect. She had been like a mother to him. The only mother he'd ever had.

"You should call me 'mother,'" she'd said to him, five years ago, at the funeral. "You would have been my son if … " She'd broken off, overcome.

She'd spoken the truth. He would have been her son. The wedding date had been fixed, and he'd sworn to Phillipa she wasn't getting out of it. *Over my dead body.* That's what he'd said to her that night. *I'll haul you back by your hair.*

"Thank you." He'd taken Mrs. Trombly's hand, but his heart had failed him. "Thank you … Louisa." *Mother.* He couldn't say it. He'd lost the right to think of her as his mother the moment Phillipa's head hit the marble of the courtyard.

He stood staring at Trombly Place, the blue door with the heavy knocker. He shut his eyes and willed himself to block out everything but the image of Louisa's kindly face.

He walked up to the door and knocked, but Mrs. Trombly had taken the coach to see the modiste.

"You could wait in the sitting room," said Rutherford. He'd been the Tromblys' butler for as long as Isidore could remember. The years had not been kind. His face was thin and heavily scoured. Phillipa had been a great favorite with him.

Isidore wanted to say something. But didn't know what. He stood looking at the man for a moment too long, awkward on the step.

You should rest, Rutherford. Sit down with a warming pan. Looks like you could use it. He couldn't think how to communicate his affection and concern for the butler without hurting the man's pride. He'd forgotten all of his social graces. If he'd ever had any. Luckily, the expression in Rutherford's pale, rheumy eyes made words unnecessary.

"Thank you," he said, "but I'll call tomorrow."

He turned from the door, and that's when the sound reached his ears. Faint. Melancholy. Someone in the house was playing a Bach sonata.

His blood ran cold. Every hair on his body stiffened, rose. How many times had he played it, that very sonata? He on the violin, Phillipa on the harpsichord.

He whirled on the step, thrust out his arm. The front door closed on his bicep, and he forced it open. Rutherford stepped back into the hall. His thin lips had whitened.

"Who is that?" Isidore advanced into the hall. He didn't wait for an answer. The music had wrapped him with silver chains, and deep in the house, in the music room, a winch was turning, reeling him in. Pulling him forward.

Someone was playing Phillipa's harpsichord.

"My lord." Rutherford's voice meant nothing. No sound penetrated except for those haunting, silvery strains. He didn't realize he was at the music room door until he saw his hand on the doorknob.

Nothing had changed in the music room. He might have been stepping back in time. The walls alternated pale-green papers and tapestries patterned with birds peeking through green-and-blue foliage. A marble bust of Bach rested on a pillar near a curtained window. A lyre hung above the mantel. The room was immaculate, not a spot of dust on any surface, yet the very air weighed upon him. It was thick with everything he'd lost.

I am mad, he thought. *I am finally utterly and completely mad.*

For the music that filled the room came from *her* fingers, the touch so light, so quick and sure. A ghost was playing for an audience of ghosts. And for him.

Dozens of empty chairs were arrayed about the room. The harpsichord stood in the center. A beautiful instrument, the dark wood of the case contrasting with the paler rosewood of the inner face. A woman swayed on the bench. Slender. Clad in black, from boots to bonnet. It took him a long, excruciating moment to realize that she was flesh and blood. To remember that ghosts don't dress in mourning, but rather, those who grieve them do.

He was at that harpsichord in an instant. The woman's fingers came down with a discordant crash, and she shot to her feet, falling backward over the bench, so that he had to catch her shoulders and steady her.

He gripped harder than was necessary. Maybe it was to steady himself.

"Let go of me." The woman's voice was rapid and low. Her head was bowed. She held so still that he wondered if her heart was beating.

He released her and stepped back. He felt like a fool, like a boor. He tried to recover his control. Folded his arms across his chest.

"Why are you in here?" he asked.

"I couldn't help myself." The woman's voice softened. Her tone had changed, filled with wonder. "I've never seen anything like it."

For a moment, his anguish flooded back.

What? He wanted to ask her. *What had she seen?*

His eyes roved the room, as though he might glimpse, in some shadow or another, the sheen of Phillipa's black hair, the glimmer of her eye, the dark rose of her wide mouth, the pale length of her slender neck. He fixed on the cabinet and imagined the sheets of music inside fanning up and scattering. Phillipa had done such things, in fits of fun or fury. Scattered sheet music. Plucked leaves from trees. Her energy was uncontainable in life. And in death … ?

No, he said to his whirring mind, his racing heart. *Stop. No more.*

At that moment, the woman turned again to the harpsichord and let her fingers brush the keys. He understood then what she had meant. It was the harpsichord that had enthralled her. Phillipa had been the same. The day it was first brought into the house, she'd played for hours, refusing to leave the music room to dine. Within a week, Michael, her father, had worried about the gift. Worried she might love it *too* much. Phillipa did nothing by halves.

She had played divinely.

He looked at the harpsichord, forcing himself. He looked at the nameboard, inlaid with ivory and mahogany. Amid the grotesque ornaments decorating the inside of the lid—beasts of the field, and serpents and capering satyrs—the massive cartouche drew his gaze. It contained the painted figures of Orpheus and Eurydice, Orpheus frozen in the act of turning back, one arm holding his lyre, the other stretched out. He stared at Eurydice. Eurydice's flat black eyes stared back, sightless. Her black hair flowed across her diaphanously robed shoulders. At any moment, she would vanish into the Underworld.

Damn her.

He didn't know whom he meant, Phillipa or this woman who had drawn him into the music room. The last place he should have gone.

"It's Italian," said the woman, curling her fingers back from the keys.

"Venetian," he said flatly, hating himself for falling so easily back into his old patterns. Macabre visions. Self-torment. Without the music to stir the air, the room seemed to close in upon him. Trombly House had once felt bright and open. Now he felt oppressed by it. The windows were shuttered. The room was dim. Every particle in the air had steeped in sorrow.

He realized he was staring at the woman's fingers, slim and white against the black fabric of her gown. He couldn't help himself. He had to examine them more closely. He closed the distance between them with a stride and caught her wrist, as gently as he could. He turned her hand and stared at the knuckles, the tapering fingers. Her hand was thinner than Phillipa's, the tendons and veins visible through the skin. Her fingernails were even in length, perfect ovals with pale half moons rising above the smooth cuticles.

What had he expected? That the fingers that had freed the music latent in those keys should resemble Phillipa's?

The woman was making a strangled noise, tugging her hand. He raised his head, and for the first time, looked full upon her. The upper half of her face was shaded by the bonnet. Her eyes seemed impossibly deep-set, swimming in shadows. His own eyes were drawn down by the deep red of her lips. Her mouth wasn't as wide as Phillipa's. Her lips were full. Fuller. Under his gaze, they parted. He heard her indrawn breath.

She was not Phillipa. She bore no resemblance to Phillipa in body, face, or spirit. But something in him thrilled with recognition. The shiver that moved across his skin was queer … a kind of fearful expectation.

He felt another tug and opened his hand reflexively. He had no right to handle her this way. He was beyond a boor. He was a cad, unfit for human interaction. The woman was a guest of Louisa's. She had been left to her own devices in the house, and she had been compelled to enter the music room by the sight of the harpsichord. Like Phillipa, she could not keep herself from touching those keys. She could not keep herself from playing that Bach sonata, infinitely sad, infinitely beautiful …

That Bach sonata. How had she known? The bust of Bach near the window. Perhaps seeing it had brought Bach, and his sonatas, to her mind.

He looked at Bach now, the blank white marble of his frozen countenance. No counsel there.

"I apologize," he said, looking back at her, fumbling for a way to end this unfortunate interview. The woman had dropped her head again, presenting her black bonnet, her tense black shoulders. Her thin, white hands. Again, she had gone still, like a wild creature alert to danger.

Or like the dead.

"My behavior … " He couldn't finish. There was no way to excuse himself. She gave a slight movement, responding to a sound he couldn't hear.

He glanced toward the door and saw Rutherford, even more stooped with apprehension, hovering on the threshold.

"You shouldn't … " he began and stopped again, knowing he should not go on. But he had done too much already. He had gone too far. It was easier to plunge ahead. He would play his part in this fiendish drama until the end. It seemed his voice took over, continued with a will of its own.

"You shouldn't play that melody," he said. He heard the harshness in his voice, though he hadn't intended to speak so. Could Rutherford hear him? He lowered his voice.

"Get out of here," he whispered. "You have no business in this room, whatever Louisa told you. You don't belong here."

The woman seemed to settle even more profoundly into stillness, into silence, as though she could disappear.

"Get out," he said, and when she made no move, he leaned toward her. He barely breathed the words.

"*I'll haul you …* " This phrase, this dark echo, pounded in his head. He broke off. He had ashes in his mouth. He could taste them. Almost choking, he wheeled around, pushed past Rutherford, and started unsteadily down the hall.

He thought for a moment that he heard the music start up again behind him. But it was only the infernal mechanisms inside his head, repeating their plaintive strains.

The house was silent.

• • •

Ella sank back onto the bench as the thundering quiet of the music room crashed around her. Her legs would not hold her. There. That muted sound was the front door slamming. He was gone. Whoever he was, he was gone.

She had thought, for a split second, when his hands had closed upon her shoulders …

Alfred. He's come for me.

She stood. The man's voice rang again in her ears, terrible with threat. Or was it warning? Either way, he was right. She did not belong here. She had sensed, as soon as she'd pushed open the door, that the music room's spell of silence was not to be broken. It was as though the room were under an enchantment. She had meant to shut the door and slip on down the hall. Yet, despite her will, despite everything, the harpsichord drew her.

Now, as she turned to leave, she could not deny herself a parting look at the harpsichord, so much darker and grander than her own.

Alfred, she remembered, thought music was dull. Any music but the hunting horn put him right to sleep. That's what he'd always said, yawning, when Papa had her play. He'd have sold her harpsichord by now. Or destroyed it out of spite. Within the little circle of calm she'd created, she felt blank, numb.

She probed along her collarbones, raised and lowered her shoulders.

How could she have believed, even for a fraction of a second, that the hands on her shoulders were Alfred's? The man's grip was hard as steel.

She left the music room, relieved that Rutherford was not waiting in the hall. Yet as she turned the corner, she ran smack into Mrs. Hexam, the housekeeper, instead. During the three days Ella had spent in residence at Trombly Place, Mrs. Hexam had never changed her expression. She stared at Ella now with that same look frozen on her sallow, careworn face. That same mixture of fear and suspicion. Ella had endured worse.

Mrs. Hexam said merely: "I've laid tea in the sitting room. Mrs. Trombly is just in." So instead of retreating to the upstairs bedchamber, Ella walked slowly behind Mrs. Hexam to the sitting room. Her soft, kid boots made no sound on the carpet. The hush that prevailed in the house had descended. Music and commotion—both were unthinkable in that heavy silence. She could almost doubt the encounter in the music room had even happened. Except for the slight ache in her shoulders. Except for the voice ringing deep in her ears.

You don't belong here.

She reached out as she walked, let her fingertips trail along the cool wall. She needed to feel something solid.

Mrs. Trombly was sitting on the green damask sofa wearing a simple but elegant high-necked gown of brown silk. Something fresh clung to her. Remnants of afternoon breezes that she'd brought into the house.

Ella's stomach twisted with longing. She hadn't stepped foot outside the house since she'd arrived. At first, she'd been in no state.

And then … she hadn't known how to ask. She wasn't sure if she could just say to Mrs. Hexam, casual as can be, "The day is so fair. I'm off for a stroll," and walk out the front door, unaccompanied, to take a turn in the park. Her position was exceedingly peculiar.

"Good afternoon," she murmured to Mrs. Trombly and took a seat.

"Good afternoon," said Mrs. Trombly. "I trust you're well today?"

"Quite well, thank you." Ella smiled, an uncertain smile she didn't doubt, and inspected the tray on the table. Sugar biscuits. Six of them. She put one on a plate, her skin prickling.

Whenever she was in Mrs. Trombly's presence, Ella felt the older woman staring at her hungrily. But when she turned her head, Mrs. Trombly's eyes were dreamy, fixed on a far-off point. It made her anxious. Sad. Guilty. It made her want to take her hasty leave. But where would she go?

She glanced up, but Mrs. Trombly was smiling shyly into the teacup at her lips. The silence stretched.

"Mrs. Trombly." Ella rested her plate on her knee. The two of them, sitting so close in the quiet, dim room with few topics near at hand for frothy conversation—it made confession the only course.

"The music room … I went there today."

This was not her fancy. Mrs. Trombly's face drained of color.

"Yes?" said Mrs. Trombly. She was holding her breath. She covered her long exhalation by blowing across the cooling surface of her tea.

"Perhaps I shouldn't have," said Ella. "It felt … "

Now Mrs. Trombly's whole face was alight. She leaned forward, hand trembling so violently the tea lipped the edge of the cup.

"It happened again," she said. "You felt it. The connection. As Miss Seymour promised you would. You sensed her, there in the music room. She came to you."

"No," said Ella. "That isn't what … Rather, I … "

"Tell me everything," said Mrs. Trombly. "Please."

Mrs. Trombly's eyes were glittering. She was waiting. Hoping. Yearning. Ella found it difficult to meet her gaze. She wanted to say something, anything, so that Mrs. Trombly would stop looking at her with that naked need.

She said, "The harpsichord … "

"It called you," said Mrs. Trombly, with something like triumph in her voice. Ella tried to ignore this insistence, to stumble on without falling into avowal or denial. It was a horrible game, and she scarcely knew how to play.

"I shouldn't have touched it, though," said Ella carefully. "Not without your permission."

"Ah." Mrs. Trombly leaned back against the sofa. The mist had settled on her face. She had lost focus again. She peered through veils toward what? Another world? Then Mrs. Trombly's misty eyes found hers.

"When I imagine her," said Mrs. Trombly, "I often see her in that room."

"The harpsichord was hers, wasn't it?" whispered Ella, curious now, unable to stop herself, leaning toward Mrs. Trombly in turn. "Your daughter who … " She swallowed.

Slowly, Mrs. Trombly nodded. Her eyes were shut. Her chin was trembling. Here it was: the perfect opportunity. Ella knew what she should do. Pitch her voice low. Speak with the throbbing authority of the spirit world.

I saw your daughter in the music room. She was standing by the harpsichord. She was waiting, and then, when I sat down to play, she moved. She moved, and the melody carried her from the shadows to the light.

That was what Mrs. Trombly hoped to hear. Was *paying* her to hear. She could not say it. God help her, it would be a mercy to them both, but she could not. It was a lie. She could not prey on Mrs. Trombly's pain.

What do you think you're doing? Living here? Accepting wages?
Playing a role, she answered herself. *Pretending. Not lying.*

"What happened next?" asked Mrs. Trombly, and Ella blinked, marshaled herself.

"I sat at the harpsichord. I started to play, a sonata," she said. "A man interrupted me."

"A servant?" Mrs. Trombly's eyes widened slightly.

"No," said Ella. "A gentleman. He must have come to call on you. He found me in the music room. He was not ... " She paused. "Pleased."

She felt the heat rising to the surface of her skin. The man had leaned so close above her. She had looked for a moment into his face, dark featured and bold, contorted by some emotion she could not fathom.

Who could he be? What gentleman would charge past Rutherford, barrel deep into Mrs. Trombly's house, and berate an unknown woman in a closed chamber? Who would have the audacity? A family member? But Mrs. Trombly had said her family was far away. That peremptory—no, *furious*—man who had burst into the music room, he could hardly be Mrs. Trombly's husband, home early from Brazil. He had exuded strength, vitality, something she could not associate with this wilted woman or her distant husband.

"A tall man," she said. "Young."

Mrs. Trombly's attention sharpened. "A tall man?" she asked. "Black hair?"

"Black hair," Ella said. "Yes." He had given the impression of storm. Dark, massive, unpredictable. His black hair had been tousled by the wind. Wild. "He must have left a card?" she asked. "He wasn't a housebreaker. I'm sure that Rutherford admitted him."

Mrs. Trombly's lips parted. A word puffed out.

"Isidore."

It was as though *Mrs. Trombly* were the one who had trances. Ella fought the urge to snap her fingers. What was it about this house that invited reverie? She feared that she was sliding into that in-between state, joining Mrs. Trombly in a kind of half life. She tried to center herself in the quiet sitting room while she waited for Mrs. Trombly to continue. She picked out sturdy, average items and stared at them. Tea service. Sugar biscuit. She lifted a biscuit, bit off a corner.

"They were going to be married," Mrs. Trombly said. "Phillipa and Isidore."

Now it was Ella's turn to stare. The man who had grabbed her ... Phillipa Trombly's betrothed? She opened her mouth then closed it.

Mrs. Trombly continued: "That night ... I lost a daughter and a son."

"But certainly ... " Ella hesitated. The way the man, the way *Isidore,* had charged into the music room and seized her, the interloper ... His violent emotion, his odd actions—they had been strange, and frightening, but they had been born, she could see now, of pain. Pain and a protective instinct. Isidore was protective of Phillipa's memory. Of Mrs. Trombly.

"He's lately come back to London," said Mrs. Trombly. "His father died. Just a few months ago." She paused. "I doubt he would have returned otherwise. Ever since the night we lost Phillipa, he has been ... different. He left England almost at once. He lived for a time in Italy, for a time, I think, in Cypress. Then in Egypt. He wrote. He returned to England, not often, but a few times. Even when I was in his company, nothing was the same. I don't know how to explain it."

It was too much. After three days of tiptoeing around the house, trying to keep herself open to forces she didn't understand, or even fully believe in, Ella had reached her limit. After three days of skirting in conversation the edges of a tragedy that defined everything about this household, she had to know.

"How did your daughter die?" Ella whispered, unable to keep her lips from forming the question.

"It was an accident." Mrs. Trombly did not seem to find it rude that she'd asked. She seemed to have forgotten Ella's presence all together. "She fell from a balcony."

"How?" Again, a word slipped out without Ella's volition. Mrs. Trombly was still gazing into space.

"Phillipa had so much energy," she said, almost as though she hadn't heard. "She was irrepressible. She preferred to run instead of walk. She liked to throw windows open and lean as far out as she could. 'Outside air is better than inside air,' she'd say. 'Even in London.' She always sat on the balustrades of balconies and kicked her heels. She was so charmed." Mrs. Trombly's eyes came to rest on Ella. "She could be careless. She slipped. She lost her balance. It was the middle of the night. My husband and I were asleep. We didn't even know she hadn't come home, that she wasn't already upstairs, when Isidore brought her back to us. He carried her. He sat with her until morning."

Ella felt as though her blood had turned to ice.

Did he lay her out here? In this house?

She kept perfectly still, but she had turned a dark corner in her mind and she did not like what she saw there.

The dark man, Isidore, holding Mrs. Trombly's daughter, stiff and cold.

Her papa's deathbed. She had sat by his side until the end and after. How strange it had been to gaze on that familiar form, the livid face framed by tufts of oakum hair, and know that Papa was gone from it.

And before that, her brother, Robert. She had not seen his body. By the time it came back to them, there was not enough intact. She had seen her papa after he saw. That was enough.

She shook herself. That's when she realized Mrs. Trombly was smiling, a lovely, luminous smile.

"Phillipa guided you to the music room," she said dreamily. "And you played at her harpsichord. You played, and Isidore came. He came back to us."

She took Ella's hand, her fingers soft and cool as sheets.

"I've missed him," she said. "Almost as much as I do Phillipa. We share a property line with the Blackwoods, in the country. Isidore was often with us, even as a boy. He had no brothers or sisters, and the lure of playmates proved irresistible." Her dreamy smile tightened. "Nothing could keep him away."

"What would have kept him away?" Ella felt that strange prickling, the hairs on her neck lifting. Mrs. Trombly's tone told her that something *had* tried to keep Isidore away. "After all, it's very natural," she said with a studied offhandedness, "and very fortunate for children to make friends of their neighbors." She didn't think she sounded wistful, but Mrs. Trombly's look was suddenly penetrating.

"The old viscount didn't share that view," she said slowly. She drew her fine brows together, forming a deep crease in the middle of her forehead. She paused again. "He was a rather … controlling man."

She squeezed Ella's hand.

"It's working," she said, eyes bright. "I never gave up hope. You can help her. I know you can." She raised Ella's fingers to her lips.

"And if you can help her," she said, "you can help Isidore."

Ella's heart was hammering again. She should get up, leave, now, at once. Put as much distance as she could between herself and Trombly Place. She had to go. If she stayed any longer, she would crush Mrs. Trombly's hope. Inevitably, she would reveal something about who and what she really was. That luminous smile would fade forever.

I don't belong here. I must leave. I must leave now.

"I believe in you," said Mrs. Trombly. "I have to believe."

When Ella freed her hand, it was only to retrieve her sugar biscuit and take another bite.

Chapter Five

The Benningtons had moved into the Bennington House on Dering Street, Hanover Square. Isidore knocked with the heavy ring then waited on the front steps. Daphne, Ben—they were good friends. Old friends. Clement had reminded him that he'd broken a dinner engagement with no word of explanation.

How does a man stop running? How does a man pick up his old life?

He makes amends. He repairs bridges.

Yesterday had been a disaster. He'd lost his head at Louisa's. That melody. That slender woman at the harpsichord.

He didn't want to think of that encounter, or what had come after. He'd fled the house in disgrace, mood black and growing blacker. He hadn't returned to his apartments, hadn't stopped by the club. He'd gone to a tavern and drank his lunch—five flips, so maybe that counted as a meal. Each flip had at least part of an egg stirred into the gin, and sugar. Dinner … dinner had been more of the same. But without the eggs and sugar.

Maybe I shouldn't have ripped up that ticket. That's what he went to sleep thinking. *Maybe I should buy another.*

But somehow—though he woke late in the morning, head filled with sand and glass, body aching—he was determined to try again. London. The *ton.* All of it. He wasn't giving up. His visit to Trombly Place had been a false start. Today would be different.

He rocked on his heels, looking up, up the façade of Bennington House. The sky above was blue. He tried to keep his mind sunny and blank.

He wouldn't tell Daphne and Bennington the truth. Why he'd failed to keep the engagement. He'd give them an airy, charming excuse then launch into an off-color anecdote from his travels.

The one about the dancing girl who stripped off her clothes and folded herself until she could have fit in a hatbox. Or the one about the Albanian cavalryman who shot his friend in the hand over a mummified crocodile phallus.

He wouldn't say what he could now admit to himself. That the people he'd cared about and who'd cared about him *before*—those were the people he had the most trouble facing. They had also been friends with—he didn't want to think her name. Not today. For today, let him be free of her.

But she was suddenly there, on the step beside him, a presence he could almost see out of the corner of his eye, could almost touch. *Phillipa.* Bennington was the only core member of their set who hadn't been at the party when Phillipa died. He was kept at home with a headache. He'd been spared that final scene. But Daphne had been there. He made his hands into fists, resisting the urge to bring them to his temples. He heard, again, Daphne's screams. Saw her, kneeling, arms twined around her own neck. She had sobbed until her face had purpled.

When the butler opened the door, he managed to smile.

He was shown through an imposing hall—gleaming white marble with Roman statues in the wall niches striking martial poses—and into the sitting room. This room too was imposing, decidedly masculine in its décor, with heavy mahogany furniture and gilt-framed oval portraits of the Bennington forbears, all soldiers, on the navy blue-papered walls. No feminine touches softened or brightened the space. Even the curtains that hung over the tall windows were thick and somber. There was a massive portrait-book and a few cheaply printed newspapers on the low table, the only items in the room that looked moveable, as though they hadn't been in the same spot for fifty years. Isidore was reaching toward them when the door opened. He turned.

"Sid," said Daphne Bennington in her sweet, high voice and held out her hand. He took it. She smiled, a dimple flashing in her creamy cheek. She wore a low-cut gown of green silk that left a great deal of her breasts exposed and little to the imagination as to the luscious contours of the remainder. "We wondered if you were halfway to Dar es Salaam by now." She gestured to the leather settee, and he sat while she moved to take the armchair opposite. She was a petite woman, almost child-sized, although her lush figure told quite another story. The chair dwarfed her, and he was struck again by the ponderous, uninviting quality of the room and by the incongruity between that room and its mistress. The furnishings weren't to Bennington's taste, either; he'd bet his life on that. Bennington was too much of a dandy. He'd always favored style over substance, form over function. He and Clement had called him "Knees" at Cambridge because he used to wear trousers so tight he couldn't sit down. This room—this whole house—reflected the style of his father, General Sir Henry Bennington. The general had died over a year ago, but clearly Bennington hadn't yet made the house his own. Or maybe he was trying to become the kind of man who'd be at home with sabers on the walls and bookshelves filled with leather-bound tomes of military strategy. Maybe he wanted to remake himself in his father's image. Like a tulip pretending to be a hickory tree.

Isidore shouldn't judge. After all, he was society's black sheep trying to sprout a golden fleece.

"We expected you last week," Daphne prompted when a few moments had passed without his offering any kind of response.

"Yes, about that … " Isidore rubbed his thumb along his jaw, the airy, charming excuse and the off-color anecdotes vanishing from his mind. Daphne was looking at him with interest, one delicate brow raised, as though she enjoyed watching him squirm. He released his breath in a burst.

"I should have sent a note, but what would I have written?" He wrote in the air with his forefinger. "Sick of it all, let's meet instead on a farther shore, Sid?"

"You could have made up a polite excuse," said Daphne dryly. "Something less dramatic. Bad cough. Pressing business. Allergic to turbot. Anything, really."

Isidore laughed. Daphne was so tiny and exquisite that people often made the mistake of thinking her a perfect little doll— masses of red-gold hair, round blue eyes that opened and closed, head filled with sawdust. But she had a keen mind and a scathing tongue. He'd heard her deliver withering set-downs to men who couldn't ever seem to grasp the fact that she wasn't cooing in their ears. She had been the Incomparable of the season her first year out in London, and even though she'd married Bennington that summer, she didn't stay at home feathering her love nest like many young wives. She attended every ball, every party, with Bennington and without him.

She and Phillipa had been thick as thieves.

He swore to himself. Fought the memories. But, looking at Daphne's bright hair, remembering Phillipa's dark head bent toward hers as they shared some whispered joke, he couldn't stem the tide of dark thoughts.

Thick as thieves, yes, but Phillipa had not confided in Daphne. There was no one with whom he could share the burden of his knowledge. Phillipa had told Daphne the same story she told everyone else.

Cynical, brooding Isidore Blackwood had dropped down on his knees in the Tromblys' music room, clasped Phillipa against his chest, and begged her to become his bride. Her heart had beat wildly. His heart had beat wildly. After so many years of friendship, they'd both realized, simultaneously, as though struck with the same bolt from the heavens, that they were in love. A perfect romance. He would never say a word to the contrary.

There was, of course, one other person who knew what he knew. The man who should have proposed to Phillipa but didn't. The man who left her in such an impossible situation that Isidore, her best friend, had had no choice but to step up and offer to make her his wife. If Isidore ever learned the man's name … Why, he would beat him within an inch of his life.

Daphne was staring. Christ, his repartee was rusty. She had joked about polite excuses. Now he must riposte.

"That is very good counsel," he said, almost hearing the creak in his voice. "But I have no need for it." He flashed his most charming smile. "I've resolved to live in a way that puts me less in need of excuses."

"*That's* not dramatic," murmured Daphne. Then she colored slightly. "I don't mean to be cutting," she said. "I hope you don't feel you have to make grand declarations on account of a missed engagement." She paused, a shadow flitting across her eyes. "It so happens I dined alone that night. Ben didn't turn up, either."

"What was his polite excuse?" Isidore spoke lightly, but he didn't take his eyes from her face.

She frowned. Then, all at once, she leapt up, widened her eyes, and spread her arms, imitating her husband. "By God, Daph, I plumb forgot!"

This excellent bit of mimicry elicited another laugh. She had looked and sounded for all the world like Bennington. The man was a study in innocence. Daphne dimpled for him and sat back down.

"He didn't remember we'd asked you over until the sixth rubber of whist. I hated to admit you'd never come. It would have been lovely to play you each for a guilty party vis-à-vis the other, but I was afraid you'd compare notes at the club and the truth would out. Then I'd be scourged as a manipulative minx."

"You *are* a manipulative mix," said Isidore. "I adore you for it. Bennington does too if he has half a brain in his head."

The arrival of the tea tray prevented Daphne from having to answer. But the tension in her rosy mouth did not escape Isidore's notice.

"How do you take your tea?" she asked.

"Black, no sugar." He took the cup and saucer, balancing both on his knee.

"I haven't seen Ben at the club. Haven't laid eyes on him in weeks. Where is he now?"

Daphne stirred sugar into her tea. "Debating the franchise, I imagine." Then, as though clarification might be necessary, she added: "The Liberals want to extend the vote."

"I may be known chiefly as an indolent rake who abandoned his mother country to live in a tent with desert nomads, but I do pick up *The Times* on occasion, if only to swat flies." Isidore leaned back in his chair and gazed at the medallion in the plasterwork ceiling. "I fancied Bennington as a backwoods peer. Showing up to the opening of Parliament so everyone could get a look at his pretty face then running for his life if anyone so much as mentioned the word 'bill' in his hearing."

"Did you?" Daphne's voice sounded brittle. Isidore turned his eyes back on her. She was still stirring her tea as though she'd forgotten what her hand was doing. The sight disturbed him. She noticed his close regard and smiled, laying her spoon on the tray.

"I don't blame you for thinking that," she said. "Ben was as frivolous as the rest of you. I won't deny it."

"The rest of us?" Isidore clapped a hand on his heart as though wounded.

"But you couldn't be more wrong," continued Daphne. "You haven't been around much in the past five years. Ben is very involved in politics. He has grown serious."

"He was always serious," said Isidore. "About his hair oil and how he knotted his cravat. Just as I was always serious about getting to the bottom of a gin bottle and betting every shilling my father ever gave me at long odds. I don't think frivolity is an apt charge, Daph. We were misapplying our talents, perhaps, but we were doing so with a great deal of focus and determination."

"My husband's focus has changed. That's what I'm trying to tell you." Daphne took a delicate sip of tea. "A piece of walnut cake? Lemon tart? The lemon tart is divine. We have a new cook who has a gift for pastry. How is your cook working out? It's so terribly hard to find a good one."

Isidore followed her gaze to the assorted cakes and sweets arrayed on the table.

"I was teasing," he said. "Don't punish me by playing the perfect hostess. You know I think the world of Ben."

Daphne ignored him, cutting a healthy portion of lemon tart. He put his tea on the table and accepted the plate.

"Delicious." He pronounced after the first bite. "Your cook is truly a treasure. I could eat a dozen."

Daphne smiled a real smile.

"I'm sure you could," she said, giving him a look of frank appraisal. "I don't know where you put it all. It's unfair you should look like that. You've seen Warren Cowper? He's produced the most alarming pair of jowls. Robert Abergavenny has gained a pound around the middle for every hair he's lost off the top. Now that you've come back, you've put all the bloated bachelors to shame. I saw Lord Averly at the Puttnams' musicale turning down the éclairs in favor of a watercress sandwich."

"And you lay this culinary heresy at my doorstep?" Isidore polished off his piece of tart and returned the empty plate to the table.

"You cut an impressive figure." Daphne poured him more tea, bending over the pot. Isidore couldn't help but take in an even more generous view of her considerable endowments. She had a tiny port wine stain on her left breast just peeking out above the silk. It was shaped rather like a heart. How convenient. He nearly rolled his eyes. She looked up at him through her lashes.

"Do you have any idea how many questions I've had to field about your intentions? Does Lord Blackwood intend to stay in London?

Does Lord Blackwood intend to marry this season? Does Lord Blackwood prefer blonds or brunettes?" She paused. "Or redheads?"

Isidore crossed his legs and leaned back on the settee. He remembered that a man had to be wary of Daphne. Daphne delighted in her powers of attraction. She flirted shamelessly then tried to flay you alive.

"It's because of my figure, is it?" He shrugged. "I've always been possessed of it. The debutantes managed to restrain themselves in the past."

"Now you are … unattached." Daphne's coquetry vanished. She regarded him somberly.

"I spent years in London unattached," he reminded her. "My engagement to Phillipa was brief."

"Formally," she replied. "But it was obvious to everyone your affections were engaged. Even before you admitted it to yourself."

He let this pass.

"Phillipa knew," said Daphne. "I used to think she rather took advantage of you. Before the engagement, of course. Then I realized she reciprocated your love."

"Of course," echoed Isidore. He felt increasingly uncomfortable with the conversation. But he'd asked for it. He should have taken her cue and begun to discuss the demerits of his cook. Daphne's gaze was too keen. He couldn't imagine what she was trying to get at. He looked at her blandly.

"So do you?" Daphne glanced down then up again, as though trying to surprise a new expression on his face. "Intend to marry?" *Or are you still mourning Phillipa?* The unspoken question hung between them.

"Marry?" He laughed. "That's what's expected of me, isn't it? London in the spring. Castle Blackwood in the summer. A wife for all seasons. An heir for the future."

He saw Daphne flinch and cursed himself. Six years of marriage and she was still childless. The fault wasn't necessarily hers, if one could speak of fault in such cases. But it couldn't be easy. He wondered if this was the source of the strain he detected whenever she mentioned Ben. Isidore had lived his life in broad emotional strokes—love and hate, devotion and fury, joy and despair. Those were sentiments he understood. He didn't consider himself particularly sensitive to nuance. But he couldn't help but feel that there was a subtle undercurrent of unhappiness in the Bennington household.

The longer he sat across from Daphne, the more he began to notice the little changes time had wrought. The light lines around her lips had been carved by frowns. She didn't move with the same fluid, boneless grace that he remembered. She was more awkward in her skin. As though something had shaken her confidence, her sense of who she was.

He wasn't surprised Daphne and Bennington's union had soured. Even if Daphne had borne a child, he couldn't see those two comfortably settled in the nuptial bower. He'd thought the match doomed from the very beginning. He knew Daphne to be, for all her intelligence and charm, a vain and jealous woman. And he knew Bennington … well, he just knew Bennington. The man was, quite frankly, too handsome for his own good. Women had always thrown themselves at him, and he'd never seemed more deeply attached to one than another. He enjoyed them all. Isidore had always wondered if some secret financial difficulty had spurred him into the engagement. He'd never asked, and he'd never caught wind of any gossip that confirmed his suspicion. Daphne was certainly desirable enough to tempt a man into marriage, even if she hadn't come with a substantial fortune. Maybe Bennington had simply fallen under her spell. He liked to fall under the spells of beautiful women. Usually it was all over in an evening's enchantment. Isidore had known him to be so ensorcelled a hundred times … before and after he'd married Daphne. But he tended to be discreet. It could be Daphne was deceived and thought him faithful. He hoped so. But he rather doubted it. The lines in her face were most likely the signs of her disappointment. He wondered if she had strayed herself.

"Well," said Daphne, an ugly smile stretching her beautiful lips. "That *is* what's expected of you. What you will do, of course, remains to be seen. We all play our roles with differing degrees of success. My life has not gone as I'd planned."

"Nor has mine." He fumbled for the right words. He wanted to comfort Daphne, who suddenly seemed perilously close to tears. "We don't always have complete control over what happens to us. There are greater forces at work."

"Sid," she said. Her blue eyes were enormous, brimming. Her voice had faded to a whisper so low he could barely hear her. "What forces do you mean?"

The sneer the question summoned was more for himself than for her. He'd wasted enough time with his mad, black thoughts about the devil. And he couldn't really bring himself to mouth platitudes about a watchmaker God.

"Chance," he said flatly. "Contingency. The random unfolding of the universe. The forces of chaos. That's all. Nothing grand. Nothing purposive."

"Sid." Daphne didn't seem to have listened. She was sitting up very straight, her hands on her lap. Staring at him. "Sometimes I think that I'm cursed. I think that she cursed me."

"Who?" he said, leadenly. He knew who. The room seemed suddenly suffocating. It smelled of old leather and dust and cooling, bitter, overdrawn tea. Shouldn't there be flowers? Daphne could have insisted on a few bouquets to add just a little life and color and fragrance. He couldn't sit still a moment longer.

"Can I open the window? It's a fine day," he said and, without waiting for an answer, walked to a window, pulled apart the curtains, and lifted the sash.

"Sid." He felt a hand on his shoulder. "Do you think it's possible?"

"I think you're mad," he said. From the window he watched men in high-crowned hats walking smartly along the street. They were utterly, intractably sane. They didn't look for the reflection of a raven-haired, black-eyed girl in every puddle, every shop window. He found himself crossing his eyes so he could see the windowpane rather than the scene outside. That dark blur was his own raven hair. Not hers.

He heard a muffled sob and turned to catch Daphne in his arms. She pressed her small, soft body against him, and he stroked her hair, the silky strands touched with flame by the afternoon light that shone through the parted curtains. The sitting room door was open, and his eyes strayed to it. All he needed was a servant to pass that door. Or Bennington.

"Daphne." He thrust her back, hands on her shoulders. "That was cruel. I didn't mean … We all went a little mad. *I* went mad. For years. You're not cursed. No one is cursed."

"She could be so spiteful." Daphne stared, not at him, but at the light streaming over his shoulder. Her heart-shaped face was illuminated. Eyes like blue fire. "She envied me. Do you think she's happy? Knowing how I suffer?"

"Stop it," he said, muscles straining with the effort it took not to shake her. Her eyes focused on his.

"You loved her," she said. "I loved her too. Everyone loved her." Daphne pulled out of his grasp, drifting to the other side of the room. She let her fingers trail across the mantel then picked up an antique pistol from its mounting and laid the barrel across her palm.

"It's heavy," she said. He crossed to her in two strides and snatched the pistol from her hand. She smiled at him as though she'd scored a point.

"Are you frightened?" she asked. "That hasn't been fired since Waterloo."

He returned the gun to the mantel.

"I'm not frightened," he said. "I'm finished. I've played every sick game, indulged every morbid thought. I let a phantom chase me from London clear into the Sahara. It's over. Five years, Daphne. Do you think she's still roaming after five years? She's at peace. Now it's our turn. If I can try to believe that, surely you can too."

"If she's at peace, why did Miss Seymour say she's still in the shadows?"

Isidore leaned against the mantel. He made his face a perfect blank. "You can't bait me with a riddle," he said evenly. "I've lived in the land of the sphinx. I don't think all riddles need to be answered."

He waited. He figured she might last a minute. She didn't.

"Miss Seymour is a medium." Daphne chose a newspaper from the table and handed it to him.

He read the banner across the top. "*Spiritual Magazine.*" He flipped the pages so hard one tore with a dull, protesting sound. "That's what this is about? Of all the faddish nonsense." He thrust the paper back at her. "Daphne, you can't be serious."

"Don't look at me like that." She flung herself into the armchair. "I'm not the one who started it. It's Louisa Trombly. She hired a woman as a private medium."

"She *what?*"

"She hired a medium," repeated Daphne.

"I heard you," he grated. "I understand the concept of retaining an employee at wages for services. But this medium, what does she do?"

"What all mediums do," said Daphne. "She uses her mystical powers to communicate with the dead." Her lips curved into her habitual smile, the teasing smile of a society flirt who wants to insinuate that she and her interlocutor are somewhat above the rest of the company. *You and I know better, of course.* But her eyes were still wide, and her smile slipped. "No one has ever heard of her. She doesn't have a following."

He made a choked sound of disbelief.

"Laugh all you want. There are quite a few very famous mediums in London. Americans mostly. You don't have to subscribe to newsletters." She threw *Spiritual Magazine* onto the table, where it blanketed the lemon tart. "You can read about them in the society pages. They're popular at parties."

"She's American?"

"No." Daphne tapped her fingers on the arm of the chair. He had never known her to fidget. Her movements had always been so sinuous, so practiced. She tried to smile again, but its falsity must have struck even her because she abandoned the effort. "I told you, she has nothing to do with all of that. She's not established as a medium. She's a non-entity. A woman from some backwater. Very shy, said Louisa. Not the sort who would ever go in for a spectacle. It *can* be a spectacle, you know."

He felt his patience thinning. "And how did Louisa come by this blushing damsel, this modest mystic who avoids spectacle but practices the dark arts in secret for a set fee? Did she find her mooning over a grave in Cornwall?"

Daphne's fingers now traced figure eights on the upholstery. She was watching them describe their unvarying loops. "She was at Miss Seymour's last séance," she said to her fingers. "Miss Seymour called Phillipa down from the shadows, and the woman sat bolt upright then toppled over and shook, and Miss Seymour held her down and felt Phillipa pass into her. Mrs. Wheatcroft was there, and she said it was undeniable. She got chills from it."

"Mrs. Wheatcroft is a twit," he said. "I could rap on her skull with my own knuckles on Midsummer's Eve and convince her it was the Ghost of Christmas Past." Dear God but he felt the desire to rap on *somebody's* skull growing stronger within him. "She's exactly the type I'd imagine goes to these séances."

"All types of people go." Daphne frowned. "Louisa went. Would you claim that *she* is a twit?"

"No." He put a hand on his forehead. "Of course not. But she's vulnerable. She's ... " *She's lonely and miserable.* That too was partly his fault. He should never have gone away. He should have weathered the storm and been a son to her.

"Louisa and I discussed it." The drumming began again—Daphne beating a march on the chair. Maybe she was transmitting a message from one of the old generals whose likenesses stared down at them. "Yesterday. She called in the morning. She feels that the woman, the medium, will help Phillipa. She trusts her."

His exclamation carried him forward. "Trusts her!" He didn't care that he was shouting. That he was looming over Daphne threateningly and he was not a small or gentle-looking man. "Trusts *who*? Who is she? Where is she from? What kind of woman hires herself out to *channel* another woman's dead daughter? A fortune hunter. A liar. A shill. A *prostitute* who realizes she can wheedle more out of genteel women appealing to their sentiments than she can out of men appealing to their ... "

He choked off the tirade before it devolved into a stream of vulgarity. His blood rushed hot and cold in his veins. The slender woman, the woman in black at the harpsichord ... Was she Louisa's medium? Did she spend her waking hours in the music room playing Bach on the harpsichord like Phillipa's very ghost? Tormenting Louisa. Tormenting *him.* He shouldn't have barked at her. He should have forcibly ejected her from the house.

"You think she's a fraud?" Daphne's face mingled too many emotions for him to decipher them all. Relief was among them. Also fear. "Of course, she may be. But ... " She swallowed. "Spirits linger when they have something they want to communicate. And Phillipa ... " She broke off again, licking her lips. Her eyes seemed too bright, almost feverish. "What does Phillipa have to tell us? What do you think she's come back to say?"

He stared at her dumbly. This was *Daphne*, not some eighty-year-old woman who got the vapors if someone sneezed in church.

If the medium claimed she'd received a message from Phillipa, would Daphne believe it? Would the whole damn *ton* believe it? This medium, this shy country lass, posed a distinct threat. What would stop her from revealing any number of secrets attributed to Phillipa's spirit, the more scandalous the better? She would certainly gain a following then.

What if one of those secrets was true?

The idea struck him with the force of a blow. What if she *knew?* What if she wasn't just a hapless fraud who had stumbled onto an excellent opportunity, but a calculating blackmailer?

"I must be going," he said. "Give my regards to Ben." He turned so smartly the Bennington forbears might have smiled approval. But the painted mouths were fixed for eternity in those grim lines. Unmoving. Silent. As they should be.

"I was a ninny, Sid," said Daphne, following him into the hall. "Wait for Ben at least. He'll be back any minute. You're planning on barreling over there right now in a rage, aren't you? Sid … "

But he was walking so fast the butler, almost running, poor man, could not beat him to the door. He let himself out.

Chapter Six

Ella let the book drop into her lap. She could see the brilliant blue of the sky from the window. What she felt for the sun—it was like hunger, or thirst. She rose from the chair and paced the bedchamber. She *had* to leave the house.

Before she knew what she was about, she'd pulled on boots and gloves and flung a black cashmere shawl over her readymade bombazine gown. Her fingers fumbled with the strings of her bonnet. Urgency made her clumsy, giddy.

She stepped out into the hall.

"Miss?" At the sound of the voice so close behind her, she spun around, swallowing hard to stifle a gasp. Lizzie, the maid, was looking at her narrowly, light eyebrows knit together. Wisps of blond hair had strayed from beneath her mobcap. She was holding a duster close to her chest, like a shield.

Ella tried to smile. She nodded at the maid and turned again to continue down the hall, but Lizzie bounded forward and was in front of her in a flash.

"Miss," said Lizzie, "I heard you the other day. In the music room."

"Oh," said Ella, trying not to flush like a guilty child. "Yes. It's a wonderful instrument." She paused. "Venetian." And then she asked, with studied indifference: "Does Mrs. Trombly play?"

"I've never known Mrs. Trombly to play," said Lizzie skeptically. That look of surprise—it was habitual, perhaps.

"And her daughters?"

"The oldest was off and married by the time I started," said Lizzie. "I didn't know Miss Edwina to play, either." She hesitated. "It was Miss Phillipa who played."

Enough, Ella told herself. *Don't pry any further. What do you even hope to discover? And for what purpose?*

The afternoon sun wouldn't wait. It would sink in the sky if she didn't go out to meet it. But before she could move, Lizzie was speaking again, speaking in a rush, with the same momentum that carried her leaping down the halls.

"She was a right one for it," said Lizzie. "Miss Phillipa. She put all the other ladies to shame with their plinking and warbling. There was musicales held in the house and all the fashionable people rolling up in their carriages and the kitchen sending out rum punch by the gallon and fresh strawberries and pastries filled with chocolate, and Miss Phillipa making the prettiest racket anybody ever heard, and her being so beautiful, too, that all the gentlemen fell in love with her and sent so many flowers they didn't fit in the house and had to be brought away and handed around at the charity school."

Lizzie blinked at Ella, and Ella blinked back, astounded.

"Course I was never there," said Lizzie. "It was before I started."

"But someone told you about it."

Lizzie stared at her like she was daft. "How else would I know about it, clear as day, like I described it? Or do you think everyone gets pictures sent into their head by the spirits like you, miss?"

There was no way of pretending this last wasn't meant as an impertinence, so Ella remained silent, taking the maid's measure.

"Sorry, miss," said Lizzie, crossly. She wasn't sorry for what she'd said, it was obvious, but she must have realized there was a chance that she *should* be sorry, or that Mrs. Trombly might see it that way if Ella brought the remark to her ear.

"Think nothing of it." Ella spoke coldly and, giving a brief nod, started again down the hall. She wouldn't have minded if a closer natural sympathy existed between her and the maid—her only age-mate in the house—but she couldn't ignore Lizzie's hostility. And her pride forbade currying favor.

"Miss." Lizzie moved so quickly she was again between Ella and the stairs. "What's it like to be dead?"

Ella's breath departed, and her chest hitched before it came back. Lizzie's pale irises washed into the whites, and the black pupils bored into her.

"I don't know what you mean." Ella refused to look away, but she wished fervently that some new impetus would send the maid leaping in another direction. But Lizzie inched closer to her, eyes fixed.

"If you can talk with Miss Phillipa, and Miss Phillipa is dead," said Lizzie, "you must have asked her. I've so wanted to know all my life." She spoke faster and faster, inching closer and closer. "Reverend Cotter says I shouldn't fear it, but I do fear it, and you trapped her soul in your body and it made you fall down and look so awful and ghastly pale that I can't help but think it *is* as fearful as I've imagined, like starting up at night with a weight on your chest and you can't breathe, but then the air never comes, and the feeling goes on and on and on like that forever."

Lizzie had come so close that Ella could smell the sour milk on her breath and see where the eyelashes rooted in her pinkened lids.

"You can tell me, miss," whispered Lizzie. "I'd rather know, I think, than keep pretending, if there's no angels and just the dark and not breathing."

"I can't tell you," said Ella, stunned. She wanted to push the maid away or run past her, escape the fetid breath, the black, pinprick eyes.

"Well." Lizzie skipped back from her with a little swish of her skirts. "If you can't, or you won't, it's all the same to me. The way I see it, *you're* the one who's pretending. You want to pretend to Mrs. Trombly, instead of earning your money by the sweat of your brow like an honest woman. I know about your kind, miss. You put on airs and stand by the harpsichord like you're Miss Phillipa in the flesh, but you're not fooling me, miss, and if you tell Mrs. Trombly I said so, then I won't thank you for that either. I only say so because she's a kind mistress and doesn't deserve to be taken in by a spirit-talker who doesn't know anything about the state of being dead, as if you could have spirits without the dead, my word." And she bounded off.

Ella took a deep breath, then another. She felt shaken, both by the maid's intensity and disdain, and by her question. She had often feared that death *was* like the darkness Lizzie described. Like the darkness that came from time to time and swallowed her. She had often feared that she *did* know what being dead was like. And it was ghastly indeed. Maybe she should race after Lizzie.

"Yes," she'd say when she caught her. "You're right, Lizzie, yes. Yes, it's dark, and you can't draw the air in your lungs and you're alone, more alone than you could ever imagine. That's exactly what it's like."

That would be cruel, though. Lizzie thought she wanted to know, but she didn't really. Anyone who already bore the burden of such knowledge knew better.

She wouldn't wish her lot on anyone. A walk. A walk was very much in order.

It was as Ella came down the stairs that she heard it. A voice. Male. Angry. Not loud, but low, urgent. It was coming from the sitting room.

She knew at once. It was the man from the other day. Isidore. Mrs. Trombly was right. He'd come back. He was talking to Mrs. Trombly in the sitting room. Saying what?

She stopped and gripped the banister. The front door was yards away but might have been miles. She would have to pass the sitting room to reach it. Impossible. She turned and stole noiselessly up the stairs. She would return to her bedchamber, come down later, and try to walk in the early evening. She gathered up her skirts, almost running.

"Miss Reed!" Mrs. Trombly called to her just as she reached the second floor. She was standing at the bottom of the stairs. "Would you join us in the sitting room?"

She didn't wait for Ella to respond but turned and preceded her into the room. When Ella entered, Mrs. Trombly smiled at her faintly. Her visitor was sitting on the love seat, but he stood immediately, unsmiling, tall and lean, in black boots, black trousers, black coat, his hair black, his face darkly tanned. Now that she saw him lit by the afternoon sun that spilled through the opened shutters, she had to draw her breath. This man—it was as though he drew all the color from the room. The room faded out. Ella could see nothing but that vibrant black figure. A fragment of poetry rose in her mind. Something she'd read with her Papa.

No light; but rather darkness visible

By visible darkness, that was how one could see in hell.

Yesterday, this man had gripped her with hands of steel, held her as though he wanted to break her bones for daring to touch Phillipa's harpsichord. *Get out*, he'd said, and he'd meant the music room, Trombly Place, London, the world. There was no denying that now. He wanted her to disappear. She could feel the hate rolling off of him.

This man was dark. He was dangerous. She wished she could grab something, grip the back of the blue damask sofa, but she knew from her dealings with Alfred that she could not display weakness. Predators respond to fear, give chase the moment they sense impending flight. This man was nothing like Alfred, but he was also a predator. She stood as tall as she could, spine stiffened. Then he was gliding toward her, his tread silent, lethal, and she saw his eyes catch the light.

Not black. Blue. Midnight blue, shadowed by the black sweep of his lashes. The eyes of a fallen angel.

He was more than dangerous. He was the devil himself.

"Miss Reed."

His voice was smoke and velvet, harsh and soft. It took her a moment to remember that *she* was Miss Reed, that "Reed" was the alias she'd given Mrs. Trombly.

"Yes." She could have cursed herself as soon as she said it. *Yes, I'm Miss Reed.* Could she sound any less convinced? She felt exposed, as though the blue lightning of his eyes had turned her dress to cinders, made her flesh glow transparent as candle wax. She felt he could see the dark shadows of her bones and read every lie in her heart. This man was not credulous like Mrs. Trombly, vague and dreamy and eager to pretend she was a conduit for family ghosts. He looked like he wanted to crush her beneath his boot and summon the maid to scrub the stain out of the carpet.

"Pleased to make your acquaintance." She curtsied, a rigid, little dip. *Don't show fear. Don't show fear. You've done nothing wrong. You are in this house at Mrs. Trombly's request.* This man projected dominance. It was his height, his muscular grace, the arrogance of his features, which were slightly too large, too brutal. It was as though a face sketched along fine, aristocratic lines had been gone over by a thick charcoal. His nose was aquiline but thickened at the bridge—perhaps by a blow; his cheekbones were high and stark, eyes deep set, lips full and sneering, strong chin deeply cleft. His hair was true black, no chestnut highlights, no auburn, and thick and coarse and too wild to be fashionable. He seemed the master of the house. As though it were his right to decide what to do with her.

He stopped before her and sketched a brief, ironic bow. A lock of hair fell across one eye, and he pushed it back with a large hand of startling beauty. His fingers looked strong, but they were exquisitely shaped, long and elegant. He could make wringing necks into an art form.

"Miss Reed, allow me to introduce Viscount Blackwood." Mrs. Trombly, with her graying hair and her lavender silk gown and faded beauty, seemed like an apparition next to this bold, black figure. Scarcely there.

Viscount Blackwood. Isidore Blackwood.

His presence was overpowering. The hate that rolled from him had a black undertow, hot and inexorable. A current that made her fight to stand her ground. She wanted to sway into him. Dear Lord, her palms were sweating inside her gloves. Her pulse quickened.

"Mrs. Trombly and I have been discussing you, Miss Reed." The viscount smiled, a lazy, predatory smile. His teeth were even and blindingly white against that sun-darkened skin. "What a remarkable power you possess."

Ella kept silent, aware that he was toying with her, prepared to pounce if she uttered the wrong word. They'd been arguing about her; that's what he meant. Mrs. Trombly had claimed she'd lost him as a son, but he was certainly acting the part of a son. He wanted to protect Mrs. Trombly from *her*. She supposed it was laudable. She wished she could explain to him that she meant no harm.

She said only: "Mrs. Trombly is very kind."

"She is," he replied, narrowing his brilliant eyes.

Ella wondered if he was about to unsheathe his claws, denounce her a charlatan and demand some proof of her ability, or if Mrs. Trombly's gentle presence would restrain him.

The look he gave her was frankly insulting. "Mrs. Trombly is *too* kind."

This last made Ella narrow her own eyes. She returned his look with as much scorn as she could manage. *Too kind*. Alfred had said the same thing about her papa.

The thought of Papa's kindness made her heart throb now. It gave her the strength to answer the man who stood before her, contempt in every line of his face. She looked Viscount Blackwood in the eye.

"I don't believe there's such a thing as too much kindness, my lord," she said. "The world is ever in short supply."

Something flared in his gaze—surprise. At her words or her tone, Ella couldn't be sure.

"Be that as it may," he said, voice dropping into a lower register to become even more menacing, "it is not for Mrs. Trombly to make up the deficit."

"Isidore." Mrs. Trombly laid her hand on his arm. "Miss Reed has done *me* a great kindness in agreeing to stay with me. She did not seek me out. I all but kidnapped her. I told you, she'd collapsed. She wasn't even conscious when I had her brought here. What greater proof of her disinterest do you need?"

"And was her performance at Miss Seymour's séance a *disinterested* piece of theater?" He put his hand absently atop Mrs. Trombly's, swallowing it whole in his grasp. A casual, tender gesture. But he kept his glittering eyes on Ella. "She fell insensible at a convenient moment. She knew it would capture your interest."

"I knew nothing of the sort." He wanted to stare her down, did he? Well, she could match him there. She knew that her eyes disconcerted. She fixed him with her gaze and stepped closer. She wished immediately she had not. His maleness flooded her. His heat and his scent, a mixture of coffee and amber, whisky and pepper, cedar and musk. It made her giddy. Her vision swam, and she almost blinked. The effort it required to keep her eyes locked on his made her clench her hands at her sides. "I had never heard of Mrs. Trombly before that night. I had never heard of her daughter. I did not *perform*. I … " Again, she had come up against the truth. She heard Mr. Norton again, his nomenclature making no concessions to her youth or gender.

When the morbid material in your blood reaches a sufficient level it operates on your brain. This causes the convulsions. It is desirable that you have these convulsions. If the vertigoes and convulsions become less frequent, this is a sign that the condition has become masked and will find other outlets. The automatisms will become more condensed, more profound in nature. Assault, homicide, arson. All of these terrible deeds have been documented.

She let out her breath. No, she could not explain herself. She would rather deceive kindly Mrs. Trombly and all her kith and kin. She *was* lying. She was a charlatan. But not in the way he insinuated. She had not orchestrated this situation. She couldn't have done so if she'd wanted to. The idea that she could have was ludicrous.

"I never dreamed I would wake up in this household," she said, hearing the bitterness in her voice. "I don't know what motivation you ascribe me, my lord, but you do it wrongly and in haste, based upon a very cursory study of my character."

This speech affected him; she could tell. His eyebrow lifted. She doubted he had revised his opinion of her, but she had awakened some new interest. A muscle ticked in his jaw, and he tilted his head, considering her. He glanced at Mrs. Trombly, whose eyes had filled, predictably, with tears.

"My dear Louisa," he said, turning to her, trapping her hand now between both of his own.

"Why don't you sit down?" said Mrs. Trombly, blinking rapidly. Her voice was a wisp. She forced a smile and spoke with more vigor. "Why don't *both* of you sit down? I'll ring for a tea tray. Cook has made red-currant scones."

"Oh." Ella looked at her in dismay. The last thing she wanted to do was sustain a sitting-room farce with Satan, to look at him for the next hour—massive, scowling—across Sevres china tea cups and the silver cow creamer. "Thank you, but I couldn't possibly intrude. I'll leave you to your tea."

"You are dressed for going out," said Mrs. Trombly, as though seeing her for the first time since she'd entered the room. "Well, it is a lovely day for a walk. You *are* going out?"

Ella hesitated.

"I'd hoped to walk to Hyde Park," she said.

"You won't be gone long?" Mrs. Trombly's voice was mild and held no objection.

"However long it takes to reach the park and take a turn by the lake," said Ella. The prospect of imminent escape almost turned her knees to jelly. She was transforming the wobble into a passable curtsy of farewell when Lord Blackwood spoke.

"I'll accompany you, of course," he said.

"Really, Isidore," began Mrs. Trombly at the same time Ella murmured, "There's no need … ." Both women stopped.

The viscount lifted Mrs. Trombly's hand to his lips and kissed it. Seen in profile, the planes of his face were even starker, his nose, cheekbones, and jaw prominent. Alfred scarcely had features at all compared to this man.

"Miss Reed has all but invited me to familiarize myself with her character," he said. "I confess I find the prospect enticing. And I love to take the air in pleasant company. You do trust me with your … medium?" He gave "medium" just enough of a lilt to make the term, rather than the phrase, the question.

Ella had already drawn a breath to decline his offer on some maidenly pretext—it couldn't possibly be appropriate to gallivant around London with an unmarried man—but his exaggerated pronunciation of the word "medium" brought her up short. She was no longer protected by, and subject to, the rules of etiquette that dictated the behaviors of aristocratic young ladies. She existed in some other, far hazier, social category. She had neither wealth nor even her name to fall back on. She was impecunious, orphaned Ella Reed, private medium to Mrs. Trombly. A fraud who needed to cling tight to the one shaky branch of security fate had thrust in her path. Cling tight and hold fast. No matter what Lord Blackwood might do to dislodge her.

He wanted to dislodge her. He wanted to send her whirling back into the storm. She had read it in his eyes. She had to treat with this man warily.

"I appreciate Lord Blackwood's offer." Ella smiled at Mrs. Trombly, what she hoped was a sunny, careless smile, then turned the smile on the viscount. "I count chief among life's pleasures an afternoon walk to the varied pace of animated, *congenial* conversation."

"Your simplicity does you credit," was the viscount's dry response. He folded his arms across his chest. The fingers of his left hand lay upon the swell of his right bicep. Long fingers, bronze skin against the black coat. "I am told you're from the country?"

"Somerset." Her smile, which had failed so demonstrably to dazzle, faded from her lips. Her tongue felt wooden. This would never work. She didn't possess the charm to win him over or the wit to deflect his questions. He looked so at ease, awaiting her reply. Such a large man shouldn't be that well formed, that graceful. The tiny Mrs. Trombly was a Lilliputian beside him; by all rights, he should have looked clumsy in comparison, an ogre best kept away from the glass-fronted cabinet of porcelain figurines. But his body was perfectly in balance. His proportions had achieved some mathematical perfection. His trousers molded to the curving muscles of his thighs; his impeccably tailored coat hugged his broad shoulders. The flick of his wrist as he swiped at another errant lock of hair made something flick inside her. She might as well be set upon by a panther as this man. She was as ill-prepared by her life thus far to meet with either.

"Somerset. But how delightful. Let me guess what part." He was playing with her now.

He shut his eyes. No wonder his eyes seemed to blaze like the cerulean centers of flames, hedged about as they were with those thick, black lashes. His eyelids darkened near the lashes, as though lined with kohl. "Glastonbury!" His lids swept up, and she was skewered again by his gaze. "You can only be from Glastonbury, resting place of King Arthur and Guinevere, his queen. And now I can guess at your lineage. You are descended from the enchantress Morgan Le Fay. What a perfect pedigree for a woman of your profession. Your American competitors must be quite put out."

"I am not from Glastonbury, my lord." Had she thought her tongue wooden? How optimistic she had been. It was heavy as lead.

"Ah, well, so I am not a clairvoyant. Where, then, are you from?"

"From farther west, my lord." She would keep as near to the facts as she could. Simpler that way, and there could be little harm in it. Only if he really were a clairvoyant would she have cause to fear he could divine her story. She could have been part of his world—the Arlingtons might easily have rubbed shoulders with the Blackwoods, with the Tromblys ... if everything were different. Papa had sold the townhouse after Robert died. He never went back to London. He had withdrawn into books, reading and writing, a world of imagination he shared with her alone. Theirs had been a society of two.

Alfred Gunning, barrister at law, would appear in Debrett's this year as succeeding to the title and estates of Baron Arlington. Her name would not be mentioned. Lord Blackwood could never guess who she really was. Unless Alfred ... but no. Alfred would *not* find her. Not here.

"Miss Reed, from farther west than Glastonbury." A half smile played on Lord Blackwood's lips. His cheekbones were so bold, the shadows beneath them dark as ink.

The current ... the current between them. She could feel it again, warm and dark and irresistible, tugging her. She wanted to rest her fingertips in the hollows beneath those cheekbones, stroke the length of his jaw, and run her forefinger along the cleft in his chin.

No one had prepared her for this. No one had told her this was possible. A man who could pull her like the moon pulled the tides. He was aware of it; he had to be. He was *doing* this to her. He was in control of it, exerting this force. Wicked. His half smile was only a shade different from his sneer. He lifted a black brow.

"So," he purred in that smoky voice, "you disclaim your ties to Avalon?"

She couldn't breathe, concentrated all her might on simply returning his stare. Where did he come by this ability to befuddle her senses? She had no charm; she had no wit. But she had always had a *will*. She had always known her own mind. Her will, her discipline, her self-control—that was what she had. Her will was her only defense against her illness; although, in the end, will wasn't enough.

This man's proximity, the heat of his body, the blue fire of his eyes, made her head fill with fog, made her unsure of her direction. She had no direction of her own. She was groping her way ... toward him.

Mrs. Trombly, clearing her throat, dispersed the mist.

"Do you want bread for the ducks, Miss Reed?" she asked. "I'll call for some old rolls."

Ella's gratitude was out of all proportion to the offer.

"Oh, why yes, thank you. That would be lovely. Old rolls. Wonderful." Relief made her babble. She angled her body away from Lord Blackwood, tying the strings of her black bonnet more firmly beneath her chin. She would not let him overwhelm her. She didn't have much, only her freedom. She wouldn't let him take that away.

Chapter Seven

She walked quickly. Isidore's legs were long, and he matched her pace easily, but she, far smaller, was taking little hopping steps, almost running. Her face was composed, but her legs betrayed her. She was nervous. Why? What exactly was she hiding?

He intended to find out.

Trombly Place was on Mount Street. Miss Reed headed straight for Berkeley Square. A few minutes into their silent ramble, he thought perhaps she might check her speed, but if anything, she went faster. *Very well then.* He slowed. The sun shone on the upper stories of the Georgian buildings that fronted the square. The bricks glowed a baleful red. The plane trees dappled the grass with shadows. He stopped and watched her as she increased the distance between them. Her skirts were swinging. She really was as close to breaking into a run as one might get without the enabling occasion of a footrace. How her heart must be pounding.

Suddenly she too stopped. She had realized he was no longer walking with her. She turned, jerkily, with that same rigidity he'd noticed before, as if clockworks determined her movements. She didn't seem to be one with her body, a continuous organism composed of flesh and its vitalizing forces. Rather, she gave the impression of being divided—a disembodied will standing against her body, holding her body in check. Her awkwardness was the result of her exerting too deliberate a control over every gesture. He'd never seen anything quite like it.

He watched her as she came back toward him. She was no longer running. Her walk was slow and stately, but she couldn't eradicate that tense, hitching skip from her gait. Lord, but she was strung tight. Good. The easier to make her vibrate. To turn and pluck her and figure out to what pitch she'd been tuned. And then to snap her. He remembered the feel of her wing bones beneath his hands. He'd almost snapped her then.

Her chin shot up. She had noticed his appraisal. He folded his arms and let his gaze wander from her boots to her bonnet and back down. He was being insolent. Parceling her out. He wanted her to know he was taking her measure. He wanted her to think he saw through her. But he didn't. Not yet. He was *more* confused, less able to guess what she was about. She presented too odd a mixture of elements for him to fit her easily into a category. As he'd charged to Trombly Place to dislodge this medium, he'd imagined she would show signs, under closer observation, of more obvious charlatanry. Cosmetics purpling her eyelids. Amulets around her neck. A voice that veered between registers as she responded to unheard frequencies. He'd expected her features, scrutinized, would appear harder. Her attitude more garrulous and theatrical.

Miss Reed was not showy. Her accent was refined. Hardly the accent of an untutored rustic from the forests of Exmoor. Her manners bespoke good breeding. Her dress and bonnet were cheap, but her boots and shawl were fine and would have come dear. Louisa had told him she was in mourning for her father. If she was the daughter of some country squire, a man of old family who drew on his high station and low income until he died destitute, that might explain both her refinement and her need for paid employment. But why hadn't she married? Surely marriage came before work in the mind of a well-bred young woman? She wasn't in the first bloom of youth, but she was hardly in its autumn; he guessed her to be in her early twenties, maybe so much as twenty-five or six. Old enough to have debuted and weathered several seasons on the catch for an eligible bachelor. She must have had prospects. Her mourning black emphasized her pallor, her straight, fragile shoulders, and long, slim neck. Her face, stark and white, was wide across the cheekbones, narrowing to a pointed chin. Those lips that had caught his eye in the music room … He couldn't deny they fascinated him now, the details he hadn't noticed: upper lip deeply indented, the full lower lip slightly scabbed. Lavender shadows beneath her dark eyes made them seem hollow. Hers wasn't a pretty face, but it was arresting. He might even say it had a peculiar loveliness. Bound to captivate some man or other.

Maybe she was some aristocrat's by-blow. A bastard cut off by her legitimate siblings upon the old philanderer's demise. She came to London and fell under the sway of some huckster spiritualist. The sort who read up on London's tragic stories and used his pseudo-scientific mumbo-jumbo to turn those tragedies into pounds and pence. He could picture the man: short and ferrety, with a pointed beard and round glasses. Always probing into past scandals, looking for a new shred of information. It would be easy to manipulate wealthy, bereaved widows and mothers if you uncovered the right tidbit. Not one of them knew her deceased husband or offspring as well as she thought she did.

Isidore didn't doubt a hundred of these men existed within a square mile of where he stood. London was always creating new breeds of scoundrel. If opportunities for honest men were created as quickly, it might go a long way toward reducing the sum total of misery for the rich as well as the poor.

He'd save that sentiment for the House of Lords.

This huckster spiritualist, he would always need accomplices, women who fit certain specifications. Delicate and otherworldly, impressionable and adrift. Along came strange Miss Reed. He lured her in, twisted her to his own ends.

The more Isidore thought about it, the more likely it seemed that some version of this scenario pertained. He didn't ascribe events generally to grand conspiracies, but criminal networks *did* exist. And they were adaptable. No sooner had London's women of fashion decided they absolutely could not be parted from their toy greyhounds and Blenheim spaniels than organized dog-nappings took the city by storm. Why wouldn't the fad for mysticism serve as a new pretext and point of entry for underworld masterminds? Miss Reed was not working alone. At the very least, Miss Seymour was involved; she made money from her séances but not enough. She probably designed her public appearances to facilitate private contacts for her girls. It was a time-tested model. Didn't some mediums even call themselves madams?

He wondered suddenly if Miss Reed really was in mourning. Maybe mourning attire made her a more sympathetic figure to those she preyed upon. Maybe she knew black became her, emphasized that moony, haunted quality. The urge to laugh rose in his chest. No vulgarity for gently bred Miss Reed. No paint and dye. She must have cultivated those hollow eyes the way a soprano cultivated her voice. Instead of practicing scales, she practiced sleeping in fits and starts.

The idea of her sleeping caused an odd feeling to wash over him. Her hair was fair; he could see twin slivers peeking from beneath her bonnet, loops swept back from either side of a center part. It was unusual to see blond hair paired with such dark eyes. He couldn't help but imagine that hair spread out on her pillow.

She came within two arm spans and stood returning his stare.

"Do we part ways so soon?" She couldn't disguise the fact that she found this idea not altogether unpleasing. He smiled. *You won't get away so easily.*

"I said I would accompany you to Hyde Park."

This flustered her. Confusion brought her thin, dark brows together. Or she pretended it did. He doubted she was as new to London as she'd claimed to Louisa. The more information she already had, about London, about the Tromblys, and the more ignorance she claimed, the more convincing her messages from Phillipa would be.

"Yes … ?" she said, searching his face for the answer. She didn't look like she was pretending. She looked off-balance and irritated and a little self-righteous, as though *he* were the one playing games. He sighed.

"Hyde Park is that way." He pointed back the way they had come. Heaven help him. He set the pace now, slower, back along Mount Street. Miss Reed walked stiffly, quivering with the suppressed energy that had sent her bounding from Trombly Place as though hell-bent to escape him.

"I didn't realize I was walking in the wrong direction." The indignation and chagrin in her voice sounded disturbingly authentic. As had her avowal that her swoon during the séance was *not* a performance. Well, what was a medium anyway if not an actress?

"You could have said something sooner."

I could have.

"I'm glad to learn that we agree on certain points." He smiled at her and watched with interest the way she compressed her full lips in irritation. He might come to enjoy torturing her. She was so jumpy and so desperate to contain her anxiety. It rather brought out the feline instincts. But he shouldn't be thinking about enjoyment. He shouldn't be savoring anything about the situation. He should be direct. Move in for the clean kill.

"Now that it's just the two of us … " he said pleasantly. *The two of us. Intimate friends.* "We can speak frankly. Why are you living in Mrs. Trombly's house?"

"She asked me to," came the ingenious reply. Miss Reed had decided to take shelter in a country mouse routine. She was making a show of looking up at the grand homes. He wouldn't be surprised if she suddenly tugged his arm and asked him to take her to a shop to buy hair ribbons. *I've never been behind those big, plate-glass windows before!*

"Indeed," he said shortly.

"You will remember, my lord"—Miss Reed flashed a quick glance in his direction—"that Mrs. Trombly and I agree on *that.* She brought me into her house and begged that I stay. The arrangement took me quite by surprise."

"What if I go and speak with Miss Seymour?" He expected to see her start in fear at this proposition, but the arrow missed its mark. Miss Reed only looked at him gravely. He wondered if it were possible that Miss Seymour was not involved. She had to be. The setup was too perfect.

Louisa had described the scene in more detail than he cared to see it. Miss Seymour had felt a presence in the shadows—young, black eyes, black hair. When Louisa stood, sobbing out Phillipa's name, Miss Seymour had stretched out her arms.

Come, Phillipa. I will bring thee where no shadow stays.

And Miss Reed had been taken, possessed, and consumed by the spirit.

How many times had they done it before?

"I wish you'd bring me." Miss Reed's voice was low and steady … and sincere. "I want to speak with Miss Seymour as well. About what she thought she saw when I … " Miss Reed broke off then started again. "She reminded me of a vulture. Or a crow. She croaked like a crow."

"Crows feed on the dead." He said it to disturb her, but she nodded as though he were raising a point she had considered.

"I thought of that," she said. "That was part of it. She was feeding on something. If not the shadows themselves, then on sadness. I'd never been to a séance. I only went because a girl at the boardinghouse … " She caught herself and changed tack. "I went imagining I'd find it silly," she said, "but I didn't. It was different than I expected. Have you ever been to a séance?"

"No," he said. Her conversation disarmed him. Its searching quality. She sounded for all the world as if she were really trying to figure out what to think about it. The séance. Her subsequent employment. That didn't fit at all with his theory about the huckster spiritualist or Miss Seymour, grand madam. "No, I haven't." He gave her what he hoped was an enigmatic smile. "But I *have* seen men walk on fire and swallow live snakes. Does that seem more outlandish to you?"

"Where did you see these things?" she asked.

"Cairo." He winked at her. "Would your answer be different if I said Berkeley Square?"

She laughed at that, a brief, halting laugh. He saw a flash of her small, white teeth. The front two angled backwards just enough for her incisors to seem slightly prominent. He found the imperfection beguiling. He found *her* beguiling. He hated to admit it even to himself. It was probably what she was counting on.

"I suppose they're equivalent," she said, a hint of smile on her lips. "Conjuring a spirit out of a cabinet. Walking on fire. England isn't any less bizarre than Egypt."

"Do you know why they're different?" he asked softly. "The firewalker and the medium?"

She looked at him, and the traces of laughter disappeared from her eyes. They were solemn again, round and black and wary.

"Motive," he said. "The firewalker is undergoing a rite of purification, a stripping away of the self to come nearer to his god. The medium is charging admission. The medium wants something from the people watching, and the firewalker wants nothing."

She dropped her gaze to her boots. Maybe she was imagining fire beneath them.

"I'm going to ask this a different way," he said. Then, as slowly as he could: "What do you want from Mrs. Trombly?"

"I want what she said she'd give me." Miss Reed still walked looking down, the brim of her bonnet obscuring her face. "A reference, so I can earn my own keep."

"That's all?" He shook his head. *Not good enough.* "Miss Reed, you've chosen a roundabout way of getting work as a governess."

"I didn't *choose* it." She sounded as though her teeth were gritted.

"I know, I know." He tipped his head back and blinked up at the blue sky. "You just happened to fall over at the wrong time."

At this, her head rose and snapped toward him. Her upper lip lifted in a snarl, baring those small, crooked teeth. "That's right." She almost hissed it.

"And you had no acquaintance with Miss Seymour before that night?"

"None." Her eyes were sparking, and he felt his own anger kindle.

"You did not know what that night was? The significance of that night?" He'd stopped walking and was shouting down at her. A couple passing with a Cocker Spaniel on a short leather lead turned their heads and looked at him with widened eyes. Hoping to sniff out some scandal. He nearly growled at them.

"I did not know." Miss Reed sought his gaze and held it. With the sun's light falling across them, her dark eyes glistened. Black pools, fathomless. And suddenly, they no longer glared defiance. They held a sorrow too deep for tears.

"I did not know then," she said. "I know now."

"What do you know?" He turned from her abruptly to hide his own response. A throng of children barreled by and forced her to step forward, brushing against him. He looked down at the curve of her cheek, the swell of her lower lip. Her lips were so red, so lush, so unexpected in that face as white as powder.

Too red, he tried to tell himself. Like a poison berry. But he watched the corner of her mouth, fascinated. He watched those lips move as she began to speak.

"I know Phillipa died that night, five years ago. I know she fell from a balcony and that you carried her back to Trombly Place. You sat up in the room with her all night."

This recital took his breath away. He didn't want to remember it. To travel back to that night. He looked away from Miss Reed, concentrated on the everyday sights and sounds of the street. The gorgeous weather had called everybody with two hale legs, and some without, into the street. He saw a man with a wooden leg on the corner selling nuts. Charwomen and countesses alike were making their way down the thoroughfare. The handsome equipages of Mayfair's finest, drawn by glossy horses, better fed than a good three-quarters of the citizenry, rolled toward the park with pedestrians weaving in and out in little groups, brightly clad in afternoon dresses and suits dyed blue and green and that suddenly ubiquitous shade of chemical purple.

What a pair they made, he and Miss Reed, both in matte black, except for the glimmer of black silk at his throat, both silent, both still, locked in struggle over a ghost.

He did not want to travel back to that night, but he could do it so easily. He could get back there so quickly.

Yes, he had sat up with her, gazing at her face, always so mobile, a thousand expressions flitting across it, gone cold and fixed. Gazing at the glimmer of her eyes just barely visible beneath the lids he'd pressed down. He had taken off her gloves and held her hands.

Yes, she had fallen from a balcony. She was drunk that night. They were all drunk. There was rum in the punch, gin in the lemonade. Everywhere: glasses of sherry, claret, champagne. Clement had lit a cheroot in the ballroom, and other men had followed their host's example, lighting cheroots, cigars, pipes, filling the house with smoke. Many lovers had quarreled that night. Tipsy spats punctuated the music. Other pairs had disappeared upstairs. The party had started late—after the opera let out—and the good little debs in their pastel silks should never have ended up there. He should have turned Phillipa around at the door. Instead, he followed her up the stairs.

No one had seen it happen. He didn't look for her on the balcony. He didn't realize she'd gone in that direction. He thought she'd run downstairs. No one knew *how* it had happened. She might have hoisted herself up onto the balustrade as she often did and toppled over. But she was so lithe. She had such balance. Even as distraught as she'd been … racing away from him … sobbing … flinging her body about as though she wanted to punish it … would she have slipped? *Could* she have slipped? Phillipa, who could stand on the back of a cantering horse? Could she have fallen … if she hadn't wanted to? If at least one little part of her hadn't desired that spiraling moment, that leap into oblivion?

Suddenly, he wanted Miss Reed to be genuine. He wanted her to *know*. He wanted her to speak the truth. He wanted her to be absolutely guileless, undesigning, no purpose whatsoever other than to act as Phillipa's mouthpiece. He wanted her to put him out of his misery. To pronounce judgment. Exonerate him or seal his doom. He wanted it so badly he would almost, in that moment, do anything to believe in her.

He became aware again of her slender, upright form. She was so close. Vibrating with that odd tension. The top of her bonnet came up just past his shoulder. If he lifted his hand, he could stroke the exposed curve of her cheek, brush his thumb across the ravaged flesh of her swollen lower lip. Catch her chin and lift her face, hold her still, and plunge into those eyes until he drank in their darkness, glutted himself on the black knowledge that brimmed there.

"How did you know that?" The words caught in his throat. He hated himself for asking in that way, with that raw longing in his voice revealing his vulnerability. His desire to surrender to blind, stupid hope. That was how it worked, wasn't it? This kind of hoax?

Even the staunchest skeptic will banish his good sense if you can whet his need, whet it until it cuts his sanity to pieces.

He started walking again, without warning, and she trotted to keep up. It was boorish of him, but he didn't care. He tried to make his tone contemptuous. "How did you know? Did Phillipa tell you?"

They were nearing Park Lane, and on the other side, Hyde Park stretched before them. Acres and acres of green hills and budding trees. Thousands and thousands of men and women, horses and dogs, carriages and phaetons. Give him a choice between Hyde Park and a country meadow, Hyde Park and a lonely Cypriot beach, Hyde Park and the rolling dunes of the Sahara, Hyde Park and just about anything … he'd take anything. Once, he hadn't minded it. He'd made light of the posturing, the preening, the gossiping, the lords and ladies making peek-a-boo into a pastime, playing like infants at the game of seeing and being seen. Now the sight of colored parasols floating above the sward made him want to gnash his teeth. So much for starting over.

"Of course Phillipa didn't tell me." Miss Reed's matter-of-fact tone restored him to sanity. "Mrs. Trombly told me. Shall we enter here?"

"Wherever you like." He shrugged to underscore his indifference, although, as they crossed into the park, he realized he did, in fact, have a strong preference for where they walked. He didn't want to go near the Serpentine, where babies were wailing in their nurses' arms and children were shrieking over swamped sailing vessels and debutantes were milling about, entertaining delicious fantasies of whose admiring eyes were trained in their direction. He didn't care that Miss Reed had expressed a desire to take a turn near the water. He didn't care that he had a stale hunk of bread crumbling in his pocket. He steered them instead onto a path that led into the thickest copse of trees.

"Oh, but I want to feed the ducks." Miss Reed looked over her shoulder. "I suppose we can circle back to the lake?" She said it as though they really were taking a constitutional. Walking for health in the brisk, bright air. As though health mattered to people like them. The corrupt.

He did not respond. He stalked along the path, and this time it was she who lagged behind. He glanced back at her and saw the rapid movements of her eyes. She didn't like it, the relative desolation of the spot. She was dragging her feet. He felt malicious pleasure, knowing that alarm bells were ringing in her head. Smart girl. He waited for her where the vegetation was thickest. Here, despite all the people that surrounded them, they would be hidden from view. A fact that was not lost on her. She approached on her tiptoes, and he could tell she was trying to formulate some excuse, some compelling reason why she needed to feed those ducks right that minute. *They must be so hungry.* She was preparing herself to whirl and dash. She was switching her weight from leg to leg in anticipation. Pity he was so much faster. She pivoted on her heel. He caught her by the wrist before she could blink.

"Why 'of course'?" he demanded, flexing his arm and jerking her closer. He felt angry, irrationally angry, for that moment of weakness, that moment when he'd betrayed himself and almost sniveled in his desire to believe she really could cross between worlds and bring him succor. Her eyes were wide and uncomprehending. "Why did you say 'of course'? *Of course* Phillipa didn't tell you. Why wouldn't Phillipa have been the one who told you? Isn't that what you do? Receive messages from the dead? Did you not claim to Mrs. Trombly that you could speak with her?"

"No." She was scared now; he could feel the tremors moving through her body. Her eyes darted here and there, trying to assess her surroundings, the chance that someone would stumble upon them. He felt, suddenly, like a monster. That too was doubtless part of her act. She was playing on his sympathies. She was no fawn beset by wolves. *She* was the wolf. A small, silvery white wolf with a fawn's liquid eyes. His head felt hot. He couldn't think clearly. God, he wanted to shake her, even as he reviled himself for his loss of control.

"I have made no claims," she said, with surprising firmness. Grudgingly, he credited her for her strength of mind. She did not give in to the animal fear that caused her limbs to quake. "I told

Mrs. Trombly that I would *try* to communicate with Phillipa. That I would remain open to the possibility. I promised nothing more. You have no right to harass and threaten me."

"I have every right to defend Mrs. Trombly." He tightened his grasp on her wrist reflexively.

"What right?" She flung the words at him. "The right of son? Mrs. Trombly told me what kind of son you've been. Did you stay by her side after Phillipa's death?"

He flinched. "She had her other daughters. She had her husband. She didn't need me." *I was the one who had nobody.*

"I see." Miss Reed yanked with her arm, but he had no intention of releasing her. "I see how Mrs. Trombly is encircled by the loving members of her family. She is nearly smothered by their fond attentions."

"You see nothing," he said dully, winning out against the impulse to twist her wrist until she screamed. "I saw her whenever I passed through London. We exchanged letters. She never asked me to come back. Edwina visits. Visits often. Michael—Mr. Trombly—he was with her. It's only a recent development that his work takes him overseas."

But Edwina doesn't visit often. Louisa makes much of her visits, but they are rare and getting rarer. With Arabella in India, there's even less of a sense of family occasion. And Michael had absented himself even before he sailed for Brazil. He threw himself into his work after Phillipa's death. It was his outlet and his refuge. Louisa had only the house with its empty rooms. Its silence. Could anyone blame her for chasing a phantom?

"She wasn't alone," he said softly. "I didn't leave her alone." It was his own conscience he was arguing with. He knew Miss Reed could hear it in his voice, because she stopped tugging and looked at him with something like compassion in her eyes. That was worse than anything. He was terrorizing *her*, and she looked at him with pity.

He let go of her arm. She stepped rapidly back, but there was a tree behind her and she couldn't back up any farther. The slatted light that filtered through the sparse crowns—only a few fresh, young leaves had yet unfurled—emphasized the chiaroscuro of her features: black eyes, white skin. If he still painted, he would have painted her like that. Pressed against the tree in light and shadow. Nude, though. No bonnet. A priestess of Avalon. No. A nymph. Her red mouth hinted at bacchanalia.

Maenad in repose. That's what he would call it. Thank the devil he'd stopped painting.

He took a step toward her. "What happened to your lip?"

She didn't expect this question. A gloved finger flew to the ruby scabs. Then she covered her mouth with her hand. He took another step toward her, and that did it. He couldn't get any closer. She swallowed hard. Lowered her hand.

"I bit it."

"Hmmm." He laid his right hand on the tree to one side of her head. Her eyes flew to his arm, a thick black bar prohibiting any move in the rightward direction. Slowly, deliberately, he laid his left hand on the tree to the other side of her head. Now her eyes flew to that arm. He leaned into the tree, leaned over her. She was trapped in the cage of his arms. She looked back and forth, from one arm to the other, frantically. As he'd intended her to.

"It must have hurt."

"Yes. No. I don't know." She licked the lip. She couldn't meet his gaze. He wondered, suddenly, if she might be a virgin. Maybe she wasn't a con man's mistress. The huckster spiritualist with his round glasses and pointy beard was just a caricature after all. A figment of his imagination. Maybe she wasn't lying. Maybe she had been overcome at the séance. A country mouse might faint in a crowd. Particularly a country mouse in a corset. He pushed the thought away before it could prick at his conscience. She hadn't fainted. According to Louisa, she had frothed at the mouth.

"I bit … It happened at the séance. I can't remember much of what occurred."

"You were possessed by Phillipa Trombly, my dearly departed." He brought his face closer to hers. Her wild black eyes fixed on his, and she froze. Even her trembling ceased. "That is the supposition believed in some corners." His eyes drifted over her face, slipped from the shining eyes to the smudged circles beneath and down the regal slope of her short, thin nose to the beckoning red of her mouth. "Unless you are willing to admit it was feigned?"

"It wasn't." She didn't move her lips as she breathed the words. She was afraid, perhaps, of inviting more attention to them. Too late for that. A little voice piped up in his head. "Stop," it said. "You are *definitely* enjoying yourself." And he shouldn't be. But stopping was out of the question.

This Miss Reed maddened him, how she flickered between timidity and ferocity, retreating then flashing defiance. How she used her body like it was a rigid little barricade between her true being and the world. She hid behind a black-and-white façade. She was elusive, entirely untrustworthy, utterly alluring. He wanted to destroy her defenses, force her into some spontaneous action, eliminate the distance she'd created between her inner and outer self. Not only because of the harm she could do if she began to prattle about the secrets that weighed on Phillipa's unquiet soul. But because she was a puzzle that didn't resolve into a picture he could recognize.

Many women tried to present themselves as puzzles. They were subtle, intelligent, mysterious … but ultimately the pieces fit together. He saw what they wanted, what they feared. Miss Reed—if that was even her real name—seemed to shift like desert sands. He couldn't get his bearings. A chasm might open at any moment.

No matter who had put her up to it, no matter how much she knew or didn't know about Phillipa's secrets, the fact remained:

she had feigned contact. She had wormed her way into Louisa's confidence. She was positioned to rip open old wounds. To bring what festered to the surface.

She was his foe. And suddenly he was glad of it. Because that meant he owed her nothing. Not respect. Not restraint. He could do anything he wanted to discover what she knew ... to see how far she would go.

"Can you summon Phillipa now?" He raised a hand and slipped a finger beneath her bonnet, pulling it back to expose her ear. "Is she with us?" He let his hot breath stir the fine hairs that covered the tiny, dark opening. Her convulsive response brought her breasts into brief contact with his chest. She gasped and jerked back, pressing herself into the tree. He fancied he could hear her spine grinding. Unless her mystic abilities extended to de-materialization, she would not escape through the wood. He smiled against her neck. She didn't smell like an enchantress. She smelled like a good English girl, smelled of rosemary soap and freshly laundered clothes, and only a hint of something else, something tangier, saltier, her own smell. He wanted to inhale more of it. To nuzzle her neck, seek it out. He raised his mouth so his lips brushed her earlobe. "Does Phillipa want to kiss her betrothed?"

He was teaching her a lesson. That was all. Showing her how dangerous it was to toy with people's emotions. Showing her there were consequences she couldn't anticipate. So what if it was ghoulish? Damnable? The whole business was ghoulish and reeked of brimstone. *She* had begun it.

He plunged his hand more fully beneath her bonnet, feeling the silky mass of hair beneath. He lifted his left hand from the tree and pressed his forefinger to her upper lip, traced that deep indentation. He'd never cared to wear gloves except when riding, or when the weather was particularly inclement. He'd abandoned the habit altogether in Egypt. His hands were bare. The fingertips of his left hand were callused from the strings of the violin. He rubbed the roughened surface of his finger down the cleft and up the peaks of her lip. She drew in her breath, and her lips parted.

"Or maybe it's *you* who wants to kiss me?" he whispered. "Only you."

She didn't deny it. Her eyes had closed, and the lids, with their faint mauvine smear, fluttered.

"Open your eyes." He still spoke softly, but it was a command. He would not allow her to retreat. She squeezed them shut more tightly. He cupped her face, pulled at her eyelids with his thumbs, stretching the thin skin, uncovering the black irises. Her eyes appeared more slanted then, more like Phillipa's. *Damn it.* He lifted his thumbs. Her eyes opened wide and stayed open.

"That's right," he said, harshly. He put his forehead on hers and felt her eyelashes sweep down, up, down, up, against his cheek. Then he could bear it no longer. He lowered his face and claimed her lips with his own.

Her lips were dry, hot. They parted slightly as he breathed against them, and he availed himself of their opening. He slid his tongue along her lower lip, felt the little scabs, tasted the hint of blood, coppery, mixing with the cinnamon on her breath. God, it was the taste of sin itself. He took the lip between his teeth, gently, and suckled it, plump and salty-sweet. He felt her lips open further. He thrilled with triumph as her breath exploded. She'd been trying to hold it in her lungs, to tamp down the air in her lungs, to withdraw into herself. But she couldn't hold back any longer. She gasped against his mouth, and her body shuddered, the clockwork mechanism winding down. He turned her face with his hands, kissed the peaks of her upper lip, the corners of her mouth, the smooth, white skin of her cheeks. He slipped his tongue along the damp crevice beneath her full lower lip, and she caught his upper lip between hers, returning his kiss, her tongue against his teeth. She pressed into him, moved her mouth on his with bruising force.

He responded with a low growl, rocking back on his heels, pulling her against him. He wanted to rip her mourning gown down the middle, expose her white skin through the ruins of those black shrouds, reveal her breasts to his plundering mouth. He wanted to lay her down on the damp ground, on the first shoots of spring still weak and tender, struggling out of the dead earth, and take her there, the heat of their bodies sending warmth into the clay, enlivening it. They would be soiled by the act, rutting in the mud, leaves in her hair, cold dirt beneath his fingernails. They would defy the sanctified dead by rolling in the mire, that compost of corpses. He bent her backwards, one hand at the small of her back. The shawl slipped from her shoulders, and he bunched the soft wool in his hand, pulled it away with one smooth motion, and let it drop. He gripped the back of her neck, and she moaned, once, loud and harsh against his lips, the sound ugly with need. He was hard, straining against his trousers. He dragged his mouth from hers, dazed, and in that moment, he glimpsed her face. Her eyes. Her wide, open eyes, black, hungry, tormented, the pain in their depths the twin of his own.

He had wanted to see how far she would go. How far she would take her little game. He had never expected he might push beyond his own limits.

He knew he really was damned. Beyond any dream of redemption. Because he wanted her there with him. Because he hoped she was damned too.

Chapter Eight

Isidore Blackwood's presence invaded her. She felt the hard trunk of the tree against her back. She couldn't sink into it. It wouldn't give. His arms, his broad chest were just as hard, just as unforgiving. There was no way out. Warmth emanated from him, carrying that heady mixture that was his scent, musky and tantalizing. She couldn't block it out. She could only shut her eyes and try not to see him. She tried to disappear. She had done this often. Floated somewhere, anywhere else. A dark, featureless place in which everything was absent. She'd escaped so much pain, hovering beyond it. She worried that sometimes not all of her came back. That she lost a little bit of her soul in the journey. But the alternative—remaining locked in her wracked body—was worse. It wasn't only physical pain that sent her drifting. When word came that Robert had been found—on the pebble beach in Porlock— she had gone away for days. She didn't need food, or sleep. Papa spoke to her, but she couldn't hear him. Though, finally, Papa was why she returned. Why she ate, why she slept, why she spoke again and listened and pretended all of her was there.

She caught her breath and held it in. But he would not let her disappear.

"Open your eyes," he said. His hands tightened, viselike, on her face, and his fingers pulled at her lids so her eyes watered and she saw smears of color. When he let them go, they stayed open. Instead of the nothingness, she saw him. His eyes—his eyes glowed a blue she had never seen. Like hellfire behind a stained-glass window. Where the light played on his face, she could see the fine grain of his skin, burnished bronze. Then the ridge of his brow pressed hard into her forehead, locks of his black hair stroked her temples, and she felt his breath blow hot across her lips. His lips came lower, closer, and suddenly they were on hers, between hers, pushing her lips apart.

She knew it was a kiss. She had read of kisses in novels. And she had been kissed herself—twice. The first kiss hardly counted. She'd been fourteen, walking her lamed horse through the fields with Mathew Sunderland, who had claimed it was no sacrifice as the riding party was an absolute bore without her. He was thirteen, and his kiss, brief and light, reminded her of when she was *very* young and used to kiss buttercups. The second was a proper kiss three years later, the musical professor Papa had hired for the summer taking a liberty. He was young and handsome— much to Papa's chagrin—and, like a man in an opera, he sang every word, from "good morning" until "good night." On his final day at Arlington Manor, he had wrapped her in his arms. His mouth felt warm and pleasant. She was worried that he would break into an aria afterwards and alert her papa that something untoward had occurred, but instead he bowed, so deeply and so dramatically she had to skip to the side, and trilled a simple "La!" She shouldn't have allowed it, but she was curious, and she knew nothing more would ever come of it. Such a silly, strutting fellow, though his voice really was a fine instrument. The next morning he was dispatched to Hanover Square, and that was the end of that. Those were kisses, and this too was a kiss, but so different it shouldn't go by the same name.

This was new. She had never known that a kiss could be so … powerful. That it could involve teeth, tongues, and burning breath. His tongue slipped over hers, stroked her, and she opened her mouth, released the air from her lungs, and pushed back with her tongue. She heard him groan, felt his suction on her lower lip. The rhythmic pulling sensation made something respond in her lower belly. It was something between a tickle and an ache and an itch that made her want to rub herself against his hard thigh where it nestled between her legs. The heat of their joined mouths was sinking through her, sending ripples all the way to her fingertips. His hands were on her head, on her back. Her own arms had twined around his neck without her knowledge. Her breasts crushed against his chest, and the tips felt like hot coals, hurt like hot coals would hurt embedded in her flesh.

This was pain, but she wanted it. She wanted to feel it. She wanted to feel every fiber of her body stretch and strain and fray. She wanted to keep every sense alive to it. She wanted him to feel it too. She wanted to *make* him feel it, for the pain to be theirs and not hers alone. She tasted his skin—pine, smoke, pepper—and the taste wasn't enough. She wanted to devour him. His breath was coming harder, and so was hers, and she realized her eyes were closed again and forced them open. She wasn't going away. She was staying. She was inside her body, and her body was thrumming, and the little moan that she gave was the sound. His tongue moved deeper inside her mouth, filling her, and she wanted to scream then, because she wanted more, and this wasn't real. It couldn't be real. This wasn't for her. This heat of skin against skin, tongue against tongue. Now that she knew what a kiss could be, everything was worse. It wasn't fair, that she could feel like this. Hot and yearning and alive. She shouldn't want to melt into him. She shouldn't want to feel his tongue filling her, to take it in, to swallow him. But her body was proving that it wanted. It could experience this other pain, this sweet agony that made the blood race through her veins. Her red blood with its dark cargo. Its taint. *Morbid material.*

He pressed into her, curved over her, and her body was bending back like a bow. She wanted it to break in half. She wanted the tension to release so she could force herself to twist away. She didn't belong in his arms. Resistance stiffened her limbs. She felt a bubble in her chest, a little hole, expanding. She was empty. She would stay empty. Nothing would ever fill the hole inside her. She was damaged beyond repair.

He was still kissing her, his eyes closed, kissing her lightly, his lips teasing hers, licking, tickling. She stared into the bronze blur of his skin, the dark smudge of lashes. Then his eyes opened too. Searing blue slits. He drew back with a ragged breath, gripped her shoulders, and looked at her. Isidore Blackwood. That brutal face still close to hers. The features so large, so strong. The most vivid face she had ever seen. But he was a stranger. A muscle in his jaw flexed as he clenched his teeth. What he found in her eyes made his eyes widen. He let her go, and she almost staggered. The air felt cold as it rushed to fill the void left by his body. *Empty.* She hugged herself to suppress a shudder. Her shawl was gone. Fallen to the ground. She bent to pick it up and shook it out, stalling for time.

He had seen something in her face that shocked him. A hint, perhaps, of the beast she could be, the beast she became. *Not even human.*

She held the shawl in her hands, staring at the soft blackness. She wanted to hide in its folds. Make it into a black tent and crawl inside. She draped it over her shoulders. The copse was not so thick that she couldn't see the open green of the park through the trees. She could hear the low roar of mingled voices, hoof beats, carriage wheels. The city that had faded away when the world condensed to lips and stroking hands was reforming around her. The world wasn't her body and his, pressed together, moving as one. The world was out there, vast and terrible, and she was alone in its midst. Not a part of it. Not a part of anything. She had to remember what she couldn't have, or she would want more. And that was a hurt she could spare herself. She must not want … more.

Now that he was out there, detached from her, a part of the world that she wasn't, she could look at him. He stood a few feet away, the angle of the light casting one side of his face into shadow. She couldn't read his expression. His chest rose and fell evenly, as though he hadn't groaned in her ear, panted against her mouth. He hadn't felt it—the dark need, the sweet, driving pain. He was unmoved. Disdainful. Judging her.

A kiss couldn't be a revelation to him.

She realized her bonnet was askew and straightened it, tucking back the hair that had fallen from her bun with a savage motion that caused a sharp pain in her scalp. This kind of pain—simple, so different from the double-edged agony she'd just experienced—cleared her mind.

He had kissed her to be cruel. Shame swept over her in a wave. Shame and fury.

"Did that accomplish what you expected, my lord?" She met his eyes, his startling eyes, blue-black rings starred with paler blue. "Do you feel closer to Phillipa?"

"Not in the least," he said, voice flat. He scrubbed a hand across his face. The creases alongside his mouth deepened. He looked almost haggard. She could imagine, suddenly, how he might look in twenty years if the care continued to eat at him: Lines etching the bold planes of face. Features even more marked. Nose like a blade. A grim face. Then his look softened, and the vision vanished. He was young again, and his stark beauty made her yearning a bodily ache. Dear lord, she would need to find new ways of ignoring her body. Her body was finding new ways to betray her.

"Miss Reed." He searched the treetops. With his head so angled, he revealed the broad column of his neck, the shape of his chin, the rich red of his upper lip, the slight bump in the bridge of his nose. "I want to apologize for my conduct. That was ... unkind. I should not have taunted you."

And what of the kiss? Suddenly she did not want him to apologize for the kiss. The taunts, yes. But his lips on hers ... Had the unkindness of the impulse been borne out in the act? Did he feel that the act had polluted him? Could he ... taste it ... her tainted flesh? He had tasted … delicious. And she … *Am I foul?* Tears pricked her eyes. It must have been so different from kissing Phillipa. Phillipa's lips must have been sweet.

"I have never been a bully." He linked his hands behind his back and rocked on his heels, studying her. He looked boyish, ill at ease. Guilty. His mouth quirked with self-mockery. "I hate bullies."

The old viscount. His father. She remembered the shadow that had crossed Mrs. Trombly's face when she spoke of him. *A controlling man.* Watching the play of emotions on Lord Blackwood's face, she suspected the old viscount had been rather more than simply controlling.

"This is a deuced odd situation. I've handled it badly." He shrugged, still distant. A male voice boomed beside them, as though the speaker were standing right there, just through the trees. A flurry of "What hos!" followed, growing fainter.

She glanced about to locate the figures and saw slivers of masculine couture—tweeds and top hats—receding. No interruption forthcoming from that front.

She fidgeted, balling her hands in the edges of her shawl. "I cannot summon a spirit at will."

Now the quirk of his lips turned sardonic.

"My dear Miss Reed," he said. "I never thought you could." He shrugged then threw his arms open in a gesture meant to communicate helplessness. Except he could not look helpless. The reach of his outspread arms was prodigious and only emphasized the breadth of his shoulders.

"This fashion for mysticism … Spirit-writing, table-tapping … " He shook his head. "I'd like to see every table in England milled to sawdust."

At this unexpected image, her lips curved. "And we all eat standing up? Even the Queen?"

He blinked at her, surprised, then grinned. A crooked grin that stole her breath.

"We would recline on couches," he said airily. "As they did in ancient Rome."

"Of course. Ancient Rome. How could I forget?" She was quite sure her own reading on Ancient Rome had never delved into recumbent eating practices. She found it difficult to imagine Lord Blackwood poring over a book. Papa was her template for the literary man: balding, stoop-shouldered, absentminded, gentle, shy, always a little bit rumpled. The tall, demonic viscount, with his fitted black suit and mane of hair—well, put a sword in his hand, he'd make war on heaven. But a pen in his hand … no, she couldn't see it.

"But if destroying all the tables is meant to discourage the table-rappers … " She hesitated. "Don't you think they would find something else to rap on?"

"The tables are not the issue. Is that what you're saying?" He sighed. "How clear-headed you are." His voice was rich with amusement.

This easy, bantering tone. The sudden familiarity between them. It was a hint of what it might be like … if they were friends. She felt emboldened.

"You subscribe to a more rationalist view of the world, my lord?" His brooding mien did not bespeak a scientific bent. He cocked an eyebrow. She tried again. "You disapprove, that is, of mystical explanations for earthly phenomena? Or perhaps you are pious? You find spiritualist practices offensive?"

He thinned his lips. "I distinguish between parlor tricks and mystical experience. And I dislike chicanery. Too many weak-minded and weak-hearted people are made the worse for it. Should I meet a true enchantress, I assure you, I would not condemn her in the name of God or science. I have seen too many things that my understanding does not compass to refute the possibility of magic. But … to return to the matter at hand … "

His face had set again in its hard lines.

"I know," she said, chilled. "I am *not* descended from Morgan Le Fay. But I promise you I have no ill motive. Mrs. Trombly has been so kind to me … "

"And you think the world is in short supply of kindness. So you said. You're right, of course." His air was bemused and tinged with self-reproach. "I do not think I have it in me to make the world a better place. But I will not make it a worse one." He was serious, his voice low and husky.

"I don't understand you, Miss Reed." He said this reluctantly, as though it pained him to admit. "You experienced something at that séance, feigned"—she opened her mouth to interrupt, but he waved a hand and would not be stopped—"or authentic. Yet you tell me you have neither ill motives *nor* spiritual powers. This is what I don't understand." He pressed his fingertips together below his chin.

She was silent. Again, this impasse. She looked up at the trees. A cool wind rustled their crowns. The fair day was fading fast, and a fouler night was coming. He stepped toward her. Dear God but she *felt* the distance between them narrow, as though stroked with a finger.

"I do not want you spreading *messages* from my betrothed abroad. I do not want you to whisper my betrothed's secrets in her mother's ear. If Louisa locks you in the attic with a writing pad and Phillipa's pen and bids you stay there until you can produce a missive from the otherworld, you will not write a word. You will sit in the attic, and when the month of your *mediumship* is up, you will take your leave. If Louisa asks you to rap on the table, you will—"

"Mill it into sawdust?" She met his eyes squarely. "Yes, my lord."

"Well ... " The wind flattened his hair against one side of his face. "A truce, then." He held out his hand. Her heart began to pound. She held out her own hand. She couldn't feel the texture of his fingertips through her gloves. Those small calluses that had scratched the skin of her lips. *Calluses.* What did he do that he should have calluses? She felt maddened by the leather that kept those calluses from grazing her palm.

"A truce," she echoed.

"Shall we give the bread to the ducks?" He smiled at her, not his spontaneous, crooked grin, but a practiced smile. "Or should I crumble it along this path so we can find our way back here?"

"Why would we want to find our way back?" As soon as the words were out of her mouth she blushed furiously. She could feel the heat cresting her cheeks. Even her forehead had to be scarlet.

"Oh, I don't know," he said blandly. "Just a bit of whimsy."

Whimsy.

"Don't you care for fairy tales?"

She smiled tightly. "Yes, my lord."

"Remind me to tell you the Egyptian story of Rhodopis." He said this casually, as though future tête-à-têtes were an inevitability.

She wanted that to be so. She wanted to return here with him, to this little scrap of woodland in the park, brown and green and redolent of rich, pure dirt. It was the closest thing to a fairy-tale forest in the whole city. She wanted to take him to Arlington Manor, to ride with him on the moors, to go all the way to Exmoor and picnic on a low stone wall and wander between oaks and look for the golden stag.

This wanting—it frightened her. She looked away from him, down the path, which was transformed by the rolling clouds above the tree crowns into pools of light and shadow.

"We should head back," she said. "Mrs. Trombly will be wondering what became of us." She was shivering as she walked past him.

It was the wind, she told herself. It was just the cold wind.

• • •

As soon as they were admitted into the entrance hall of Trombly Place, Mrs. Trombly came to meet them. She wore a reproving look. Ella handed her gloves to Rutherford and almost touched her bare finger to her tender lower lip.

But Mrs. Trombly was not looking at her lips. She was shaking her head at Lord Blackwood.

"No hat?" Mrs. Trombly tsked at him, hands on her hips. "If I'd seen you go out I would have insisted you take one of Michael's."

Lord Blackwood raked his fingers through his hair, disarranging what few locks the wind had neglected.

"I go hatless to improve myself," he said with a winning smile. "The air stirring the hairs stimulates the intellect."

"What nonsense," said Mrs. Trombly, but the fondness in her voice was unmistakable. Ella tried to fade into the wall. She had no place in this, what felt like the greeting a fussing mother hen would bestow on a wayward chick. She began to sidle sideways toward the stairs. Rutherford made a discreet evaporation seem so natural. He'd already vanished from the hall.

"Did the Greeks wear hats? Or the Romans? Miss Reed … "

Lord Blackwood's drawl caught her by surprise. She blinked, froze in mid-sidle, and straightened.

"Miss Reed knows something of the Roman proclivities." Lord Blackwood's eyes glinted.

"Are you asking me if the Romans wore hats?" What funny notions of the classical world he harbored! She thought of senators, hatless, strolling by the Tiber, then returning to the capitol to swallow grapes in complete prostration. "Oh, not until the *decline* of the empire, I'm sure, my lord."

She shouldn't feel warmed by the quirk of his lips, the suppressed smile that indicated his appreciation. She shouldn't be looking at his lips at all.

"I rest my case." He winked at Mrs. Trombly.

"Nonsense," she repeated. "You should have worn a hat in Egypt at least. To keep the sun off your face. The other day, Mrs. Wheatcroft told me her daughters are calling you 'the gypsy.' And the Wheatcroft girls haven't had one original notion between the five of them for as long as I've known them. If *they're* calling you 'the gypsy,' that means it's all over London."

"The gypsy is such a fashionable figure." Lord Blackwood cocked a black brow. He looked every inch a gypsy king. "Everyone tells me this is the season for gypsies. They're in the highest demand."

"At costume balls," said Mrs. Trombly. "Where the effect is achieved with boot polish." She glowed as she said it. Lord Blackwood tilted his head, striking an even more raffish pose. He knew what pleasure Mrs. Trombly derived from scolding him. His absurdity was calculated. It was … kind. Watching them together made a lump rise in her throat. She had enjoyed scolding her papa.

Is that jam on your nose? Papa, surely you could put your book down to eat.

"Miss Reed, how did you enjoy your walk?" Mrs. Trombly's melting eyes swung in her direction. "Did it strain your sensibilities to appear in public with this vagabond?"

Damn her pale skin. She wished *she* had taken more sun. If she had a fraction of his tan it might disguise the flush that she felt again creeping up from her breasts.

"I enjoyed the walk," she said carefully. Lord Blackwood was watching her with undisguised interest.

"Was it crowded near the lake?" Mrs. Trombly's benignant smile was turning ever so slightly quizzical.

"Very peaceful, in fact," she answered in a strangled voice. "Except for the ducks, of course. They were so … animated when presented with their bread."

Lord Blackwood made a movement, and she nearly gasped. He wouldn't produce the old roll now to prove her a liar. That would teach her to make a truce with the devil. But he only reached into his waistcoat for a pocket watch. He'd done it to torture her; she was sure of it. His low laugh could have nothing to do with the hour he read on the face of the watch. What man chuckled over the time? Mrs. Trombly's smile was *definitely* quizzical.

"Well," said Ella. "I *am* feeling a little fatigued by the exercise. I'll just go upstairs now, to rest, if you don't mind." She smiled at Mrs. Trombly, then once she was sure the smile was fixed in place, turned to Lord Blackwood. "Thank you, my lord, for the walk. I … " Drat it, why couldn't she think of another word? " … enjoyed it."

He grinned, that same crooked grin she had seen in Hyde Park, and again the breath fled her body. She wondered if their truce was more a threat than open hostility.

"Well," she said again. And all but scurried for the stairs.

In the bedchamber, she untied her bonnet and threw it at the wardrobe. She paced the worn carpet. She was a fool. He had kissed her on a whim, a malicious whim, to test her. She had no right to keep thinking of his kisses. Hers was to be a life without kisses, without a husband, without children of her own. She knew that. Her dear papa, who had loved her so much, *he* had known that.

Maybe Alfred was right in Papa's case. Maybe Papa's kindness hadn't helped her in the end. If he hadn't always seen the best in people, if he had suspected Alfred was a selfish, climbing sort of bastard, and that he would not do right by her, he might have made some other arrangements. He might have found a way to leave her with something.

She had told Papa that Alfred had no love for him or for her. He was sly and jealous. He'd often complained that his mother had married beneath her. He held his own father in contempt and spoke slightingly of the man's "insufferable bourgeois habits." By "insufferable bourgeois habits," she took him to mean decency. A resistance to turning every hunt into a massacre. A willingness to go to his office and work for his clients.

Alfred is a sporting man, not a poet, Papa had said. *He's clumsy with his words. He cares for you, Ella. He'll look after you.*

Papa had assured himself that Alfred would allow her to stay at Arlington Manor. He had taken no precautions. Made no provisions. He had left her with nothing.

No thought had ever felt so much like betrayal. *I'm sorry, Papa.*

She hurled herself onto the bed and vented her agitation in gusty, tearless sobs. She dug her fists into the coverlet and buried her face in the pillow. Her hiccupping breaths drew the pillowcase into her open mouth. The fabric tickled her lips, dampened against her teeth and tongue. Her breasts, flattened by the weight of her body, felt full and sensitive. She sat up abruptly. Phillipa's photograph stood on the bedside table in its silver frame. *She* was the woman Blackwood loved, even now. Even dead, she had a greater claim on him.

Phillipa had danced with him. She had felt the hard muscles in his arms and shoulders and dreamed …

Enough. She lunged forward and grabbed Phillipa's photograph. She couldn't look at her anymore, that fetching, slightly blurry face. *She could never sit still.* She would stuff the photograph into the writing desk. It was such a pretty satinwood desk, with one long drawer and two short drawers, each with a brass-ring handle. She pulled open the long drawer; there were pens inside, and a writing pad and blotter, the pasteboard backing cornered with red satin. Mercifully, the pad and blotter were bare.

Papa always said handwriting was an expression of the soul.

Writing unites the hand and the word. In that unity, a man finds himself.

What would Papa have thought of London's rabble of spirit-writers?

She could almost hear him: *They can take dictation from the dead? And it's all marmalade recipes from someone's Aunt Barbara? No sonnets from Donne? Bah.*

She slid the photograph inside the drawer and shut it hard. There. That was better. She turned around and caught her reflection in the mirror on the wardrobe door. So white, her face. Sunken eyes. Sharp nose, sharp chin. Sharp, crowded teeth. Her hair the color of ashes.

She was a ruin, but without former glory. A ruin born. She flung open the wardrobe door. Now she saw only her black dresses, neatly hung. She knelt down, and her fingers found the ring of the wardrobe's single drawer. She tugged the drawer open.

It was filled with Phillipa's relics. Gloves in kid, satin, and lace. Beaded reticules. Embroidery rings. Ella sifted through the neat piles and selected a cream-colored purse embroidered with roses. She opened the purse and drew out her velvet pouch, weighing it in her hand before she untied the strings and shaped each of the items inside with her fingers. Bracelet, watch, hair clips, spoon, ring. Everything that remained after she'd sold what she needed for food and lodging and cab fare when she'd first arrived in London. She returned the pouch to its hiding place. She checked twice a day to make sure its contents were accounted for. If something should go wrong here, with Mrs. Trombly, those small pieces of metal would once again provide her only security.

She covered the purse with a pair of opera gloves. Then hesitated. She lifted the opera gloves and ran her thumb over the cool ivory leather.

How did you find the third act, Miss Trombly?

Orfeo's aria made me shiver, Lord Blackwood. So mournful.

Mournful, yes. But Amore herself rewards him for it with the return of his Eurydice. And so it is the happiest of songs.

And if Amore had not favored Orfeo? If Eurydice had remained below?

Were I Orfeo, my darling, and you, Eurydice, then only one course of action would lay before me should Amore prove so cruel.

Yes, my lord?

I would join you in Hades.

She laid the gloves back down. Her imagination had always been vivid. It wouldn't take much to convince herself that her fantasies were visions. Maybe she really could be a medium. A reticule in the back of the drawer caught her eye, bronze beads against black silk. She slid it out, picked at the knot in the black ribbon drawstring, worked her fingers inside the narrow neck, and spread it open. She brushed something soft and pulled. A fold of white emerged from the black bag like a magic trick. She turned it in her hands—a creased linen handkerchief—and touched the initials embroidered on the corner in thick blue thread.

IHB.

She lifted the handkerchief to her nose. Dust and the faintest whiff of gardenias. The scent had nothing to do with the man who'd held her in his arms, who smelled musky and hot, who smelled of wood shavings and smoke.

Once he had daubed himself with perfume and gone courting, this prince of darkness.

It was quiet in the room and getting darker. She remained on her knees in front of the wardrobe, the black reticule in one hand, the white handkerchief in the other. She didn't want to move just yet. Maybe if she stayed in that attitude a little longer, peace would find her.

Chapter Nine

As soon as Miss Reed had made her way down the hall with that halting clockwork gait, Louisa turned to Isidore.

"You aren't leaving?" She didn't wait for a reply. "I would speak with you a moment." She followed him into the sitting room and shut the door.

"You didn't quarrel with her?" She did not take a seat but stood, peering anxiously into his face. "You think I'm behaving foolishly, and maybe I am, but *she* isn't to blame for it. She's a dear girl, without an ounce of presumption. And she's been hurt very badly by something; you can see it in her eyes. I want her to stay with me. She reminds me … Well, actually, she reminds me of … "

"Don't say Phillipa." Isidore stepped around her and flung himself onto the sofa. He sprawled there, regretting his words, feeling clumsy and rude. He had always taken the liberties of a son with Louisa. He didn't deserve them. He had failed, in the end, to perform a son's duties.

"I wasn't going to say Phillipa." Louisa walked to the sofa and stood over him. "I was going to say that she reminds me of *you*, Isidore. The look that would come upon your face at the end of day when it was time for you to leave us and return to Castle Blackwood—it used to break my heart. Resigned and defiant at once. Like an innocent man at the scaffold. Such a terrible expression for a boy to wear."

Isidore pressed his fingertips into his jaws to loosen the muscles. His face felt locked.

I am no innocent. Not anymore. And neither, I think, is your Miss Reed.

In the hallway, he had watched the dusky blush stain her pale cheekbones. She looked so wretched, so undone. He would have pitied her. Except the kiss had affected him too. Had left him scorched. Restless. The only way to soothe the burning in his body would be to hurl himself back into the flames.

Bitterness stabbed through him. He'd certainly made a hash of things. The black knight, storming in to save the day, spurring his horse to a lather, and himself spurred on by demons, usually did.

"Sometimes I catch Miss Reed wearing that very expression." He heard Louisa speaking as if from far off. "Wounded and hopeless, but with the same mulish tightness about the mouth. Unyielding."

For a moment, he felt almost like a boy again, looking up at her, so much taller than he, and so much gentler than anyone he had ever known. He almost wanted to pull her down beside him and weep upon her breast. He had never allowed himself to do that when he was a boy. Too late now. When he spoke, his voice was thick.

"Tell me," he said, "are you so very lonely?"

"Isidore," she said, searching his face. She leaned over and put a finger beneath his chin. She used to do that when she wanted his attention, wanted to make him listen.

Let Michael go back with you. Let Michael try to talk with him.
She said, "It's not your fault."

His jaw worked without his volition. He would not look at her. She pulled back and straightened.

What's not my fault? He wouldn't be able to ask without sneering. He would not subject her to his scorn. Louisa was a sweet, uncomplicated woman. She'd never understood him. She'd never understood Phillipa. He would not punish her for having a simpler nature. A *better* nature. But her exoneration meant nothing.

"You could leave town." He smiled bleakly at the vase of roses on the table. "Shut up the house. You could stay with Edwina."

"I wouldn't want to impose." As Louisa spoke, the room dimmed. The blinds were open, but the sunlight no longer beamed bright squares upon the carpet. The red of the roses deepened. Blood-dark.

"She'd be happy to have you," he said, but he knew it for a lie. Edwina found her mother's presence cloying. Always had. She took after Michael. Practical, efficient, active. Displays of strong emotion displeased her. Two weeks after Phillipa's death, Edwina had already lost patience. *Sid, she's not trying to get better. She likes to be miserable. I can't endure another minute of it.*

Still, he pressed on. "You'd be a great help to her, I'm sure. I could settle things here. You could go at once."

"And take Miss Reed?" Louisa sat gracefully in a seat across from him. The last rays shining through the windows thinned, and the room swam with shadows. Clouds were rolling in from the country, filling the sky, replacing that pale, scrubbed blue with a dome of gray.

"Miss Reed wants nothing more than to work as a governess." He realized as he said it that he believed it. Well, why not take her at her word? He had offered her a truce. If she would refrain from voicing histrionic transmissions from the other side, he would not malign her to Louisa. "Find her a position. She won't regret an early dismissal if you honor your agreement."

In the murky room, Louisa's face was indistinct beneath her upswept hair, the gray strands luminous. She was young to have gone so gray. That hair used to be warm, chestnut brown. Her eyes were soft as moss, shading between green and brown. All of her daughters had inherited Michael's coloring. Phillipa's eyes had been like chips of obsidian. .

He heard her sigh. "You know, I *have* thought about it." For a split second, he thought she meant going to Edwina, releasing Miss Reed from her service. But even before she continued, he knew she had never considered the suggestion. She had barely registered his words. She was picking up a different thread, the one always unspooling in her mind.

"I've thought about why it's so hard," she said. "After all, other women have lost their children."

"No consolation there," he said gruffly. "Each person's suffering is only a small share of the great sum of suffering in the world. Just makes you sorrier for the world."

"But other women bear it better."

What could he say? "People are different."

"I've often thought … " She started again, "It would be easier if it happened … differently. Illness. Childbirth. It's not that I would have been prepared, but I could have wrapped my mind around it. Understood it somehow. Come to terms with it. The way it was … so sudden. I always think … there was one last thing she had to tell me."

"She was twenty years old." He realized he was digging his nails into the damask of the sofa arm. "She had *many* things to tell you. A lifetime's worth."

"No." Louisa's whisper floated from the depths of the chair. "That isn't what I mean. I think … she died with something important unsaid." She had sunk into herself.

He wanted a drink. Or seven.

"It's dark." He rose abruptly to light the lamps. Rutherford wasn't coming. The man was too discreet to knock on a closed door. The hiss and flare of the lamps, the warm yellow light, was a relief.

"There," he said.

"That's better. Thank you. I hadn't realized." Louisa stirred in her chair. "Sit."

But he couldn't sit down again. Rising had been a victory. He needed to quit that room. He had a bottle of whisky in his apartments that was already aged to perfection. He would go.

First, a concession.

"Take this month with Miss Reed," he said. Perhaps Louisa would even benefit from her presence, albeit not in the way she intended. Mothering Miss Reed might take her mind from Phillipa.

Then, a request.

"But after this month, I beg you, put an end to it. No more séances. No more strays." *However lovely.* He paused. Played his last card. "Michael would be concerned if he knew. He too would think you need a change. If I saw more cause for alarm … I might feel compelled to write to him." Louisa did not notice, or did not acknowledge, the implied threat.

"Michael. He's so reasonable." She shrugged. "He was a good father. A better father than a husband."

Isidore stirred uncomfortably before he could stop himself.

"I'm sorry," she said. "I shouldn't talk like this in front of you. You always looked up to him." She shifted in her seat, and her skirts rustled. She smoothed the silk, a gesture too absently tender, too intimate for Isidore to watch. He looked away.

"You would be a good father." This snapped his head back toward her.

"You would have had children by now," she said. "I think of that sometimes too."

Christ almighty. "Maybe, maybe not." He should look at her. Not meeting her eyes, rocking on heels—those were his tells. He should look at her. But it was impossible. "Not every married couple produces children."

"You would have." He could hear the smile in her voice. "Beautiful children."

Before she could begin to name these phantoms and place dimples in their cheeks and ribbons in their curls, he cleared his throat.

"It's time I go."

"Of course," Louisa said at once, rising with a little shake of her head. Banishing the grandchildren that never were. "You came on foot? I'll have the coach sent around to take you back." He demurred, but she could be insistent. "The weather has turned," she said. "It's the coach or a hat. I thought so," she said with a gleam in her eye as he gave her a rueful grin. "You're coming to the Tenbys' party on Saturday?"

He'd almost forgotten. He frowned. Polite excuses.

"I'm allergic to turbot," he murmured. Now it was Louisa's turn to frown.

"Then confine yourself to the turtle soup and capon," she said. "You talk to me about loneliness, but really, Isidore, you're the one who acts like a social gathering has the appeal of a tooth extraction. Roger Tenby was a good friend, if I recall."

Yes, damn it, they were all good friends. Five years ago, six years ago, seven years ago. The whole glittering crowd. Young, wild, in love with themselves, and, for a week here and there, in love with each other. One big, happy family.

He'd have to remember to send Tenby a letter. *Frightfully sorry, old boy. Sudden toothache.* He couldn't just pick up where he'd left off. Didn't have it in him. These last two days had proved it to him.

"I'll consider it," he said.

She waited with him while the coach was brought around.

"I'm going to bring Miss Reed," she said. "I'm aware that I've put her in a gloomy situation. Gay company will do her good. She's very serious. Didn't you find her so?"

This merited a shrug. He *had* found her serious. Among other things. Intelligent. Quixotic. Fascinating.

"It will be interesting to introduce her to Mr. Huntington."

The suggestion in her voice caused his eyes to fly to her face. She wore a tiny smile.

He scowled. "Now you want to play matchmaker? Do you hope to tempt a member of the *beau monde* into a mésalliance with your medium?"

Louisa ignored his scowl. "Mr. Huntington is a sober-minded young man. And Miss Reed is a woman of good sense and good breeding. Don't protest! I may know very little of her background, but certain things are self-evident."

He snorted. Even Huntington would want to know that his *well-bred* wife hadn't dropped down from the moon. A mysterious past could be an asset for a woman who wanted to play medium. For a woman who wanted to walk down the aisle it was a distinct disadvantage.

He said only: "Miss Reed expressed interest in a paid position, not an advantageous match."

"Yes. Unusual, isn't it?" Louisa mused.

Unusual. Try suspicious. Red flags. Alarm bells. He didn't want to dwell on the mystery Miss Reed presented. It might make him reconsider his truce. And if the truce were called off …

He would have to renegotiate terms. The idea of a renegotiation caused his veins to constrict. He would, slowly, so slowly, disrupt the mechanism that powered her, coil the springs tighter and tighter, until they shot in every direction. He would melt her steel will and hold her molten in his arms. Take her hot tongue deep into his mouth. Part her quicksilver flesh and slide his fingers …

"Her father died quite poor, I believe," said Louisa. "I wonder if there might be a sad story there."

"Ah," he interrupted. "The coach."

He didn't want to reprise Miss Reed's sad story. Come up with more flattering variations. Sad stories didn't interest him. They were the air he breathed. They suffocated him. He needed to stay far away from her. And he would.

He had done what he had to do. He had assessed the situation, kissed the daylights out of the suspect, and neutralized the danger. Now all that remained to him was to ride, boldly ride in the other direction and not look back. If he managed that, it wouldn't be a complete rout.

But he couldn't keep himself from a parting remark.

"Huntington needs an heiress. Or at least, his creditors would prefer it." *Sober-minded. Huntington. Indeed.*

As he bent to kiss Louisa's hand, he did refrain from murmuring, "See you in a month."

Chapter Ten

A month can feel like a very long time. A *minute* can feel like a very long time. Clocks tell a man nothing about how he experiences the duration of the passing moments. Isidore looked at his pocket watch often, staring at the slender hands, which seemed frozen in place. Surely the watch had wound down? Surely the hands would have shifted by now around the dial? Somehow every activity, every errand, produced some new reason for him to pay a visit to Trombly Place. He grew restless waiting these reasons out. Yes, Louisa loved irises, but he'd managed to pass costermongers daily for weeks without having to fight the inclination to dash over to her with a bouquet. He was going soft in the head.

On Friday afternoon, he stood in the street staring at the flowers like a lunatic until the woman sitting behind them, Irish by her lilt, asked him if he mightn't prefer planting a seed between the cobbles and staring at *that*. He bought a bouquet of irises then, but as soon as he turned the corner, he saw another woman selling potted plants and flowering sprigs—laurel and myrtle, geraniums and hawthorn—and he couldn't help but buy a budding hawthorn branch. Miss Reed's lips would curve if he gave it to her.

"From Avalon," he would say, and her lips would part into a smile that revealed those slightly crooked teeth. The smile would flit across her face and vanish, and he would have to tease her until she smiled again. She responded to his teasing. It rallied her; she became arch, confident, uninhibited. Playful. She forgot, for an instant, her reserve. Maybe he should buy a laurel branch too. Something he seemed to recall that the Romans bent into wreaths and wore about their heads ... instead of hats. Presenting her with a laurel wreath might even make her laugh. Miss Reed had felt the shared fun of his poor jokes about the Romans. Her iron self-control had melted just a little.

Remembering Miss Reed's self-control, he remembered—belatedly—his own. He returned at once to his apartments.

"Yes?" he snarled when Brinkley's mouth fell open.

"Nothing, my lord." His valet recovered quickly. "Very lovely. Shall I put them in the breakfast room?"

He wanted to snap, "You can put them on the refuse heap," but instead he responded with a curt, "As you please," handing over the irises and hawthorn, and silently resolved to take his breakfast in his study for the rest of the season.

Saturday he dedicated entirely to business. He had plenty to keep him occupied. He'd made strategic investments in Egypt and gotten involved with several commercial houses in Alexandria. Cotton cultivation. He'd done well, and he'd needed to. His father hadn't been happy when he left England. In fact, he'd lunged across his desk with a dagger and tried to cut off his ear. The left one. The one he hadn't sliced when he was a boy. That was a prelude to cutting off his income.

He was lucky Michael Trombly had drilled the basics of business into his head, and he'd prospered. Now he was in the process of selling. Exports were bound to go down with the War Between the States over and America poised to reenter the market.

There was also this continuing issue of what to do about his hereditary landholdings. The Blackwood estate required radical restructuring, not only of the land use and terms of tenancy, but also of the relationships between the Blackwoods and the families who lived and worked on their properties. He would not follow in his father's footsteps. He would not run the viscountcy as though nothing had changed since the Restoration.

Technological innovations and political reforms *were* slowly disintegrating the calcified hierarchical system, freeing men of all classes to move from their ancestral homes, to find new occupations. England would see the day when all men met on equal footing. Of that he had no doubt, even if the majority of his cohort of lords insisted on denying it. The act of trade, not the fact of birth, would define social relations. And feudal ties … they would fall away. The estate had to become economically viable and socially satisfying for everyone involved, or it would crumble.

Paternalism had always struck Isidore as a rather bad model for running affairs. The well-being of the group depended entirely on the benignity of the father.

And sometimes the father was a brute. A perverted, pitiless fiend.

Yes, there was plenty to do. He moved his breakfast tray from the desk to a chair and spread out his papers, arranging them into stacks. He picked up a pen. He could develop plans for farm organization, brainstorm methods, sketch out the balance of inputs and outputs. He shifted his papers again to make room for a writing pad. He put the tip of the pen to the paper.

He had the capital to invest in machinery; he would take advantage of innovations in agricultural science. He would counteract years of inertia, implement improved drainage systems, educate the farmers on crop rotation and fertilizers, and shift the distribution of profits so they realized more income from their labors and felt more responsibility for, and pride in, their achievements.

It would be a monumental task. The Blackwood estate had stagnated for generations; the changes would have to happen in stages. Every decision presented a challenge and an opportunity. Focus was essential.

He looked down at the writing pad. He'd scrawled a zigzag line, a series of peaks and troughs. Not unlike the repeating shape of a finely molded upper lip, with a deep valley and two crests … He dropped the pen. It was too soon to draft a plan anyway. Before he could educate farmers, he needed to educate himself.

He stalked to his library, returned with a copy of Morton's *Agricultural Cyclopaedia,* and settled back at his desk. He read for what felt like a decade then checked his watch. Definitely broken. He let the *Agricultural Cyclopaedia* bang shut and picked up a copy of *The Journal of the Agricultural Society of England.* He leaned on his elbows over the journal, furrowing his brow, aping concentration in the hopes that the posture would penetrate to his brain. *Concentrate.* Ah, soil complexity. Fascinating. As he blinked at tables listing crop yields in trial plots fertilized with different quantities of superphosphate of lime, he found that his knee was vibrating. His eyes kept wandering up to fix on a wall sconce, and he had to push back his chair again and again to stand and stretch the bunched muscles in his thighs.

His chair had grown remarkably uncomfortable. His study smelled stale. A bit of fresh air ... a walk to ... Berkeley Square. *No.* It was imperative that he remain in his study, that he persevere. His estate manager had arrived in London the previous evening; they had an appointment for three that afternoon. He needed to be ready with questions, proposals ...

He checked his watch. Still eleven a.m. Maybe more coffee. He could ring, or better yet, go down to the kitchen for it himself. *No. No coffee. Soil complexity.* He leaned again over *The Journal of the Agricultural Society of England.*

Soil. Who would have thought it was so goddamn complicated? Wasn't anything simple?

He pitched *The Journal of the Agricultural Society of England* across the desk and watched it sail through the air. The edges flopped against the mantle as the journal fell, making one of his carvings—a basswood donkey, braying, big eared—skip closer to the mantel's edge. He should give the thing to Clement. But it was crudely done. The donkey's ears were a little *too* big. Clement himself was a perfectionist; he should give him a better example of his craft. He tried to turn a dispassionate eye on his woodwork.

His gaze lingered on the carving of the deer—its slender legs rising from a hunk of unfinished wood as though it stood on rough forest ground. It was his finest piece, his finest animal, at any rate. Anyone with knowledge of both woodcarving and instrument-making would judge the clumsiest of his violins finer than the best of his figurines. He had a calling as a luthier.

He loved to make violins, loved every aspect of the process: plotting the curves on paper, selecting the wood, planning the top and bottom plates, cutting and bending the ribs, shaping the neck. He sometimes fancied he could *hear* the particular sound the violin would make even before it was completely assembled. Rocco, the violinmaker he lived with in Agerola, shared that fancy. One day, while they sat together varnishing instruments so they shone a rich red-brown, Rocco described harvesting the wood.

He wandered the Alps, he said, pressing his ear to the spruces in search of the perfect tone; only when he heard that tone singing out through the bark would he chop down the tree. Rocco was a dark, short, bandy-legged man with a crooked spine and bright blue eyes—Norman eyes—strange to see in that most Neapolitan of faces. He always had a tale on his lips. He said he never lied, which was true, if you accepted, as he did, that reality was something you could invent. His optimism was staggering.

"The first fifty years of my life," he told Isidore, "I carried spruce trees down the mountain on my right shoulder. You see how my back is bent to the right. The next fifty years of my life I will carry spruce trees down the mountain on my left shoulder. That will straighten me out again."

Isidore had looked at Rocco's twisted shoulders, then at his battered hands, fingernails cracked, skin stained with varnish. Rocco's hands were so different from his father's, so different from the hands of any man he'd ever known.

"I understand." Isidore had met Rocco's twinkling eyes. Sometimes the Italian offered wisdom in parables. "It's not too late to change the direction I'm heading." He shook his head. "But I need to have patience. It will take a hundred years for me to find the right path."

"I don't know," Rocco had replied. "I was talking about me. You, it might take two hundred years."

And he had laughed so hard he fell off his bench.

If Giuseppe Pietro Rocco, cobbler, vintner, violinmaker, had been his father instead of Gore Morbury Blackwood, tenth Viscount Blackwood, maybe he wouldn't need centuries to find his way. Everything would be different. Simpler. More wholesome. He often thought that those months he spent with Rocco and his family had given him the strength to stay alive.

The donkey he'd carved was in the likeness of Rocco's donkey, Geppetto. Quite possibly the loudest donkey that ever lived. His alternately deep and squeaky brays carried for miles. Rocco seemed proud of this when he wasn't threatening to walk behind him with a stick and beat him until he jumped into the volcano.

Isidore had taken a liberty with the story he'd told to Clement. Rocco only slept in the same room as Geppetto when his wife got angry and sent him to the barn.

He would keep the donkey carving. Miss Reed, though, might appreciate the deer. He could give it to her when her month with Mrs. Trombly was over. To make whatever tiny garret she occupied as a governess seem more like the wilds of West Somerset.

Well. He was certainly making progress. Discharging his lordly duties. He dug his ledger out from beneath a stack of folded letters and glared at the numbers.

His neck felt stiff. He had to look up, tilt his head from side to side. His neck cracked as he pressed his chin to his chest. *Getting old.* Amusing thought for a man not yet thirty. He was in the prime of life. At this point, the *ton* diagnosed his bachelorhood as a persistent but not yet incurable condition. Clement was his age and remained one of society's most enticing prospects. But Clement was unmarried because he was still looking for the right woman. Whereas *he* was unmarried because … well, the Blackwoods had destroyed enough. He would not pick a bride and watch while proximity to his blighted heart withered her hopes and ate away at her dreams of happiness. Blight her he surely would. He could not take a young woman into the dark circle of his confidence. Intimacy with him could bring only misery.

Come with me; the marriage bed is in the ossuary. You don't mind, my love, that we sleep with skeletons between us?

Miss Reed had looked at him with eyes like black wells, wells so deep no ray of the sun could ever reach the bottom. They were eyes that reflected the night sky, even at noon. They stripped the sky of its mask of blue and showed eternity: endless black spangled by stars.

She had looked at him as though she too carried a great burden. She did not bow beneath the weight, even though it made itself known in every step she took. He could almost imagine that together they could bear both their burdens more easily.

He checked his watch. Eleven a.m. He went to check the clock in the hall. Eleven a.m. Had *all* the timepieces broken? He breathed easier once he was in the hall. So much easier that he continued on down the stairs. A short walk would do him good. He donned his overcoat and waved off Brinkley as the man tried to present him with a heavy, old-fashioned top hat of felted beaver fur. The other option was a hat of silk plush with a towering crown and a broad, swooping brim that tilted up at a dramatic angle. He tried it on gingerly.

"You could empty an entire water glass into this brim," he said, running his fingers down the brim's steep slope. "Was it made to hold liquid?"

"I doubt expressly for the purpose, my lord." Brinkley too was eying the hat critically. "But the shape does put one in mind of a rain gutter."

That settled it. He snatched the hat off his head.

"Thank you, Brinkley. I'll go without."

The day wasn't dreadful. He turned his collar up against the damp as he walked through a pocket of brown fog. Not absolutely dreadful, no. The sun was struggling to burn through the mist, and it wasn't out and out raining. A few suspended water droplets never hurt anyone. After the confinement of his study, he felt downright giddy with the circulating air. Perhaps, though, a hat was in order. Something similar to the hat he'd lost, nothing made of pelt or with a brim like a trough. With that mission in mind, he decided that his short walk in Pimlico would have to become a cab ride to Mayfair followed by a stroll along Bond Street.

Once he had purchased a hat at a gentleman's shop—tasteful, black silk, the crown high but not vying with the chimneys, the brim nearly straight—he found himself too close to Mount Street not to drop in on Louisa and show her his acquisition.

As he waited for Rutherford to open the door, he imagined tipping his hat to Louisa.

"I tried to purchase a turban," he'd tell her. "But they'd sold out, so a topper it was."

He would ask after Miss Reed, but he wouldn't ask to see her. Of course, if she happened to be in the sitting room …

Rutherford opened the door.

"Good afternoon, my lord," he said, and Isidore grinned at him.

"It *is* afternoon, isn't it?" He stepped into the hallway, handing Rutherford his hat. "Not eleven?"

"No, my lord." Rutherford regarded him evenly. "It is not eleven."

"Heaven be praised. I could have sworn the day got stuck somewhere in the forenoon." He nodded at the hat. "Do you approve?"

Rutherford did not so much as glance at it. "A great gain for civilization, my lord." The deep creases alongside his mouth deepened as though a smile were being sternly suppressed. Isidore listened for the sound of feminine voices: Louisa's high and thin, Miss Reed's low and breathy ... the kind of voice a man wanted to hear close to his ear. Her little moans had sounded such sweet, low notes.

He grimaced. "Is Mrs. Trombly at home?"

"No, my lord. She should return shortly."

"Ah." He flicked his cuffs. Really, he was a master of nonchalance. He ran a hand through his hair. "Well then," he said. "Is Miss Reed at home?"

"No, my lord." If Rutherford had divined the question before it was asked, he tactfully gave no sign. "She accompanied Mrs. Trombly."

"Well," said Isidore again. "I suppose I'll wait."

"Yes, my lord," said Rutherford.

"I'd leave my card, but I seem to have forgotten them." Isidore smiled weakly. "I'll wait for just a few minutes. They'll return shortly, you said?"

And before he knew it, he was in the sitting room again. He hadn't expected to find himself back in that room until late April. May, even. His will was not made of iron. Aspic, perhaps. He rubbed at an ache above his left eyebrow. *Well done.*

There were fresh roses in the vase on the table. The room smelled of roses and of powdered sugar. He couldn't sit but roamed about. One of the watercolors framed on the wall was Clement's. Blue borage flowers, petals arrayed like stars. The others—all of birds—were his. The flaws screamed at him.

He checked his watch. It was getting on toward two o'clock. Time had sped up and escaped from him. He needed to get back to Pimlico soon to meet Mr. Chadwick.

He couldn't tell if he was relieved or disappointed. When he saw the maid at the door, he shook his head.

"No tea, thank you. I'm just leaving." Then he noticed she held no tea tray. Her hands were working at her sides, and she cast a quick glance around her before she gave a queer little hop that launched her into the room.

"Your lordship." She curtsied, a dip down that jettisoned her up again. She was a bouncy creature. Round faced, young, and not unattractive. He recognized her, vaguely, from prior visits.

"Miss … " He nodded at her, bemused.

"Lizzie," she said. "Lizzie Bradshaw." Again she shot a look around her. It was almost comical—even her desire for circumspection was brash. She approached another pace.

His eyebrows shot up. He wondered suddenly if she meant to make some kind of advance. She was chewing on her lower lip and blinking at him with a most determined expression.

He did not tryst with servants. Ever. It was a rule with him. Too unfair to the woman and too messy. Lizzie came yet nearer with a twitch of her skirts. He cleared his throat. But at that moment Lizzie burst into speech, and his warning "ahem" was drowned out in the rush of her words.

"I need to talk to you," she said. "Mrs. Hexam'd have my head if she knew, but she didn't see what I saw, and she's like Mrs. Trombly, thinking Miss Reed is pure as a dewdrop because she's pretty and talks in a pretty way and pretends she can hear the spirits, but she can't. She's clever with her pretending, but she's a liar and a thief too. I saw the proof of it, and you being so closely connected to the family, and what with the master away, I had to say it to you when I saw you'd come back. I wanted to say it to you when you came before, but I never had the chance." She paused after this remarkable outburst, sucking in a breath like a hiccup. "Miss Reed," she added, "is a *nasty* baggage."

Isidore gaped. Then he almost laughed at his own shock. He really had been expecting a stream of seduction to issue forth from the maid's lips. Daphne's flattery must have swollen his head. Thank God he hadn't given any sign of his gross misperception.

"You think it's funny, my lord? That Mrs. Trombly is nursing an ass to her bosom?" Lizzie Bradshaw's face was screwed up into an expression of intense dislike.

Ass to her bosom? What the devil … He comprehended her mistake and exploded into a coughing fit, hitting his own chest with his fist until his eyes watered.

"You're laughing." Her voice was filled with wondering disgust. "I tell you that night she was carried in and put in bedclothes I took her dress to the laundry room and found a pouch filled with all kinds of valuables sewn inside, and you're laughing at me."

He sobered instantly. "What are you talking about? What pouch?"

"A pouch of valuables," she said. "Jewels and the kind of spoon you'd give a little lord."

"They might belong to her," he said, even as his heart sunk.

"Oh, aye," said Lizzie. "Maybe she talked to Prince Albert's ghost and he got Queen Victoria to make her a gift of sapphires and pearls. I don't think so, my lord."

He didn't think so either. "Why don't you tell Mrs. Trombly?"

"I told you." Lizzie thinned her lips until they went white. "She makes such a fuss over Miss Reed, it'd be like telling her that biscuits ain't made of flour or that butter ain't made of milk. She wouldn't believe me, and I have no proof."

"You left the pouch in Miss Reed's dress, then?" The ache above his left eyebrow was starting to stab into his brain.

"Course I did." She drew herself up so rapidly she had to hop backwards to keep her footing. "*I* am an honest woman. Just because I see something's been stolen, it doesn't give me the right to steal it meself, now does it? It'd tell pretty black against *me* if I stole what her stealing tells black against her. If you understand my meaning, your lordship." She was affronted, but he couldn't muster an apology. He thumbed his eyebrow, mussing and smoothing the hairs.

Miss Reed … a common criminal. She wasn't a puzzle that he could linger over. She was a problem that he needed to eliminate. At once. She would have to leave Trombly Place. He could not tolerate a thief. Why did he feel this creeping sensation of disappointment? The thought of driving her out of the house made him sick. She would return to her madam, her pimp, return to whatever den she'd crawled from. What could that mean to him?

Sad story there. Yes, she must have some sad story. Genteel poverty produced its criminals as surely as squalor. But she couldn't be allowed to fleece the family who had all but raised him while he pondered what sad circumstances could possibly have led her to this pass.

And so Miss Reed, the truce is over. Nullified as if it never were. He would show her no mercy, and he would show himself no mercy. No game of cat and mouse. No deluded dalliance. Severance. Swift and final.

"I've looked for it since," said Lizzie when it became apparent he was not going to speak. "In her room, but she's hidden it good. She's probably adding to it, too. Building up her little hoard. Not that I've noticed anything missing; I keep a look out, your lordship. But you can't be too careful with a woman like that."

"No." He checked his watch. Another few minutes of this, and he'd end up late to his appointment.

"I did right to tell you?" Lizzie was wheedling now. There was a protocol for this kind of exchange. In his ill-humored distraction he'd almost forgotten. He produced a guinea and handed it to her.

"Thank you, Lizzie," he said through clenched teeth. "It was most proper of you."

Lizzie smiled, plummeted into a curtsy, and popped up again. The guinea had disappeared like a magic trick.

"You're going to talk to Mrs. Trombly, then?" Emboldened by the tip, she inched toward him. "And when might that be? You won't say my name? Not at first? Not until she believes you? Not until she knows how black it all tells against Miss Reed without hearing it's from me?" She was agitated, eager. He could *smell* her nervous energy, sour and metallic.

His headache made it difficult to think. He nodded curtly at her as he headed for the door.

"I'll come back this evening to speak with Mrs. Trombly. Your … " He searched for the phrase. *Vindictive meddling?* "Keen perception will be appreciated, I'm sure."

"Tonight's the Tenbys' dinner party!"

Her shrill reminder made him wince. He muttered something indistinct as he continued down the hall. Back on the street, he hailed a hack. He climbed inside and shut his eyes, rubbing small circles on his throbbing temples. Christ. He'd already sent Tenby his polite excuse. Should he send a polite excuse for failing to keep his polite excuse?

He would be dining out after all. He would corner Miss Reed at the party and hear what she had to say before he went to Louisa. He would give her that much of a chance to explain herself. But he had a feeling Miss Reed would offer him nothing satisfactory. She would offer him her back, most likely, as she turned and fled back into the shadows from whence she came.

Chapter Eleven

It was between the fish course and the entre that Ella took her first easy breath. The party was not an unmitigated disaster. No one was interviewing her about her relationships with the dead. No one was paying the slightest bit of attention to her. Even her dinner partner, Mr. Huntington, had abandoned her. They had suffered through two false starts—he asked what events she was planning on attending this season and who her connections might be in London—before settling on a sufficiently general subject—the weather.

Throughout their painful dialogue, Mr. Huntington had kept his ear pricked to the low tones of a far more interesting têteàtête taking place across the table. Ella had just made the observation that the fog and the smoke in London shared several qualities and was beginning, after his prolonged silence, to enumerate those qualities, when he jerked his head around and cried, "Why Cliveden never said any such thing! What rubbish. I was *there*. Out with your sources."

The orbit of the very entertaining conversation about what Cliveden did or did not say, and to whom exactly, widened to include Mr. Huntington. And only Mr. Huntington.

Cliveden could have nothing to do with her.

Seated at the long, candlelit table, wine flowing and conversation sparkling all around her, she might as well have been alone. If she were attending the party not as Miss Reed but as Miss Arlington—a *different* Miss Arlington, healthy and whole, with a brain bright and spotless as new bunting—the situation would have been cause for tears rather than quiet celebration. Slighted by a dinner partner! Ignored by everyone of consequence! The horror.

She smiled faintly, toying with her sherry glass. For her, even "wallflower" had been too lofty an aspiration. A wallflower might at any moment be chosen, picked out from amongst the other languishing maidens. A wallflower might suddenly be led onto the dance floor, swept into a couple in the midst of other couples. A wallflower was *eligible*. A wife in potential.

She was *not* eligible. She had dreamed of being, at best, a fly on the wall. Allowed to remain in her home, in proximity to others, but on the perimeter. Allowed to take vicarious pleasure in other people's love, other people's children.

Until Alfred had squashed her meager, stupid dream. She could imagine his riposte. *Let you remain as a fly on the wall? My dear Ella. Flies are the handmaidens of contagion. One does not harbor flies.*

She gazed toward the head of the table. Mrs. Tenby presided, an attenuated woman, everything about her long and thin. She wore a gown of lemon silk, which gave her too much the appearance of a yellowed bone. She was talking animatedly, waving a long arm, throwing back her head again and again, overcome with laughter. The gesture exposed a considerable length of thin, white throat.

It would be more charitable to think of her as a swan instead of a bone. Doubtless, swan was the effect she was going for.

Ella tipped her sherry glass against her mouth to hide a smile that must strike anyone who glanced her way as a little too wide for one so neglected. People tended to be suspicious of those who enjoyed their own company. The last thing she wanted was to stir suspicions. She wanted to fade into shadows between the pools of candlelight and watch without being watched herself.

But she couldn't fade away completely. *He* was looking at her. Isidore Blackwood. She could feel the heat of his gaze the moment he turned his eyes on her. The blood rose to the surface of her skin. He was seated at the other end of the table. She had been trying not to look toward him.

When he'd walked into the parlor, she'd felt his presence too, even before the announcement sent a flurry of consternation through the guests. She was standing beside Mrs. Trombly, looking down into the velvety nap of the Wilton carpet. The air changed, became charged, like the air before a storm. She turned to the doorway. He'd run a comb through his hair; the wild black locks were swept back from his forehead. The grooming only brought out the angles of his face. He looked even bolder. More predatory. His black evening suit seemed painted on his body so perfect was the fit, so easy were his movements. His blue eyes brushed over her as he lazily surveyed the room.

Her stomach dropped.

"Blackwood!" Mr. Tenby, corpulent and ruddy, walked over to him immediately. He was the kind of man whose confidentially lowered voice had the effect of a stage whisper; it whet the audience's curiosity and was audible to all. "What's this? Didn't expect to see you here." He signaled to his butler. "Another place setting." The butler did not share Mr. Tenby's attitude of bemused toleration. The man looked distinctly irritated, almost injured, as he exited the room.

Mr. Tenby shook his head—a massive object—at Lord Blackwood. "You'll have to walk into the dining room alone, but I suppose you'll manage. Tooth's all better, I take it?"

Lord Blackwood answered with a smile. A wide, white, flawless smile. "As though the problem never were."

Mr. Tenby harrumphed at that. But he seemed pleased at Blackwood's appearance. Ella noted—and her stomach gave a strange twist as she did—that the ladies assembled in the parlor seemed doubly pleased. Mrs. Hatfield, a statuesque widow with a wide, feline mouth, nearly purred her pleasure to Mrs. Trombly.

"A rare sighting," she murmured, her tone leaving no doubt that it was also a pleasant one. "You don't suppose he comes with a *particular* purpose?" She cut her eyes at Miss Tenby, who was herself gazing at Lord Blackwood with a wolfish mien.

Or perhaps, Ella thought, frowning, she was hungry. Blackwood's unexpected arrival had pushed back the dinner by some minutes.

Mrs. Trombly glanced at Miss Tenby. "I haven't the faintest idea. Does a man require a particular purpose to dine out?"

"No," said Mrs. Hatfield with a voluptuous smile. "Not when there's such a wealth of beauty, good sense, and virtue in the company at large. A man should dine out with an open mind."

To Ella's satisfaction, Mrs. Hatfield had ended up quite as far down the table from Lord Blackwood as it was possible to get. She was forced to lavish her "beauty, good sense, and virtue" on her dinner partner, Lord St. Aubyn. Not exactly a hardship.

The names and titles of the various dinner guests swirled in her head, but she could definitely remember Lord St. Aubyn. The man was a baron. Unmarried. Tall, blond, classically handsome. He had a chiseled face. Lips finely molded. Nose straight and thin. Never broken. His eyes were pale, a green-blue, and peculiarly inquisitive. When Ella had been introduced to him in the parlor, he'd studied her as though he were shortsighted. There was no judgment in his look but rather a clinical detachment. Then he'd smiled. A warm, frank, lovely smile. He was a *very* attractive specimen.

Any woman in her right mind would declare him better looking than Lord Blackwood. Lord Blackwood's countenance too was built along classical lines, but the lines were rough, dark, mobile. Lord St. Aubyn reminded her of a Grecian statue. Lord Blackwood's expressions could never be captured in marble. There could be no mistake; he was flesh and blood. Powerful. Perishable.

She moistened her lips with sherry. Why *not* look at him? They had made a truce, after all. They had walked together. They had laughed together. His tongue had stroked her earlobe.

That's why not.

She did it anyway. She couldn't help herself.

He was separated from her by half the table's length, sitting between Mrs. Trombly and Miss Tenby. Miss Tenby was speaking to him, her head inclined coquettishly. Her head was not so overlarge as her brother's—its size deemphasized by the row of curls curtaining her forehead—and his ruddy corpulence was in her a rosy plumpness. Her blue gown was *very* low-cut. She looked soft and appealing. Ella felt a pang. Miss Tenby could flirt and gossip to her heart's content. They were probably the same age. She felt years older. Lifetimes older.

Lord Blackwood wasn't listening to Miss Tenby. She could tell from his posture. His body was angled away from her. He was swirling the wine in his glass, looking down into the ruby liquid. The warm candlelight lent a richness to his bronze skin. Played upon the sensual curve of his lips.

Then he looked up. His eyes met Ella's. Her instinct was to glance away. But she did not. She held his gaze. She imagined the whole party disposed around the room on couches, dining in the Roman style, and her lips twitched. Roman women had never contended with crinolines. She smiled, letting him see the laughter in her eyes. Would he too smile, guessing at the reason for her amusement?

His mouth flattened. His face set into hard lines. Deliberately, he turned his gaze away. He said something, and Miss Tenby laughed, blushing.

Her smile crumbled. She felt as though her throat had filled with dust.

"More sherry?" The question came from close at hand.

"Oh." She put her sherry glass down hurriedly on the table and nearly upset a salt cellar. "No, thank you." *Only fidgeting.*

She hadn't expected any courtesy from Mr. Penn. Along with Mr. Huntington, he was her neighbor at the table. He was sitting on her left but had been turned away from her, speaking intently with his wife, since the dinner began.

Maybe he wasn't intent on snubbing her, as she had supposed. She tried to revive her smile.

"I'm quite all right," she said. "One glass is enough."

She heard a thin sniff from across the table. Mrs. Bennington, a strikingly pretty woman, though not so strikingly pretty as her husband, caught her eye. The footman was filling her wine glass with Bordeaux. Not for the first time. Or the second. Mrs. Bennington tilted the glass this way and that, then took a dainty sip.

"Delicious," she murmured. "Even better than the last."

Ella cursed herself. *And* the lull in conversation that had made her comment audible. She hadn't meant it to be pointed. She did the only thing she could think of to remedy the situation.

"That is, I don't care very much for sherry," she said to Mr. Penn, brightly, shooting a glance at Mrs. Bennington. "I'll have a glass of wine, of course, with the roast."

The roast was just then being served.

"Certainly," said Mr. Penn, politely. Mrs. Bennington's rosebud lips parted as she laughed a pretty, silvery little laugh. She poked at the meat on her plate with her knife then picked up her wine glass again.

"I'll have *two* glasses of wine *instead* of the roast," she said, dimpling at Ella.

"How frank," said Mr. Huntington, looking around at them as though he sensed the dinner conversation had found a new center of gravity. "Most women leave that an unspoken policy."

"It is a *good* policy, unspoken or otherwise," said Mrs. Bennington. "For the figure, at any rate. Mr. Penn will have to tell us if it is as beneficial for the constitution."

"Mr. Penn would have us drinking water and eating leaves," said Mr. Huntington, shuddering as he helped himself to the side of sweetbreads.

Ella looked quickly at Mr. Penn. There *was* something on his plate that looked suspiciously like leaves. Green salad, perhaps.

"Would you?" asked Mrs. Bennington, fixing her light-blue eyes on Mr. Penn, widening them with sham curiosity. "Is that the current wisdom amongst medical men? Leaves and water?"

Mr. Penn … a doctor? Ella nearly choked on her first sip of Bordeaux. Mr. Penn looked nothing like a doctor. That is, he looked nothing like Mr. Norton. As a thought experiment, she tried to dissociate Mr. Norton from the idea of "doctor," but it proved almost impossible. Mr. Norton was the exemplar and determining figure of the whole category. He was ancient, easily three times Mr. Penn's age. His longevity alone seemed a significant testament to his knowledge and ability. Papa had had absolute faith in him. And it wasn't only Papa. Mr. Norton was widely admired. He was called away to attend to difficult cases up and down the coast, and inland, deep into Devon. Sometimes he went as far as Cornwall. He was a legendary figure. The supreme authority on everything from the common cold to childbirth to … convulsions. His manner was peremptory, even harsh, and he had no tolerance for weakness. Whimpering, weeping, trembling, sneezing, excessive coughing—all of these incurred his wrath. They interfered with his work.

She supposed it was understandable. Mr. Norton was locked always in combat with Death, and Death could not be defeated. That had to tell on a man. He looked a little like her image of Death, his skull coming close to the thinning skin. When she was a girl, he frightened her. His cold hand felt like a claw when he sat by the bedside and pulled her cheeks from her teeth, articulated her limbs, tapped her chest, probed her abdomen.

Mr. Penn didn't have a peremptory bone in his body. He was elegant and thin as a whippet, with curling dark hair and mild, luminous eyes. He had a soft, cultured voice. She couldn't picture him crouched over a man, bleeding him by cups.

"I don't recommend drinking water," he said as he took a sip of wine. "But leaves won't do you any harm."

"Two glasses of wine and a pile of leaves, you heard the doctor, Daphne." Mr. Bennington turned from Lady Berners to enter the conversation, laughing. Mr. Bennington made a strong case for the return of the exquisite. He seemed to have stepped out of an earlier era, a time when men wore jewels and powder and lurked in opera boxes waiting for assignations. His oval face was perfectly symmetrical. Ella found herself mesmerized by it; its beauty was uncanny.

Mrs. Bennington ignored him. She leaned forward, showing even more of her pale décolletage. "Water is harmful, Mr. Penn?"

Mr. Penn leaned back, as though restoring balance to the table. He glanced to his left, read something on his wife's face, hesitated, then shrugged.

"If it's contaminated," he said.

This remark caught the general attention. A hush fell over the table.

"Lord Berners, you and Lady Berners were recently in Paris?" Mrs. Tenby addressed the earl with a strained smile. "My niece just arrived in Paris."

But Lord Berners didn't give a fig for Mrs. Tenby's niece. His eyes were alight, and his jowls quivered.

"Contaminated, you say?" Lord Berners craned his neck to see Mr. Penn.

Mr. Penn cleared his throat. "I refer, of course, to cholera."

A clatter from the head of the table as Mrs. Tenby dropped her cutlery.

"You really shouldn't, of course," declared Mr. Tenby from the foot of the table. His face was bright red with drink.

"Shocking," said Mrs. Hatfield with evident relish.

A dark laugh rang out.

"Ho, Blackwood," muttered Mr. Tenby. "Why don't you tell us about the tombs of caliphs or that coral from the Red Sea the ladies are mad for?"

Lord Blackwood smiled. Ella had begun to recognize his smiles. This one, dazzling, was entirely sardonic.

"It's never the fact, but the fact of the fact being mentioned, that causes surprise in the best society," he observed, eyes roaming up and down the table. "How dreadfully earnest those people who have it the other way around."

"How dreadfully *tiresome* those people," replied Lady Berners tartly. "We have no power over facts, Lord Blackwood. But we can choose whether or not we acknowledge them."

"It is the great privilege of the aristocrat." Now Lord Blackwood's smile looked dangerous, even as he nodded graciously, as though conceding a point. "And why, perhaps, his days are numbered."

Lady Berners was a large woman, but nothing about her seemed soft. Her hair was steel-gray, and her back was straight as a spear. She lifted her chin. "I, for one, *do* find it less shocking that a few people should die diseased in *Stepney* than that an earl's son" —here she allowed herself an accusing look at Mr. Penn—"should judge it a meet topic for mixed company at a dinner party on *Park Lane*. To me, it indicates even more clearly what the world is coming to."

Lord Berners cackled, and for a moment Ella had the disconcerting impression that his teeth were floating in his mouth. *False uppers.* She averted her eyes. She heard Mrs. Trombly's low voice; the dear woman was trying to draw her little region of the table into a conversation about Victoria Gardens in Bombay. The man on her left side obliged her, and the murmur of their voices broke the tension.

The footmen were setting out the plates of preserved fruits and nuts and cheeses. Ella looked at the sage cheese, the white skin mottled with green. Mrs. Bennington was eying it too, with revulsion. The whole evening had taken on a distinctly queasy cast. Ella understood why her abstracted, rumpled papa, who'd liked to take his dinner in the library and who always had crumbs on his waistcoat, had never fit in with high society in London. She couldn't imagine him excelling at the barbed banter that seemed its mainstay. The pursuits of the *ton* would have struck him as pointless and empty. No wonder he gave it all up so easily.

Every member of the glittering party suddenly seemed to her desperately unhappy. Gorging themselves on rich foods, swilling wine, laughing brittle laughs, doling out set-downs and blandishments, nursing their private agendas. They were all so keen on presenting brightly glazed versions of themselves. Pretending that the world too was glazed. Everything fixed in its place.

Except Isidore Blackwood, who pretended nothing.

And perhaps this Mr. Penn. An earl's son. With a generous allowance, no doubt. She wondered what had motivated him to choose a profession, and an unlikely one.

"The thing is we *do* have power over facts," said Mr. Penn quietly but clearly. Those involved in speculations about whether Mrs. Trombly's daughter had exaggerated the dimensions of a stone elephant in her last letter took no notice. But a few heads turned back to Mr. Penn.

"I believe we're going to see another epidemic in the East End, and sooner than later," said Mr. Penn. "But it can be avoided if we take preventative measures now. For example, if we hold the East London Water Company accountable to the Metropolitan Water Act."

"It's *water* that causes epidemics?" Mrs. Hatfield's nose wrinkled. "What a discouraging notion. We can't avoid water, Mr. Penn."

"I can," declared Mr. Huntington, holding up a glass for Madeira.

"Indeed," murmured Mrs. Bennington, following suit.

"It's bad water that needs to be dealt with," said Mr. Penn. "Unfiltered water pumped from the river."

"Surely it's dirty habits that cause disease." Miss Tenby was looking around for confirmation. "*Vice*," she said, meaningfully, but would go no further. She lowered her eyes meekly, as though far too delicate to say any more.

"She's right," agreed Mr. Tenby. "You're bound to come across all kinds of nasty things if you go looking for patients in places like St. Giles, Penn. They live like swine, all piled on top of each other, men and women alike."

"Miasma," bellowed Lord Berners. "Miasma is the killer. You remember The Great Stink. That's why we built the sewers."

Mrs. Tenby was pouring powdered sugar on her brandied fruit as though sugar were the only antidote to words like "stink" and "sewer."

Miss Tenby tittered nervously.

"Whatever the case," interjected Lord Blackwood, "we can't ignore what happens in the rookeries forever." He didn't raise his voice, but he had the ability to command attention. All eyes were on him. "Public health will become a more pressing issue when a larger share of the public gets a political voice. And that can only be to the greater good." Lord Blackwood meant to look at Mr. Penn as he said this, Ella was sure of it, but his eyes met hers.

She felt herself nodding in agreement, before she froze, blushing. He didn't care what she thought. But *she* cared what he thought. She was glad that he considered the suffering of those less fortunate as something more than a vulgar dinner topic. That he supported this dedicated young doctor. It conformed to her assessment of his character. Beneath the brooding exterior, behind the sneer, he *was* kind. She shouldn't care, of course. As long as he didn't interfere with her arrangement with Mrs. Trombly, his character could be of no interest to her.

"The people in Stepney, or Bethnal Green, for example," continued Lord Blackwood. "They cannot rely on the elite to act in their interests." He turned his gaze on Lord Berners. "If their only recourse is to depend on the beneficence of the rich, they will die in droves without ever seeing improvement in the conditions under which they live their lives. One or two judged deserving might get a pair of donated boots. It can't continue. The tide of history is turning against the few in favor of the many."

"You're talking about the Reform Bill now," said Mr. Bennington, lowering a dried apricot from his lips. "Unless you're proposing something more radical?"

"You think *workingmen* can be trusted to support 'the greater good' as you call it?" Lord Berners sputtered. "Of all the sentimental rubbish. Blackwood, I wouldn't have suspected you of it. Might as well let my horse, or a Hottentot, decide the fate of the country. My horse, at least, never beats his mate or starves his children so he can spend his last ha'penny on gin."

"Well," said Mrs. Tenby, and she shot out of her seat like a jack-in-the-box. "If it is time for the gentlemen to discuss the Reform Bill, that means it is time for the ladies to depart for the parlor."

Things only went downhill from there. Amongst the ladies in the parlor, the reprieve Ella had enjoyed over dinner ended abruptly. Mrs. Bennington initiated the inquest.

"You are from Somerset, Miss Reed?"

"Yes." Ella smiled. The chair she had selected was less comfortable than it looked.

"But you have no relations in London?"

"No." Ella glanced around and saw far too many eyes fixed on her. Mrs. Tenby was hunched in her chair, clasping her elbows, trying to recover, no doubt, from her failure to rescue the dinner conversation from doctors and radicals. She had powdered sugar on her chin. Mrs. Penn was perched on the edge of the sofa, explaining hospital administration to Miss Tenby, who looked as though she might cry with boredom. But the other women had made her the center of their circle. Lady Berners's lips were pursed, fine lines fanning out around them. Mrs. Trombly nodded encouragingly. Mrs. Hatfield stifled a yawn. Mrs. Bennington wore an inscrutable smile.

"My mother was an orphan," Ella explained. "My father's family confined their activities to Somerset."

"There *is* so much to do in Somerset." Lady Berners might have intended her smile to be friendly.

"And your father, while he lived … ?" asked Mrs. Bennington.

"Wrote poetry," said Ella. A startled silence descended.

"And he was principally occupied in … poetry?" asked Lady Berners.

"A poet!" Mrs. Hatfield shook her head pityingly. "How vexing that must have been."

"And he never remarried?" Mrs. Trombly hadn't pressed her for any more information than she'd offered at Trombly Place, but she couldn't restrain herself now. "You said your mother died when you were very young."

"Of course he never remarried!" For the first time that night, Lady Berners looked scandalized. "You heard the girl. He was a *poet*. If a poet can't be counted on to let the wasting sickness of true love gnaw eternally at the core of his being, who can?"

"He never remarried," said Ella.

"He wrote poems about your mother, I'm sure," said Mrs. Trombly with sweet conviction.

It felt like sacrilege to talk about her father's poems in such company. Looking around at their faces, she saw she had no choice.

"I suppose they were all about her," she said. "In a sense. Many of his poems had to do with love, but some dealt with nature, or time. They could be beautiful, but also abstract. He took great inspiration from philosophy. His metaphors were often—"

"And now, Miss Reed," interrupted Lady Berners. "Before this discussion delves into prosody and becomes unsalvageable, let us discuss matters of more interest."

She *did* mean to be friendly when she smiled, Ella decided. She just wasn't very good at it.

Lady Berners bent her lips up even more severely and blinked her deep-set eyes. "I hear from Mrs. Trombly you are a necromancer. Don't look so alarmed! I adore necromancy. I believe it accounts for the preservation of *several* ladies of my acquaintance. One of them a duchess. I won't name names!"

She waved a finger admonishingly. Mrs. Hatfield shrugged and settled back in her seat. Bored again. Lady Berners leaned toward Ella.

"I hope myself to be animated long beyond the span of years allotted to mortal woman," she said, with a smugness that suggested this was entirely within her reach. "My great-great-grandchildren will be the better for it. I shudder to think what will happen to them if they are raised outside my sphere of influence. They might become *doctors*." And she did shudder.

"Coffee?" asked Mrs. Tenby in a high, unnatural voice. Ella felt almost sorry for her. Lady Berners waved her off.

"What I detest about this *modern* spiritualism," she continued, "is that it is so *democratizing*. The oldest families always had their ghosts. The Elphinstones have a ghost, if I recall. And the Giffards, of course. The Blackwoods have a ghost. A weeping lady. She appears from time to time in a lancet window. She was Scotch, the story goes. The third viscount, or maybe the fourth, who can keep track, brought her back from Culloden, but she never took to him, languished, and died. Very proper. A man could write a poem about that." She nodded at Ella. "But the way spiritualists today go on, you would think *any* family has a right to a ghost."

Mrs. Trombly looked pained.

"Do you think it takes a title to make a shade?" asked Mrs. Bennington, eying Mrs. Trombly with a touch of malice.

"Well," Lady Berners considered for a moment. "Yes. There are haunted castles, not haunted haberdasheries, after all."

At that moment, the men entered the parlor, and the shades, titled or otherwise, were sent back beyond the mortal veil. The men's arrival reconfigured everything. The circle around Ella dispersed. Mrs. Tenby began to pour the coffee. Miss Tenby drifted away from Mrs. Penn toward Lord Blackwood. Mrs. Hatfield, with a few undulations of her impressive physique, maneuvered Lord St. Aubyn into a corner.

Ella took the opportunity to stand and walk a few paces to the other side of the room under the pretense of admiring a framed engraving. Really, she found nothing to admire about the parlor, except the piano, which was tempting—mahogany with ebony inlay and sheet music on the music rest that she wished she'd gotten a better look at—and, of course, the carpet. On the whole, it was too ostentatious, every ornament multiplied by three. It would be lovely when it was time to leave. And loveliest if no one spoke to her again until that blessed hour arrived.

"I hope you didn't take Lady Berners seriously." Mrs. Bennington was suddenly at her elbow. "None of us do."

Just her luck. Sometimes Ella thought the surest proof of God's existence was the swiftness with which he denied her supplications.

Mrs. Bennington's cheeks were flushed, and her eyes sparkled. She took Ella's arm as though they were intimates.

"It's so wonderful that your father was a poet and immortalized your mother in verse," she said. Ella regarded her warily. Anything could be happening behind that china-doll face. "So few women find men who truly love them," she added, almost wistfully.

She glanced back at the guests milling about the parlor, and Ella followed her gaze to Mr. Bennington, who stood conversing with Lord Berners by the fireplace.

"And sometimes the ones who do don't deserve them. Do I sound terribly jaded?" Mrs. Bennington leaned closer, applying pressure to Ella's arm. Her perfume was too strong. Ella wished she could inch away. The realization she'd had at the dinner table came flooding back to her. Well, why not out with it? Why play a game?

"You do sound jaded," she said, and Mrs. Bennington's eyes widened. Ella looked at her steadily. "I think it's because you're unhappy."

A mistake. She knew it immediately. She should have made some flippant remark or a vague protestation. Mrs. Bennington sucked in her breath. She dropped Ella's arm and drew back.

"Unhappy," she repeated. Her eyes looked slightly unfocused. The effect of the wine perhaps. "What makes you think I'm unhappy?"

"Nothing," said Ella hastily. "I shouldn't have said it."

"You say whatever you want, don't you?" said Mrs. Bennington slowly. "No matter who it hurts. That's what people like you do. I don't know how you stand it. You even look the part. You look … morbid." She shook her head. "*Necromancer.* Lady Berners *is* a funny woman. But it fits, doesn't it?"

She clutched at herself, as though suddenly cold. "I was Phillipa's dearest friend, you know. We were like sisters."

Her face wasn't quite so perfect as it had appeared from across the table. One of her eyes was slightly larger than the other. She used powder to hide the light tracing of broken capillaries on the tops of her cheeks. She didn't seem to be talking to Ella at all, but to herself, or to something unseen, something hovering between them.

"I told her everything," she said.

This is a nightmare. Mrs. Bennington's eyes were so pale. Her perfume filled the air. Ella felt as though she might gag. *Dear God, don't let me have a fit.* Her head swam. She put her hand discreetly against the wall, propping herself up. She breathed to steady herself.

"She must have been a good listener," she said, although that didn't accord at all with the image of Phillipa she'd formed.

"No." Mrs. Bennington's lips curved. Dimples formed. "She didn't listen to anyone. *He* was her betrothed. Lord Blackwood."

Ella would not risk a look in his direction. She looked instead at the teardrop earring dangling from Mrs. Bennington's left ear. She tried to think of it as an anchor. A tiny, diamond anchor.

She had to ask.

"Lord Blackwood," she said and stopped. She feared for a moment her voice had given something away. "Lord Blackwood," she began again. "He loved her truly, didn't he?"

Mrs. Bennington was silent. Then the teardrop earring swung dizzyingly as she laughed her musical laugh, a shower of notes. She laughed like a pianist playing scales. A practiced laugh. No feeling in it whatsoever.

"He loved her blindly," she said. Then she caught Ella's arm again and stroked it, absently.

"You aren't really a medium, are you, Miss Reed?" she asked. "You can tell me."

And make Mrs. Trombly a laughingstock? Ella stiffened. *Don't trust her. Don't trust any of these people.*

"I am employed by Mrs. Trombly in the capacity of medium," she said, as proudly as she could. "You may discuss my credentials with her."

Lord St. Aubyn was approaching. His arrival broke the tension.

Mrs. Bennington turned her dimpled smile on him. "You've escaped from the man-eater?" She raised a delicate brow.

Lord St. Aubyn made a face. "Only just," he said. "You might have come to my aid."

"I was speaking with the enthralling Miss Reed." Mrs. Bennington stroked at Ella's arm again, more demonstratively.

"An enviable situation." Lord St. Aubyn accompanied this gallantry with a slight bow. "And about what were you speaking? Or is it to remain shrouded in feminine mystery?"

"I'm sure you can guess." Mrs. Bennington raised a conspiratorial eyebrow. "We were speaking about Miss Reed's powers."

"Ah." Lord St. Aubyn smiled, and Ella felt a flutter in spite of herself. "I'm sure Miss Reed has many powers."

"Her *spiritual* powers. Miss Reed"—Mrs. Bennington gave her arm a squeeze—"have your ears been burning? You've been much discussed this evening. Up and down the table, everyone was whispering your name."

"Surely I couldn't have competed with London's sewer system," said Ella, and Lord St. Aubyn laughed appreciatively.

"Perhaps it would be vulgar to suggest that sewers and mediums have a certain similarity?" Mrs. Bennington seemed to relish Ella's slight start. "They are both, after all, conduits for corpses."

"From any other lips it would be the *height* of vulgarity," said Lord St. Aubyn. "But you can get away with anything. Of course, you're just teasing Miss Reed. Really, Daphne, you go to such lengths to be provocative."

He was trying to soften Mrs. Bennington's remark. Ella could have told him not to bother.

"But Miss Reed," Mrs. Bennington persisted. She was going to *bruise* her arm if she didn't stop squeezing. Ella extracted herself with difficulty. "Are you really a conduit?" That peculiar intensity had crept back into her voice.

"Let's get away from *conduit*," said Lord St. Aubyn. "I've had enough of that for one evening. Miss Reed, I believe Mrs. Bennington is asking you, rather indelicately, if you can, in fact, speak to the dead?" His posture belied his casual tone. He was leaning toward her.

The two of them, quite unconsciously, it seemed, were crowding her into the wall. Ella shut her eyes. *Just for a moment. Leave just for a moment.*

How wonderful to shut out their inquisitive gazes. To escape that parlor. To drift away from the palatial home, away from Park Lane, away from London, toward the forests in the west that exhaled such sweet air. The library window was open. In the dark garden, the glow worms shone with faint, green light. She could hear her papa as he read aloud to her, the morocco leather-bound volume open in his hands.

I saw eternity the other night,
Like a great ring of pure and endless light

She would always hear his voice. Her papa would always be with her. And that knowledge gave her the strength to answer them. Her eyes flew open.

"Yes," she said. "I can. I can speak to the dead."

She heard her certainty ring through in her words.

Mrs. Bennington frowned. She looked to Lord St. Aubyn, but he was staring at Ella. Intent. Mrs. Bennington glanced at the rest of the party over her shoulder, and her frown changed. She looked almost ugly, her face twisted.

"Oh, hell," she murmured.

Mr. Bennington was sitting on the sofa with Mrs. Hatfield. Their heads were very close together.

"Excuse me," she said coolly to Ella and Lord St. Aubyn and stalked toward her husband.

Ella stood awkwardly under Lord St. Aubyn's stare. He was handsome, yes, but he didn't make her skin tingle. She didn't worry that she was about to tumble into him, crash against his chest like a wave against a rock. *Thank God.* Thank God only one man seemed able to harness the elements and override all the senses.

Lord St. Aubyn was doing it again. Peering at her with his sea-green eyes as though he sat behind a microscope. Suddenly something clicked in her head.

"Are you an artist?" she asked. His eyes narrowed.

"Blackwood told you."

"No." She waited before elaborating. She wasn't versed in drawing-room theater, but she understood the basics of dramatic timing. Maybe she would get the hang of this after all.

"It's the way you look at things," she said at last. "Dissecting them. Though I suppose I might as well have guessed you were a zoologist."

"Yes," he agreed dryly. "Or a doctor."

"But there's also a watercolor signed *St. Aubyn* in the Tromblys' sitting room."

"A detective *and* a medium." He laughed, a surprisingly harsh sound. "No secret will be safe." A muscle ticked in his jaw. She saw the sudden turbulence in his eyes.

Classically handsome, tall, blond Lord St. Aubyn wasn't a statue, after all. He was a man, wracked by some torment she couldn't comprehend. Her intuition stirred, guiding her.

"Oh, I can keep a secret," she said, smiling. "But secrets can eat away at you, my lord."

There. He flinched. She wasn't mistaken. He struggled under some terrible burden. She stepped toward him, pursuing her advantage.

"Perhaps some secrets need to be told," she whispered, focusing all of her attention on his face. Letting the rest of the room fade away. "Perhaps, my lord, it's time to tell."

He recoiled.

"Are you a witch?" he rasped.

"No, she is not." Lord Blackwood stepped between them. His approach had been silent. *That lethal tread.* "She is not a witch. She is something else entirely."

His eyes flicked over Lord St. Aubyn, noting his pallor.

"Clement," he said, but Lord St. Aubyn shook his head warningly.

"Don't speak to me," he said. "Sid, I can't … " He almost lurched as he left them. Ella watched him make his way to Mr. Tenby. Making his excuses, it seemed. He was leaving. She had shaken him badly.

It wasn't witchcraft. No one's conscience was clean. Give a hint. Make an insinuation. A man's guilt supplied the rest. She was learning lessons she wasn't sure she wanted to learn.

"What did you say to him?" Blackwood stood no closer to her than St. Aubyn had a moment before, but she could feel the heat from his body. She could smell his spicy scent—not cologne, something subtle, natural. It made her want to step closer. Everything about him drew her in. The black current …

She couldn't form a word. She could only study him. Midnight blue. Ivory black. He was made up of so many contrasting colors. So many irreconcilable elements. The planes of his face were so harsh. But his lips could be so tender. She *had* to look away from his lips.

Music began to play. Her lips parted. For a moment it seemed like magic. It wasn't, of course. Mrs. Hatfield, dislodged from the sofa, had sat at the piano. She had opted for Beethoven. A bold choice. Her touch turned the notes to mud.

"Let's talk about something else then." Lord Blackwood leaned over her. "How did you come by the jewels that you carried hidden in your skirts?" His voice was barely above a whisper. The question hit her like a sledge. She felt pain in the crown of her head, and a sheet of darkness came down to obscure her vision. *This* was the nightmare. It was being set into motion now. The tempo of the sonata was all wrong. She couldn't think.

"Tell me where they came from." His face was tense; his eyes brilliant.

Had he searched the room? But how would he know she had hidden the pouch in her dress? Someone knew, of course, in the Tromblys' house. Whoever undressed her when she was first carried into the house unconscious … Whoever took the gown into the laundry room … *Stupid.* Stupid of her to count herself lucky the articles were all there and think nothing more would come of it. That it wouldn't be mentioned. Who had told him? Mrs. Hexam. Lizzie.

"Are they under your skirts now?" His gaze slid down from her face. He stepped closer to her. Everyone else was arrayed around the piano, watching Mrs. Hatfield torture the keys.

This was why he had not returned her smile. He thought she was a thief.

"Tell me," he whispered. Was there the hint of a plea in his voice? Did he hope she would give him an explanation that he could accept?

She couldn't. She tried. *They were left to me by my father, Mr. Reed. A simple, poor man, a poet, yet possessed of a few very fine pieces of jewelry and silver. As poets sometimes are.* She tried, but no sound came out. Why would he believe her? She could produce no proof. If he began to look into the Reeds of Somerset and found nothing that matched her stories, what then? If he began to investigate her identity …

She shook her head mutely.

"Miss Reed," he said. Cold. Detached. "Do you know the punishments for theft?"

She took a shuddering breath and met his eyes. She said nothing. The room fell silent. Mrs. Hatfield had finished the first movement.

She heard Lady Berners's acid voice. "Do stop there, Mrs. Hatfield. I can't imagine the other movements add a thing."

And Mr. Huntington. "Bravo! Miss Tenby, won't you oblige us? Perhaps something lighter? A Celtic air?"

Blackwood stepped back from her. His chest heaved as he drew a deep breath. He spoke rapidly, as though he needed to get the words out before he could reconsider.

"I will pay a visit to Trombly Place tomorrow afternoon. If you are no longer in residence at that time, I will consider the problem taken care of by itself. If you *are* there when I arrive"—he lifted his hands, considering them before they folded into fists—"then you will leave with me," he finished. "And I will drag you straight to Newgate."

She had moved beyond fear. She gave a short nod. Tomorrow then. She would be back out in the storm. Her gaze wandered across the room to Mrs. Trombly. She would leave without saying goodbye. It would be easier that way.

"You have nothing to say?" Again, that faint note. So faint she could almost believe she had imagined it. But she knew she hadn't. He wanted to believe something better of her than this. How strange that she felt she could understand him, the complex of emotions that raged within him. Maybe he would understand her too.

My name is not Miss Reed. I am not a thief. I am …

"Nothing, Miss Reed?" The note was gone. His voice was like black glass. Blank. Smooth. Hard. His lids half hooded his eyes. He was dispassionate. Absolutely unmoved. Unconcerned.

Nothing. Nothing. Nothing.

"I won't be there, my lord," she said. "You won't see me again."

Chapter Twelve

The London night matched Isidore's mood. The city looked like lead; the rain ran down like ink. Sleep would be impossible.

"Covent Garden," he told the coachman. He wanted to watch a fight, or pick one. The coach rolled east, away from the splendor of Mayfair. Soon the wheels rattled on broken pavements and cobbles. The vibrations set his teeth on edge. He stared out the window at the heaps of bricks that passed for buildings, at the hovels, booths, and stalls. He caught a whiff of the air as the coach slowed. Pestilential stench.

Disease billowed from these winding alleys. Maybe it was in the water. Maybe it was in the foul vapors that rose off the river, or in the saliva of the rats that scurried in mobs over the refuse. Most likely, it was in the city itself. The opulence of Park Lane produced the squalor of Seven Dials. The only thing to do was raze the metropolis, the whole thing, not only the flash houses but Buckingham Palace, and start again.

He pressed his forehead to the glass and focused his eyes on the beaded water glowing sickly yellow with the light from the coachman's lamp. Bennington had accused him of radicalism. He wasn't a radical. His mind went to extremes so he could reject taking action and resign himself to doing nothing. He was a fatalist.

Penn, on the other hand, acted with the courage of his conviction. He made a difference, a small difference, every day. He was a good man. He'd never been a member of their set. His older brothers were—both of them notorious rakes—but David wouldn't carouse. Too serious. Isidore regretted that he hadn't made the effort, years ago, to get to know him. He'd been too busy drinking and climbing in and out of windows. Back then he was far more interested in the Mrs. Hatfields of the world than he was in skinny, bookish medical students. He *had* saved Penn from a beating at Eton. He recalled grabbing the boy's two assailants and knocking their heads together. Bloody mess that had been. He wondered if Penn remembered it.

How different they'd turned out. Penn helped people. Saved people. Isidore only hurt people. Even when he meant to do the right thing, someone ended up bleeding.

And now he was driving into the slums, hoping to find a strongman he could punch until his knuckles split. That was the one difference between him and his father. He didn't target the weak. But he was filled with the same violence, the same hatred, that he had seen so often glittering in his father's ice-blue eyes. Nights like this he couldn't deny it.

The coffeehouse he remembered, across from St. Paul's, always open until the wee hours of the morning and filled with pugilists pounding one another in mills both sanctioned and spontaneous, was abandoned. By men. Not rats. He could hear them squeaking as he stood outside the moldering hulk, looked up at the chimneys from which no smoke rose, black against the leaden sky. He climbed back into the coach and rolled away from the open square; the coach turned onto narrow streets, moving further east, or maybe south. It was impossible to get his bearings in that warren of mud and stone, plank and brick.

After a time, he stopped the coach. He chose a public house with music filtering out into the street. An iron signpost stuck out above the door, but the sign had long since fallen. There was a dead crow by the door, wing outstretched. He stepped over it. Not everyone had.

The Sign of the Dead Crow, he thought. *Perfect.*

Once inside the taproom, the fight went out of him. Such a grimy, greasy, undernourished lot. Men in threadbare coats fastened by pins. The comic vocalist who accompanied the piano was hunched and gray as a gargoyle.

Isidore ordered a glass of raw gin and sat on a deal bench to drink it. A woman swayed at a nearby table. Drunk. Her cheeks were sunken. Her left eye was bruised and swollen. Who had done this to her? It could have been any or none of these wretches. She saw him looking.

"Ain't you a swell." She winked at him with her good eye. "Two penn'orth of gin."

He glanced around for the potboy and saw him sitting by the bar fire with his own pint pot. His apron may have been white once. Isidore signaled, but the potboy, shooting to his feet at the proprietor's call, went in the other direction, through the red curtains that blocked the passageway to another room. Isidore rose, shouldered his way to the bar, and bought two glasses of gin and a few biscuits from the basket. He put one glass and the plate of biscuits on the table in front of the woman. She laughed at the biscuits.

"Plenty of sawdust on the floor without paying for it," she said. "Sit ye down. You ain't ugly."

He sat with her. Gloom weighed heavier and heavier upon him. Luckily, she didn't want to talk but lapsed into vacancy. The room was warm and smoky. The comic vocalist retired to a table, and a sailor leapt up to begin an Irish melody. He had a rumbling, deep voice and sang the notes true.

"'Tis never too late for delight, my dear. And the best of all ways, to lengthen our days, is to steal a few hours from the night, my dear."

Isidore finished his gin. The glass had sweated a new ring on the table. The table's surface showed easily a dozen such rings. Some overlapped. He thought of chains. Chains symbolized bondage. They symbolized forever.

He set his glass down. The woman snapped to attention.

"Not a drop," she observed. "Me neither. And warn't I a nickey to think you'd buy me another?"

He bought her another, which she took without thanks. What could he do for the woman other than this? Buy her a drink. Treat her like a human being. She had a story too, a story similar, no doubt, to many others, but her own nonetheless. She was an individual, though her life, with all its particulars—petty cares and great loves, memories, dreams—would go unrecorded, unremembered. Drudge. Whore. He caught her ungloved hand—cold, the skin dry and yellow as parchment—and kissed it goodbye. She laughed again at that. The eye that wasn't swollen shut was a muddy green.

His mother's eyes had never been blackened, swollen like hers. His father was almost surgical in his precision. He aimed to instill the most fear, to inflict the most pain, and to leave the least visible traces. He wasn't crude, like the man who had marked this woman. The upper classes beat their women below the neck. Or cut or burnt. Or relied on threats and humiliation.

Sometimes he wondered if the world had in it already every kind of monster. Or would new monsters arise, specializing in brutalities as yet unimaginable?

Had he thought *London* should be razed? Make it the whole miserable world of man.

It was a quarter after twelve. He left the Sign of the Dead Crow feeling darker than he had when he'd entered. He wasn't ready to return to the coach. He walked through streets so narrow his shoulders almost brushed the bulging bricks on either side. It reminded him of Cairo. But Cairo didn't smell as strongly of pig shit. Must be sties in the courts that opened here and there, behind the butcher shops and taverns. The rain had stopped. He headed toward the water, the wind coming hard against him, sweeping away the pig and replacing it with a thick, briny smell. Tide was running in.

Clement had left the party looking as though Miss Reed had stabbed him through the heart. Isidore should have followed him. They could have gone to the club, talked it all out over brandy and cigars. Clement would tell him what Miss Reed had said to him, and he'd tell Clement that she was poison. A liar. A thief. Clement would tell him he'd done what he had to do. Discharged his responsibility, and as mercifully as could be expected. He'd be home by now in front of the fire, sleepy, relieved, instead of wandering by the riverside. But for some reason, Isidore hadn't been able to let Miss Reed out of his sight. He couldn't go after Clem when she was still in that parlor, standing in the far corner, slim and strange and silent, those dark eyes so full of pain.

Earlier in the evening, he'd told himself he needed to look at her, because he was assessing her, coolly evaluating her every gesture, squaring his impressions with Lizzie's revelation.

His impressions did *not* square with the revelation. This irritated him immensely, his inability to see her as the larcenous, *nasty* baggage Lizzie had described. Maybe that was why he'd needed to keep staring. He wanted to see it, the mercenary strumpet. The filcher who would violate any trust. The woman who spoke of the world's need for kindness then took advantage of kindness when she found it.

Without that hideous bonnet, she looked even more unearthly. Her head capped with that shining, silvery blond hair, upswept to reveal the delicate curve of her neck as she stared into the candle flames. He knew how those tresses felt, slippery and soft.

She didn't speak at dinner. Made no attempt to dazzle the company or ingratiate herself. She was the *opposite* of crafty baggage. She was utterly withdrawn. Even absent. She had looked at him once, and smiled. That smile transformed her features, illuminated her pale face, kindled something darkling bright in those enormous black eyes.

He'd had no choice but to devote his attention then to the tedious Penny Tenby, who was bland as a dinner bun, and whose agenda was almost pitifully clear. She wanted to make a brilliant match. With him, if she could. If not, with someone else. Flattering, to be sure. He couldn't feel too badly about disappointing her.

He hadn't looked in Miss Reed's direction again until he'd let the table's reaction to Penn gall him into idiot speeches. She was nodding as though in perfect agreement. He could tell she was in sympathy with Mr. Penn and had little patience with Berners, Tenby, and the rest. That irritated him too. Everything he liked about her chafed. Desiring her was bad enough. *Liking* her … It was out of the question.

After dinner, in Tenby's parlor, he very nearly failed to do it. He'd stalled, reconsidered, and recommitted himself. Daphne and Miss Reed standing close together across the room presented a startling contrast. Daphne, with her auburn hair and red silk gown, was so richly colored, small, rounded, and supple. Miss Reed, in black, so slender and straight, was pale as a moonbeam piercing a dark cloud. Day and night. He preferred Miss Reed's eerie beauty, which seemed to go through phases like the moon. Sometimes she dimmed, vanished into herself. Sometimes she was wan, glancing. Sometimes she turned to him, full-faced and radiant. He felt that he could watch her forever. That it would be a rare delight to come to understand her cycles, what made her show her face, what made her slip away.

But he couldn't just watch. He'd had to steel himself and approach her.

Afterwards, he expected to feel some release, but he felt worse. He'd joined the circle by the piano and waited there until she and Mrs. Trombly departed.

The expression in her eyes had nearly unmanned him. Like a wounded deer awaiting the *coup de grace*. He wished she had tried to defend herself. If she had lied to him, pleaded with him, displayed any kind of cunning … he could hold her in contempt. But she had only looked at him, unwavering, until *he* felt like the criminal. There had been no hint of accusation in her face. That too would have made it easier. He could have felt the comfort of righteous indignation.

She was possessed of innate nobility. This charlatan housebreaker.

He could see the river now. Black and high. Barges moving slowly out on the little waves. The red lights of coal fires winked as they bobbed up and down. Smaller boats were drifting beneath the arches of the Waterloo bridge.

And he could see a figure walking along the embankment. Not a typical waterside character. A cloaked woman, straight and slender, with a peculiar gait, as though she walked with stiffened limbs, as though she were powered by a mechanism tightly wound. A clockwork walk.

He had to stop in his tracks. Blink. Convince himself she wasn't a figment. A conjuration of his inflamed brain. How could it be? But it was. Miss Reed, walking in the dead of night alongside the dreary river. She had stepped out of his very thoughts. He was too stunned by her appearance, at this hour, in this chill and desolate place, to call out. What was she doing, walking so close to the shelving-wall, the river at flood tide, moored boats floating? She risked assault. Robbery. Rape. Murder. His muscles tensed.

She stopped and faced the water, and the wind blew her cloak around her.

He remembered the bleakness in her gaze. *You won't see me again.*

A dog barked nearby. She didn't turn. She stepped up on the wall.

Christ almighty. She was so small and the river vast and foul, tons and tons of black water surging with the blind power of annihilation. It had swallowed who knew how many miserable souls.

No, he thought. *No.* And some more obscure voice from deeper inside him cried out too. Cried, *Not again.*

He ran. He threw himself across the uneven ground, threw himself into the teeth of the wind. He splashed through puddles, vaulted rotten wood, reached her in moments. He launched himself onto the wall behind her, barely checking his momentum as he hugged her against his body, grabbed her shoulders, the two of them carried forward even as he jerked them back. They balanced on the river's edge. Her body went rigid with shock. Then she thrashed her head, threw her elbow into his side, and kicked and screamed, fighting him like a wild thing. He tried to still her, whirl her around so she could see him, know him, the whole time saying her name, but she was beyond hearing. Her feet slipped out from under her on the dank stone, slick with deposits, and she was suddenly clinging to him, pulling him forward.

"Don't fight me," he grunted. "Little fool, don't fight." But she twisted again in his arms, crazed, off-balance, pitching her weight, and then they were both of them over the edge, falling down into the black water that closed—frigid, filthy, final—above them.

Chapter Thirteen

Cold. She had never been so cold. She tried to struggle, but fabric wrapped her arms, her legs. She was paralyzed in the freezing, breathless dark. No air in her lungs. She didn't know if her eyes were open or shut. No way of determining up or down. She opened her mouth to scream, to breathe, both impossible, and the water rushed in, choking, thick, and now her chest burned, burned like fire, even as she sank like a stone in the icy fathoms. Was that the sound of her blood, that rushing in her ears? She had to get out, to claw her way out, out of the clothing that was weighing her down, out of her *body*, it was too clumsy, too heavy, if she could only wiggle free and rise, but she was trapped in wet wool and silk, in cold, cold flesh. She was squeezed from all sides. She could feel her heart beating, beating, beating, but the water, which had no rhythm, was beginning to cancel everything out. The terrifying darkness—silent, featureless—filled her. Still. Blank.

She could see a light, far off. The moon floating on top of the river. All the talk of heaven and hell … empty bluster. It was just the moon in the end. Papa was waiting on the moon. He beckoned, or it was the light waving, waving through the water as it found her. Cold, and a little frightening, the light waved. How strange that it could find her, even here.

Something was pulling her. Pulling her away from the light. She wanted to move her limbs, fight against whatever it was, but their weight was the weight of the river itself. She was being sucked down, down, and the light was receding.

Let me go. She tried one last time to reach for the light. *Papa. Papa.* Then there was only black. She screamed and heard a gurgle, oily water and bile pouring from her throat, and air rushed in. Air that felt like claws, scraping all the way down into her stomach.

More water, hard, hurting, moved up through her body to pour from her mouth. She was wracked, shaking. Through the pain in her ears, she heard a voice. Deep. Harsh.

"Breathe. Breathe, damn it. Breathe, my angel. Breathe, darling, breathe."

It hurt to breathe. But the air came rasping in, and this time it went again, without water. She felt something hard digging into her back, became aware of her soaking dress plastered to her skin. She couldn't stop shaking. She opened her eyes and saw only blackness. *No.* She shut them again in terror.

"Open your eyes." She recognized that voice. That command. She felt the scratch of callused fingers moving on her face, the pressure of warm hands. "Look at me."

This time she could see. A dim figure bending over her, dripping onto her. From the shadows of the face as it drew nearer: a glimmer of blue. Blue eyes. The color of midnight—that absolute black that signaled the day would come. Bright. Shattering the dark. Blue beneath black. Blue eyes bringing her back into her body. She tried to sit up, and strong arms wrapped around her.

"Don't fight me. Can you stand?"

She could. Shakily, his arm around her waist.

"Come," he said. He led her, half crawling, half climbing over slippery stones. She stumbled, sinking in sludge and scum. *God, that stink.*

"This way. We can't get up the wall there."

The bell of a church clock tolled in the distance. Once. She could hear the creaking of iron chains and men's voices, indistinct, coming in and out across the water. An enormous ship was passing slowly, close by, on the river. No one from the deck would notice the two figures, wet, shivering, struggling on the shore. And that other sound—chugging, nauseous—that was the paddles of a steam ship churning.

"Wait, wait." She pulled against his arm, and he held her while she vomited, doubled over, more filthy water. It gushed even from her nostrils. Stinging. She heaved again. Nothing. His hand was smoothing back her hair, kneading her back. His voice was murmuring near her ear. "Easy, love. Easy. Let it out. Breathe. Ready?"

He was gentle but firm. Already urging her on. She wanted to collapse, but she forced her legs to move. Suddenly they were out of the lee of the pier, and the cold wind slapped against them. She gasped, and the wind snatched her breath away.

"Stay still," he commanded and ripped off her sodden cloak, dropping it in the mud. He caught her beneath the knees and armpits, carrying her the last few yards up to the riverside streets. She heard his breath sawing as he went on his knees to lower her to the cobbles. She drew in her legs, clutching herself, and rocked. He crouched beside her. He withdrew a knife from his boot and pulled her arm across his thighs. He worked the blade between her wet, shrunken glove and the skin of her inner arm. He slit the fabric to her wrist and spread it apart. She gasped as the cold moved up her arm, air brushing across the exposed skin. He pulled the ruined glove from her hand. He did the same with her other arm. Then he rubbed at the clammy flesh, caught her numb fingers between his hands, and chafed at them. God, they hurt too. Everything hurt.

His teeth were chattering. Blades of hair plastered his cheeks. He put his lips against her forehead, the hot breath providing a temporary focal point—one thing in this world of pain that felt good.

"We need to get to my coach." She felt his lips move. "We're going to stand at the count of three." She couldn't bear to imagine him standing, removing his body. The wind would blow through her. She clutched at his shirtfront.

"Stay," she whispered. This feeling—it was almost like the convulsions. Her body was frozen in a slow-motion spasm. Clenched. "Stay here."

"We'll be warm soon," he said. "I promise. Now we're going to stand. One. Two."

At "three" they rose. She made it to the alley before she wavered, too dizzy to take another step. He lifted her up into his arms. She pressed her face into the wet cloth of his shirt. His heart beat steadily, but so slowly. She must have lost consciousness. The next thing she knew, she was being wrapped in a greatcoat that smelled of camphor and horses and settled on the padded bench of the coach. The movement of the coach jolted her. She huddled back into the greatcoat. The light from the coachman's lamp gleamed through the window, playing upon the face of the man beside her.

He had saved her life. He had also nearly killed her.

Now that her senses were returning, questions followed.

"What … " she began and coughed. Her throat felt raw.

"You swallowed a great deal of water." He slid across the seat until he was pressed against her side. "Don't overtax yourself." For the first time, his presence failed to make her skin tingle. Her skin was like rubber.

"I can't feel my feet," she said. She couldn't tell if her lips moved when she spoke. Her face had stiffened, become a mask.

He got his arm under her knees and lifted her legs, pulling them across his lap. His fingers, so beautifully formed, so clever, moved clumsily as he tried to untie the laces of her boots. His hands were trembling. He lifted them before his face, opened and closed them, shook them viciously from the wrist, then spread the fingers wide. Still, they trembled. He swore and reached for his knife. Then he cut through her bootlaces with two crude motions, tugged off her boots, and tossed them to the coach floor. She felt the tip of the blade as he slit her stockings and pushed them up her calves. She wiggled then, resisting, back pressed to the side panels of the coach. Her legs, from bare calves to heels, rested on his damp trousers. His palms slid across the tops of her feet. His thumbs pressed deep into the arches. He bent her feet up, then down, sliding his thumbs in little circles.

"Can you feel this?" he asked, pressing harder with his thumbs.

She felt it. She had never felt anything like it. She swallowed, wincing at the ache in her throat. He lifted her feet, leaned over, and … breathed against her toes.

She jerked involuntarily. If his grip were any looser, she'd have kicked him in the face.

"Lord Blackwood," she whispered unsteadily.

"Isidore," he said wryly. "I am, after all, blowing on your toes." And again that warm, tickling breath seeped across her skin.

She tried to control her breathing and felt, remarkably, a blush rising. Heat moving from her core up to her neck and face. *Thank God.* It meant her blood hadn't congealed in her veins.

"I would have had the foot warmer prepared, if I'd known we were bathing in the Thames tonight." He lifted his head, hands still gripping her feet, rubbing the soles, the heels, rubbing up to and around the ankles, sliding up the curve of her calves and back down. He looked worn and grim, jaw hardened against the cold, but his lips quirked.

What was he about?

"You *attacked* me," she said wonderingly. One moment she'd been staring out at the black forest of yards and masts across the river, the next she was battling an unknown assailant, larger than she, and far stronger, battling for her life. That instant, when the iron arms closed around her, had been more terrifying even than the fall into the water.

The river, at least, was indifferent. Men, on the other hand, exulted in cruelty. Mastered all of its forms. She would rather drown than become fodder for such delights. But it wasn't a cutthroat who'd grabbed her. It was Isidore Blackwood. She could not assimilate this knowledge.

"Attacked you?" The mockery in his eyes puzzled her. "Is that what happened?" His cheekbones stood out like blades as he thinned his lips, suppressing a shudder. She tried to open the greatcoat, to spread it over both of them, but he tucked it back around her.

"Keep it," he rasped.

"You're freezing." She tried again to open the greatcoat. He swore again and pulled her onto his lap, wrapping his arms around her, holding her and the greatcoat firmly in place.

"I can't freeze," he said, shifting her to the side so his cheek was near hers. "Too much gin in my blood."

She couldn't smell the alcohol on his breath. All she could smell now was river slime. The fumes rising off both of them. And to think, the poor *drank* this fetid liquid, redolent of feces and decay. She shoved Mr. Penn's voice from her head. Her stomach was still making noises.

"I doubt the coat is doing you much good." Blackwood braced her with one arm and used the other to hook her wet hair and tuck it behind her ear. "Your dress is soaking." His voice was low, lips against her earlobe. "I should have cut it off you."

He sounded as though he were still considering the option. She half expected him to reach for the knife.

"I'm quite warm now," she said hastily. He laughed against her neck, a little gust of warm air.

"Come, Miss Reed, we both know you're a better liar than that," he said.

"Ella." It felt good to speak the truth. "You may call me Ella."

Be careful. Be on guard lest you tell this man too much.

"Ella," he repeated.

How could she be on guard? She was fighting to keep herself from dissolving into tears. After the shocks of the last few hours, physical and mental—it took the last remaining bit of her strength to remain clam. She *wasn't* warm. The icy dress was a torment.

They would both be so much warmer if he did cut the clothing off their bodies. If they clung together, skin to skin. The hard muscle of his thigh had pressed between her legs when he embraced her in the park. Now she was resting on those long, hard thighs, cradled against his chest.

She supposed, in a sense, the coat was doing her *plenty* of good. It kept her from feeling the heat of his body, yes. But it also kept her from feeling the contours of his body beneath her. The ridges of lean muscle. The rise of his hipbones.

"Why aren't you asleep in bed ... Ella?"

It seemed unfair that he would ask her that. He knew what tomorrow held. She was to be cast back on the world. The fragile calm she'd known at Trombly Place would shatter. Mrs. Trombly would be told that she was a thief. Mrs. Trombly would sit mute on the pretty sofa, a sorrowing, foolish woman, her misguided attempt to connect with the spirit world eroding her faith in the living, leaving her at the same time farther from the dead than ever.

And she would be friendless again and would feel it even more acutely for having had—though briefly, though she had won it falsely—the promise of help.

She said only, "Sleep doesn't always come at the appointed hour." There was nothing he could say to that. He wasn't asleep, either. "I needed to think."

She had to clench her teeth then, bite back the torrent of language that threatened to spill from her mouth. Her body wanted to void everything now. River water. Her inner ravings. She wanted to say more. Gush the words out.

I was going mad.

I was going to wear through the carpet, pacing.

I felt as though I really were a criminal, stealing out of the house, walking the streets in the night when all the innocent maidens are tucked under coverlets, dreaming sweet dreams with their curls spread on scented pillows. Perhaps I belong to the streets and the wharves and the drear, anonymous night. Insofar as I belong anywhere.

I felt as though I couldn't stay another minute in that bedchamber, where Phillipa once dreamed her own sweet dreams, of her wedding, of her children.

I felt as though I were a nightmare that troubled Phillipa's sleep. If I disappeared, she would wake up. None of it would ever have happened. She would be beside you now, in a tester bed, the two of you dry and warm. She would murmur as the memory of the nightmare faded, and you would smooth the worry line from her forehead and whisper, "It was just a bad dream."

A dream sent by a jealous fairy. Morgan La Fey, lonely on her misty island, longing for the love of mortal man.

Insane fantasies. She'd been beside herself.

Thank God her lips stayed closed. The words did not spew forth. She forced them back.

She felt his chest move as he took a deep breath, preparing to question, to accuse. She couldn't handle an interrogation. Not now. She was too cold, too tired, too defeated.

"Please," she said and heard her voice break. She had the mortifying sensation that she needed to expectorate and did so, discreetly, into the fold of the coat. Funny, how she had swallowed half the Thames and could suddenly feel this desperate thirst.

She tried again. "Tell me the story of Rhodopis," she said. "You asked me to remind you."

He let his breath whistle out. Said nothing. The silence lasted so long, she began to drift away from herself. She was drifting away from her huddled body and the vibrating coach, up over the wide lanes of mansions, the dense, evil-smelling rookeries, the factories with their smokestacks like iron trees, up over the river that curved through it all, carrying disease, lapping against stone walls and marshy shores and causeways. She was drifting up over everything great and small, so high nothing could reach her. Then he spoke, and she heard him as though from far off, and at first his words sounded alien, as though she were no longer part of the human community. But they tethered her. She could follow them back down.

She turned her face so her cheek touched his before she realized what she was doing. His cheek was clammy. The soft rumble of his voice resolved into meaningful units.

"Rhodopis was a Greek girl," he said. "She lived on a rocky island where cyclamen grew pink and white, and the sea was clear as glass. She tended goats and ate figs and honey."

She could *see* the island as he spoke. He conjured it with his words, with the cadence of his voice. She curled up more tightly, burrowing into the coat, into him.

"One day," he said, "raiders came and slaughtered the goats and burnt the fig trees and smoked the hives, and they took Rhodopis to Egypt, where she became a slave. She was sold to a cruel master who took her to his city. It was called Hephaestopolis. Can you guess what that means?"

"City of the fire god," she whispered. She could see that too. City of metal, scorched clay, living coal.

"Yes," he said, stroking her hair, then resting his hand on her brow. The comfort she derived from that gesture. It made the tears stand in her eyes.

"It was always hot in Hephaestopolis," he continued. "And Rhodopis was forced to do the hottest work. She had ashes always in her hair, and she turned the oxen on spits all day and night for her master. But her spirit was unbroken. Every now and then she would creep away to the river Naucratis and dance and sing for the fish and the birds and shake the ashes from her hair and wash the soot from her skin. The animals loved her and wanted her to be happy. But they knew not how to help her. Then an eagle flew down while she bathed and stole one of her slippers. He flew with it to the Pharaoh, who was driving his chariot through the desert. The Pharaoh trusted that the eagle had presented him with the slipper for a reason, and he vowed to test it on every woman in the land until he found its owner. Rhodopis was found and brought to the Pharaoh at Memphis, and though his advisors cried out that she was only a slave and worse, a Greek, no fit queen, he swore that none other would be his wife. He married her at the river Naucratis with the fish and the birds and the eagle in attendance."

"And she was happy?" Ella stirred, and he took his hand from her head, clasped her again around the middle.

"Ever after," he said. "So the story goes."

"Cinderella." Her eyes had closed, and she could not open them. Her tremors were getting worse not better.

"The first Cinderella," he said. "The earliest known tale. The third pyramid was built for her."

"Did you go there?" She wanted him to keep talking, to keep telling her stories. He could be whimsical. She already knew that about him. He had alluded to Arthurian legend. To Hansel and Gretel and their trail of crumbs. This demon viscount—so tall, so broad, so strong, so harsh and unbending—he reminded her of the heroes she'd read of in books. He did not seem like a man who would stroke her hair and murmur fairy tales into her ear. But he was full of contradictions. He loved myths as much as she did. How odd that they had this in common. Imagination for her had been a refuge. Imagination was for the weak.

She lifted her lids partway and peered down at his hands, one folded atop the other on the greatcoat. They were large, brutal, the knobs and hollows of the wrists pronounced, roped by veins, but the fingers were long, sensitive, just the slightest bit tapered. When she'd first seen them she'd been struck by their menace. Their beauty. The hands of a strangler or a sculptor. She was beginning to think it wasn't one or the other; he had proclivities for both, destruction and creation.

"I went there." He nodded, the roughness of his cheek abrasive. She wanted him to nod again. Anything to make her know her skin was living, connected to sensation. Not wax. Not clay. "I climbed the pyramid at sunrise. I could see in front of me the Nile valley, white mist parting above green plains and black soil, and behind me the desert, vast as the ocean. The sands looked purple. Inside, the chambers are filled with bats."

"What else?" She used the excuse of speech to move her face ever so slightly against his. His voice lulled her, rising and falling, as he painted pictures in the air.

"What else?" He paused. "I met a party of Frenchmen and rode with them to their camp. They'd raised a tent in the shade of a palm grove. But most of them had passed the night like the Arabs, wrapped in blankets, burrowed in the sand. They were proud to tell me that. We drank coffee and smoked pipes. They showed me their booty, collected from the tombs and caves. I remember one had a mummified child, an infant really, curled up. He wanted me to hold it. Feel how light it was. They invited me to go with them to watch a beheading in a nearby village. I made it to the courtyard and turned around."

She felt the tension in his jaw. "This isn't what you meant," he said. He barked a bitter laugh that turned into a cough. "Why am I telling you these things?" He shook his head slightly. "Another legend says that Rhodopis was never a queen. She was a great courtesan. She rubbed gold powder on her skin and glowed in the sun. Her eyes were like fire … " His voice trailed off.

She whispered, "I could listen to you for hours," but her voice was fading. It was almost inaudible, even to her. Right then, Egypt sounded like paradise to her. Blazing sun. Burning sand. But it was more complicated than that. What he said, and what he didn't say, revealed so much. He had seen things, maybe even done things, that troubled him. She wanted to be someone to whom he told his stories. Someone with whom he shared his troubles. This desire frightened her as much as anything.

"You're a good storyteller," she said in a stronger voice.

"No one has ever complimented my storytelling." She thought she could detect a hint of pleasure in his ironic drawl.

"It's important," she said. "Storytellers pay attention. They care about the little details. They're awake to beauty."

"And ugliness."

"You can't have one without the other." She coughed too, muffling her mouth in the coat. "They exist as a dyad, together." It was one of Papa's favorite topics, culture as composed of oppositions—good/bad, beautiful/ugly, life/death. "Only art, poetry, music, by *intensifying* experience instead of merely identifying and delimiting, can rupture the binary system. Make it overflow. The beautiful and the ugly, each in excess, no longer divided. One is carried into the other and back again. A vortical motion." She stopped, her scratchy throat closing. She'd never voiced anything like this outside of the library at Arlington Manor, where she and Papa had discussed philosophy, religion, the hermetic tradition, neo-Platonism, metaphysical poetry— everything unfashionable. These notions, these abstractions, *mattered* to her. She shouldn't have attempted to explain them. She'd sounded embarrassingly earnest.

But he didn't jeer. He shifted her again on his lap, so she sat turned to the side, his arm supporting her back. In this position, they could see each other face-to-face. His gaze was a snare. She couldn't look away. He was thinking about what she'd said. He was intent. *Interested.*

"And this motion?" he asked. "This motion by which the dyad becomes other than what it is? Do we know it when we experience it? What is the effect?"

Every word now caused a tickle in the back of her throat. But she forced it out.

"Communion," she said. Their eyes were locked. "Recognition." She swallowed with effort. "You feel it. It's a touch … that's not a touch."

Their faces were an inch apart. His eyes traveled to her lips and back again. She could see the rays in his irises, the black tips of those blue starbursts. His eyelashes were wet, clumped.

"Yes," he said softly, and her heart skipped a beat. "I understand what you're saying. It's a force that brings you out of yourself. Music can do it. Art. A force that moves you over the dividing line that separates you from everything else. Brings you forward. Toward another thing. Another self."

Art. Poetry. Music. *Love.* The forces that overcome the tidy order man imposed on the universe, the valuations, the rules, the either/or. She was spinning. There was chaos in his eyes. Vortical motion. He *understood.*

Their lips were so close. Nearly brushing. A touch that's not a touch. That's less and more. She could feel the air sliding between their mouths, just a sliver of air, thin as a knife blade. That's all that kept their mouths from joining.

The coach rolled to a stop. They were staring at each other. He had to feel it too. She couldn't be imagining it. Not alone.

I want this to be real. The confession was painful. Exposed too much. It wasn't for her to want such things. But she couldn't look away first. He, however, could. He broke the connection. He glanced toward the window then pressed her shoulder. Pushed her onto the seat. "We're here."

"Where?" she asked, hating the catch in her voice. Hating the longing that throbbed in her chest. He had pushed her aside. Casually. It had cost him nothing to break that moment of contact. The cold had reached her very center. Good. Numbness was preferable.

She looked out the window at the unprepossessing terraced houses, considering the possibilities for the first time. Had she expected he was bringing her to Trombly Place? At one in the morning? Shaking and drenched in river water? But to go anywhere else … seemed equally impossible.

"My apartments," he said. Ironic again. Distant. "If my lady does not object."

She must have looked miserable, because his tone softened.

"Come," he said. "We'll get you dry and tucked into bed."

"Mrs. Trombly," she began, and his look darkened.

"I will send her word in the morning," he said, and she leaned her head back against the seat wondering exactly what words he would send. Wondering what the morning would bring.

He lifted her out of the coach and did not put her down. Of course. She wore no shoes. She would make her introductions to his staff in his arms. Well, what did she care, really? Would their opinions of her be better if she walked in under her own power? The coachman was opening the front door. He was thin and hunched with cold. That too should come as no surprise. She had been hacking into the poor man's greatcoat for the entirety of the drive. She wanted to thank him, but he was preceding them into the house, rousing the servants.

The house came alive. Gaslights flared. Voices rose in alarm then hushed to murmurs. Servants scurried here and there, linens in their arms.

"Put me down," she said, twisting. She saw a glimpse of a maid's round, shocked eyes as the girl hurried past.

"So you can fall down the stairs?" He headed down the hall. "No, Ella. I didn't pull you out of the water for that." He sounded matter of fact. Curt. Lord of the house. "Mrs. Potts, have a bath drawn."

The stout woman who bobbed along at his elbow nodded. She had to be his housekeeper. She was more advanced in years than the maid. But by the look on her face, she had encountered nothing in those years that better prepared her for the sight of her master coming through the door in the middle of the night, fully clothed and soaked to the skin, a kicking woman bundled in his arms. "Appalled" was too mild a word. Poleaxed, perhaps.

The *reek* of them couldn't have helped matters.

"The bath is filling, my lord." Mrs. Potts was breathless, either with the excitement or the attempt to keep his pace. "The kettles are on. The stone bottles are heating. Violet is hanging the blankets in front of the fire. What else will you be needing?"

"A nightdress," he grunted as he took the first stair.

"My lord?" Mrs. Potts frowned.

"For my guest, Mrs. Potts. Ask Violet. I'll buy her a new one. I'll buy her ten new ones. Just get the nightdress."

At the top of the stairs, Ella twisted again.

"You can put me down now," she said.

"Now I'll drop you," he said. "With pleasure." But he didn't drop her. He lowered her feet slowly to the ground, and when she tottered under her own weight he steadied her without raising his eyebrow nearly as high as he was able. Showing her a small kindness. Or perhaps his brow was simply too chilled for him to achieve maximum ironic lift.

"Don't thank me," he said. "I make it a point to carry damsels great distances whenever I can. It's part of my physical regimen." The corner of his mouth lifted in the faintest of smiles. In the gaslit hall, she could see the lavender tinge to his skin. His lips too had a purplish cast. Gin in his blood or not, he looked half-frozen. He looked exhausted.

"Mrs. Potts will help you bathe and show you to your chamber," he said. "So. Good night." This commonplace had a strange ring after the urgency and intimacy of what had passed between them. Signaling a partial return to … what? What were they? Acquaintances? Friends? Enemies?

He turned abruptly. She watched him go. If she'd thought his clothing molded to his form *before* he fell into the river … She hadn't imagined that a man's hindquarters could *be* so muscular. A satyr's perhaps. She squeezed her eyes shut.

"Miss." Mrs. Potts took her arm gingerly, flinching as she touched the cold, slimy silk of her sleeve. "Lord, but you're quaking like a leaf!" She firmed her hold. "You've had a night of it, haven't you?" The horror in her voice neutralized the curiosity. It was obvious she wanted to know, and at the same time *didn't* want to know, what had happened. She shook her head. "And Lord Blackwood purple at the gills. Dear me, whatever … " She trailed off, then said briskly, "Well, nothing gained by hashing it over. A hot bath is what you need. And a hot cup of tea by the fire, and warm blankets on the bed."

"That sounds wonderful." Ella let the wizened little housekeeper lead her to the steaming tub. It was even more wonderful that it sounded. An hour later, Ella was sitting in an armchair pulled as close as she dared to the crackling fire, a blanket wrapped around her. She felt sick and strange, but at least she was dry and the smell of her skin no longer triggered her gag reflex. Her hair was clean. The blanket was thick and soft.

She should never have sat in the chair, should have crawled straight into the bed, but the fire had proved too tempting. Now she didn't know if she'd be able to get up again. She glanced at the bed. The room was small. Surprisingly small. And plain. The house itself was small and plain. Isidore Blackwood proved himself again and again a figure of mystery. He could certainly have established himself in far grander lodgings.

She wouldn't wonder now what motivated his decision. The frost in her bones had turned to fog. Everything was hazy. Even though the bed stood a mere two strides away, it might as well have been a mile. She was too tired to move. She was maybe even too tired to sleep. Her head kept nodding, but her eyes seemed to stay open. Or if they closed from time to time, she kept seeing the dancing flames.

When the door opened, she was still in that state. Chin on her chest. Eyes on the fire.

She didn't hear him cross the room. Of course she didn't. He moved like a cat.

"Ella." His voice eddied from the darkness. Ah, her eyes were closed then. With effort, she lifted her lids. He was kneeling beside her chair. He too had bathed. He'd lost that ghastly, lavender pallor. His drying hair had begun to twist into serpentine waves. The anguish etching lines in his face surprised her.

"How do you feel?" He took her hand and brushed her knuckles against his lips. Her body tightened. She felt more awake. More alarmed. The precariousness of her position struck her. She was in his house. Without protection. There was nothing in the world to keep him from taking any liberty at all. She was at his mercy.

He didn't let go of her hand. He was rubbing her palm with his thumb, almost absently. Staring at her. It made her nervous. The blanket hung loose around her shoulders. Beneath, she wore only a thin nightdress. He should not have come into the room. She would send him away. She could appeal, perhaps, to his sense of honor. But he thought her a woman with no honor at all. What respect would he think her due?

"How do you feel?" he asked again. Was that a slur in his voice?

"Very well," she said. "Considering."

"Considering," he said. He rose onto his knees and put his elbows on the arms of the chair. He blocked the firelight. The warm glow made a nimbus around him, but his face, his form, were shadowed. "Considering you might have died? Or considering … you lived?"

She sucked in her breath. He leaned forward. She could see the darker shadows welling beneath his cheekbones, the curve of shadow between his parted lips. He smelled of brandy.

He was drunk. That was the explanation. He was powerfully drunk. Her alarm heightened.

"Ella." Such roughness with which he uttered her name! As though the syllables grated in his throat. "Tell me … " He couldn't finish. She was wide awake now, the pulse throbbing in the crooks of her arms. Her chest felt tight.

"Tell you what?" she whispered.

"The devil take you." He sank down in front of the chair. He swayed for a moment then bowed his head. She swallowed hard as he bent farther. He laid his head down on her lap. She felt the hard bone of his cheek pressing into her flesh. He seemed almost broken.

She hesitated then lifted her hand. After a moment, she lowered it. Slowly, so slowly. With her fingertips, she touched his black hair. She let the weight of her hand rest on his head. Moved her fingers. The strands slipped between them, thick and damp and cool.

The sound that came from his mouth might have been a sob. She snatched her hand away. She slid off the chair, forcing him to lean back and raise his head. They were knee to knee on the thin carpet. She tried to meet his eyes, but she couldn't find them through the shadow. She touched his cheek. It was hot and dry. Tearless.

He crushed her fingers in his hand. The flames illuminated only the side of his face, the hard mound of his cheekbone, the plunge of his cheek, the chiseled line of his jaw.

"Tell me." His breath came raggedly. "Tell me ... did you mean to jump? Did I drive you ... " He couldn't finish. His grip was hurting her, grinding the bones of her hand, but she was no longer afraid. *He* was afraid. The realization astounded her. He was afraid of what she might say. He was waiting for her to speak, trembling like a man awaiting the executioner's blow.

The fog cleared. Everything came into focus.

He had seen her on the wall above the river and thought she intended to cast herself over the edge. He had seized her to prevent her self-murder. He thought he had driven her to it.

"No." She shook her head violently. "No, that wasn't it. I never ... " But "never" wasn't right. She *had* imagined it, so many times. Casting herself into the river. Ending finally what nature had seen fit to ruin by stages. She had thought there might be some comfort in it. Choosing, when the time came to die, to die as Robert had died. Sharing that with him. Whenever she gazed at the water, she saw Robert, struggling, a small body buffeted by waves, disappearing. She saw herself sucked down. Joining him at last. But she knew now there was no reunion to be found in the black terror of those heavy fathoms. How could she have ever imagined it would feel peaceful? That it was, at the last, a gentle death? She had fooled herself. She'd wanted to believe that Robert had not suffered.

"I would not have jumped." Her voice had thickened. "I went only … to look."

"I saw you on the edge. I saw you falling. I could see it." He laughed without humor. "As though I had a view from Avalon. I could see the future. And the past."

Dear God. The firelight licked across his face. A man put to the rack would have worn that expression.

"You think she did it on purpose." The whisper tore from her. "You think she jumped."

She did not add, "And the guilt consumes you." She didn't have to. She could see it in every line of his face. Egypt. England. He didn't care where he lived. Now she understood. What did it matter? He was already living in hell.

He staggered back from her, rose to his feet. She scrambled up too.

"Isidore … " She could say nothing more. What succor could she give to a soul in torment? She was no angel of absolution.

As he stared at her, his face changed. She realized she had risen without the blanket. The white nightdress was too small. The shape of her body was visible. Shame flooded her, but she crossed her arms over her breasts and stared him down.

His throat worked. He made as though to move toward her. Stopped.

"Forgive me," he said. It came out a low growl. He walked past her, leaving her standing by the fire. Hugging herself. She felt that she could crawl into the embers and still not be warmed.

For what did he ask forgiveness? And of whom?

Chapter Fourteen

When Isidore arrived in front of Clement's house, the morning fog was thick as soup. As he climbed the steps to the front door, the skies opened. He rang the bell and stood beneath the portico. He wore hat, gloves, and a heavy Inverness coat. His chill had retreated like a beast from the fire, but it had not fled. It had hidden inside his bones, inside his bloody *molars*. His teeth ached, and his joints cooperated with his movements under protest.

He listened to the rushing, pattering sound of the downpour. No melody. No harmonies. Rain made music unconnected to scales, pitches, phrasings. So did sand, whispering across the desert on the back of the wind. The unintelligible music of the world. In Egypt, the many Arabics he heard in the city bazaars and the villages washed him at first in the same kind of noise—resonant and meaningless.

After last night, everything had changed for him, and nothing. He had risen from that stinking river with Ella in his arms. He had temporarily lost the power of speech and had poured forth into her ear the primal sounds that continued the world's music, no words, but a guttural crooning, letting her know she was not alone. And if *she* wasn't alone, then *he* wasn't alone either. She was with him. He was with her. It was simple. It was profound and transformative and shook the foundations of his being. He'd knelt beside her on the shore, waiting for her to open her eyes, *needing* her to open her eyes. When she did, the exultation he felt was near to violence. A ferocious joy the likes of which he had never known.

The first word she had said, before her eyes focused: *Robert.*

He stamped his feet to bruise them out of numbness, to vent his rage and self-loathing. Robert, she'd said, a hoarse cry, rough with longing. He was a fool, a fool to have felt the name like a blow, and later, after he'd nearly boiled himself alive in his bath, a fool not to have locked himself in his room and waited out the hours until morning. Instead, he'd gone to her. He'd buried his face on her lap and felt as though the chambers of his heart were leaking. He'd had to ask her, needed to know if she'd meant it, to know if, when she'd climbed up on that wall overlooking the river, she had courted destruction, and she had guessed it then. His darkest suspicion. More than suspicion. It was the certainty that had hounded him across the globe.

He had forced Phillipa into death's open arms.

She didn't guess the sordid details, of course, but now she would wonder. *Why did she jump? Why would Phillipa have jumped?* If she needed fodder for her spiritualist antics, for blackmail, he had given her plenty. Five years ago, he had closed everything inside him, set seals upon his heart, and now, this woman, this stranger, was opening them one by one.

Part of his mind whispered to him that he should trust her. Trust her even though circumstances told against her. But she had no connections he could verify, no one who would attest to her identity. She had adduced no evidence to exonerate herself from Lizzie's charges. She hadn't even attempted to deny them.

That irrational part of him countered, seductive, insistent: *Trust yourself then.* What facts could he collect that would weigh heavier in the balance than his own impressions? She was intelligent, courageous, stubborn, intuitive, awkward, shy, beautiful. She made him want to talk, to invent stories just to amuse or soothe her, to tell her things he'd never told anybody. She made him want to throw caution to wind, dismiss every rational measure, and rely on his instinct to guide him. His *animal* instinct, which would guide him straight into her bed. *Christ.* Before he did anything else, he needed to talk to Clement. Get another perspective.

At last the door opened. Jenkins let him into the hall and took his coat, hat, and gloves. Isidore rubbed his hand across his roughened jaw. He hadn't shaved. Or eaten.

"Is Lord St. Aubyn at breakfast?" He started for the breakfast room. Clement always breakfasted from half nine to half ten.

"No, my lord." Jenkins intercepted him.

"He isn't out?" Isidore studied the butler's face. Clement was a creature of habit. At ten a.m., he wouldn't move from *The Times* and two eggs soft-boiled if the house were on fire.

"No, my lord."

Was it his imagination, or had Jenkins the Expressionless grimaced?

"Well, where is he then?"

Jenkins hesitated. Something thudded above them. Isidore glanced up then at Jenkins, eyebrow raised.

Jenkins sighed. "I believe you'll find him in the library, my lord. I'll send up a tray. Perhaps … " He hesitated again. "It would do him good if you could convince him to eat."

It was unlike Jenkins to offer a comment that could so nearly be described as opinion. Foreboding made Isidore's jaw clench. *What now?* He climbed the stairs, silent as a prowler.

Most libraries smelled like … well, libraries. Leather and vellum and wax and dust. Isidore's nostrils flared as he pushed open the door. Turpentine. There was a large canvas on the easel silhouetted against the south-facing window, an enormous Venetian window, rain streaking the panes. He listened at the threshold for movement, breathing. Nothing. Just the muted sound of the rain.

"Clement?"

He stepped into the room. Floor-to-ceiling bookshelves lined the west wall. Smaller, glass-fronted cabinets flanked the fireplace with its curving marble surround, scrolling rosettes supported by acanthus-leaf corbels. Coals glowed in the iron grate.

"Clem?"

He walked over to the center table, the surface piled with papers and books. A delicate, hand-stitched volume lay open to a vividly colored print: a man, naked, heavy flesh marbled blue, eyes staring, mouth open. A man flaming in hell. He turned the pages. A naked man unhorsed, he and his mount upside down, falling together into fire. Isidore's eyes skimmed the words.

Those who restrain desire, do so because theirs is weak enough to be restrained.

He lifted one heavy sheet, then another. He came to a page densely scripted; little drawings interspersed the words, washed with blue.

Proverbs of Hell

He closed the volume. Clement's tastes had changed. Once it had been *The Annual of British Landscape Scenery* that lay thumbed open on the table. *Isidore* was the one who'd loved Blake.

He sifted through an adjacent stack of engravings, a wolf-like beast rendered by many different hands. Now it stood in profile, leering with red lips. Now it leapt from the trees at peasants who ran toward their hayricks, arms stretched out. Now it crouched atop a woman, open jaws prepared to fix on her neck.

"The beast of Gevaudan."

Isidore let the print drop.

"You have quite a collection," he said. He turned toward the voice. Clement was slouched in a leather chair in the far corner of the room. He wore the evening dress he'd worn the night before at Tenby's, minus the cravat. His coat was spattered with crimson blood.

Isidore almost started. *Paint.* It was only paint. Blood didn't stand out on black fabric, thick and red. Blood darkened. Blood dried and flaked away like rust. The blood in Phillipa's hair had turned sticky, then, quickly, so quickly, it had stiffened. Her black curls had swallowed any hint of its color.

Clement laughed. He tapped his head.

"The beasts are in here," he said. His voice was thick. "My friend." He laughed again. "Go 'way," he called at the footman's knock.

Isidore frowned. "Put the tray on the lamp table." He waved the footman toward the marble-topped table. He rocked back and forth on his heels, studying Clement, until the servant had positioned the tray and made his hasty departure. There was a bottle of whisky standing by Clement's left foot.

"You didn't leave much for breakfast."

Clement tracked the direction of Isidore's glance to the bottle and smiled thinly.

"Didn't know I'd have guests." He knuckled his eyes. "It's early for you, isn't it, Sid?"

"Early or late. I don't know." Isidore approached him slowly. "The days and nights have been running together." An album lay on the floor to the side of the chair. Clement must have knocked it off the arm. Isidore went and picked it up. *Los Caprichos.*

"Goya?" He lifted his brows. "I remember you preferring Girtin. More hills and clouds. More topography, less torment. Herbs, not hobgoblins."

"Don't push me, Sid." Clement's voice was strained. He had a faint golden shimmer of stubble on his jaw. His eyes were bloodshot.

"No, of course not." Subdued, Isidore handed Clement the album. They didn't know how to be easy with each other anymore. Clement accepted the album with indifference. He had paint on his knuckles. Isidore resisted the urge to look toward the easel. He would wait for an invitation. He and Clement had always respected each other's privacy. That was part of why they'd been able to share so much.

Not even Clement. Those had been Phillipa's words when she swore him to secrecy. *Sid, promise me. No one can know.*

He sniffed the air. "There's ham on that tray." He walked over to it. "Toast?" he asked. He carried the tray back to Clement, resting it on the windowsill. Clement ignored the proffered round of bread, sinking further into the chair. Isidore had seen Clement worse for drink hundreds of times, but never quite like this. Never slouching and sullen. Usually alcohol intensified his fastidiousness. Made him enunciate his words like an Oxford don and walk as though he followed a chalked line.

"You left before I could talk to you last night." Isidore leaned his hip against the wall, buttering the toast. He folded a piece of ham on top. The explanation for Clement's odd behavior had to lie in the exchange he'd interrupted.

"What did Ella say to you? You looked … " *As though you'd seen a ghost.* He took a bite of ham and toast. Crunching the hard crust of the bread with his molars, he felt a twinge of pain. He swallowed. "You looked as though the conversation was not agreeable."

"Ella?" Clement lifted his chin from his chest and tried to focus his eyes. "You use her given name?"

Isidore placed his toast carefully on a plate. He was conscious of a strange, nervous energy thrilling through him.

"After the party, we became … better acquainted." *I knocked her into the Thames, dragged her to shore, carried her half a mile in my arms, cut off her boots in my coach, and gained an intimate knowledge of her toes. Her toes, by the by, are beautiful.* He took a breath. "I will lay the whole matter before you. Your opinion will be very valuable to me as I decide my course of action."

"Get rid of her." Clement lurched out of the chair, and *Los Caprichos* fell again to the floor. "You want my opinion? There it is. Send her away. Give her money if that's what it takes. Buy her a cabin on a steamer to America if you can and be done with it."

Isidore felt an icy wave rippling through him. The chill creeping out.

"Tell me what she said to you."

Clement staggered forward. His arms wrapped Isidore's throat. Isidore's hands twitched, but he did not strike. He stood motionless. Clement's weight pulled his neck down, and he tensed his muscles, standing straight, allowing Clement to hang from him, half strangling, half embracing. Clement smelled like turpentine, liquor, sweat. Isidore pushed him, gently, and Clement released his hold. He stepped back, and Isidore saw that he was crying, soundlessly, tears coursing down his cheeks.

Isidore had never seen a grown man cry. He couldn't bear to look in Clement's face. He turned away and stared blindly at the wall of books. Clement touched his shoulder.

"Let me show you my nightmare," he said.

Isidore followed him to the easel. The room felt cold as a tomb, but maybe it wasn't the room. *He* was cold as a tomb. All of his organs had turned to ice.

Clement kicked away the oilcloth he'd laid over the floorboards. He stood to the side of the canvas, turned away from it, facing Isidore. His cheeks were livid and tear-tracked. Isidore glanced at him. He let his eyes slide over the canvas and rested his gaze on the rain-streaked window. He didn't know how long he stared at the thin panes of glass.

He was afraid. He was afraid of Clement's tears. He was afraid of the paint drying there on the canvas. He had faced every kind of brutality with unflinching calm, and these little, harmless things—a few drops of salty water; crushed pigments—threatened to undo him.

Finally, he forced his eyes back to the canvas. The brush strokes were small. The colors jewel-bright. A beast on a balcony loomed over a young woman in a black-and-red gown. The glazed black of the night sky contrasted sharply with the white marble of the courtyard beyond the balcony. The light that spilled through the French doors glossed the beast's black fur, the young woman's black hair. The beast was on its hind legs, like a man, wore trousers like a man, and a waistcoat. Its furry chest split its white shirt wide open. The feet were furry, tipped with cruel claws. The claws on the furry hands were crueler; they dangled over the woman, ready to tear her to ribbons. The beast had a lupine face, rapacious jaws. One of its pricked ears was notched. Its eyes were blue.

His mouth had gone dry.

"I could show you more. I have a dozen of them." Clement stepped beside him and examined the painting. "The beast changes. Wolf. Ape. Bat. Donkey." He laughed, a harsh sound, almost a sob. "Its eyes are the same."

"What does this mean?" Isidore was trembling. The cold, he couldn't fight it.

"Isidore." Clement's voice was steady now. Isidore felt physical relief as he tore his gaze from the hideous beast, the terrified girl, but Clement's hectic face provided no comfort. His sea-green eyes shone, the whites threaded with red veins. "I found her. I found her on the balcony. Her skull … "

The cold had numbed everything. He couldn't feel his limbs. He didn't trust himself to move. Didn't know if he *could* move. He listened to his own voice as though a stranger were speaking. It was a stranger who said the words with such calm.

"I don't understand you." As though it were an abstract point of logic they were discussing, or a mathematical equation.

"I heard you fighting. I heard her tell you that she was running away to Paris."

Isidore said nothing. His frozen organs had stopped his blood. How long before his eyes would frost over? He saw white light at the corners of his vision.

Clement's features were unrecognizable. Contorted by his inner struggle as he formed the words.

"She was not … faithful to you. She was breaking the engagement. She was leaving you for a lover. I heard you threaten her. She screamed at you. She was hysterical. I couldn't listen. It was wrong of me to stay as long as I did. I went downstairs. I thought you'd come down, and when you didn't, I went back up. I couldn't find you. The balcony doors were open. I went onto the balcony. Oh God."

The recollection of that horror overcame him. He blinked his eyes rapidly, as though to banish the vision.

Isidore's hands found Clement's collar. He bunched the fabric and shook him with all his strength, shook him until he heard his jaws clack together hard enough to chip the teeth. He let go, panting. The color had drained from Clement's lips.

"She was dead." Clement's voice held the wonderment he must have felt when he first saw her. Disbelief. Awe. "The blow had cracked her skull. I lifted her up … and I rolled her over the railing. There wasn't much blood. Wiping it away was the work of a moment."

Isidore didn't realize he was on the floor until he heard Clement drop to his knees beside him. Those green eyes were more familiar to him than his own. But the face was a mask. The pale lips moved.

"I know you couldn't have meant it."

He understood the words, but the sentence made no sense. He shook his head.

"You were out of your mind." Clement was shaking his head too, but his eyes seemed to stay in the same place. Fixed. Isidore could see nothing else.

"I thought I could bear it. For your sake, Sid, I thought I could. I cannot. I cannot."

They sat in silence. The rain still pattered, as though the world had not turned upside down.

Isidore made his fingers into claws on the polished wood of the floor. "You never spoke of this to me."

"We both knew," Clement whispered. "An unholy covenant. Made in silence. Kept in silence. There isn't a day that goes by that

I don't wish I hadn't done it. Then I picture you dragged into the street, hung for murder before a crowd of thousands."

The ice floe inside of him began to break apart. He didn't know what would happen when it shattered completely and feeling returned. Would he scream? Would he hurl himself through those panes of glass? For years, he had carried the burden of his guilt. But Clement had carried a burden just as terrible. To protect him. Each had suffered alone a hell of his own making.

"I didn't kill her." It gusted out of him. "I would have lost my arms at both shoulders before I lifted a hand to her." *I didn't kill her.* For an instant, he felt a wild surge, the desire to run, to skip, to clap his hands, like a slave whose manacles have fallen open, whose chains are broken. She hadn't leapt from that balcony in wrath and desperation, to punish him, to punish herself.

She had been murdered. Now the chains wound about him tighter than ever, squeezing the breath from his body. She had been murdered.

Clement was staring at him. "She was dead. I saw her."

"Someone else dealt the blow." *There.* That piercing crack—the ice had broken. His breath stuttered. He crossed his arms around his chest and heaved forward and back with such violence he would have dashed his forehead on the floor if Clement hadn't braced him, brought him up short.

"Sid, don't lie to me. It's the one thing that could make this damnation worse. Don't lie to me."

He couldn't catch his breath. He wrenched free of Clement's grasp and scuttled backwards on the floor. Not even a beast. A beetle. His back hit a table leg. Blake's proverbs were poised above, ready to spill down, to bury him. *A dead body, revenges not injuries. The most sublime act is to set another before you. The crow wish'd every thing was black, the owl, that every thing was white. The tygers of wrath … The cut worm … The bones of the dead …*

"She betrayed you." Clement's look blended compassion and repulsion both. "You were furious. I'd never heard you sound like that. Like a baited bear. You said you'd die before you let her go to him."

"She didn't betray me." Now the truth would out. He should have told Clement years ago. He'd kept his faith with Phillipa and in doing so nearly destroyed his best friend. "Our engagement was not what you thought. It was … " What was Clem's phrase? *An unholy covenant.*

He needed fortification for this confession. He stood in stages. He felt his muscles lock then tear apart. A knife was scraping them from his bones. He stumbled to the whisky bottle.

"I am going to finish this whisky," he said hoarsely. "And then I am going to tell you the truth. I'm going to tell you everything."

"If you didn't kill her … " Clement remained on the floor, one leg tucked beneath him, one knee bent, forehead propped upon it. His golden hair curtained his face. "Who did?"

"I don't know. Yet. I'm going to find out. " He took a burning pull of whisky. "And I swear by God's wounds, I am going to kill him." He barked a laugh. "Now if they hang me, they'll have to use a silken rope. I am a Peer of the Realm." He kissed his left fingertips and bowed. A lord at the gallows. He laughed again, swallowing more whisky.

Excess of sorrow laughs. Blake had worked feverishly on the day of his death, sketching scenes from Dante's *Inferno.* In his engraving, *The Circle of the Lustful,* he depicted those gray bodies twisting in a whirlwind, those men and women whom love bereav'd of life. He wondered if Clement possessed a copy. He wondered if throwing it in the fire would break the circle, end the agonies of those weary souls. His lips twisted.

Of course it wouldn't. The flames would devour the paper, mimicking the action of the blacker, infernal flames.

He was done with symbols, with futile gestures. Finding and killing Phillipa's lover, Phillipa's *murderer*—that was the only act that remained to him. An act of vengeance. Pure. Absolute.

He felt composed, suddenly. Lucid. The way was lit before him. Light shining on the dark path. All he needed to do was take one step. And then another.

"What of Ella?" he asked. "Miss Reed? How does she fit in to this? What knowledge does she have?"

"Most likely none." Clement rose gracelessly. They were both moving like old men. "I overreacted."

"She didn't speak to you of ... the murder?" The word "murder" still tripped up his tongue. Phillipa had been *murdered*.

"All she said was that I kept a secret that ate away at me." Clement walked wearily to the leather chair he'd vacated and fell upon it. "Tell a man he keeps a painful secret. Tell a woman she dreams of love. Simple enough. Put me in a Gypsy caravan, I too could astound customers with the clarity of my visions in the crystal ball. It's not what she said so much as her very presence, the suggestion that she might *conjure* Phillipa ... " He gave an involuntary shudder. "Stirs it all up, doesn't it?" He paused, staring into space. "She's an unnerving woman besides. The way she looks at you ... " He shut his eyes. "Christ almighty," he whispered. "I let Phillipa's murderer go free. Covered up his crime."

"For me." Isidore smiled a bleak smile. "All these years, I've wondered. I couldn't figure out why you pulled away. We sat for hours together by Phillipa's casket, and you never looked at me. Never said a word. I felt ... " *Betrayed. Abandoned. Forsaken.* "But you thought ... " His throat threatened to close. He tilted his head back, tipping the whisky bottle until it emptied. "I don't know how you endured sitting by my side."

The last drop of liquor rolled back down the neck of the bottle. He put the bottle on the breakfast tray. Jenkins wouldn't thank him when the tray was collected, the food virtually untouched, the empty bottle testifying to the morning's less wholesome repast.

Clement's head was nodding. The sleepless night catching up to him.

"Clement," Isidore said, and the head jerked up. The green eyes opened.

"I'm listening," Clement rasped. Isidore leaned again against the wall. He took a breath. Ella had told him he was a good storyteller. She meant he told stories well. Not that he had good tales to tell. Most of the stories he knew were tragic. He was going to tell Clement one of them. Phillipa's story. He couldn't tell it through to the end, because it wasn't over. Phillipa's murderer walked among them. Phillipa's soul *was* unquiet—Miss Seymour had been right.

He spoke dully, mechanically. By the time he'd finished, he knew what course of action he would take. Ella's presence stirred things up. That was exactly what he needed. He needed to unnerve, and then unmask, a murderer. He needed to hire a private medium.

• • •

"Coffee" was all he could mutter when he arrived back at his house. He took the stairs to his study two at a time. He expected his footman to appear, but it was his housekeeper who came with the tray. She put the tray down with an abrupt motion and fisted her hands on her hips.

"The young lady's dress is ruined, my lord," she said.

"I imagine it is," he said, pouring himself a cup of syrupy coffee. His cook might not have a gift for pastry, but he'd given her detailed instructions as to how he liked his coffee and he had no complaints. Mrs. Potts was still standing by his desk. In a twit about a bloody dress.

"Burn it," he said. The curt tone was meant to act as a dismissal.

"I'm not concerned about how to dispose of the dress, my lord." Mrs. Potts's chins multiplied as she drew back her head like an angry bird. "But Miss Reed needs something to wear. She hasn't set foot outside the bedchamber."

Good. He hadn't intended her to set a damn foot anywhere. He meant for her to stay exactly where he'd left her. He sipped his coffee. He needed to collect himself. His sanity was hanging by a thread. Mrs. Potts, though, showed no sign that she was ready to leave him in peace. She had warmed to her topic.

"I couldn't believe my ears when Mr. Brinkley told me you'd gone out this morning without making any arrangements for her comfort," she said. "After what she went through! Lor', don't mind my saying so, but it's hard of you. Why, she's such a sweet thing too. I haven't heard a cross word from her, and she thanked Violet for the nightdress with such language as made the silly girl blush. She's not high at all in her behavior, for all she's a lady through and through. I brought her a shawl, and some cough drops, and she had a bit of omelette for breakfast, and she's taken tea and a scone. It's a miracle she's not dying of the shock she had." Mrs. Potts shook her head.

It's a miracle she's not dying of your neglect and vulgar treatment. He could all but hear Mrs. Potts's unspoken reprimand. It seemed Ella had made the most of her morning's confinement, winning over his staff. Last night, Mrs. Potts had looked at her as though she was the Whore of Babylon. Now she was willing to challenge the master of the house on her behalf.

Good work, Miss Reed, he thought.

"Will Miss Reed be continuing in the house, my lord?" *Without clothing?* Mrs. Potts pressed her lips together as though preparing herself for a bitter blow. His answer was bound to scandalize her even more.

"For the night, at least, Mrs. Potts. Beyond that, I can't say. Send a porter to Trombly Place for a gown, shoes, and necessary items." He stood. Mrs. Potts opened her mouth, no doubt to continue her harangue.

"Thank you, Mrs. Potts," he said. "Your interest in the lady's welfare does you credit. I assure you I have the situation well in hand."

"Don't take the situation *too* much in hand, my lord, if you catch my meaning," said Mrs. Potts. The knowing look she leveled at him was so much at odds with her prim demeanor that his coffee went down the wrong pipe. He spluttered for a moment, at a loss.

"Will you be needing anything else, my lord?" she asked, and while he was still coughing, she turned on her heel and left the room.

Maybe he deserved it. He'd treated Ella badly, leaving her to wait for his return and wonder what fate he'd decided for her. He hadn't intended to keep her waiting as long as he had. Hell, he hadn't predicted any of this when he'd quitted the house. The morning had taken an unexpected turn. He'd stepped out of his own nightmare into Clement's and then into yet another.

He stood. It was time to invite her to join him in darkness. He rather wished he had something else to offer.

• • •

He tapped softly on the door before he pushed it open. She was standing by the window, looking out at the rain. He felt a stab of disappointment to see her wrapped in Mrs. Potts's woolen shawl. That nightdress pulled taut across her hips and breasts, firelight sliding up and down the curves and planes—he hadn't forgotten the sight. Her hips were wider, her breasts fuller, than he'd imagined. The delicate bones of her face, her posture, and that severe black mourning gown made her appear thinner than she was. Her body was lush.

He cleared his throat. She turned. The lavender shadows that hollowed her eyes were darker today. Her hair had been hastily done; only a few pins anchored the twisted mass. It would be so easy to pull them out and watch her hair fall about her shoulders. He hadn't gotten to appreciate her unbound hair last night, when it was tangled and coursing with foul water. Quite a few activities last night he hadn't gotten to appreciate. His eyes fell to her feet. They were bare. The nightdress was too short. He could see her ankle bones, see up to where her heel curved toward the lower calf. His groin tightened.

"Leave the door open." She reached out her hand as though to stop the door from closing as he stepped into the room. He looked at her a moment. And shut the door deliberately behind him.

"The servants will talk." She stepped behind a chair, hiding her exposed ankles. This show of modesty amused him. Why not admit it? It excited him. Cat and mouse …

"I carried you past them all in the middle of the night," he reminded her. "They won't talk of anything else for months. Unless a volcano erupts and blocks out the sun. Even then." He crossed the room slowly, stopped in front of the chair. "Unless Queen Victoria marries the ghost of Abraham Lincoln … "

Her smile flashed then vanished. He felt absurdly gratified. He knew how to conjure those rare smiles. Serious, philosophical Miss Reed had an undeniable taste for nonsense. She appreciated the ridiculous. Her life had made her dour and dark and awkward with her body, as though she were an operator working a badly oiled industrial machine. But nature had made her warm, imaginative, *sensual.* She had moved against him in the coach, unconsciously seductive, while he whispered the tale of Rhodopis in her ear. She had sighed with satisfaction. She *desired* such stories: romantic, impossible. She dreamed of happy endings. He wanted to whisper all kinds of foolishness into the curve of her neck, tickling her with his breath until she laughed helplessly, gasping for air, begging for mercy. He wanted to have that power over her. He wanted to make her writhe in his arms, respond to his words, his touch, spontaneously, unable to divide her mind from her body. He wanted her fused, mind-body-soul, and opening, to him.

It might take another dip in the Thames to shrink the signs of his arousal.

"I'm sorry I kept you waiting." The effort it took not to reach over the chair and run his thumb along her jaw made his voice harsh. "I'm glad to see you're not much the worse for last night's ordeal."

"I would have left before you returned, but … "

"But you haven't anything to wear," he drawled. "I noticed." The image of her standing before him in just the nightdress rose again in his mind. Wonderful piece of luck that Violet was so small in stature.

"Where would you have gone?" he asked, watching her closely.

"To Trombly Place," she said immediately. "To collect my belongings." He heard the split second of hesitation before she said the word "belongings." She numbered among her *belongings* not a shilling but quite a few jewels. He narrowed his eyes. "And to take my leave of Mrs. Trombly," she rushed on. "She must be quite … That is, when she discovered this morning that I was not in the house … " Her lips parted. She could not hide her discomfort. As she stumbled over the words, her mortification only increased. She looked like a debutante caught kissing in a garden. Her lips were red, as though she had been kissing. Red and full. "I wanted to write, but … "

He was staring at her too intently. She dropped her gaze. Her eyelids too had a lilac tinge. She needed more rest. She needed someone to take her cares away from her. And here he was, preparing to introduce her to greater horrors.

"You needn't have troubled yourself about it," he said. "I wrote to Mrs. Trombly."

"You wrote?" Ella's eyes lifted. She always mastered herself quickly. She took an audible breath. "And you've had a letter back?"

He hadn't opened Louisa's response. His letter to her had been brief. He'd written it and posted it at Clement's.

"I don't know why I worry what you told her." Ella's lips curved. A faint sneer, self-mocking. He recognized the type. It was similar to the one he often wore himself. "She won't think well of me as a thief if she has less cause to think ill of me as a woman."

"I told her you had another vision," he said, and she jolted, brows winging upward. "You walked out into the night in a trance, and I found you staring up at Clem—St. Aubyn's house. The scene, as it were, of … " *The crime.* "The misfortune," he finished. "I detected the signs of spirit possession. I took you here at once so as not to disturb her household."

Her eyes were wide. She was gripping the back of the chair.

"Why?" Her pink tongue moistened the corners of her mouth. "Why would you tell her such a thing?" She lifted her chin. "*How* could you write such a thing? You accuse me of playing with her emotions, and then you write a lie that needs must excite and terrify her. That needs must raise false hopes."

"I regret raising her hopes falsely," he said. "But she will talk of your latest trance to Mrs. Wheatcroft. And Mrs. Wheatcroft will talk to Mrs. Hatfield. And Mrs. Hatfield will talk to *everybody.* And before too long, rumors of your stunning feats of mediumship will reach the ears of someone whose hopes are *not* raised by the news that you have opened a powerful channel to the otherworld. Someone who feels nothing but fear at what you might say."

She shivered. Perhaps the cold was creeping out of her bones now as well. *No sweet dreams for the likes of us,* he thought. Strange that he should now think of that agonized coach ride as a hallowed interlude. They'd been inside a magic circle, everything complicated and insoluble locked beyond the glass and the wooden panels, their bodies close together, struggling to exchange animal heat. Protection.

"I have a proposition for you," he said.

"A proposition?" She stepped back from the chair. Suspicious. Outraged, even. Too late, he realized he had been infelicitous in his word choice. She would leave his house without shoes, in that sheer nightdress and bulky shawl, before she would accept a *proposition*. Her situation didn't permit her the luxury of such pride. But he couldn't help but admire it. She was as stubborn as he.

He didn't want to coerce her. To threaten her with Newgate.

"Let's call it a devil's bargain," he said. "To free an immortal soul from its bondage."

She gave him a measuring look and drew the shawl tighter about her shoulders. She nodded slowly, as though considering. As though she were free to make her own choice. A lady through and through.

"I will hear your proposition," she said.

Chapter Fifteen

The porter came before dinner with her gown of black bombazine. Ella dressed but ate alone in the room. Waiting for the summons. It came, and she went to Isidore's study. He sat behind his desk, and she sat on a chair across from him. There were sconces on the walls fitted with gaslights, but he'd opted for oil lamps. The light they gave was low, intimate.

"Brandy?" he asked.

She shook her head. He poured two glasses and put one down in front of her.

"You'll need it," he said. They stared at each other. Two generals at a war council. He looked tired, tired as a general in the field, and as determined.

"Yesterday I told you in no uncertain terms that you were to leave Trombly Place." He took a sip of brandy, but his eyes remained locked on hers. "You made no answer to allegations that you are a thief." He paused, as though to give her time to make answer now.

She said nothing. What was the use? Protestations of innocence rarely swayed opinions founded on the bedrock of preexisting prejudice. Nothing could be easier than assuming the worst of her. She wouldn't embarrass herself with declarations or appeals. He didn't care if she was a thief. Not anymore. You don't ask an angel to make a devil's bargain. She waited. His eyes narrowed.

"I wasn't happy that Mrs. Trombly had hired you in the first place. I did not conceal my misgivings."

No, he hadn't. He had made his misgivings plain. She glanced at his mouth then quickly away, but not before she saw those lips curve. He'd noticed. *Damn him.*

He leaned forward but not to taunt or tempt her. The tempest in his eyes obscured their blue light. They were black, fixed. "I worried that your position as medium would give you the power to make claims about the dead. Claims that might gain currency. People tend to be credulous when it suits them. The *ton* has an insatiable appetite for scandal, the more sensational, the better. Séances just extend their reach—gossip from beyond the grave."

"Surely it isn't only gossip people want." She sounded so brittle. Why did his cynicism provoke her? Maybe she was more of a contrarian than a cynic. Maybe he just flustered her.

He shrugged as though the point weren't worth debating. "In some cases, spiritualist fervor is prurience disguised as sentiment. In other cases, it's sentiment disguised as prurience. For the practitioners, the mediums, the spirit-writers, it's money in the bank."

"Your thoughts on spiritualism are known to me, my lord," she said stiffly. She didn't disagree. But she'd be damned if she admitted as much now.

He tipped his head. Relaxed his posture. He wasn't challenging her anymore. The weariness crept back into his face.

"Phillipa died with certain secrets," he said. "Secrets that I wanted buried with her. I felt I could not allow any tapping from beyond the grave to spell out some message—however cryptic—that hinted toward the truth. I even feared that you may have discovered something about Phillipa, through spiritual or worldly means ... " He smiled a faint smile. "And that you had planted yourself in Trombly Place to turn this knowledge to your advantage." He paused again. She couldn't keep herself from shaking her head slightly.

"No," he said. "I begin to believe you. I begin to believe your presence is a dark coincidence. Or, if you prefer, the workings of fate. I believe you are to be the instrument of justice. Of retribution. Divine or demonic—it matters to me not in the least degree."

She clutched the glass of brandy. He was right. She needed it. To hold on to if nothing else. The snifter was cool and smooth in her hand, narrowing from the wide base, delicate enough to crush. He could crush *his* snifter certainly. His long fingers cradled the transparent curves. He tipped the glass this way and that, absently, swirling the brandy. Watching her.

"Until yesterday," he said, "I thought that my fiancée had thrown herself from that balcony."

"Why?" Her face burned as soon as the word slipped out. She sipped at the brandy. Now her lips burned as well. Heat rolled down her throat. The question had pounded in her head all night.

"We had a row." He leaned an elbow on the desk. She saw the muscle in his arm bunch as he raised his hand to rub the back of his neck.

"It must have been a bad one." She could have bit her tongue at the inadequacy of this remark.

"Worse than you could imagine," he said slowly.

What was it about? She wished for him to continue with every fiber of her being. *Was it about these … secrets?* But he lapsed into silence.

"I was wrong," he said at last. "She ran from my presence. I pursued, but … " He shook his head. "I tripped. While I lay there on the floor in a stupor, too drunk to give chase, someone followed her onto the balcony and broke her skull."

Her involuntary cry checked the brutal flow of his speech. She put the brandy on the desk before it could slip from her nerveless fingers. It was hard to look at him. Someone had broken Phillipa's skull. Smashed the life from her. If he could bear this revelation, so could she.

For a moment, his gaze gentled, responding to her shock and horror. It was amazing to her that he could spare her a look of such compassion, before his own torment again marked his features.

"I wanted the world to believe Phillipa's death was an accident. I encouraged that interpretation. A suicide—it would have

destroyed her family. If an inquest had discovered more … "
He stopped. She glimpsed it again—the man he might become.
Grim, lined, haggard. His beauty the beauty of a ravening wolf.

"I thought I was protecting her," he said flatly. "Instead, I was
protecting her murderer."

"What do you want me to do?" she murmured. Her heart
thudded in her chest. She realized he could say anything, make
any demand, and she would consent. She was giddy with the
peril and with the power she felt. He thought *she* could help him.
Isidore Blackwood, so large, so strong. He had hands that could
break her in half. *He needed her help.*

"I want you to enter my service as a private medium." The
irony of the situation made his lips quirk despite the blackness
brimming his eyes. Then a rueful, crooked smile spread across
his face. "It's deuced inconsistent of me. I suppose I should
apologize." The smile transformed his features. And stopped her
heart. *Heaven protect me from that boyish grin.* It made her want …
That was it. Plain and simple. It made her *want.*

"It's not necessary." She averted her face. "Nothing is consistent
in this world. Some things we can more or less rely upon. The sun
rises in the east. We wake with a roof over our heads. Our loved
ones are with us as they were the day before. We think things will
be the same tomorrow as they were today. But one day, we wake
… and everything is different. One day, we don't wake at all."

Her wandering gaze settled on a row of wooden figures on the
mantelpiece above the fire. In the low light, they were a menagerie
of shadows. Animal shapes. Relics, perhaps, from Egypt.

"You are philosophical for one so young."

She looked back at him. He wore the look that most
disconcerted her. No mockery. Just an earnest, avid interest. His
eyes were considering. Curious.

"I had few amusements in the country," she said. "I was often
reading books with my father."

"A cloistered life," he said. His lifted brow was quizzical. "Were there no opportunities beyond the library? Perhaps you lived with your father in a hermit's cottage deep in Exmoor forest?"

"You are whimsical, my lord, for one so grim." She feared she had overstepped herself, but his other eyebrow shot up and he laughed.

"It's true the hermitage I imagined was excessively picturesque. Thatched roof. Briars of blooming rose along the stone path. A lantern burning in the window."

"It wasn't a hermitage." She smiled at him, beguiled by the image. There would be linnets chirping in the thatch. The roses would climb the walls. "But it might as well have been." The question she read on his face forced the lie. "My father was an invalid."

Understanding flared in his eyes. As though she had given him a piece of a puzzle.

"That must have been difficult," he said, and his sympathy only deepened her shame. He must have seen in her face that she could endure no further questioning. He pushed back his chair, unfolding his long body with that fluidity that characterized all of his movements.

"You have come from your country cottage to the city of shadows," he said. "And here you will help me apprehend a murderer." There was regret in his voice. The way he described it, it sounded like a fairy tale. She was like Rhodopis in the city of the fire god. Ripped away from everything she knew. But there would be no miraculous resolution. In real life, eagles didn't speak to pharaohs. Strawberries didn't bloom in the snow. A dead brother never reappeared, alive, in a cloud of smoke. He knew it too, that there was no such thing as happily ever after. She couldn't help him bring Phillipa back. The love of his life. She hated herself for the jealousy that gnawed at her.

"Who is he?" *The murderer.* The idea of him didn't produce terror so much as a welling sadness. He had ended Phillipa's young life and warped so many others. Man was the cruelest beast. No other creature would kill a female of its species for pleasure. Or in rage.

She too rose, without grace. Her body never moved fluidly, all of a piece. Her limbs were too ungainly. He had drawn his brows together. A deep crease scored his forehead. He was looking at a point above her head.

"I don't know," he said slowly, low and thick, voice like a black cloud. "But I know things about him. He's a friend. An acquaintance, at the least. He's young. Handsome. Rich." That smile he wore, so full of loathing, seemed the precursor to an act of violence. He seemed to have forgotten she was there.

"How do you know?" she asked, a trifle breathless. "Young, handsome, rich?"

He blinked at her, returning to himself. He rocked back and forth on his heels. "He was at a party at St. Aubyn's."

"Ah," she said. But his answer didn't satisfy. It could have been the butler. Or a footman who'd long since left St. Aubyn's employ. Or some ugly, penniless aristocrat. God knows there were plenty of them. Young. Handsome. Rich. What made him so sure? *Phillipa's secrets.* He kept them from her.

"I want to use his guilt, his fear, to flush him out," he said. "Who could have more interest in what Phillipa Trombly might utter from the tomb? Who could have more dread? Every word you speak will be a dagger in his heart. He'll reveal himself. He'll give some sign, and I will be watching."

The distant look was back. He was flexing his hands. The glint in his eye was murderous. He too was capable of violence. She could see it all unfolding. Violence begetting violence begetting violence until the destruction of the world. Bards had been singing of exactly that for millennia. She looked down at the carpet, red and blue, a Turkish pattern.

Then he said: "I will pay you, of course."

Her breath rushed out. She needed money. Why should his offer of payment wound her?

"I'll double Mrs. Trombly's wages. When it's over, I'll see to it that you find the position you seek. As a governess. As whatever you like. Will you help me? Ella?" At the sound of her name, she looked up. She hadn't gotten used to hearing those syllables on his lips. Her name sounded husky when he said it, laced with dark promise. He circled the desk. Nothing stood between them but a foot of supercharged air.

She nodded jerkily. All at once, she wanted to cry. For the pity of it all. For the promises unfulfilled. She turned in a rustle of skirts and approached the fireplace. She held out her hands.

"Are you cold?" He was by her side, nearly brushing against her. "I can ring for more coals." The concern in his voice—she couldn't bear it. His kindness made the tears push out the corners of her eyes. She lowered her lids to trap the moisture in her lashes.

"Thank you, I'm not cold." She strove for composure. "I wanted a closer look at these figures, that's all."

"Do you like them?" he asked.

"Yes." She moved closer to inspect them. That low, sinuous curve of dark wood was an alligator. Those birds—ibises. She smiled at the braying donkey. "I can almost hear that donkey."

"Everyone in Italy could hear that donkey." She heard an answering smile in his voice.

"This donkey was known to you personally?" She turned toward him. He had folded his arms across his chest. He looked *too* nonchalant, too disinterested. Suspicion kindled.

"You carved these, didn't you?" She turned back to the mantle. "They're beautiful." *Beautiful* wasn't quite the right word. Some of them seemed purposely crude. Totemic. Each seemed to hold some essence of the creature it represented. And of the wood itself.

"This deer … " Her fingers hovered over the curve of its neck. It was alert, poised to spring from its base if she made a sudden movement. She curled her fingers.

"I'm afraid I might startle it." She almost laughed. "It's so alive." She felt him move closer. He reached over her shoulder. If she turned her head she could rub her cheek against it, the muscle swelling beneath the thin fabric of his shirt. His scent enveloped her, that complex mixture: coffee and pine and his hot, hard flesh. He adjusted the carving, shifting it so the deer faced her.

"I knew a man … " she began. She felt him vibrate with sudden tension. She stopped. She shouldn't say anything more about her past.

"Go on," he said. His voice was soft. The heat emanating from the fireplace warmed her front, and his body so close behind her warmed her back. It felt so good. She felt so safe, exactly there, where she stood, gloved by these two different kinds of warmth.

"A hunter," she said. "He would have loved to shoot a creature so lovely."

"That's hardly unusual," he said. "Every man in England hunts. Foxes. Pheasants. Deer."

Suddenly, she wanted to make him understand.

"For him, it's different. It's not about meat or even sport," she said. "It's more than that. He lives for it. He comes alive when he takes life. His study is filled with heads. Sometimes, though, he leaves carcasses to rot. He kills so many animals the party can't carry them all back."

"You don't like this man." It wasn't a question but a statement that prodded for more.

"I hate him," she whispered. There it was, violence surging, even in her. She hated Alfred. She would hurt him if she could. In these lovingly carved figures, she saw an alternative to destruction. She focused on the resonant forms.

"You *respect* this creature." She touched the slope of the deer's back lightly with the pad of her thumb. "You didn't have to kill it to understand something about it."

His hands closed on her shoulders. He turned her around to face him. His thumbs stroked once along the tight muscles then settled near her collarbones. The weight of his hands awakened the ache in her body even as it soothed.

"Did you run away from him?" His eyes were infinitely gentle.

"He wasn't my husband, if that's what you think." It would be too easy to tell him everything. Tell him about Papa, about his love for her and his mistaken trust in Alfred. Tell him how Alfred wanted her locked away, erased from the family record. Tell him how she had fled, friendless and frightened, and that she had never meant to foist herself upon Mrs. Trombly. She had never stolen what wasn't hers to take. But she would have to explain *why* Alfred loathed her. *Why* she couldn't marry. *Why* she could never hope to lead a normal life. She would have to quote Mr. Norton. *There are anatomical abnormalities in my brain.* She would have to tell him that *she* was the invalid. Papa had stayed at home for *her*, not the other way around.

His face would change. Revulsion would replace the tenderness. He was looking at her as though she were a woman. What if he knew she turned into something else? Not even human. Hideous.

"My cousin." She couldn't remain silent with his coaxing eyes so close. "I was his dependent. He turned me out."

She broke his hold and walked the length of the small room. The walls were dark—polished mahogany panels. The light of the oil lamps didn't reach into the corners. The window was shuttered. She stopped by a low table. A large case rested on it, leather-covered, studded with gold nails.

"A violin?" She understood, suddenly, the calluses on his fingers. She imagined those fingers sliding over the strings, changing the pitch with the finest modulation of pressure, the angle of his touch. "May I?"

"Please." He came toward her as she opened the case, revealing the red-velvet interior and the varnished wood of the instrument. She glanced about for a plaque inscribed with the name of the workshop.

"I learned how to make violins when I was in Naples." Her eyes flew to him. He was smiling, a smile she'd never seen, almost shy. "That's when I met Geppetto."

She raised a brow.

"The donkey," he clarified. "He belonged to a man named Rocco. Rocco is not a famous luthier by any means. His workshop is small. Just him and a brother, his son, and a few nephews." His voice was warm with remembrance. A pleasant memory of a pleasant time. She wondered how many pleasant memories he had.

"You too have a love for music," he said.

An image of that first meeting hung for a moment between them, she frozen at the harpsichord, he a storm of black energy rushing toward her.

"Yes," she said simply. She closed the violin case. "There were times when it was my only solace."

"The sonata you played … " The light in his eyes was difficult to interpret. He started again. "You played it well."

"It's one of my favorites."

"Ah," he said, still with that odd light in his eyes. "And so you don't always play so well?"

It would be ladylike to agree. *Oh yes*, she should say. *That was one of the few pieces I've mastered. I am only an indifferent player.*

She said: "Often I play better."

He laughed, surprised. Not unpleased by her arrogance.

Her lips twitched in return. "My mother used to read music the way other women read novels. She could hear the music in her head." She had grown up with her mother's collection of sheet music. Some of the manuscripts were very old, hand-written scores passed down through the generations. Alfred had them now. Her chest tightened.

"I didn't know her," she said. "She died when I was born. My father told me.

He loved music too."

"My mother also played." The corner of his mouth turned down. "Until my father smashed her violin."

She exhaled, wanting more than anything to brush away the lock of hair that had fallen over his eye. To stroke the crease from his brow.

"That's when you decided you would learn to build them?" Her question hung in the air. He moved his jaw from side to side, releasing tension.

"Yes, I suppose it was." He spoke slowly. "I never thought of it quite like that." Something had ignited in his eyes. They were brighter. Burning through her. He pushed the hair away from his eyes, and the disordered black locks stood up around his head. He looked wilder. He belonged in an enchanted grove, not a staid, paneled study in a terrace in Pimlico.

"Ella," he said, the timbre of his voice dropping lower.

"Yes." She meant to make it a question. *Yes, my lord?* But it emerged as a throaty assent to a question he had not asked. Or had he? He closed the distance between them as though her response was exactly what he was waiting for. His hands slid over her shoulders, pressed into her back. She had no choice but to step into him. The fullness of her breasts flattened against the hard plane of his chest, forcing the air to rush from her mouth in a gasp. His fingers dug into her spine. They moved up and down from the curve of her neck to the small of her back, unlatching her. She was spilling forward, melting into him. He moved his hand around her throat, wrapping it, so that she felt the slight constriction as she swallowed. Then his fingers were sweeping along her jaw, tilting up her face.

"Do you know how often I've thought of exactly this?" His voice was gruff, his thumb tracing her lips. She wanted to make some disbelieving noise, but the blue intensity of his gaze fringed by lashes black as night transformed the protest into a sigh. She strained against him, lifting onto her toes, and moved her fingers through his hair, felt the shape of his skull. She pulled his head down to hers. The shock of his lips made her groan. The heat of his breath, his tongue, radiated through her. She kept her eyes open, watching the bronze skin, the black brow, until the proximity made her vision smear, blur, disappear, and she shut her eyes, not to escape but to sink more deeply into her body. To feel the sensations rippling through her.

She slid her hands down his back. The heavy slabs of muscle in his shoulder blades shifted as he wrapped her tighter in his arms. Tentatively, she kneaded the muscles in his back, moved her hands lower. She felt the dramatic curve of his buttocks, hard as rock. When she cupped them, he made a low noise, shifting his mouth to kiss her jaw, her neck. She lifted her hands away, abashed, but he reached behind him, caught her wrist, and brought her hand down again, trapping it for a moment in place. She gripped him. He was kissing down the line of her throat, undoing the buttons of her high-collared gown. He worked his hand inside. Only the thin linen of her undergarments separated her skin from his hand. She shuddered as his hand grazed her nipples. His fingers closed on her breast; the sensation centered in the nipple. The flesh puckered, tightening. This was the pain she craved, the sweet agony he inflicted upon her. She kissed his chin, running her tongue through the cleft, nipping beneath his jaw; his stubble abraded the delicate flesh inside her lower lip. Sweet agony. She wanted more. She was always so *restrained*, always holding herself in, keeping vigil over her body lest a moment of inattention permit her disease to gain ground. Now she felt abandoned. Greedy with the possibilities.

His other hand stroked her backside through her skirts. Suddenly his arm was beneath her buttocks. He was sweeping her off her feet and depositing her in a leather chair. He never took his mouth from hers. He followed her down, dropping to his knees before her.

"You've bewitched me." He spoke against her lips, voice ragged. "I don't care if you were sent to me by the devil himself." He pushed her skirts over her knees. His hands were sliding up her legs, over the knees, up to her garters. She clapped her knees together, and he parted them easily. The strain in her muscles as she tried to close her legs, pushing against his hands, dear God, it only aggravated the shivering tension in her inner thighs, the sweet throbbing in her lower belly that he seemed intent on reaching. His fingers brushed the very tops of her thighs. His thumbs slid lower, slid over the bare skin, then delved into her linen drawers. He delivered one stroke to that most private region of her body. She bucked. Gasped. Shot back in the chair, her head and shoulders sliding up the smooth leather.

"No," she breathed. She pushed his chest. She might as well have tried to move a mountain. His weight drove her into the chair. She couldn't breathe. His hands came up to her face, tugging the pins from her hair. She felt the cool mass against her cheeks, her throat, heard his gasp of appreciation. He lifted away from her to unwind its length, let it coil upon her breast. The dingy blond, dull as ashes—she could *see* it suddenly as he saw it.

"Like moonlight," he whispered. His hand slid again into the opening of her gown. The sound of ripping fabric startled her.

"Isidore." She grabbed his wrist. His fingers closed with bruising strength around her nipple. "Stop."

He was breathing rapidly. He released her breast and braced himself on the arms of the chair. She looked up into his face. The way he looked down at her—with tenderness and brutality merging into one. A look of *hunger*. Of *need*. He wanted too.

"Do you have a lover?"

The question slapped her like a wave of frigid water.

"No, I—" Her breast heaved as she caught her breath. Shivers were still running up and down her legs. Her shins were pressed against his thighs.

He bent his head and kissed her, a feather-soft kiss, his hair stroking her cheek. When he pulled back, his eyes held a steely light.

"Did he … hurt you? Tell me he misused you, even disappointed you, and I will make him regret that he was ever born."

Confusion cast her gaze down. He thought she had been spurned by a lover. That she had been turned out of her house for her wantonness. Her cheeks flamed. She was hardly proving herself a model of chastity now, panting beneath him on a chair with her skirts around her waist. What could she have been thinking?

She wiggled, smoothing her skirts over her knees. He pushed off the chair and stood. She stood too. He looked at her a moment. Something he read in her face made him swear to himself. He pulled her into his arms, molding her body to his. He was so tall he had to bow his head to lay his lips against the part in her hair.

"Ella," he said, his voice raw. "I want you in my bed."

She closed her eyes, breathed in his musk. She placed her hands on the dense muscles of his upper chest and felt their contours before she pressed against them and stepped away. Her senses erupted. Craving his heat, his weight, his scent, his taste. Mutinying against her judgment.

Why not put her hand in his and let him lead her into his bedchamber? He wasn't asking her to marry him. She would never have to tell him the truth. Never have to disclose the tainted facts of her existence. She could share his bed and when their devil's pact had ended, she could leave. She could remember the feel of his arms and his lips when she was all alone.

Nothing could be easier.

Nothing could be more difficult.

It would destroy her more surely than the Thames. She wouldn't be able to walk away without a part of her dying.

She shook her head.

"I can't." Her voice broke. He stepped toward her. "Please," she said. "I'll help you find Phillipa's murderer. But that's all I can do."

"Ella." His breath was still unsteady. His lips were swollen. She felt the tug of his body even though he made no move toward her. His eyes shone like dark stars.

She had to put more space between them. If he reached for her, if he asked her again, she wouldn't be able to say no. She would go with him and her ability to live her life, reconciled to loneliness, grateful for her freedom, would be shattered forever. The want would consume her.

She turned on her heel, aware of his burning gaze. She didn't flee like a deer. Her steps were heavy, awkward, ugly. She wasn't sure even when she reached the hall that she'd escaped in time. Her life had already shattered. He'd already changed everything. It was just as she'd feared.

She'd seen the danger too late.

Chapter Sixteen

"The cornet player's foxed." The voice at his ear was Huntington's. Isidore looked toward the band. He shrugged.

"Not compared to the cellist." *Or to you,* he might have added. Huntington, true to form, frowned at his empty glass.

"Punch won't stay put," he said.

"Try the scotch," Isidore suggested. "It's older." He gestured with his glass toward Clement, who was standing on the other side of the hot, crowded ballroom, Granville at his elbow. "Ask St. Aubyn where he's hiding the bottle."

"I think I will." Huntington mopped his brow with a crumpled handkerchief. "I'll tell him his punch is positively coltish. I've broken a sweat chasing it around the room. I say, you missed a riveting show at Astley's tonight."

Isidore hid his impatience. If the mention of scotch hadn't sent Huntington off like a shot, he didn't know what would.

"I've seen it," he said shortly. "The one with the female Mazeppa mounted naked on the wild horse of Tartary?" He paused. "Bareback, of course."

Huntington blinked at him. "That sounds marvelous. I almost wish I'd thought to pay attention to the drama. I assumed it was *Richard III.* No." He leaned closer with a confidential air. "Bennington got punched in the nose and nearly fell out of the box into the pit. By whom, do you ask?"

Isidore didn't. He sipped his scotch. The band struck up a waltz, and a few couples moved through the figures. The dancing was as clumsy as the music. Had these late-night parties always appeared thus? The company should, by all rights, have scintillated. The gowns rippled in all shades, frothed with ruching, ribbons, and lace. The jewels twinkled. Champagne bubbled in crystal flutes.

Tapers set in silver six-light candelabra burned in the wall niches. Fresh strawberries glowed on platters on the sideboards and tables, amid candied fruits and pastries brightly glazed. Above the sad strains of the gay waltz, female voices lifted in false, high cries. The drone of male conversation filled the lower registers. Everywhere was sound, motion.

The sounds seemed tinny; the motions defined meaningless arcs. The whole thing was flat. Dull as ditch water. He only hoped it would answer to his purpose.

"The lovely Mrs. Bennington herself!" Huntington slapped his thigh with delight and nudged Isidore in the ribs. If Huntington hadn't been such a harmless puppy, better ignored than anything else, Isidore might have felt inclined to nudge him back. *Hard.* He smoothed his evening jacket.

Poor Daphne, he thought. It must have been a riveting show indeed.

Huntington looked deflated by Isidore's cool expression. Then he smiled broadly, revealing too much of his reddened gum-line.

"What an uproar!" he continued, shaking his head. "As soon as she finished with Bennington, she jumped on Mrs. Hatfield. Went straight for the eyes." The smile was more of a leer, really. Huntington had clearly found Daphne's display of temper titillating in the extreme. She must have looked a tiny Valkyrie.

"Mrs. Hatfield put up more of a fight than Bennington." Huntington laughed. "She's a bruiser. I would have laid my money on *her* out of the three of them. Abergavenny broke it up. He's planning on proposing to Mrs. Hatfield. Had you heard? He's been moaning about it for days. But *she's* holding out for St. Aubyn."

He shot Isidore a speculative look. "I can't see that happening, can you? He'll go for a little virgin with curls, I'd wager."

Isidore tried not to snort. Huntington would wager on anything. He could respond, "St. Aubyn's holding out for the

Empress Dowager of China," and Huntington would snap to attention and lay him long odds. He didn't rise to the bait. He turned his gaze on the crowd, letting his eyes wander until he fixed on Bennington. Ben seemed fine, smiling his dazzling smile at some dazzled-looking brunette. Not a mark on him. Maybe Daphne needed to practice her punching.

"Bennington's here," he said. "His nose is on straight."

"Too bad, eh?" Huntington poked him in the shoulder. "I wouldn't have minded if she'd dented it a little. Give the rest of us a chance. Now where's our talented Miss Reed? Does St. Aubyn have her hidden away with the scotch?"

Isidore smiled briefly. "No one has seen her."

"But everyone came here to see her!" Huntington scanned the room. "She wanted this party is what I heard. Or Miss Trombly did. Spoke through her and demanded it. Specified it had to be at St. Aubyn's, for obvious reasons." His sudden flush indicated his awareness that the mention of the "obvious reasons" might have been in poor taste. He rubbed the back of his neck, casting his glance up around the ceiling as though a graceful transition might be spelled out in the gilded plasterwork.

"Dammit," he muttered. "Put my foot in it. Sorry, Blackwood. Must be uncomfortable for you. All this talk of, ah … " He raised his empty glass to his lips and tipped it back to save himself from further fumblings. Isidore watched with faint amusement as he smacked his lips, savoring the nonexistent punch. He realized Huntington had given him an opening. He shifted his weight, turned, and stared for a moment at the French doors. He'd stood by them since the party began. As though compelled. The doors were closed; the glass reflected the blazing ballroom. He stepped closer to peer through the glass into the courtyard. Lights from the mansion's many windows illuminated white rectangles of marble. He could make out the curved basin of the fountain, a hint of the pedestal rising from the center, carved in a cluster of masks spouting black water from their open mouths. The flowerbeds and yews swam with shadows.

Huntington cleared his throat uneasily.

"It's quite all right," Isidore murmured, letting his fingertips rest on the glass. He sighed and turned back to Huntington. "I find it all fascinating," he said. "Painful, but fascinating. At first, I was dubious, of course, about the authenticity of Miss Reed's trances, but there have been certain proofs … " He trailed off, aware that Huntington was looking at him eagerly.

"I had it from my sister that she got examined by a … a … " Another inspection of the ceiling yielded nothing. He snapped his fingers. "A what-do-you-call-him … "

"Psychical researcher," supplied Isidore. "From University College." He nodded significantly and, with effort, managed not to rock back and forth on his heels as he continued. "Professor Urquhart said he'd never encountered anyone quite like Miss Reed. His tests revealed unprecedented facilities." Huntington nodded too. Isidore could see the wheels in his head turning. He'd be holding court on the topic of psychical research in no time at all. The seed had been planted. Isidore could change the subject. And, with luck, get rid of the man so he could think.

"Tenby's trying to get your attention," Isidore said, waving. "Over there." Tenby was standing near the band, shoulder propped against the wall. His hair was brushed back, and his head loomed above his shoulders like the dome of St. Paul's Cathedral. Mrs. Tenby, dressed in cream-colored silk, sipping champagne at his side, was easier to miss. She blended with the pilasters.

Huntington's eyes settled on them. He grinned at Isidore, that wide, gummy grin, cocking his finger for another poke. "And where's *Miss* Tenby, I wonder? You were stuck to her like cobbler's wax at dinner last week. Has she caught your fancy? I don't think I could join my giblets with a woman who looks quite as much like

Tenby." He poked and chuckled. "But that's just me. Wouldn't want to discourage anyone."

Isidore seized his shoulder.

"Don't look yet," he said, "but Miss Chartwick is unattended at the moment. You must remember when her father came into that trust a few years back? No? It was a rather famous case. I was sure you'd have heard of it." He lowered his voice to a whisper. "The fortune had been invested at *compound interest* for a *hundred* years. The old man is inordinately fond of her. Apparently, she loves racing. Will hear of nothing else."

Huntington gave his arm a conspiratorial squeeze. "You're not such a croaker as they make out," he said. "I'll take that tip. Where is she?"

"Under the chandelier. If you go quickly, you can save her from the dripping wax."

He gave Huntington a shove, not gentle but not precisely vicious. Encouraging, he'd call it. He watched as Huntington glided toward Miss Chartwick. The young lady's blue silk gown was so heavily adorned with bronze brocade that the bodice looked more like a breastplate. Good luck to her. Were she Joan of Arc herself, he doubted she'd be able to discourage Huntington's attention. The man would follow compound interest to the moon.

For a moment, Isidore stood alone in the ballroom, the French doors at his back, perfumed groups forming and dividing in front of him. One of these black-clad men was Phillipa's murderer. Had to be. He'd gone over the guest list a dozen times. Clement had invited everyone they could remember from that night, and Jenkins had been instructed to permit anyone to enter, regardless of invitation.

He was here. Phillipa Trombly's name was once again on everyone's lips. London buzzed with rumors. This was *her* party. Her spirit had grown restless. She had something to say to the living. A weighty secret that kept her soul from rising. A confession. An accusation. Every time Miss Reed made contact, the message became clearer. Soon it would come into focus, with terrible clarity. Miss Reed would give it voice.

How could he have stayed away?

For the past six days, Isidore had made innumerable calls, attended dinner parties, balls, the opera, spent late hours at the club. He had taken every opportunity to drop tantalizing tidbits about Miss Reed's revelations into conversation. He wasn't a gifted actor. He spoke in stilted language, shuddered and sighed and broke off his exclamations like a hero in a penny dreadful. But his interlocutors seemed to take his forced, halting speech as a sign of his sincerity, of raging emotions held in check. They ate it up, regurgitated it to others. Yesterday, at the Marchdale ball, he'd listened with satisfaction as gossiping women traded versions of his own words: altered, intensified. *I heard she walked in a trance to Lord St. Aubyn's and crumpled on the* very spot *where it happened. I heard she materialized Miss Phillipa in the Trombly parlor. It was a terrible shock for Mrs. Trombly. I can't even imagine. She's taken to bed, I hear. Miss Reed will be holding a séance this coming week? At Blackwood mansion? How terrifying. I'd be too frightened to attend. I don't suppose the invitations have gone out? I might be persuaded, of course ...*

It was nearing midnight. Over the tops of heads, he saw Jenkins whispering in Clement's ear. Clement caught his eye and nodded. He expelled breath. The wait had begun to strain his nerves. He began to make his way along the perimeter of the room. Voices quieted as he passed then exploded again behind him. He glimpsed the excitement in the fresh, unfamiliar faces. It wasn't only the members of his old set in attendance tonight. The youngsters were here, too—the next generation of the fast and the wild. They laughed too loudly, drank too quickly, then brandished their champagne flutes like victors in Olympian games. *They* didn't think the soirée flat or dull. They were in ecstasies to find themselves at a private party with no gray-haired chaperones glaring them down. A party that had barely begun, although the clocks were about to toll midnight.

Is it true? Is the house haunted? They were hounding older siblings for details. The whispers floated around the room. *Were you here when it happened? Was it horrible?*

"*That* was her betrothed." He heard a woman's eager voice. A slender girl in pink silk, pink gauze floating over her shoulders, drew back and shivered as he walked by. Her round eyes shone. Her shiver expressed voluptuous pleasure, unalloyed by even an ounce of sympathy. A girl her age *died* at a party just like this one, at this very house. It was a ghost story to her, plain and simple. Thrilling.

He kept going, barely looking at the women or at the gawky youths. It was the men who drew his gaze. The men who had gathered many times before in this ballroom to drink and laugh and sneer and dance and drink yet more.

Some of them were thick-waisted now. Some still slim as blades. Some were married. Some were still enjoying their bachelorhood. All of them were known to him. As his eyes slid over their faces, he ticked them off. Greenfield. Munns. Linley. Dorset. Granville. Cowper. Averly. Tenby. Abergavenny. Bennington. He considered each. Huntington—damn him—appeared in the periphery of his vision, waggling his fingers to attract his attention. He winked ostentatiously as he led Miss Chartwick to the punch.

Huntington he'd already dismissed. Like many others, he'd been infatuated with Phillipa, but from a distance. She'd thought he was a hopeless case. In those days, he'd had terrible spots, and the London spring made his nose drip. He'd sent her a sonnet once by Sir Philip Sidney he'd tried to pass off as his own.

Isidore winked back.

Luke Pearsall, lounging against the wall beside the massive fireplace, glanced up at him as he neared and raised his glass. He tossed back the amber contents. He too was drinking Clement's scotch. He was one of Clement's oldest friends. Clever, handsome, fun-loving, fickle, impossibly rich. He'd been less of a drunkard back then, less self-indulgent.

He'd guessed Luke was her lover straight off, years ago, and she'd shaken her head frantically. *No. Stop. If you keep guessing I'll scream.* Christ, he'd already gone through this very thing—scrutinizing the whole bloody *ton.* He'd failed to fix on the man who had stolen Phillipa's heart. And, as it turned out, her life.

That day in the music room, Phillipa had sobbed in his arms. Then she'd pulled away. She'd hunched over and refused to answer any of his questions, chewing on her lower lip, picking at the skin around her cuticles.

"I *itch,*" she'd said. "I itch all over. It hasn't stopped. It's been days and nights of it. I can't *breathe.*"

"Why didn't you tell me sooner?" None of the condemnation he felt was for her, but she whimpered, stuffing her fingers in her mouth. He'd never seen this side of her, fragile, fearful. As children, they'd once cut across a pasture too near a watering hole. She hadn't cringed before the charging bull.

He'd tried to ask gently. He'd coaxed. He'd begged.

"I'll make this better," he'd promised. "I just need his name."

He should have wrested it from her. He should have *known* who it was. He hadn't been paying the right kind of attention. She'd never given the appearance of preferring one suitor to another. Somehow he'd missed the signs.

He reached Clement.

"She's here," Clement said quietly. "She came in the back entrance. She's dressing upstairs."

"She came alone?" He'd told Louisa not to accompany her, but he'd been worried she would force the issue.

Clement nodded.

"Good." Then it would be any minute now. He moistened his lips with the last of the scotch. His strained nerves had begun to jangle. He wondered how *she* felt. He hadn't seen her since Wednesday afternoon, when he'd called on her at Trombly Place to discuss this evening's entertainment. She had returned to Mount Street the morning after he'd tried—and failed—to seduce her in his study. The joy that flared in his breast when he learned she no longer had a lover had been doused by her rejection. She didn't want to share his bed. Why should it rankle? He couldn't blame her. Women had more to lose from those kinds of arrangements. He knew that better than anyone. Well, better than any *man*. When she'd turned to leave, he'd wanted to follow. Assurances had sprung to his lips. He wouldn't let anything happen to her. He wasn't a green boy who couldn't control himself, whose seed shot forth without forewarning.

He hadn't been able to think of a formulation that didn't sound crass. He'd let her walk away, his body all but splitting open with bottled desire.

It wasn't too late to make her a better offer. Instead of inviting her to share his bed for a night, he might ask her to become his mistress. He could establish her in her own apartments. No more stealing. He'd provide for her every need. He'd give her all the jewels she wanted, although he imagined she would prefer books. He'd give her both. Descartes and diamonds. Byron and pearls. With pleasure. For pleasure.

"More scotch," he said hoarsely to Clement and passed off his glass.

Years went by. Decades. There was a lull. The music paused. The pianist launched into Chopin's minute waltz. The other members of the band had abandoned him, also refilling their glasses. To occupy himself, Isidore observed the pianist. He was a lively fellow, dashing through the waltz in record time; his fingers must have been flying over the keys.

Suddenly, a woman screamed. The pianist's fingers slipped and crashed down on a sour chord. A hush fell over the room, relieved by the creaking of the French doors. They were opening, the panes of glass reflecting waving light. Now gasps and rustles broke the silence as the women nearest the doors shrank away. The men too fell back, faces registering bafflement, shock, wonder.

A woman stepped into the ballroom. As she entered, the cool air from the courtyard came with her. A gust of wind made the doors bang. Another scream, quickly stifled. Candles guttered. Several flames went out. The woman walked forward, the only moving figure in that frozen crowd.

She was tall, slender, dressed in a gown of black and red silk. The short, ruched sleeves were red, and red silk draped the low neckline, gathered at the lowest dip of the V by a cluster of rosebuds, their red-silk petals edged with green-silk leaves. More silk roses adorned the black fall of the skirt, which stopped short of the ground to reveal flaring red underskirts. Her elbow-length gloves were black. The ringlets piled high on her head were black. Her skin was white. Dead white. Black eyes seemed to fill that small, white face. Black eyes brimming with mystery. And torment.

Isidore had known what to expect—had ordered the wig, sketched the dress for the modiste—but still his mouth went dry. Phillipa had been smaller, more rounded. Her skin had a warmer, olive tone; her mouth was wider. There was no real resemblance between them. But the differences worked to his advantage. Ella looked like a pale reflection of the original. Attenuated. Shimmering. The way her black eyes sparkled as she looked out across that room, head held high as she endured a hundred appalled stares—he could tell she was blinking back tears. He had subjected her to this. Her eyes grazed his. Returned. He wanted to hold her up, to send all of his strength out through his eyes. But he tore his gaze away. He couldn't allow her to command his attention. He needed to examine the faces around him, gauge the reactions.

Footsteps sounded. Daphne, running from the room. He glanced about to see if Bennington would follow. Bennington stood stock-still, staring at Ella. His face had gone whiter than hers. Isidore looked for Luke. The man's languid attitude had altered. He'd stepped away from the wall, body rigid.

"What the devil?" The exclamation burst out from the ballroom's far corner, and the eerie stillness shattered. Commotion reigned. Excited clamor swelled all around. Guffaws. More gasps, now theatrical. Nervous titters. Low murmurs of disgust. Speculations.

"Awful prank."

"Do you suppose St. Aubyn planned it?"

Isidore pushed through the crowd.

"My brother says that's the *exact* gown she wore, the very one!"

"It couldn't be the *very* one."

"How ghastly."

"Is it a Worth?"

"Look at Lord Blackwood."

"Poor man."

"What if this ensures that he *never* marries?"

"I would pay Miss Reed to tap out a blessing so he'd change his mind."

"Flora! He might have heard you!"

"Is she in a trance, do you think?"

He felt a hand on his arm. "Blackwood." It was Granville. Breathing hot, beery breath into his face. He smelled like a farmer. He must have stepped in horse dung at Astley's and was too drunk to care. "What's the meaning of this? My stomach almost came out of my mouth."

"Glad it didn't." He removed Granville's hand. "I can't say what the meaning is."

"Did Mrs. Trombly put her in that gown?" Granville twitched his thick shoulders. Something between a tic and a shudder.

"I don't know." Isidore spoke slowly. "Maybe Miss Reed requested it. Every day she's been deepening the connection with … " He broke off. Laughed a low, dark laugh. "All I know is that strange things have been happening. Stranger than this. I wouldn't have believed any of it a few weeks ago … but now … "

He searched Granville's square-jawed face. Did apprehension dilate the pupils in his hazel eyes? Or was it the play of light?

"Come to the séance on Monday," he said. "I think we'll all learn something."

He turned away and continued on toward the middle of the room. Ella stood beneath a chandelier, alone in a circle of light. The band had begun another waltz, but no couples had formed. People ringed around her in clusters, heads together. Watching. Her chin was still high. A defiant angle. He wondered if anyone else could tell how much effort this attitude cost her.

"Dance with me," he said, reaching her, holding out his hand. She didn't take it.

"I can't dance," she said. He made a noise of disbelief and took her in his arms. Together they began to move through the steps of the waltz. She was stiff in his arms, but her step was light, and she turned with him effortlessly, in time to the music. It was odd to look down at the mass of black curls. Some other woman's curls.

"You dance well," he said.

She looked at him. Another woman, glancing up at a dance partner through such thick, black lashes, would have been playing the coquette. Smiling at the compliment. Her lovely eyes were serious. Her red lips did not curve.

"I know *how* to dance. It's that I shouldn't."

What an ass he was. She still mourned her father. There was nothing he could say. *I'll make this all up to you one day.* How hollow that would sound.

They danced in a widening circle as the floor cleared. Still, no one joined them.

"I felt like a ghost." She spoke at last, her voice ragged. "When I came through the doors … "

He tightened his arms around her. "You're not a ghost," he said thickly. "I can feel you in my arms. I can feel your warmth against my body, God help me. I'd like to show you right here and now that you're flesh and blood." He tipped her chin up with his finger. She fluttered her lashes, as though she weren't sure whether she wanted her eyes opened or closed. Fighting with herself. It looked like an absurd affectation. He was convinced of its authenticity. He ground his teeth to keep from lowering his mouth to hers.

Maybe he should do it. The murderer was watching. It might drive him over the edge, this ghostly vision of the woman who'd loved him, the woman he'd killed, caressed by her betrothed. It might stir his jealousy, and he would slip, give something away.

He couldn't do that to her. She was the one who would bear the shame of it. He'd already pushed her so far. He wouldn't publically claim her as his lover. Not yet. Maybe ... when this was all over ...

"Smile," he said as her eyes opened, fastened on his. "I want him to see us smiling at one another." She tilted the corners of her mouth. Good enough. He whirled her, watching the crowd that watched them.

They would pour into Blackwood mansion for the séance; he was certain of it.

There was only one piece of the act left, for this night, at least.

"Are you ready?" He touched one of the curls that hung down to frame her face. He'd like to yank it, pull the wig from her head. Her eyes flitted to his hand. She nodded jerkily.

He'd only heard her play a little, a few bars of the Bach sonata they would play together, now, in full. That day, he had hardly been focused on gauging her degree of musical accomplishment. It was of no consequence, though, if she wasn't as good as she'd claimed to be. The spectacle would be enough. The waltz ended, and he led her across the room. The crowd parted before them. As they approached the band, the pianist rose and offered her his seat. Isidore watched Ella settle herself on the bench. He couldn't turn away as she drew off her gloves. Her delicate wrists and slim, white fingers slid free of the black leather. He was sure his intake of breath was audible. He knelt hurriedly by the violin case and took out his violin.

He stood facing the room. Everyone still. Staring. How many of those assembled had seen him perform with Phillipa? How many of them felt the hairs lift on the backs of their necks as Ella touched the keys?

She hadn't misrepresented her skill. She played well. Better than well. Her touch was expressive, ardent. Her posture relaxed as she leaned forward. *This* was what he wanted to do to her with his caresses. Make her muscles loosen. Make her body bend, supple, unselfconscious. Make her open.

She was doing it now, opening, her tense, withholding figure swaying with lyrical grace. Music allowed her to transcend the barriers she'd erected. It unified her, body and soul. She flowed forward, and the sound flowed from her fingers.

He listened to the first sweet notes of the sonata. He let his eyes close, briefly, drinking it in, drinking *her* in. The notes, so familiar to him, interpreted by innumerable hands, seemed new. She spoke to him through the notes, called to him. He lifted the violin. Waited until the summons could no longer be denied. He had no choice but to answer. He drew the bow across the strings.

• • •

Ella forgot the crowd staring at her back. She forgot the heavy, hot wig itching her scalp. She forgot everything but the music. She already knew the Bach well, and she'd practiced every day since Isidore had told her about the party and explained what he wanted. But she'd never played it on piano. The strangeness of the sound only excited her. Her excitement made the notes louder; harpsichord didn't respond in the same way to pressure.

Her playing rose with her emotions, fingers moving deftly across the keys. She wondered, briefly, if she would overpower Isidore, if she should hold back.

Then the violin entered, the slow, sorrowing phrase pulling through her, turning her inside out so her softest, most vulnerable recesses were exposed to the rasping perfection of his intonation. This was his other voice, a voice she had never heard, the sound his soul would make if it could sing. Darkness audible. She ached with the resonance. It faded, and she played alone again, the notes bright, the tune steady, but somehow transformed. Waiting for the violin's return. She felt the loss, the brightness of the slow tune she played suddenly bare, translucent. In that second, she looked at him. He stood, body angled toward her, the violin pressed between chin and shoulder. His head was tilted, lips pressed together, the shadows stark beneath his cheekbones. His eyes were open. He glanced up from the strings and saw her. As their eyes met, he moved, slid the bow, the tones emerging full, throaty, and dark, the tight gut-strings bending as his fingers traveled up the bridge. His hair fell across his forehead; his lips parted. Now the sound moved back and forth between them, the melodic lines mingling, infinitely richer, sadder, than before. She leaned closer to the keys, face turned so she could watch him, watch his lean, black-clad form curve, his beautiful hands shaping the notes, as her own hands responded and invited. Neither could overpower the other in this conversation. He sustained the slow notes until they scorched her, and she balanced him, supported his flourishes, and when the music got faster, she matched him, the notes sparkling, her ornamentation transmitting to his muscles, his body jerking, sensitized to each stroke of her fingers. He made the violin purr, bloom. She felt the urgency that throbbed in his phrasing, felt it inside her. This warmth, this intimacy—it wasn't gentle. She was scraped raw. The black current between them, that force that flowed from him to her and from her to him—now she could *hear* it too. Now he was everywhere.

Surging into her even as she invaded him. The tears she'd held back since she'd first stepped into the ballroom fell now, but she was safe. No one could see. Except him.

They played the last notes. Sound vanished, but her body still thrummed, still ached. She was afraid to move. She folded her hands on her lap and stared down at the ivory keys. She heard the coughing, sighing, shifting of the crowd behind her. No applause. She felt dizzy. The debutantes smelled so harsh, the alcohols of their various perfumes clashing in the air. She was going to faint, roll off the bench onto the polished floor. She rose. She had a role to play. So what if everyone could see the tear tracks shining on her cheeks? Let them know she was moved. Let them read the pain and wonder on her face. It would be more powerful than any claim she could make, any grand pronouncement. *I have made the connection. She is here.*

She pivoted slowly. Her eyes skimmed over the silent men, the whispering coteries of women. They lit on Lord St. Aubyn. He stood in the front of the press of people—his guests—all of them properly stunned, aghast by the evening's unexpected turn. St. Aubyn had consented to all of it, but he appeared more aghast than anyone. A muscle in his jaw ticked convulsively. Were those tears in his eyes? He looked away from her.

She had mentioned to Isidore on Wednesday that St. Aubyn's conscience was not easy.

Have you considered Lord St. Aubyn? she'd asked. His face had tightened.

No, he'd said. *I've taken St. Aubyn into my confidence. Everything I'm planning happens with his knowledge.*

But at Mr. Tenby's … she'd begun, and he'd interrupted, his voice flat with finality.

I trust him with my life.

Clearly, Isidore had trusted Lord St. Aubyn with information he hadn't shared with her. Yet. He'd alluded to something he needed to tell her before the séance.

Not here, he'd said, rising from the sofa, casting a meaningful glance at the open door, a door through which Mrs. Trombly might have entered at any moment. *We'll discuss things elsewhere, later. For now, concentrate on the party.*

She had. She had spent days dreading it. Dreading the moment she would have to push open the French doors and march into a ballroom filled with strangers. Her imagination hadn't carried her past those doors. She hadn't had the energy, the courage maybe, to begin to dread all the moments that would follow. Now it was almost over. She needed only to move from this corner across the ballroom and out into the hall. Her coach would be called. She could climb inside and sag and tremble and sob.

Stare them all down, she told herself. She didn't glance toward Isidore. She squared her shoulders, lifted her chin, and swept through the crowd. People parted to make way for her.

Here it was, her dream, perverted. Her dark Season. Her London debut. She had danced in the arms of a man who held her close, as though her body were something precious he wanted to protect. She had done it dressed as a dead woman. The gown she wore, so beautiful, drew attention to the woman she *wasn't.* The man who had taken her right hand and spun her through the steps of the waltz, whose fingertips and wrist had rested against her back, who had pulled her nearer than the dance required—he was only repeating what he had done with *her*, with his betrothed, on the last night of her life.

She made it into the hall without her tears blinding her. Mrs. Bennington was there, standing by the wide staircase. She was weeping, her small hands covering her heart-shaped face. Ella turned from her sharply, almost banged into Mrs. Tenby. The thin woman's face was pinched with displeasure. Ella flushed with guilt. These women had been Phillipa's friends. She bit back an apology and kept going. Other partygoers were in the hall as well, some newly arrived, handing off their coats. Didn't anyone in London sleep? She moved toward the front entrance against the stream of latecomers. She needed to find a footman.

A hand on her bare elbow made her start. Skin on skin. She hadn't taken her gloves from the piano bench. Isidore. He'd come up behind her. She could feel his presence.

"Jenkins is sending the coach around." His voice came from far above. A footman appeared with her cloak and Isidore's coat and hat. He was leaving with her. He'd never said he was going to leave with her. That wasn't part of the plan. She didn't speak, just stood by his side, reminding herself to breathe. The coach he helped her into was not Mrs. Trombly's coach. It was his coach. And he followed her inside.

She fell back against the bench. As soon as the coach began to move, he slid toward her. He drew her head down on his shoulder and held her while tears leaked from her eyes, dampening the wool of his coat. It was grotesque, her crying, and ludicrous that he should comfort her. He thought she was compassionating with him, no doubt, crying for the bride he'd lost, or out of horror, knowing her murderer had stood among those elegantly clad gentlemen. She didn't deserve sympathy. She was crying in a helpless rage, but not for Phillipa, not for him. She was crying for herself.

"Let me go." She straightened, wobbled a smile. "I'm fine."

"I shouldn't have forced you to dance." He studied her, his expression shuttered. "That much of your mourning I could have respected."

He thought she was crying for *Papa*? Shame made her shrink. Her woe was entirely selfish. Papa was dead. She was the one doomed to live.

"But I wanted it too badly." His voice was soft. They were together again in a tiny, vibrating box, the wet, black night held at bay beyond the windows. The lamplight gave her the golden tones of his skin, the proud planes of his face. The darkling blue of his eyes. It wasn't fair that his face could still startle her. It wasn't fair that his looks could lay siege to her senses.

"Indeed." She defended herself with irony, unnerved by the intensity of his gaze. "I was the belle of the ball." She laughed. He didn't.

"You are the belle of the Elfin grot." His mouth quirked. "Now I've heard your faery song." He took her hand. Her fingers were cold. She swallowed at the firm heat of his grasp. He bent her hand back and spread her fingers with his, so their palms pressed together. The callus on his thumb rubbed the soft fold between her thumb and first finger.

"Keats." She tried to ignore their joined hands.

"Her hair was long, her foot was light." He slid his free hand into the mass of black curls anchored to her head. "And her eyes were wild."

His hip bumped hers. Thank God for the crinolines, for all the gathered folds of silk that cocooned her. He leaned over, leaned down until she could feel his exhalation against her eyelids.

"I made a garland for her head. And bracelets too, and fragrant zone." His breathy recitation made her shiver. She closed her eyes to shut him out.

"She looked at me as she did love … " Her lids flew open. *His* eyes were wild as they traced her features. His lips were parted as though to utter the next line. He hesitated. He cast his gaze up as though the words eluded him.

She couldn't stop herself. "And made sweet moan." Too late she saw the trap. His gaze snapped back. Flared with triumph.

"Ah," he whispered. "Did she?" His head dipped, and his lips nuzzled her throat. His teeth scraped her earlobe. The moan this elicited made him smile. She felt it against her neck. His weight pressed her back into the padded bench. She was still inside out, that was the only explanation for the intensity of the sensation. Skin couldn't be this sensitive. Her undergarments felt as though they rubbed on raw nerves.

"Witch." His lips found her jaw. "Fairy."

She wanted his touch.

But he hadn't made a garland for her head. He had given her a black wig. The wild desire in his eyes was not for her but for that black-haired girl. She did not move a muscle, but she retreated nonetheless, fighting to detach herself from her shivering skin, from the tension gathering in her belly. Somehow, he sensed it. He was still attuned to her, interpreting cues so subtle she had barely formed the corresponding thoughts.

"Where did you go?" He pulled back, eyebrows lifted in question. "You know, I could learn from you. I always escaped the hell I was in by train, by boat, by gypsy caravan." His smile was enigmatic. He was teasing, but something deadly serious underlay his playful tone. "But you … " His fingers laced hers more tightly. "You just … float away."

She glanced down at their hands. His fingers were so exquisitely shaped, so sensitive, it was a shock to feel her fingers stretch to accommodate their width. They were so much larger than hers.

"Will you tell me why?" His smile had faded.

When she spoke, she found that her voice had dropped an octave. "I never had such means at my disposal. No Nile barges." She tried to smile. "Besides," she said hoarsely, "trains, boats … they don't help you escape from who you are."

His face changed. "Ella."

No. She pressed a finger to his lips, silencing him. His mouth was soft. The breath that hissed through his clenched teeth moistened her skin. *No.* He didn't see Ella. He didn't want Ella. And suddenly this fact no longer caused her pain. It was the very condition of her freedom. If she wasn't Ella, she could have him. They could press together—flesh and blood—and incarnate a fantasy, a make-believe love.

He caught her finger between his teeth, sucked it, his cheeks hollowing. The wet, gloving pressure made her gasp. She felt a twinge lower down. That night, if Phillipa hadn't been murdered, they would have done *this*. Sucked. Stroked. Phillipa had been reckless. Passionate.

She pushed off the seat so that their clasped hands were trapped between their bodies, flattened, her wrist straining. She pulled her finger down over his lower lip, down over his chin, skimming the length of his throat. She brought her lips up to his. Surprise made him growl against her mouth. She wrapped her arm around his neck, knotted her fingers in his hair. He kissed her, devouring her with teeth and tongue. With a ragged breath, he broke her grasp and caught her face between his hands.

"Decide." He grated out the word. "Decide now. I will take you to Trombly Place if you wish." He left the alternative unspoken. *Or …*

She could go home with him. She could share his bed.

He hovered over her, dark as shadow, but so dense, so heavy, inundating her with his heat. He smelled of smoke and peat and wool and that heady, tugging musk she couldn't define that made her want to twine her whole body around him, to sniff and suckle, to claw at his skin until she got inside. Heaven help her, she wanted to tear him to pieces. Wild. Like a beast. *Inhuman.* She would not let Alfred's voice intrude. There was no room for Alfred here.

She kissed him in answer. She opened her mouth, delved with her tongue. Deeply, yes. No timidity now. She wanted to force herself inside him. He yielded beneath her then pushed back, tilting her head up so he could slide his tongue over hers, filling her. His hand moved inside her cloak, working down beneath the taut red silk, stroking the slope of her breast. The roughness and the warmth of his caress made her shudder. He dragged his thumb down her cheek, along her jaw, callus scratching the flesh inside her lower lip.

Pretend. She was safe if they pretended. But, oh God, the light flicks of his tongue didn't feel like make-believe. His lips pressed against her temples, against the wet corners of her eyes, licking the salt.

She turned her face away sharply, breathing hard. Now his lips were in those shining black ringlets. *Yes. Like that.* Phillipa's crown of curls. It wasn't real. It wasn't her. She could let it happen. She fell against the panel of the coach, the rattling cold a relief.

Take Phillipa home.

His ragged breath was at her ear.

"You're with me now," he said. "Stay with me." She buried her face in his coat, clinging to him, humming deep in her throat so she wouldn't have to listen. She couldn't hear what he was saying. She didn't want to understand. She felt the pounding of his heart, heard only that beating. Flesh and blood, speaking to her, at last, without words.

Chapter Seventeen

He let himself into his house. The hall was dark. He'd given his staff the night off. He led her up the stairs. When they reached the top, he looked back at her.

"You're still there," he said, softly, wonderingly, foolishly. Of course she was still there. He held her hand in his, too tightly. He was grinding those delicate, bird-boned fingers. Becoming brutal in his haste. His eagerness. He lifted the hand and kissed her fingertips. The music they made could put the birds to shame.

He couldn't master the urgency that made his heart hammer in his chest. Now that he had her, he was afraid she would disappear. He backed into his bedchamber, never taking his eyes off her. The room was cool. The fire had dwindled to embers. Nonetheless, he helped her out of her cloak and threw it on the chair along with his coat and waistcoat. She wouldn't be cold for long. He lit the candles. She turned a circle on the carpet, looking around his room. He watched her. Was she gazing at his bed or trying to make out the title of the book on the bedside table? The shadows that hollowed her eyes made them seem even larger. She looked so fragile—an illusion, perhaps. Assurances, promises, again rose to his lips. But when she turned her gaze on him, he could only say, "Come here."

He reached for her, and she stepped forward into his arms. The rustle of her dress maddened him. One by one, he ripped the roses from the bodice. The sound she made was like the sound of the tearing silk. He slid his fingers along her collarbones and followed the edges of the bodice down, his two hands meeting at its lowest point. He let his fingers rest there, feeling the rise and fall of her breasts.

"I can't stand the sight of this dress," he murmured. He gripped the bodice and pulled his hands apart, splitting it down the middle, all the way to the waist. He pushed the two halves from her shoulders. Now her slender torso in its white undergarments rose from the masses of red and black silk. Aphrodite emerging from a sea of gore. Yes, he would burn the gown himself. He would buy Ella new gowns, silks silver as starlight. Green as moss. Forest shades. Colors Phillipa would never have worn.

Ella's dark eyes were wide open. Her lips were parted.

"I want to see you," he said. No gown was best. No fabrics padding and pinching, distorting her shape. Her hair loose around her face, her throat, her breasts. She caught his wrist as he felt for the pins holding the wig in place. The expression on her face didn't change. She looked mesmerized. Almost blank. He couldn't allow that. He couldn't let any part of her vanish, not by any means.

He fumbled with her lacings in his impatience. Almost reached for his knife to slice the corset from her body. The air sawed in and out of his lungs. There. He tugged skirts, crinolines, petticoats, corset, linens, down around her hips. She made no move to help him. She was watching his hands work with fascination.

He felt, suddenly, like a snake charmer. He didn't like it. He didn't want her hypnotized, pliant. He wanted to rouse her. He wanted to take her into his mouth, taste her, feel her break against him. *Communion.* Like the moment they'd shared in the coach, freezing, desperate, fiercely alive. He wanted this experience to feel like the sonata, give and take, sun and moon, joy and sorrow. He *would* rouse her. But first, he had to step back and look at her. Luminous. Darkness pooled in the hollow at the base of her neck, spilled along her collarbones and between her breasts, curving beneath, highlighting their pale swells. Her body was not symmetrical. Her hips were slightly uneven, the right riding higher, closer to the lower ribs. The dip of her waist was slightly shorter, shallower on that side. This irregularity moved him, queerly. He couldn't have predicted this hint of displacement in her contours, couldn't have composed her correctly in his mind with abstract formulae. He felt suddenly humbled before her, by her presence, frail, naked, mortal, facing him. Singular. For the briefest of moments, he had a glimmer of who he could become if he accepted her, if he carried, instead of guilt, the burden of love. Responsibility for another. Grief and jubilation mingled with his desire.

"You're beautiful," he whispered, closing the distance between them, grazing her nipples with his palms, sliding his hands down the smooth curve of her belly, veering just below her bellybutton to grasp her hips and pull her against him. She staggered, feet tangling in the puddle of ruined silks, and threw her arms around his neck to catch herself. He hoisted her, hooking her knees around his waist. She was panting, wiggling to get free, and he cupped her soft, full buttocks, holding her firmly, grinding the sensitive folds between her legs against his arousal. He looked down into her face. She wasn't watching any longer. Her eyelids fluttered; the deep, rosy indentation of her upper lip held a bead of sweat. In two strides, he deposited her on the bed.

He put a knee on either side of her, pressing kisses to her throat, sliding his head to her breasts. He kneaded them, forcing them up, kissing the damp creases beneath. He closed his teeth on her nipple, teased it with his breath, his tongue. She arched against him. He kept his palm flat against her breast and found the rim of her ear with his tongue. The black curls tickled his nose. They didn't smell like her. The wig had been scented with citrus in the shop. His nostrils flared. He wanted to inhale *her* only, not scent, not soap, just the salty-sweet essence of her skin. He dug his fingers into the chignon. Her arm shot up. She was trying to pull away his hand.

He hadn't expected it—this particular battle—but he knew how to rout her. He caught her bicep, kissed the tensed muscle, and bent her arm back, kissing the hollow inside her elbow. He pushed her arm down to the bed, trapping it above her. He kissed her forehead, her eyelids, her cheekbones, parted her lips with his tongue, sweeping the silken inner flesh. Ah, now her tongue followed his, entered him, mouth opening fully. He broke the kiss, face hovering an inch above hers.

"Open your eyes." He meant to coax her, but the words emerged as a command. Nothing. The lids didn't lift. He let go of the arm and inched himself backwards, pressing kisses between her breasts, down the curve of her belly. He laid his hands on her thighs, felt them shiver. He dug into the flesh of their inner slopes with his thumbs. As he moved his hands up, she squeezed her legs together.

"Do you want me to stop?" Nothing. She was breathing quick, shallow breaths. He spread her thighs, roughly, wide enough to fit a knee between. Then the other. He splayed her. Feasted his eyes on the sight, the darker flesh glistening. Like glimpsing a fruit in a briar. He pressed his palm to her, felt the pickling heat, the softness beneath. She gasped. Her eyes snapped open.

"Ella," he said, rubbing, giving her this broad, crude pressure: a chord in the key of the finer melody he was preparing to play. Now. He stroked with his thumb. As he flicked the nub at the top of her moistening folds, her upper lip lifted in a snarl. *Yes.* She was fighting her way back through the mists. *Here.* He slid a finger partway inside her, groaning aloud as the wet passage constricted. She jerked up, and he pushed her chest with the heel of his hand, pinning her with his weight. He slid the finger deeper, rubbed harder with his thumb, forcing her legs farther apart with his knees. He wanted to lower his head to taste the slick skin, but he couldn't. Not yet. He had to watch her as her head tipped back. He saw a flash of white as her eyes rolled toward the ceiling.

"Look at me." She didn't meet his eyes, but her gaze followed his hand as he removed his finger. He could work with that. He smiled slightly, lifting his hand, sliding the finger into his mouth. His mouth flooded. Rich, coppery. *Blood.* Her eyes flitted to his. Did she read his surprise? Confusion slowed him. He lost focus as his mind raced, and he lost her in that moment. Her gaze fell; she took a deep, steadying breath. He felt her limbs stiffening. *Goddamn it.* He leaned over her, pushing two fingers inside, noticing now the narrowness, so slippery, but so tight. She struggled to rise. He dropped his face to her breast, bit her nipple, hard enough to make her gasp. He pressed up with his fingers, searching for the sensitive, roughed patch … She bucked against him. Moaned, sweet and wild. The urgency of the cry ignited the passion he'd tried so hard to bank, to keep at a low smolder. He slid his arm beneath her back, lifted her into a sitting position. Her weight drove her down on his fingers. She rode him, thrashing her head from side to side. He lowered her upper body slightly, her buttocks sliding up, resting just above his knees. Her bent legs butterflied, opened wider. His wrist burned with the angle, wedged between them. Again he moved his fingertips, working the ridged center inside her. A short cry burst from her. Sharp. Staccato. He gritted his teeth as her convulsive movement sent a tremor through his legs to his groin.

Her head hung back, the wig askew. A glimmer of fair hair peeked out, slanting across her forehead. He had always fancied that her beauty was like the moon, mutable, shifting its portion of light and shadow. It was true; she could dim herself to a sliver. She could slip behind a cloud.

"Don't hide from me." There was more he wanted to say. *I want all of you.* But the constriction in his throat didn't allow speech. His words became motions. He thrust his fingers rhythmically inside her, and she jolted. He couldn't wait any longer. He pulled her up so her chin ground into his shoulder. He gripped the back of her neck, buried his fingers in the wig, and yanked. The pins that held it in place had loosened, but a few silvery strands of her hair still went with them. Pale, drifting, like spider silk. He threw the wig from the bed, surging with a triumph so strong, so primal, he nearly spurted. Restraint *hurt*. He cupped the back of her skull, turning her head, claiming her lips. She was whimpering into his mouth. He felt the first contraction grip his fingers, the pulse of her pleasure. She shuddered, and he pulled her head back, exposing her face, her features blurring, straining, mouth opening wide. He hungered for this, this moment. *She looked at me as she did love.* The horror in her eyes froze the blood in his veins. Her sweet moan changed pitch, became a wail. She kicked, clawed, and he let her break free, too stunned to hold her. She scrambled back on the bed, huddled against the headboard, knees drawn up, face pressed into them, arms crossed, knuckles white where she gripped her own elbows. Her body twitched. Shook.

He was sweating beneath his clothing, and the air made his skin feel clammy. He struggled to quiet his breathing. It sounded harsh in his ears. Shock, disappointment, concern, and self-reproach warred within him. He approached her slowly, as though she were a wild creature that might startle.

"Ella," he whispered, stroking the nape of her neck, fingers sliding into her hair to massage her scalp. "Talk to me."

• • •

His caress was as soft as his voice. She couldn't endure either. Her body still thrummed. She wanted to wiggle, scream, burst out of her skin. *Biting and knocking.* Oh God. What was happening to her? *Excitation of the nerves. Loss of voluntary movement.* She dug her fingernails into her skin. She clamped down on her tongue so hard she tasted blood. No good. She could still feel it, the fluttering between her thighs. Her calves were cramped. At any moment, this tingling would reach her brain. Inflaming her white matter. *Deranging that portion of the nervous center that governs intelligence and sensibility.* She had the same vertiginous feeling she recognized as the precursor to her fits. The abyss yawning open.

First, volition fled. Then consciousness.

For a delirious interval, she had almost imagined she *was* Phillipa. She was Isidore Blackwood's beloved, responding to his lips, his fingers. His tenderness was her right. His touch *worshipped* her, and she gloried in it. The sensation that flooded her was sanctified. She rolled with the waves, her body light, undulate, floating on the surface. Then everything changed. Feeling overwhelmed her. She was tempest-tossed, battered. She couldn't catch her breath. The sediment stirred in her blood. Madness crested through her.

The arches of her feet had spasmed with the force of it. Her face ... it must have become livid. Had he glimpsed it? Had it appalled him?

Her disease transformed sweetness into savagery. Pleasure into violence. And she had *craved* it. For the first time, she had wanted to lose control. She had nearly surrendered, nearly seized in his arms.

"Leave." It was absurd of her—she couldn't banish him from his own bedchamber—but she said it again, her voice oddly high-pitched. "Leave me, *please*." Panic closed her throat. A fit was coming, and he sat on the bed beside her, fingers tugging gently through her hair. He would see what she became. She shuddered, waiting for the disorientation, the blinding pain, but the fit did not take her. The signs had lied. She gulped air noisily.

"I should have stopped." He stroked her arm from shoulder to elbow. "When I realized ... " He paused, knuckles resting on the curve of her neck.

She tensed.

"You're a virgin," he said. She raised her head. His eyes were brilliant. Grave.

She almost laughed at his simplicity, but the sound lodged in her throat like a sob. Should she admit that she hadn't spared a thought for her virginity? That she had been imagining herself a ghost's vessel in a marriage bed that never was?

"I frightened you."

"No." She shifted, raising her shoulders slightly and, when his gaze fell, remembered that she was naked. She hunched, pressing her breasts against her thighs. What did virginity matter to her? A fallen woman is still a woman. She was different. She transformed into a beast.

"You're frightened of yourself." He tilted his head, the promontory of his cheekbone rising. "The way you hold yourself … the way you move … " He smiled faintly. "You walk as though your body's a hired conveyance that you find uncomfortable. You'd jump out of it if you could."

She'd never imagined that her very steps betrayed her.

"I walk with one foot in front of the other." *Too defensive, Ella.* Her tone was sharp. "It's hardly worth remarking."

"You think about every gesture you make." He said it slowly, trying to penetrate her with his gaze, to see inside her. "Such discipline. Such self-command." His voice burred with amusement. He stroked her arm again, and her breath caught. "I haven't been able to figure it out. Why you need to soldier yourself through the world. What battle you're fighting beneath your own skin. Why you want to be other than who you are."

Her skin was shivering under his touch. Whatever battle she was fighting, she was losing now.

"I thought you'd been mistreated by a lover."

"I have no lover." His look made her want to run. It was suddenly predatory.

"You *had* no lover," he said softly. "You're here with me, now. In my bed. You, Ella." *No pretending otherwise.* He didn't have to say it. Somewhere on the carpet that black wig lay like a dead animal. "You're here," he said, fiercely now, as though he needed to convince them both. His hand came up to cup her face. Warm palm against her chin. Fingertips on her cheekbone. "You're beautiful."

He had said that before, when he ripped away the gown. She had accepted it then, because she told herself it wasn't her he was seeing. Now she couldn't bear the words. She shook her head.

"There's something ugly inside me." Her voice was hoarse. It was the closest to a confession she could come. He didn't contradict her. He nodded.

"You can't have one without the other." He leaned over, brushing her lips with his. "Intense experience makes them flow together. Or so you said to me."

She shut her eyes, felt his hot breath, then the pressure of his lips against her eyelids.

"I want all of you," he whispered. "That's the beauty I mean. Beauty and ugliness both."

She opened her eyes. All of her. Damaged. Tainted. She felt the midnight blue of his gaze like a touch.

"Don't hold anything back."

It seemed unfair to her then, that he should challenge her like this when he sat fully clothed in his own bed, daring nothing. She rose to her knees, tugged at his collar.

"Take this off." Anger made her voice guttural, made her gestures even clumsier. He bowed his head, black wings of hair falling across his face as he unbuttoned his shirt.

The sudden fury that goaded her fled as she beheld the lean lines of his torso, the ridges of muscle contracting as he drew in his breath. She traced the shadows that limned each muscle in his abdomen, scratched her fingernail down from his belly button, fascinated by the dark trail of hair. He made a strangled noise. She laid her hands on the hot, smooth skin of his arms. He felt hard as metal, but molten. As she considered this paradox, his sinews knotted. He reached for her. She brushed his hands away, gratified that he let them fall. Submitting to her.

"More." Her audacity acted like a tonic. She was giddy, issuing demands. But she couldn't bring herself to fumble with his trousers. He had to undo the buttons, tug them off. "Dear God," she breathed. *This* was ugly, the length of muscle that protruded from the dark curls between his thighs. Somehow she'd imagined this part on a man would be different. It was so animal. Thick. Veined.

Her eyes flew to his face. He looked wary, grim, reading, no doubt, the judgment in her stunned expression.

"Both." She got out that one syllable, and he raised a questioning brow before his face cleared, and he grinned that crooked grin.

Both. Not ugly. Not beautiful. Something else, the two together, more than either.

He pulled her against him, and she gasped. The friction of skin against skin. Satiny heat. The solidity of his arms closing around her. She slid her hands down the slabs of muscle stretched taut over his ribs, felt the angular jut of his hipbones, thumbs brushing the dampness of the curling hairs that thickened beneath. Another inch and she would touch the base of it. But he didn't let her. His lips teased her throat as he bent her backwards. He lowered her to the bed, and she slid her hand up, clung to his shoulders. His broad body covered her, heavy, squeezing the air from her lungs, that hard length digging into her thigh, and then he was up on elbows and knees, crawling backwards, silky strands of his hair tickling as he moved lower and lower.

She wound her fingers in his hair, trapping his head against her belly. She felt him smile against her skin, the wetness of his teeth, then the shocking probe of his tongue into her navel. She tightened her hands in his hair, but he reached up for her wrists and with just the pressure of thumbs and forefingers made her release. Light kisses, licks—he continued to explore her, his hands now pushing her thighs apart.

She clutched the blanket. His breath blew hot *there,* in that spot his fingers had already tortured. She couldn't endure it, not again, she would shatter this time. She had barely held on to her sanity. *I want all of you.* He'd said it, but he didn't know what all meant. If he struck deep enough, he would find the rot. The putrefaction would billow up. She couldn't allow it.

"Isidore."

His murmured response was accompanied by a rush of air. Her mind went blank as her flesh kindled. She arched in protest, but this movement brought her into contact with his mouth. He made a pleased sound that she *felt* vibrating down her thighs and up into her belly, a buzzing in her flesh that had to be madness itself. His hands slid under her bottom, keeping her pressed against his lips. He was sucking her, licking her, and she writhed, twisted, fought to get away, before it was too late, before the tension that was coiling around the sudden pressure of his tongue became unbearable, before her reason broke and she ceded her humanity and howled.

"I can't … " She gasped. "I can't … "

He dragged his head from her, but now his fingers … Oh God, the madness was pushing into the center of her being, and this was worse, far worse, because he was watching her, his mouth glistening, his eyes locked on her face.

She put her knuckles into her mouth and bit hard, covering her eyes with the other hand. Sounds came out of her throat she'd never heard. Mewing, sobbing, rasping sounds. She felt his teeth close on her earlobe as his fingers thrust to her very core. She wasn't going to convulse, she was going to explode.

He pulled her hand from her eyes as the buzzing became a keening, high and wild, the noise of her nerves, her tissues, her blood, and she was crying out with it, jerking helplessly, as the ugliness burst from her. Her body heaved and heaved again, opening and closing, rippling with something beyond her control. It wasn't pain. It was as powerful as pain, but it was the opposite. She had moved through pain into this sweeter, hotter fire. She tried to breathe, still trembling, his weight against her side, his hand buried between her legs. She could feel herself beating around his fingers, as though her heart were suddenly lower in her body.

The ripples were subsiding, and she felt delicious, swollen with sweetness. It wasn't like a seizure after all. The moment of peril had felt the same, the leap into darkness seemed also to threaten with annihilation, but the descent was different. It was like a dream of falling, and suddenly she could fly.

There wasn't less of her returning. There was more of her. She had lost control, but she had gained something else. Trust. In her body. In him.

"Breathe, my love." He kissed her throat. "You can breathe."

Chapter Eighteen

Ella lay curled in bed, on her side, knees bent. She often slept in that position, protecting herself, conserving her warmth. This morning, though, her knees pressed the back of Isidore's thighs. Her arm wrapped his side; his arm crossed hers. She wiggled closer, nestling the hard curve of his buttocks against her belly. Her lips rested in the hot groove beneath his shoulder blade. She'd slept without dreaming. She woke knowing exactly where she was.

She let her breath puff out so her lips opened, and she tasted the salts on his skin. She tried to memorize the feeling. Time was running out. The clock hands were moving forward. The clock hands were like iron bars, levering them apart. Soon it would be over. She shifted, drawing her arm down, exploring. Her hand descended the ladder of his ribs, dropped into the taut, steep valley between rib and hip. She slid her fingers around his hip, dipped her fingertips into the depression beneath the bone then down the ridged muscles of his stomach. She bumped the silky, hard length of him and felt it twitch. She jerked her hand away, flushing. He rolled over, tipping her onto her back and coming up on his other side to look down at her. Somehow, she kept herself from pulling the covers over her head.

His hair was tousled, his eyes heavy-lidded but alert. Stubble darkened his jaw. The lazy smile on his lips made it start again, that beating between her legs.

"My dear Ella," he drawled. "Were you ravishing me as I slept?"

Her face had to be crimson—purple, even—with embarrassment. But her curiosity was whetted. Why not satisfy it? She'd come too far to turn back. The remembrance of these hours she spent with him—she would cleave to it during the lonely years to come. It would be a balm and not a torment. She wouldn't long for what she couldn't have. Instead she'd think fondly on what she once—albeit briefly—possessed.

"I don't know," she said breathlessly. "Were you asleep?"

His eyes glinted. "No."

She rolled onto her side too, inching toward him, pushing her leg between his so that they fit together.

"And what exactly," she whispered, "constitutes a ravishment?" She had one image in her head for a ravished man, a god, really. It came from the first poem she'd read that she hadn't wanted to discuss with her papa. "The Vine" by Robert Herrick. The speaker dreamed his mortal part became a vine and writhed all around his beloved.

So that my Lucia seemed to me
Young Bacchus ravished by his tree.

She twined her leg around his and wound her arms around his neck.

"That depends on you." She heard the catch in his voice. His smile had faded. *It* twitched again, and she felt the movement high against her hip.

"Do you control it?" she asked.

"Do I control what?" he asked, dryly.

"This." She worked her hand between their bodies and touched it, deliberately this time. "Your … mortal part."

His eyebrows shot up. "Mortal part? Ah, yes, of course." He cleared his throat. "Mortal part." He couldn't suppress the low rumble of laughter. "I've never heard that one. Your coinage?"

"Herrick," she muttered. "What do you call it then?" She curled her thumb and forefinger around it, and he gasped. As though being … ravished. She smiled up at him, pleased with herself. He wasn't laughing anymore.

His voice was husky. "Cock."

She tightened her grip. "How do you make it … stand?" She slid her fingers down to the soft, heavy base, cupping it. The hot skin slid over the roundness within.

He gritted his teeth. "Inside every man's body," he rasped, "there is a system of pulleys ... "

She giggled, and suddenly she was on her back. He was braced on his arms above her.

"What else do you want to know?" he asked softly. His face was serious.

She looked up into his eyes and saw the fierce emotion that burned there.

"Everything," she said, and his gaze grew hotter. He lowered himself so he lay full upon her, his weight so welcome she gave a little cry of triumph, pressing the muscles of his back, wanting him to drive her even harder into the mattress, wanting their bodies crushed together. He slid down to suckle her breast, pulling the coverlet and sheets back with him, and the sweet, tugging feeling—like a tide moving out, rolling from the crown of her head to her toes—stunned her with its familiarity. God, she wanted this, but what if she was growing to need it? *Worry after. Worry when it's gone.* She touched his hair, and as she ran her fingers over his ears, she felt the difference between them: the one rounded on top, the other truncated, cartilage slanting at a steep angle. Lopped. What had happened to mangle him so? Then he moved lower, and she stopped thinking coherently. His hands swept her hips, her thighs, kneading her, stroking her. There was a thump; he'd gone over the side of the bed. He knelt on the carpet, flicked away the sheets, gripped her ankles, and took her toes into his mouth. It tickled, and she gave an involuntary cry—loud, far too loud—something between a laugh and a gasp. He kissed his way up her calves, climbing back onto the bed, nuzzling between her thighs. His new growth of beard scratched the delicate skin. He lifted his head, and their eyes met. No smile on his face. Nothing soft. Raw desire. Blazing joy. He lowered his head, and she reared as she felt the slow, long lick. He was on all fours, muscles bunched in his arms as he leaned in, pushed with his tongue. She released a shuddering breath.

"Please," she gasped. He stroked upward, and she rolled her hips helplessly, no longer sure if she was trying to ease herself by escaping his lips or by pressing harder against them. Again he stroked, and again, and sensation shivered out from that pulsing center. She moaned, and he rose to fit his mouth on hers, swallowing the sound, drinking in her cries. His lips tasted odd, tasted faintly of the sea, and she knew this must be *her* taste and part of her marveled.

He lay between her legs, and when she lifted her hips she felt his cock rubbing that spot, which still quivered, still throbbed.

"Ella," he said, and she realized her eyes were closed. She opened them and looked up at the brilliant blue, his gaze focused, burning. "We can stop."

We. Her hunger intensified because it was his hunger as well. *Our hunger.* She kissed him, but this wasn't answer enough. He gripped her face, thumb lifting her chin.

"There may be pain," he said, as though warning her, but this was the one thing she already knew for sure. Pain had been her constant companion. With him, the pain changed. It was no longer isolating. It was as though they shared one fever, one wound.

"Yes," she said and raked her fingers down his back, digging her nails into the hard curves of his buttocks. His body was thick and heavy as a tree, pinning her to the bed. He shifted, and the blunt pressure between her legs became acute. No vine, this. No tendril, no unfurling fern. There was nothing supple or yielding about it. *Her* flesh had to yield, had to split to accommodate the length and girth of him. She panted, tensing. It wouldn't work. It couldn't.

"Open," he whispered, hands on her breast, tongue on her ear, tracing the rim. He meant her eyes; he meant her mouth; he meant *there* where he pressed; he meant everything.

"Ah," she gasped, and he moved his hips. His cock slid deeper, stretching her, filling her. He groaned as it sank to the hilt, his hipbones pressing her thighs apart. She bit savagely at his shoulder, sucked his neck, and twisted her lower body. Her flesh was *around* him. She contained him, his heat, his hardness, and as she let her breath rush out so she could take even more of him inside, he began to push. His movements were gentle at first, the friction making her sigh, making her press her knees to his sides, rising and falling along with his rhythm. His face was tilted down; he was watching their joined bodies surge together. He liked what he saw. His face was flushed, lips parted. She shuddered, and his eyes locked on hers. He caught her hands, pressed them up above her head, and trapped them with his forearm, his other hand closing on her breast then sliding down to caress the heated junction of their bodies. The flick of his fingers made her cry out. She bucked under him, almost sobbing, the fullness leaving no room for anything inside her but him. He thrust faster now, harder, his groans mingling with her cries. His teeth mashed her lips, tongue sliding deep into her mouth. She was inundated, spilling around him, unable to hold anything inside her anymore but unable to wiggle away, to free herself. Suddenly all the sensation in her body contracted into a knot, pulling tighter, tighter. She strained against him. She moaned and burst, broke into pieces, her skull shattering, rib cage exploding, his pumping buttocks sending more and more heat shooting through her. His body went rigid, cords in his neck standing out, and he rolled from her, burying himself in the bed with a shuddering groan.

She caught her breath, staring up unseeingly, skin tingling, inner thighs sore. He too had lost himself in that moment; she had seen it in his face. They had both been subsumed in the motion, the merging force of flesh made one. She didn't realize her lips had curved until she heard his inhalation. He was propped on his elbow, staring at her.

"Your smile … " He touched the flat of her chest, followed her collarbone to her shoulder. "What it does to me."

He pulled her against him. She was lulled by the gentle movement of his broad chest, by the heat emanating from his densely muscled limbs. Their breathing fell into rhythm.

She stirred first. The longer she indulged herself, the more difficult it would be to tear herself away. She heard footsteps in the hall. The servants would know what had happened. There was no way around it. But she shouldn't be caught in his arms.

"Ella," he said as she pulled away and sat up, clutching the sheet to her throat. She looked down at him but gained no sense of power from the perspective. Even stretched out naked, limbs relaxed, he seemed ready to command an army. His hand wandered to her thigh and rested there. He drew his brows together. He rose to sitting and took her by the shoulders. "I'm going to say it all wrong. You … " He paused. "That is … I … "

"You don't have to say anything." She cut her eyes toward the door. She willed herself to stand, to leave the bed. It was impossible to guess the hour. The shutters on the windows were closed. The room smelled thick: his musk, sweat, the sea. *Remember everything. No regrets.* She didn't move.

"This is new to me." He stroked her hair back then held a lock between his fingers, turning it this way and that as though it were something wondrous. A miracle.

"Stop," she said. "Please." Whatever jealousy had rankled in her heart, she couldn't bear to listen to him speak as though Phillipa never were. There was no honor in it. "It isn't necessary. This was what it was."

His face was setting into grim lines. "Was?"

She made her face blank, her voice crisp. "You can trust that I'll make no demands on you. I don't consider anything changed. I will perform the séance. You will help me find a suitable position." She looked at the strong column of his throat, watched his Adam's apple move up and down. "We are united by that arrangement. Nothing else. I'm not a romantic."

"Like hell you're not."

Startled, she lifted her eyes. He smiled his mocking half smile.

"You're as romantic as they come," he said. "You're as wild as a deer. You're as elusive as a song." His voice dropped to a seductive murmur. "You open like a rose."

Now *she* was spellbound. She tried to shake her head. He laid a finger on her lips.

"You were made for ecstasies," he whispered.

Ecstasies. Fits of pleasure. But there were other kinds. Her eyes clouded.

"You still mistrust," he said. "Lie here with me a little longer." He leaned back into the pillows.

She hesitated.

"Please, Ella."

She couldn't resist him. *A little longer.* She settled her head on his shoulder.

"I want to tell you about Phillipa," he said. She bit her lip, stiffening. She had waited for this, had wanted it, and now she felt as though the air had been knocked out of her.

"I loved her," he said. "I loved her with all my heart." He paused. She tried to regulate her breathing. In, out. In, out. Whatever he had to say she would bear it. She nodded and laid her arm across his chest. Yes. She could listen to the story of their love. She begrudged Phillipa nothing.

"We were like brother and sister," he said, and she felt a queer tension grip her. He continued haltingly, as if each syllable was being dragged from him. "I agreed to marry her because she was pregnant." Ella pulled away to look at him. He met her eyes steadily, the words hanging between them.

"She was pregnant with another man's child," he said slowly. "He refused to have her." Hatred twisted his features. Those grim lines scored his countenance. Making it haggard. Lupine.

She felt dizzy. "You couldn't ... force him?" The image rose in her mind: Isidore with dueling pistols in the mist of the morning.

Preposterous. How could he force a man to marry? But she knew that he would have tried. Emotions roiled within her. Admiration for his loyalty. And something like relief. *Brother and sister.* Not lovers.

He slid up and leaned against the headboard.

"I would have had to force *her* first." His hands were clenched into fists. "Force her to reveal his name. And I could not bring myself to threaten her. Not until that night. The night she died." He shut his eyes, grief replacing the violence in his face.

If she kissed him, perhaps she could silence him and spare him these painful memories. His lips were compressed, stark creases around his mouth cutting from nose to chin. But that would be distraction. A short flight from the bitter reality. She fought the impulse to bend toward him. She wouldn't help him flee. She would help him face the pain. She owed him that.

He opened his eyes. "She told me he'd agreed to run away with her. Paris, of course. She was very excited, drunk and excited, more animated than I'd seen her in weeks. *He* was jealous, she said, of our engagement." He laughed, the blackest sound Ella had ever heard. "I was a fool. When she first came to me and confessed everything, I thought she'd given up hope of him. I should have known better. Reasoning with Phillipa was like reasoning with a thunderhead. She was a force of nature. She never gave up. She hadn't resigned herself to becoming my bride. She'd hoped the announcement of our betrothal would goad *him* into action. In a sense, she was right."

She could hear the awful sound of his teeth grinding together. She reached out and touched the edges of his hair hesitantly, pushed a lock from his brow.

"He didn't know that Phillipa told you the truth?" she asked softly. "That you were not his rival?"

"A hoodwinked lover was more to Phillipa's purpose than a loyal brother." He shrugged. "Part of her throve on intrigue. She liked to manipulate, to provoke confrontations. She was always maneuvering, always pushing everything and everyone to the limit." He looked at her, brows knitted together.

"Believe me when I say I don't think it was a flaw in her. In different circumstances … " He opened his hands, turned them palm up, stared into them.

"She didn't have enough scope for her movements," he said. "Her theater of operations was so small. Society stifled her. She should have been born a man and gone into the navy. She was a swashbuckler by nature. Brilliant, as well. She might have been a Nelson." His face softened. Some fond memory was slipping in amongst all the horrors.

He shook his head. "She sounded like a deluded child that night. She was elated. Spouting the kind of nonsense she would have jeered at if she'd heard it from another woman. Infatuation, or wounded pride, made her too eager to trust in empty promises. Her sense of strategy deserted her. Run away to Paris! With nothing to hold him accountable. He would have dallied with her and left her a humiliated exile nursing a bastard." His jaw clenched again.

"So you tried to stop her."

His bleak gaze spoke volumes. "I'd never lost my temper with her before, but I did then. I cursed. I yelled. I swore I wouldn't let her out of my sight, that I'd haul her back by the hair. She ran from the room, and I tripped chasing, fell, maybe even blacked out. I was that drunk."

She almost flinched away from the self-loathing in his eyes. But he would interpret such a gesture as condemnation. He would think she reviled him as he reviled himself, and she could not allow that. She took his hand by the thumb, pulled it against her leg, and clung to it.

Young, handsome, rich. She understood now Isidore's description of the murderer.

"Why did he kill her?" she breathed.

For a long moment, Isidore stared into space. Then he shook himself and spoke. "Maybe he spotted us together going up the stairs. His jealousy became a rage."

"He refused to marry her." She was trying to remain calm, to act as Isidore's anchor, but a hint of the same fury and contempt that marked his face edged her voice. "He had no right to jealousy. What other option did he leave her but to wed immediately?"

The question required no answer. He didn't give one.

"Maybe she listened to me. Maybe she confronted him and said she wouldn't go. Maybe she insulted him. Laughed in his face. Ridiculed him. She enjoyed stormy scenes. I don't know." He pulled his hand away to scrub violently at his face. He had paled. "I was a beast to her. The last thing she heard from me I shouted in anger."

She couldn't let him speak so. "A beast? How can you think it? You would have married her *knowing* … " Her heart clutched as she considered the enormity of it. He would have claimed her child as his own. If she had borne a son … She stared at him. "You would have claimed another man's son as your heir."

"*Her* son," he said. "*Her* son would have been my heir." He laughed. "The end of the Blackwood line. I relished the idea."

It couldn't be that simple. He was stubborn, refusing to acknowledge the sacrifice. She wasn't fooled. She kept her eyes on him. "Not many men would do such a thing."

"I don't deserve that look," he said gruffly. "I'm not a hero in this. She used to call me her black knight. But *she* was the knight. I owed her, not the other way around." He took a breath, as though debating whether or not to continue. "I betrayed her once, out of cowardice." He said this last almost defiantly, glaring. *Admire me now. I dare you.* She would take that dare, and gladly.

She settled back against his shoulder. "Tell me."

"You know that I lived near the Tromblys as a child?"

"Yes." She smiled faintly. "Louisa told me she'd known you since you were a boy."

"My father did not approve of the friendship." His voice was eerily flat. She felt a cold lump forming in her stomach.

"What objection could he have?" she murmured. She heard the sneer in his reply.

"Objection? The Trombly fortune was made in living memory. Michael is a businessman. Louisa is Irish on her mother's side. My father could marshal any number of objections. The main one was that I was happy when I was with them."

She pressed her cheek harder against his chest, moved her body even closer to his, knowing no other way to give comfort. His arm came around her.

"Go on," she said.

"It was Christmas Eve. Holidays were … gruesome with my father. I felt my loneliness even more keenly. He never allowed me a fire in my room. He thought I should be impervious to cold, to damp, to everything, really. 'Blackwoods do not bend,' he'd say. That December was frigid. I climbed out of my window and ran through the woods to Trombly House. I thought I could creep back after dark, that he wouldn't notice I was gone. I was playing snapdragon with the girls when he came for me. I remember it so clearly. We were in the darkened parlor, flinging the flaming raisins into our mouths. Arabella was terrible at it. She'd start yelling before her fingers reached the bowl. The one time she grabbed a raisin she shrieked and threw it, not toward her own mouth, but away. The raisin lodged in Phillipa's hair. We were all screaming, laughing until the tears rolled down our cheeks. At that moment, I heard my father in the hall. He rarely left our property, and nothing but wrath could have induced him to set foot in that house. The parlor door opened. The cold air clung to my father's cloak. He hadn't bothered to remove it. In his mind, the Tromblys were beneath contempt. Louisa stood shrinking beside him. What could she do? She had no claim to me. And he was terrifying. I remember looking at the last blue flame winking in the bowl as the brandy burnt off and then at my father's face. His eyes were bright as those blue flames but so cold, so very cold. He could turn your blood to ice."

Goose bumps had risen on her skin as he spoke. She couldn't suppress a shiver. He lifted the sheet and tucked it around her shoulder, smoothing it down beneath her chin. This gentle gesture was so at odds with his grim monotone.

"How old were you?" she asked.

"Eleven." His voice was tightening. "Phillipa was only seven. But she tugged at my arm. She whispered to me. She said I didn't have to go with him. She said her father would protect me. I rose anyway, but she was quicker than I was. She was at the doorway in an instant. No one ever stood up to my father. It was unthinkable. But she put her tiny body between us, and she looked right into his face. 'Isidore wants to stay with us,' she said."

He fell silent, struggling with himself. Ella waited.

"My father didn't so much as glance at her. He fixed me with those eyes, and he asked me if it was true. Did I want to stay with them. And I said no. I left with him and without even looking at her. I didn't have the courage to stand by a girl of seven. I hated him, but I was his creature. That night, he had a fire built in the parlor, and we played snapdragon. He made me kneel, and he held my hand in the flames."

She wanted to weep, but what good would her tears do for that little boy on his knees, suffering in that long-ago winter? The skin of his hands must have reddened, blistered, blackened. He must have screamed for mercy and hated himself for it all the more. She was mute.

"She never mentioned that night to me." His voice, so close to breaking, held. "But I never forgot. How brave she was for my sake. How I failed her."

"It's easier to be brave when you're loved." She swallowed hard. "Phillipa was surrounded by love. You had no one."

"I had her after that," he said. "And you're right. It was easier."

In the silence that intervened, she listened to his heart, steady and strong. His life was precious to her. She wanted to make things easier for him, brighter, more joyful. But she wasn't fashioned to bring happiness. Ah, but it was a cruel thing, their meeting. She wasn't sorry, wouldn't be sorry. But it was cruel, cruel, cruel.

"Your mother … " She didn't know what she wanted to ask.

"Died in childbirth along with the babe. I wasn't six."

"But you remember her."

"I remember her," he said. "She was dark-haired and gentle. And sad."

Of course. She would have to have been sad married to such a man. But she would have known happiness as well, in Isidore.

She said: "The fact of your existence must have comforted her."

He breathed out heavily, almost a sigh. "She would come into the nursery and weep by the window. I would try to get her attention, but she wouldn't look at me. It was as though she didn't see me. Sometimes, if I clung to her long enough, she would touch my head and sing. Sometimes she would play for me."

Until my father smashed her violin. She was spinning now. It was too much to comprehend, the sorrow and the violence. How had Isidore survived? How could he reach out to another human with tenderness? As if he listened to her thoughts, his fingers slid through her hair, a soothing motion.

"Louisa gave me a violin after my mother died so I could practice with Phillipa. I used to play in the woods and pretend my mother could hear me. One day … the groundskeeper told my father."

She made a strangled noise, her throat constricting. "He cut your ear."

"For my own good," he said. "To keep me from womanly pursuits."

"What makes a man so vicious?" she whispered.

"Tradition." His fingers paused in their stroking. "It's the Blackwood way. I saw the scars once on my father's chest. Each the size of a farthing. I've thought often of how long you'd have to hold a cheroot against the skin to burn a mark so large ... " His fingers tightened, straining her hair at the roots. At her sharply indrawn breath, he relaxed his hand.

"Christ," he swore and lifted her off him. She knelt by his side, watching him, aching at the misery in his eyes.

"I hurt people," he said, with finality. "I am a Blackwood through and through."

"You're a Blackwood." She looked into his blue eyes, which must be so like his father's. He was born of Blackwood blood and had suffered for it. She knew what it was like to suffer from an accident of birth. "You can decide what that means," she said. "You don't have to be the same kind of Blackwood. And you're not." She said it fiercely. "I *know* you. You're ... " She stopped, gulped, shook her head wordlessly. Tears threatened to fall.

"What?" He was looking at her strangely.

The man I love.

She buried her face in her hands. He sat up and gathered her against his chest.

"Shhhh." His lips brushed her temple, nipped the rim of her ear, and pressed there, seeping warmth.

"You help me believe it," he said. The strength of his embrace made her bones creak, and then she melted into it.

"Come," he said at last, roughly, kissing the top of her head. "That's enough talk before breakfast. You must be hungry. How do you feel about ham?"

• • •

Isidore fetched the breakfast tray himself. He wanted to protect Ella from the stares of the footman. It meant that he exposed himself to the stares of Mrs. Potts. The good woman passed him in the hall outside the kitchen with an odd, abrupt signal, as though warding off evil. He nodded cautiously, and she spun on her heel.

"You'll do right, my lord, I'm sure," she said. She wasn't sure at all. Her chins were quivering.

"Yes, Mrs. Potts," he said, with a docility that surprised her.

"Well." She snapped her mouth shut and bustled off to strike fear in the dust. The rhythmic jingle of her keys underscored her words. Do right. Do right. Do right. He *would* do right, or die trying.

When he reentered his bedchamber with the tray, Ella was sitting at the table with Xenophon open. She was wearing the robe he'd put out for her. It was very plain, gray wool; she'd tucked one side tightly behind the other and cinched it with the sash. A nun might have worn such a garb without complaint. Her hair was still loose, hanging down her back like a spill of light. She looked up and smiled. His pulse accelerated. What unexpected pleasure, this. To open the door to his chamber and see her, wrapped in his clothing, curled up with a book, waiting for him, looking at him as though she were happier now that he was there.

He felt as though whatever rush of excited blood made his cock "stand," as she put it, was now doing the same thing to his heart. Dear God, an erection of the heart. This was why he was not a poet. He grinned stupidly, and she didn't seem to mind. Two thoughts came to him simultaneously.

He could have this every day.

He wanted this every day.

Greed made him rush to her and set down the tray with an inexpert crash.

"Eggs, toast, ham, coffee." He arranged the plates and silver on the table. She pounced on the food, buttered a piece of toast avidly, and bit into it. The crunching that ensued was not delicate. She caught his eye and coughed, choking on crumbs. He handed her coffee and slapped her back while she wheezed, color rising in her cheeks. She took the coffee in both hands and swallowed. Her smile was sheepish.

"I am hungry," she said, and her blush deepened. She added more milk and sugar to her coffee, and he took note. Almost white and sweet as golden syrup. He didn't approve, of course, but he'd remember. He'd prepare it for her just like that. Next time. *Next time.* Those words filled him with delight. She bit again into her toast with a loud crunch. He even liked the way she ate. Determined. She examined the toast as though looking for the best angle of attack.

"You're not?" she asked pointedly.

"What?"

"Hungry," she said.

"Oh." He laughed. Christ Jesus, she'd made him forget the ham. He folded two slices on toast with an egg hard-boiled and dispatched it within the minute. They didn't speak, concentrating on chewing, and the silence felt companionable. Yes, they could eat together, read together, sit together without conversation, their silence a knowing silence, a conspiracy of contentment ... The coffee vitalized him and reinforced his sense of well-being. He'd shown her the dark corners of his consciousness, and she'd blown away the cobwebs. He glanced up and saw her watching him with those unfathomable, dark eyes.

"You read Greek?" he asked, gesturing, and she looked down at the book, closed now on the edge of the table.

"A little. I didn't take to it. I preferred Latin." She tipped her head, giving him an oblique look. "I never would have guessed you liked to read, let alone in Greek. When I first met you, that is."

"Why's that?" he asked airily, as though he wasn't hanging on her every word. He helped himself to more ham.

"You're too tall," she said.

"For books?" He put down his fork. She nodded gravely.

"By four inches at least." Her mouth quirked. She was *teasing* him. He wanted to leap out of his seat and whirl her straight back to bed.

"No spectacles. No whiskers. No ink stains." She shrugged. "You just don't look the type."

"I've been told I'm more in the Byronic mold." He glowered at her.

She raised an eyebrow. "Very good," she said. She sipped her coffee and added—dear God—yet another spoonful of sugar. "I suppose there are all sorts of literary men."

"But the spectacles, whiskers, and ink stains … ?"

"My father." She smiled. "He lived in his books."

"It was your father who taught you Greek and Latin?" He watched the slight change in her expression, a melancholy stealing across her features. She sucked in her cheeks. The action plumped her lower lip distractingly. Her gaze drifted up to a distant point.

"He didn't always have time for supper, but he had time for the classics." She laughed, a low, throaty sound, reminding him that he hadn't heard nearly enough of her laughter. She and her father had laughed together. He could see it in her eyes.

"You enjoyed each other's company," he said. The smile still lingered on her mouth as she looked at him.

"He was my best friend," she said simply.

"Ella." He poured himself more coffee. He considered the steaming liquid then her. "Why did you leave Somerset?" She continued to butter her second piece of toast, which suddenly required all of her attention.

"My cousin," she said. "I told you." Her cousin. The hunter. She'd worn this same look the last time she'd spoken of him. A hunted look. He supposed it was fitting. She sighed and laid the toast on her plate. "He never liked me. I didn't think he would inherit. No one thought it. But my brother died, and then my cousin Charles, then Benedict. When my father died last year … well, the estate fell to him."

She *was* wellborn. No shock there. But … "The *Reed* estate?" He lifted his brows. Her toast had again become interesting. She broke it in half then broke the halves into quarters. He leaned back in his chair, tipping it back onto two legs. It was that or drum his fingers on the table.

"Reed is not my name," she said.

"No?" *Damn it all.* He hadn't meant to strike that tone of mock surprise. She bristled.

"No," she said slowly, warily. "I adopted it as a precaution. I don't want my cousin to find me."

"He's looking, then?"

Her posture began to change: chin tucking in, shoulders drawing up to her ears. She was trying to disappear into herself.

Confide in me. He pushed aside the plates and took her hands, holding them on the table, trying to press this message into her palms.

"The valuables you had in your possession," he began.

"Were mine!" She was magnificent in her defiance, her back straightening and her eyes throwing sparks. He released his breath in a low whistle. She didn't hear it, swept away by her sudden passion. "The law that declares it theft is unjust. He has no claim to them I recognize. They were gifts my father made to me. And to my mother." She sagged in her chair. "I have so little of her," she said. "But I didn't take those things for sentimental reasons. I took them to sell." Her voice turned almost cold. That restraint he had seen in her from the beginning was taking over. Even her hands felt cooler, stiffer, like claws. At any moment she would try to pull them away.

"So your cousin pursues you for trinkets?" He watched her closely. He had gained, perhaps, a few more pieces of the puzzle, but he had come no closer to putting them together. She withheld too much. "And you have no friends, no other relations, no one to turn to?"

"That's right," she said icily. "So you see why it is important I find paid employment immediately." She tugged her hands, and he tightened his grip. "I am quite alone in the world."

"You have me." She went dead white when he said it. He wondered if his face too had drained of color. He'd surprised himself. But now he had to press forward. "Reed is not your name. You're afraid to claim your real one." He looked at her widened eyes, her parted lips, the pulse fluttering darkly in her neck. "Take mine."

Her pallor had a greenish cast. She looked positively sickened. He squelched his misgivings—*She doesn't want to hear this, not a word of it*—and plowed on.

"I know I've said nothing to recommend my name. I've considered it a curse more often than not. But perhaps, if you too were a Blackwood ... " *Spit it out, man.* "Perhaps if we shared the name ... I wouldn't find it so distasteful."

Even when she'd vomited river water she hadn't seemed so overset. A clicking sound was coming from her throat.

"I've despoiled you of your virginity," he said. God, it was clunky. "I want to make right by you." He wouldn't thank Mrs. Potts for this phrasing when he saw her next. Ella's nostrils pinched.

"You do me great honor," she intoned. It was the very voice of death. "I regret I cannot accept your offer ... " She stopped, rigid, even her vocal cords paralyzed. He pushed back his chair and circled the table, falling to his knees at her side. He wanted to shake her until she woke up, until he saw *her* again peering through the dark glass of those distant eyes. But he jerked her chair around and laid his arms on her knees, gripping her legs, staring up at her fiercely.

"I don't care what you did," he said. "Whatever it is, you can trust me with it, now, later, never. I won't let your cousin hurt you. I can protect you with my name. With my life."

This, at least, cracked her iron control. Her breath whooshed out. Hectic spots of color bloomed across her cheekbones. "You would do this twice." She shook her head frantically. "You would make this sacrifice twice, binding yourself to a woman to save her." She looked at him with something kindling in her face. He couldn't interpret her expression. Desire was there. Tenderness, gratitude too, and regret. Then her face hardened into a mask. "I cannot be saved."

"Ella." He'd bungled the proposal with his chivalric cowardice, his talk of his name and her virginity and making right. He didn't give a goddamn if marrying her made anything right. It could send them straight to hell, and he'd want it anyway. He wanted *her*, wanted to stare into her odd, angular face and discern her moods and spout fooleries until she laughed and made some unexpected sally of her own. He wanted to make her sigh as he tasted her everywhere, learned every crease and hollow of her body. He wanted to listen to her muse about her favorite books. He wanted to play music with her in Castle Blackwood with all the windows open until the ghosts flew with the notes out into the high blue sky. As a thousand sentiments warred for precedence and tied his tongue in knots, she spoke again.

"It's nothing I did," she said, her chest rising and falling rapidly. "It's who I am."

He reached up and gripped her by the nape, her hair flowing cool as starlight over his wrists.

"You can decide," he said, echoing her own words. "You can decide what that means."

"I have." She exhaled. "My answer is no. What happened between us … it can't happen again."

He sat back on his heels. He realized—and the realization did nothing to flatter his ego—that he must look stunned. He stood.

"You accept my answer," she said uncertainly.

"Of course not." He forced a grin, and when he saw the fear and confusion dawning in her face he almost pitied her. "But we can agree to disagree. The fun will be in trying to convince each other."

"Fun." She said it with disbelief.

"Mmm," he murmured. "Fun." He put his hand on the back of her chair, leaning over her. "Marry me, Ella."

"No." Her eyes were enormous.

"Tell me no again," he whispered, leaning closer. "Like you mean it."

"No." The word barely crossed her lips so he met it there with his own. The kiss was soft and sweet and fleeting. She turned her head away.

"No," she said again, not looking at him. He pulled away and crossed back to his chair. His coffee was tepid, but he made himself drink it anyway. Her head was still turned. Her hair had fallen forward and partially veiled her face. He could see only the tip of her nose, the curve of her lips, and the trembling point of her chin. He steeled himself to stay in his seat. He wouldn't push her harder. Not yet. He would change her mind in time.

What if there wasn't time? What if her mind could not be changed?

His heart, which had felt engorged, shriveled. She didn't want him. He'd been drunk on the fiery liquor of her kisses, on the promise of more nights like the one they'd shared. Now his head ached. His eyeballs felt dry and tacky. Revenge would be bitter if he lost her. The peace he gained would afford him the opportunity to contemplate this new emptiness. If he listened, he'd hear that shrunken muscle in his chest knocking with every beat.

Chapter Nineteen

Blackwood Mansion was a severe, three-story building with a broad exterior staircase leading into a chilly entrance hall. Ella kept out of the way of the servants who trooped back and forth, conveying chairs, candelabra, and rolled rugs into the dining room. She felt awkward standing useless in plain view, ignored by Isidore and subjected to unabashedly curious stares by everyone else, and drifted at last into the massive library. She sat in a cold leather chair. She thought she'd read, but she ended up sitting stock-still, hands in her lap, staring vacantly. The ponderous atmosphere depressed her. A library should be intimate, cluttered, even shabby, because it was *used*. The books thumbed through and returned to the shelves willy-nilly, pushed in at different depths so the spines made a scalloped pattern that beckoned to browsing hands. Everything about this library was forbidding. She couldn't imagine extracting a volume from the ordered ranks that lined the walls. If she selected the wrong one, a trapdoor might open, and she'd fall into a dungeon, or the wall would groan around a secret pivot and disclose a torture chamber. Fantastical thoughts, she knew, but enough to send her jumping to her feet, hurrying on through the suites of rooms. In the ballroom, she stood and gazed at the enormous plaster decoration above the fireplace: the Blackwood arms, a blood-red chevron between three wolf heads guardant. No wonder Isidore kept this house closed.

Her skin prickled. She turned, and there he was, coming toward her with that fluid, graceful tread. He made no attempt to soften his face with a smile. Hair fell across his brow, and her fingers twitched with the desire to brush it back. She wadded her black skirts in her hands. She had no right to touch him. *Never again.* She had said *no,* three times *no,* and he had not renewed his offer. During their subsequent interactions, he'd been aloof, not cold precisely, but distracted. The *fun*, perhaps, of convincing her to become his bride had spent itself in that first attempt. He had made a noble gesture that she had nobly refused. That was the end of it. He was relieved, most likely. She should be relieved too.

She wasn't. She felt like the ruin of a ruin. Like the ruin of a ruin's shadow.

She tried to smile as he approached, as she had tried to smile last night at supper before retiring to the guest chamber. As she had tried to smile this morning when they breakfasted together, not in his bedchamber but downstairs in the drab but cozy breakfast room. As she had tried to smile this afternoon when they sat side by side in the coach, both erect, silent, their shoulders swaying slightly with every bump but never enough to brush together. As she had tried to smile when he led her into the dining room at Blackwood Mansion and swore over the rugs—*Don't just hang them. It's a séance, not a bazaar. Tie another rope. Make a kind of tent. Christ, give that to me*—striding away from her with a "Make yourself comfortable" tossed over his shoulder.

It wasn't getting any easier. But she couldn't fade away now. He still needed her. She could see the strain in his posture. Tension corded his neck. Of course he was tense. Tonight he hoped to catch a killer. She was afraid his plan wouldn't work, and she was afraid that it would. What would he do when the man revealed himself? Attack him in front of a hundred witnesses? She hadn't asked. She wondered if he'd thought that far himself. A vision of the future flashed before her, both of them in cells, her in the asylum, him in the prison. Suddenly she wished she had a gun. If she had a gun, she could shoot the murderer herself, shoot him as Isidore leapt forward. She would become the deranged murderess, the violent lunatic of Mr. Norton's predictions. It would be the sanest thing she had ever done. With one bullet, Isidore would be freed. Released from his revenge and its consequences. Her incarceration would be brief. She put her hand to her throat. What would she say on the gallows?

Love cured me of my life. I'm not sorry.

But she had no gun.

He stopped before her, and she caught her breath, lowered her hand. The smile wobbled into place.

"You should go upstairs," he said brusquely. "It won't be long now before people begin to arrive." She thought she saw him wince, regretting the peremptory address, and the next moment he was leaning forward confidentially, adopting a waggish air.

"That is ... the Wheatcrofts have the irritating habit of showing up to things on time." His lips quirked. Sardonic Isidore Blackwood, lord of the manor. But he couldn't quite carry it off. His voice sounded strangely hollow. He was pale beneath his tan. Sweat glimmered on the skin above his lip. He did not look well. She knew he would not appreciate a show of concern. She tried to match his careless tone.

"Perhaps you should come upstairs too," she said. "And sit for a bit."

He shook his head. "I should see to the dining room." He lifted a brow, as though wryly amused. "The chandelier still wants its cerement. Brinkley promised me he'd transform the table into a catafalque. I must make sure a zealous footman doesn't spoil the effect with place settings." This heroic display of humor deserved a reaction. She laughed, and the room gave the laugh back to her from every corner: thin and false.

They looked at each other as the echo went on and on, lasting longer than seemed possible.

"Do you like Blackwood Mansion?" he asked softly.

"It's ... " She searched for the right word. *Dreary. Doleful.*

"Drafty," she said. He tilted his head. His eyes raked over her body, and she fought the urge to shiver, to give him an excuse to step closer. He had proven himself so adept at warming her with caresses. His tongue was hot as a brand. She swallowed. Even his furtive glance—speculative, covetous—sent a heated wave rushing through her. "I'm not cold." She spoke quickly, avoiding his gaze. "But I noticed the draft. In the hall, of course, but also in the library. A numbing patch of air. Clammy, as though it wafted from an uncovered well. I attributed it to the Blackwood ghost." She curled her lip, striving for a light, mocking tone. *I too can be coolly ironic under pressure.*

No appreciative chuckle. He looked at her blankly.

"Lady Berners mentioned you had a family ghost." She felt a peculiar thrill, making a joke at Lady Berners's expense. She hadn't enjoyed her forays into London society, but she had gained insight into *his* world, his circle. There was something pleasing in alluding to a shared point of reference. "To hear her talk, you'd think they came with the coronet."

Now he did bark a laugh, folding his arms across his chest. "The ghost is at Castle Blackwood. She's Scotch. Wouldn't be caught dead in London."

"So to speak," she murmured, registering the width of his forearms. For the hundredth time.

Fool, she said to herself. *Ella, you're a fool.*

"My illustrious ancestor took her as a spoil of war, and she defied him by dying. Did Lady Berners tell you that?" His eyes had narrowed.

"Something like."

"Morbury Blackwood. He rode with the Duke of Cumberland at Culloden. He killed a hundred clansmen that day and carved his monogram into their chests with their own claymores, or so the story goes. There's a rusting claymore on the wall in the gallery, at least, alongside Morbury's sword and musket. He's the pride of the family." His sneer was a sneer for the ages, for generations of the damned. "The great Blackwood butcher. Every firstborn son takes his name. Isidore Morbury Blackwood. *Tradition.*" He injected the word with scorn.

"Isidore Morbury Blackwood." She said it slowly. Why did it sound wrong?

"At your service." He straightened, expanding his chest, exaggeratedly martial in his bearing. "A Blackwood never bends." Suddenly it seemed he couldn't catch his breath. His face twisted, and he pressed a fist to his forehead. He stared over her shoulder, but she didn't turn. She knew what he saw. The three Blackwood wolves, their watchful heads molded in black-painted plaster, staring back at him.

"What am I doing, Ella?" His voice rose in pitch, and the walls whispered it over and over. She could feel the blood pounding in her head. She moistened her lips. He'd sounded wrathful in her presence, sorrowful, anguished, desperate even, but never uncertain, never helpless.

"Louisa's coming," he said, brows pulling together. "I just had her note." His hand went to his waistcoat as though to produce it then dropped, empty. His breath hissed out. "I am about to subject her to a humiliation she never dreamed of."

"Don't let her come in." She feared that she too might cry out and tried to modulate her voice. "Bar the door to her. If—"

"She'll hear of it," he interrupted. "Everyone in London will hear of it. Tonight or tomorrow … What difference does it make?" His jaw flexed. If she put her ear to his cheek, she would hear the teeth gnashing. "I lay awake all night, trying to think of another way."

She flushed. She had lain awake all night as well, waging a war with herself. Right before dawn, she'd lost. She'd risen to go to his bedchamber. The sight of her thin, white hand reaching out to turn the doorknob stopped her. She saw herself, rotted from within, wasted by disease, skeletal, clinging to him, an albatross around his neck. She crept back to the bed and watched the darkness divide into meshes of gray as morning broke.

His eyes were still locked on the wolves. Beads of sweat now stood out on his forehead. She touched his sleeve.

"Come upstairs with me and sit," she said. She recognized the physical signs of acute psychic duress. His composure was close to cracking completely. "Come." She led, and he followed, although she didn't know her way. Panic made him tractable. A glance behind her confirmed that he had no will but hers. He walked with his fingers running along the wall. Afraid he would lose his balance. She linked her elbow with his and took him firmly by the wrist with her other hand. He didn't lean on her, but she heard him take a deep, shuddering breath, and they ascended the stairs together.

"Left," he said when she hesitated at the top step. His stertorous breathing had quieted. "Here." She opened the door to a sitting room. He'd had the house opened, but the third story had yet to be properly aired. The room was stale and cold and dark. They sat in front of the fireplace on chairs with claw-and-ball feet and shield-shaped backs. He put his elbows on his knees and rested his face on his hands. His back was rigid.

"We don't have to go through with it." Her voice sounded muffled now that they no longer stood in that vast, echoing ballroom. "Say I fell ill and call it off. Say I'm a fraud. Say whatever you like."

"No." Isidore lifted his head. His color was coming back and with it his self-command. "He must be discovered. He must be punished." His smile was so bitter she felt her throat squeeze. "I wish to God I didn't have to expose her like this. But I'll do it. I can't give up this opportunity." He was convincing himself. A new and dire conviction made his eyes flame. "There's no other way," he whispered. "It's the one thing you can say that will prove to him that Phillipa speaks through you. It's the one thing he thinks no one living knows."

She nodded jerkily.

"Very well," she said. The séance would go on. She would sway and stagger and scream with a ferocity that would put Miss

Seymour to shame. She would claim she'd made contact. And then she would do exactly as he'd coached. She would look out at the audience members, and she would wail in a throbbing voice.

A murderer sits among you.

She would say that he stood accused. By Phillipa.

And by his unborn child.

Come forward, she would howl. *Or drop where you sit into boiling blood and fire.*

His hands closed on hers.

"Thank you," he said. "In the ballroom … I wasn't myself. You steadied me. Calmed me." His throat worked as he released her. He leaned back in his chair. "Your father was lucky in you."

Her father. The invalid. She could not bear to be praised as a nursemaid. She could not bear to be reminded of her lies. She dropped her eyes. There was a silence. Then he spoke.

"I swore to myself that after … *this* … all of this was over, I'd make it all up to you. What I put you through." She could tell he was staring at her. She could feel his gaze. She always could. Her skin was sensitized to it. A touch that wasn't a touch. It fluttered on her and in her. "I swore I'd erase the bad with the good. It doesn't work like that, does it? In life, a negative and a positive don't cancel each other out. Tell me." His soft voice had a raw finish. "Tell me, my dear philosopher."

She looked at him and saw his expression, the one he wore when soliciting her opinion: earnest, inquiring, intensely interested. She couldn't resist it. It called to her. She spoke slowly, carefully, thinking her answer through.

"If actions canceled each other out, we'd always stay right where we are. Nothing would move forward." She fumbled for how best to express the idea. She knew how her father would have explained it.

"Think of a bow," she said. "The string and the wood. You pull the bowstring back, and the wood curves in the other direction.

The movements don't nullify each other. They create tension. It's what allows the arrow to shoot forth."

"Love's golden arrow." His gaze slid down. It shot through her breastplate and drove straight into her throbbing heart. His lips turned down as he shifted his eyes toward the fireplace. Wood had been laid there. A tidy pyre, unlit. "Death's ebon dart." He tipped his head, chin jutting forward. In silhouette, the black angles of his face and throat looked rough-hewn. Crude.

"They're in the same quiver," he said. "I feel both barbs. Each wound bleeds. Ella, I don't think I can save you. I don't think you can save me. But we can live more fully together …" She thought for a moment she'd hallucinated his low, urgent murmur. But she hadn't. He was looking at her again, but the darkness whittled his face; she saw only his eyes.

"Limning the shadows with light," he said. "Breathing the same air as the flames that consume us." He took a quick breath, and in that pause she tried to defend herself, but she had no armor against these words. She was pierced. Dear God, she was leaking out of herself, flowing toward him through a thousand ruby holes.

"Sometimes I see you, and your beauty is like a sickle moon, a mowing scythe. Sometimes I see you, and the fullness of your beauty pulls my blood in swells. It's the rhythm of life itself. Ella—"

She sucked in her breath. "Please." Warning him. Begging him. "Don't."

"Ah." With that simple sound, he fell silent again, lifting his hands, palms up, fingers open. He contemplated them for a long moment. Thinking, most like, of what the night might bring.

"You're right," he said. "It's not the time to speak. But Ella, there *will* be time. Afterward. There will be." He wanted her confirmation, wanted her to tell him, *Yes, yes, there will be time*, but even this yes was more than she could give. He thought time would be a boon. But to her, time was a bane. Every passing moment hastened her disintegration, her descent into living death. Time wouldn't treat with them equally. When it became clear that she would offer nothing, not a word, he sighed. "After this is over … this macabre piece of theater … "

The curtain of the final act was about to lift.

Ella Reed, she thought. *Medium. Tragedian.*

He stirred in his chair. "If you *could* summon a spirit … " He sounded thoughtful. "Would you summon him? Your father?"

The question caught her off guard. She bit her lip hard. To hear Papa's voice … really hear it … . Her eyes stung. But she shook her head slightly.

"He's with me already," she said. "Not just *in* my thoughts. Sometimes I catch myself thinking his very thoughts. Sometimes I see things through his eyes. We were so close." The lump in her throat made it difficult to speak. She lowered her head. "He would have liked you." She didn't look up, but she felt his small movement.

"I would have liked him too," he said, voice clotted with emotion. "A man with ink on his hands."

Instead of blood. He didn't say it, but she heard it in the glottal tick that choked off the phrase.

"A man who raised a fairy for a daughter," he continued. She heard the smile in his voice. "And taught her to value kindness."

"I would summon Robert," she said and risked meeting his eyes. They were brilliant with emotion as strong as her own. "My brother. He drowned when I was twelve. His friend's father had a small schooner, and the two of them decided to sail it. They wrecked at Gore Point, not far from Porlock Weir." She wiped at her nose. Silently, he handed her his handkerchief. "It's been so many years. I've grown up, and he hasn't. I'm so much older than him now. It makes him feel farther away." Trying to stop the tears from falling made it worse, made her chest burn and her throat clog. "I'd just like to say hello," she whispered.

She pressed the handkerchief to her face, inhaling deeply. A piney smell. No more gardenias. She remembered the faint, floral odor of the handkerchief she'd found in Phillipa's reticule.

Her mouth went dry. She spread the handkerchief open on her knee, ran her fingers over the embroidery. *IMB.* Isidore Morbury Blackwood. But Phillipa's handkerchief had read *IHB.*

"Some day you'll tell me about Robert," he said.

"Isidore." He must have heard the change in her voice for he looked at her questioningly.

"What is it?"

She traced the *I* on the handkerchief. "Who else of your acquaintance has a first name that begins with the letter I?"

He didn't hesitate.

"Ben," he said. "Bennington. His first name is Ivor."

Ivor Bennington. "His middle name?" It emerged a dry whisper.

"Heathcote." Confusion lined Isidore's brow. "Why do you ask?"

IHB. The handkerchief in Phillipa's reticule belonged to the exquisite Mr. Bennington. Young, handsome, rich Mr. Bennington.

"Bennington." She rose from her chair, mouth opening and closing soundlessly. She gasped, stuttered. "Bennington. Bennington killed her." She waved the handkerchief as though this would explain it to him, her tongue thickening in her mouth. Isidore dug his fingertips into his jaw looking up at her. There was compassion in his look, and a weary patience. He gave no credence to her outburst; she could read it plainly in his face. He thought perhaps she was trying to spare him, and herself, the ordeal to come by pointing the finger at random. She hadn't made her case. She tried to frame a coherent account ... the evidence, her intuition, her sudden *certainty* that Bennington was Phillipa's lover. The room swirled around her. He had to believe her.

He cut her off before she could really begin, gentle but firm. "Bennington wasn't there," he said and regarded her with resignation as she gaped at him.

Not there? But everything fit so perfectly.

"Sick," he said. "Bennington gets terrible headaches. Has to take to bed two or three times a month. It's always been like that, ever since I've known him." He stood, faintly apologetic.

"The Wheatcrofts"—he consulted his pocket watch—"will knock on the door within the minute. Or I'll eat my hat." He attempted a grin. "Hat-eating. What would the Romans say to that?"

She couldn't smile back. Not now. She was wringing the handkerchief, mind working frantically. "Bennington and Phillipa were friends?"

Isidore's brow creased again. "They liked each other well enough. Phillipa and Daphne were friends."

"Daphne?" Her voice emerged unnaturally high.

"Bennington's wife." Isidore cocked his head, listening. "That was the front door." He stepped toward her, stroked her cheek with his callused thumb. "They're here." He bent and pressed a kiss to her forehead.

"Soon," he said, softly. "We'll know soon. Brinkley will come for you when we're ready to begin." The rough pad of his thumb traced her lip. "Until afterward," he said.

• • •

She paced until Brinkley opened the door. Her palms were sweating as she followed him down the stairs. All of the gaslights in the hall had been turned off. Brinkley held a lamp, and when she looked away from it she realized that she couldn't see the floor beneath her feet. She might have been floating. She might have been falling. Brinkley stopped outside the dining room. The door was propped open. Rustles, murmurs, creaks came from inside. She entered silently behind the rows of chairs. So many chairs. So many people. So many pairs of eyes that would fix upon her. She hesitated. No one had heard her enter. She could turn and run.

She walked forward. Two girls flanked the aisle that ran through the center of those chairs, each holding a candle. She nodded, and the girls turned and preceded her up the aisle, marching with their candles held aloft. She walked behind—*slow*, she told herself, *stately*—and whispers rose as people shifted in their chairs to watch her pass by. The room was pitch-black, no light save for those two slender flames. Again and again those flames caught the wet gleam of eager eyes. Her legs felt weak.

She knew the shadowy structure up ahead was defined by a dozen suspended rugs. They formed a tent enclosing the table, no the *catafalque,* at the front of the room. A makeshift spirit cabinet. The girls reached the tent and pulled open the flaps. An eight-branched candelabrum stood on the draped table, throwing shadows. She climbed onto the table and lay down on her back. Even draped, the table felt unyielding. Her tailbone ground against it, her shoulder blades, the back of her skull. She tucked in her chin and folded her arms across her chest. Entombment is different than sleep. The final bed is not soft. It had been her idea to begin like this, to assume the posture of death, but as the girls dropped the flaps, every particle of her being protested. She didn't want to be interred, closed away, divided from the hopes and cares of ordinary men and women. Even though it wasn't real, she wanted to sit up, to push her way out.

Alfred is here. The thought made her blood congeal. Her veins turned to wires, tightening around her arms and neck. If he were in London, if he'd heard of the gathering, if his curiosity was piqued … why wouldn't he come? Doors opened to Baron Arlington. *He's here. He's sitting in the dark. He will see me.*

Suddenly, leaving the tent seemed as impossible as remaining inside. She would step out holding the candelabrum, and Alfred would send up a cry. *Thief! Madwoman! Savage!*

She breathed a deep breath to calm herself, but the thick smell of smoke and wax made her cough. She covered her mouth with her hand, lest the sputtering be heard. She felt as though the world were tipping over; she was going to slide off the table. She tried to find a focal point in the dim, swimming light. She couldn't make out the patterns of the rugs, only glimpses of color as the shadows moved: indigo, periwinkle, rose, green. She heard one of the girls call out.

"'Hymn to the Night,'" the girl said and began to sing. No one joined her. She sang alone, but her voice—thin and sweet and lonely—wavered on. Ella had told Isidore that an invocation was in order. Chanting, she'd said, or a song sung in chorus. That's what had set the mood for Miss Seymour's eerie performance. Yet this tremulous solo in the darkness was equally powerful, more powerful even, than the vibrations that issued from many throats. One plaintive female voice rising and falling, colorless and insubstantial, almost as though the voice had traveled from another world. The hairs lifted on her arms. She didn't stir when the girl fell silent.

Make them wait in that blackness. Let the tension mount.

The murderer. The hunter. She would face them for Isidore.

If Alfred charged her, she would not seek shelter. She would bellow like a stag, yip and scream like a fox; she would meet his charge with a stampede, the ghost of every slain creature of the forest squawking and crying through her throat. She would fly at him with beating wings, with reddened claws, with antlers honed to dagger points. She could already feel it at her back as she sat up: the dark might of a thousand bodies. Love made her many, made her legion. If that meant she was impure, insane, so be it.

She took up the candelabrum. She stepped out of the tent. She could see the shifting shapes of the seated crowd, and the twin lights of the girls' candles as they moved to either end of the first row of chairs. Someone had lit incense. The scent, overwhelming and resinous, wafted around her. The candelabrum was heavy. The wax from the candles had begun to spill over, splashing her ungloved fingers. She bit her lip but didn't cry out, didn't jerk her hands away. The pain was simple. It was such a small fraction of what she felt in that moment. Pain was a part of her, but it could not dominate her. She was so much more.

She walked back and forth, head tilted up, peering into the dark corners of the vaulted ceiling. She stopped and gave a low cry, rolling her head on her neck. Gasps from the audience. *Good.* She knelt and placed the candelabrum on the floor. On her knees, she swayed now, side to side, backwards and forwards, flinging open her arms. She controlled these wild movements, and the pantomimed frenzy gave her an odd feeling of mastery. She directed this fit. It was as though she were riding on lightning. She shuddered then froze.

"She's with us," she said. "I feel her."

More gasps, more whispers, a short burst of nervous laughter from the back row.

"She's coming down," she said, drawing the last word out into a wail. "She's coming down from the shadows. She's begging for my voice."

She stood, lurching, staggering toward the chairs. Women pulled their knees to the side. Men half rose. She saw in a flash Isidore's face, gaunt, etched with misery, and Mrs. Trombly's, bright as a star with hope and fear. Ella stumbled back and hugged herself, rocking.

"She won't know peace until she says what she has waited five years to say." She opened her mouth in a wide, soundless scream. She put her hands to her neck. Her rapid movements had made the candles in the candelabrum flicker, and she shut her eyes against the unsteady light. The incense made her mouth taste like soap, made her want to gag. She fought to stay present, to stay on her feet.

"Come to me, Phillipa," she howled. "My throat is yours. My tongue is yours. Speak!"

She let her head drop. Her chest was heaving. Her rasping breaths were audible in the silent room. She opened her eyes.

Now she would wreak havoc on the Trombly family. Now she would reveal Phillipa's secret.

There was no other way.

She pitched her voice higher, a reedy whisper. "I am ready to speak." She couldn't help but look to Isidore. He nodded once, his face terrible to behold.

No other way. *Do it.*

Her eyes slid to Mrs. Trombly. The woman was standing up, reaching out her trembling hands. The soft cry that accompanied her motion did not come from her lips. It came from Mrs. Bennington's. The lovely woman sat on Mrs. Trombly's other side. The candlelight scattered across her hair like rose petals. Her shoulders were shaking. Before she covered her face with her hands, Ella saw her eyes, the whites encircling the blue. Those eyes shone with terror beyond terror. The terror of the condemned on the day of judgment.

She heard Mrs. Bennington's voice, wistful, wrathful, in the Tenbys' parlor.

So few women find men who truly love them. And sometimes the ones who do don't deserve them.

Bennington *was* Phillipa's lover. And Mrs. Bennington knew. And she thought Isidore, deceived in Phillipa, was a love-stricken cuckold.

He loved her blindly, she'd said.

Phillipa and Daphne. Dearest friends. Sisters.

Phillipa had betrayed her dear friend Daphne. And Daphne had killed her for it.

Little lights exploded in the periphery of her vision. Her skull was lifting off. She wasn't the master of her movements any longer. She touched her face, felt her lips peeling back. A breeze blew over her. It was happening. Her arm began to move without her bidding. She had to speak now, before she couldn't. The world was collapsing into a tunnel. She fixed her gaze on Isidore. She stared into his eyes. Midnight-blue at the end of the tunnel. Not light, per se, but darkness visible. A destination.

Focus. Hold on. Speak.

"Mama." She didn't recognize her voice. She had never addressed her own mother in life. Now she said *Mama* at last, for Phillipa, and for herself. "Mama, I love you."

Her fingers were stiffening. She clenched her hands, but her arm was writhing, still writhing. Her stomach rose higher and higher. Her head rippled.

"Daphne!" She cried it out, because the scream was building within her. She was going to kick; she was going to fall in front of Isidore, biting, knocking. She clenched her teeth. *Hold on.*

"I forgive you," she whispered, and the tunnel closed.

Chapter Twenty

Ella hit the floor with a sickening thud. Isidore was kneeling beside her in an instant. He lifted her torso, cradling her head on his legs. The back of her skull banged hard against his thigh muscles, banged again and again as she shook, body clenching and relaxing.

"Breathe," he begged her. She gasped. Grunted. She wasn't getting air. Her face was turning blue. He heard voices behind him, the clatter of chairs.

"More light."

"Dear God."

"Is this another prank, Blackwood?"

"Stand back. Give her room."

All at once she was breathing again. Her head and limbs stilled. He rocked her in his arms, heart nearly bursting.

"Let me take her." He recognized the voice, mild but brooking no argument. It was David Penn. The slender man dropped into a crouch, insinuating himself between Isidore's body and Ella's, fingers probing the back of her head, moving along her jawline. He tried to pull her out of Isidore's arms.

So what if the man was a doctor? So what if he was a goddamn *saint*?

"No." He shook his head, gathering Ella's limp body, holding her more firmly to his chest. He could see Penn staring at him, reading his face and recalibrating some judgment.

"Fine." Penn spoke curtly, rising. "You carry her then. To the closest bedchamber."

Isidore stood. She was lighter without the soaking gown. Too light. Too fragile. He was afraid to ever let her go.

"Sid, what's happening?" Clement appeared at his elbow.

"I don't know," he said. He'd seen this happen to a person before, during his travels. He didn't know what it meant. But he was certain it was a medical issue, not a supernatural one. "Don't let Daphne leave. But get everyone else the hell out of my house."

Once in the bedchamber, he laid Ella on top of the coverlet and sat on the edge of the bed, the mattress dipping under his weight. Her eyelids were twitching. Her blued skin had paled, and now her face looked waxen. The smudges beneath her eyes were darker than he'd ever seen them. Her lips stood out, shapely and vivid. They beckoned to him, bidding him believe in the fairy tale. *Kiss me, and I'll open my eyes.*

"Blackwood," said Penn. "I can't examine her unless you move aside."

Isidore looked up at him.

"I love her," he said hoarsely.

Penn's serious face registered no surprise.

"Then for Christ's sake," he said. "Get out of my way."

Isidore stood and walked to the foot of the bed, watching Penn pull down her lower lids to peer at the balls of her eyes, part her lips to check her teeth and her tongue. He swallowed hard.

"I made her do it," he said. "The séance." Penn didn't answer. He was lifting her arms, testing their rigidity. "Even though this very thing happened to her before. I thought it must have been an act."

"It's not an act." Penn looked up. "Would you light another lamp?"

He did so and resumed his post.

"I know that now," he said. "Is she … hurt? Is she going to be all right?"

"Miss Reed has had an epileptic attack." Penn eyed him, rising. "She didn't tell you she suffered from epilepsy?"

"No." He steadied himself by leaning on the bedpost. "When it happened before, a medium identified it as spirit possession."

Penn smiled wryly. "I don't think epilepsy has been considered supernatural in origin since the Renaissance. At least not amongst medical men." His smile vanished. "It's a neurological disorder. A disease of the brain."

"What causes it?" He looked at Ella, her chest moving up and down, steadily. *There's something ugly inside me.* She was afraid of it, this disease that gripped her and made her fall, that surmounted all of her defenses and left her helpless. Senseless.

Penn hesitated. "The pathology of the disease is uncertain. There are competing views. And much remains to be discovered. A friend of mine, Jackson, has been doing clinical observations of epileptics at the National Hospital. I believe his work will advance our understanding. His study of epileptic phenomena is quite interesting when considered in combination with post-mortem findings—"

"Enough," Isidore gasped. *Clinical observations … Post-mortem findings …* A red cloud was rolling in from all directions, coloring his vision, making everything look lurid, hazy and violent. He raised his fists and lurched toward Penn, convinced—irrationally, he knew—that the gentle young man was about to whip a saw from his waistcoat and use it to open a window in Ella's skull. Penn's eyes widened slightly, but he didn't cower from the threat. Maybe he did remember that Isidore had once saved him from a pair of bullies at Eton. Maybe he remembered that Isidore wasn't a bully himself. It took Isidore a moment to remember it. He stood an inch from Penn, itching to grab him by the throat and wring the answers out of him. Penn was so much slighter than him. He could snap the man in two. The red cloud parted, and he saw Penn's face with sudden clarity: cautious, composed, the face of a man who has surprised a wild creature in the woods and wants to soothe it. That was Penn for you. Any other man would be looking for stones. Isidore blew air through his nose. He stepped back. "Are you saying she belongs in a hospital?"

Penn frowned. "Some convulsions are caused by lesions in the cortex, others by instability in nerve tissues. There are also convulsions caused by tumors, syphilis, injuries to the cranium. Even fright or other profound excitation." He shook his head. "In short, there are many kinds of fits. You could even say there isn't such a thing as epilepsy, but rather, there are many epilepsies, both anatomically and physiologically speaking. Jackson circulated a paper recently that—"

"Can it be cured?"

"No," said Penn. The sympathy with which he softened the word made it all the harder to hear. "As of right now, no. It cannot be cured."

Isidore stared at Ella. *Open. Open your eyes.* He tensed every ruddy fiber of his anatomically impeccable body, willing it. He took his own lip between his teeth and ground down until he tasted blood. It tasted coppery and clean, vital and hot. He'd never thought much of it before, of his possessing strong and well-formed limbs, every physical system operating in perfect coordination. He'd hated himself, certainly, damned himself for his thoughts and deeds, but he'd always felt at home inside his skin. What would it be like to feel otherwise? To feel that your very consciousness was situated in enemy territory? He understood now why Ella battled with herself, why she tried to float above her flesh.

Her eyelids lifted. He pushed past Penn and sat again at Ella's side, kneading her cold hands with his thumbs. "How do you feel?" Her dark eyes were dreamy, unfocused. She blinked at him without any sign of recognition in her face.

"She doesn't know me," he grated. "Why doesn't she know me?"

Penn's hand came down on his shoulder. "Go easy, Blackwood. People often emerge from fits in a state of mental twilight. Give her a few minutes to recover. Be prepared if she doesn't seem like herself. Sometimes speech and memory are affected."

"How long does it last?" He didn't take his eyes from Ella's face.

Penn gave his shoulder a friendly shake and withdrew his hand. "It's variable," he said and sighed. "You won't get any satisfaction from me, I'm afraid. Not until I've talked with her at least. There are too many unknowns."

"Leave us." Now he did glance at Penn. The man's lips had set in a brooding line.

"I don't think I'll do that," he murmured. Isidore's incredulity trumped his temper.

"Is she in danger?" he asked.

"She's not in medical danger, no," said Penn. All at once Isidore realized what he was implying.

"She's not in any moral danger, either," he said, and Penn looked at him ruefully.

"I don't think that she is," he said slowly. "I like you, Blackwood. I always have. I always thought you were better than the company you kept. But there are a hundred people milling about this house, and it's my professional opinion that a woman's reputation is, by and large, more fragile than her health."

"You see to her health, and I'll see to her reputation." Isidore scowled but couldn't maintain his black look in the face of the doctor's steady regard. Penn's quiet air of commitment moved him. He considered every factor, and he stood by his patient, even if it meant defying his belligerent host. Admirable indeed. But it wasn't in him to give Penn his due, to speak out in praise, not then. He was too raw. His heart was still beating too wildly. He managed, though, to compromise without snarling. "Will you wait outside the door then?"

Penn inclined his head. "Call if you need me."

• • •

He didn't know how long he sat holding Ella's hand, watching her eyes track listlessly here and there. When she finally spoke, her voice was lusterless, wiped clean of emotion.

"Isidore," she said, and relief coursed through him.

"I'm here, my love," he said. "Do you know where you are?"

"Are we still in Blackwood Mansion?" She tried to sit up, and he helped her, propping another pillow behind her head.

"Yes," he said. "You ... fell down. During the séance."

Her eyes shut again, but this time it wasn't weariness that closed them. She was afraid to look at him. She knew that he knew. What did she fear she would see in his face? Contempt? Pity? He touched her cheek, stroked her hair, trying to think of what to say.

"You had an epileptic attack," he said at last. "That's what Penn called it. Before, at Miss Seymour's séance ... it was the same thing?"

She nodded, eyes still squeezed shut, and winced.

"Are you all right?" he asked.

"Headache," she muttered.

"You don't have to talk," he said, and, for a time, she didn't. She hadn't fallen asleep though. She was gnawing on her lip, her eyes moving visibly beneath the lids. Her agitation was increasing.

"Ella," he began.

"They started when I was a child," she whispered and heaved for air. She brought a hand up to cover her face. "I am ... defective. I should have told you before you ever ... " She groaned into her palm. "Before I could pollute you."

"Pollute me?" He kissed her knuckles. Taking her hand in his, he lifted it away from her face and kissed her forehead and her eyelids and the tip of her nose. "This is nonsense. You can't pollute me."

"I have a taint in my blood." She was so pale, so exhausted, he wanted to silence her. *Rest,* he wanted to tell her. *None of this matters.* But it did matter. She had lived with this affliction, had been defined by it. He wouldn't silence her. He would let her speak even if it wounded them both.

"Papa loved me anyway."

"Of course he did." He couldn't keep himself from interrupting. "He took care of me."

He held his peace, but more of the puzzle slipped into place. Her father hadn't been sick at all. It was *she* who'd been sick. It was for her sake that they had made their house a hermitage.

"He thought I would get better, and the fits *did* come less frequently. Sometimes a whole year would pass … " She licked her lips. He wished he had water to offer, or brandy. There was nothing in the bedchamber but old linens and dust. "He wouldn't put me in an institution even though Mr. Norton explained to us … "

"Explained what?" His whole body was tightening.

"The deterioration of the epileptic character," she said, so softly he had to put his ear near her lips. "The irritated nervous system erodes the reasoning faculties. There are lapses into uncontrollable aggression. Increasingly violent behaviors."

"No." He shook his head. "I don't believe it."

"Base. Selfish. Wanton. Depraved." This was her litany. The words streamed on and on. "Brutal. Duplicitous. Hysterical. Dangerous. Vile. Papa was foolish, perhaps, to keep me at home. Alfred thought so."

"Your cousin."

Her closed eyes squeezed tighter. Her hands rose, fingers hooking in the collar of her gown, twisting restlessly. "He sent me away. He said it was generous of him, to pay for me to go into a colony instead of an asylum. He said I was the blighted apple on the family tree. I had a fit in front of him when I was just a girl. He said I looked like a monster, gobbling in the dirt. That I wasn't even human."

"No, Ella. No." He wanted to go back in time and wash away those hateful words. He could hear in her dull singsong how familiar this story was to her, how often she'd repeated it to herself.

"I don't want to be locked up," she whispered. "I ran from the train station as soon as Mr. Norton turned his back. Even if I am degenerate, I don't want to live like a caged animal. I'd rather die."

With that, she began to cry, ugly, stormy sobs that contorted her face and wracked her body. He held her until she was spent; it wasn't long. The fit had drained her strength and left her little energy even for tears.

"I want to die," she said, pulling away, lowering herself back to the pillows. Her eyes were still closed. "I want to die before I go mad."

He felt colder than he had when he'd crawled from the Thames.

"You won't go mad," he said, but how could he be certain? He knew nothing about the epileptic character, about the progression of neurological disease. His assurance was empty. It wasn't the one he could give.

"I love you," he said. "We can face this together. Look at me, Ella."

Her lashes swept back, and she looked at him for the briefest moment, her luminous eyes glancing away immediately, skittish. He could have cried aloud at the shame he saw lurking in their depths.

"I saw you on the floor," he said, making his voice brutal. "I saw you shake and kick. I saw your face turn blue. I touched your body, and it was rigid. Your limbs were jerking without your control. Your eyes were only half-closed. There was spittle on your lips. I saw it. I watched the fit happen. I saw the whole bloody thing. Look at me. *Look at me.*"

She looked at him, and he held her gaze.

"It wasn't a monster I saw," he said. "It was you. Ella. *My* Ella. Not beautiful, not ugly, both. Everything I ever wanted." He smiled raggedly. "Everything I thought I would never have."

She was staring at him now, breathing rapidly.

"I'm not going to get better," she said. "You can't believe that I am. Papa believed it, and every time I had a fit I felt that I was failing him. You can't have hope. There *is* no hope."

"I can live without hope," he said. "I just can't live without you."

This time when he pulled her against his chest, she wrapped her arms around his neck. She held him so tight he thought he might choke, and he took the air noisily into his burning throat, not caring if his lungs burst, if he spiraled into darkness in her arms. He detached himself reluctantly.

"You should rest," he said. Her lower lip bore the impress of her teeth, little dents and torn skin. Tears still hung in her lashes.

"Mr. Bennington was Phillipa's lover," she whispered. "We assumed it was her lover who killed her, but it wasn't."

"It was her lover's jealous wife," he said. He should have seen it earlier, all of it. Somehow Ella *had* seen it. She'd seen it in time to spare Phillipa and her family a final humiliation.

"What are you going to do?" she asked. He hadn't allowed himself to think of what he was going to do until this moment. Nor had he allowed himself to think of what Ella had murmured before the convulsion took her.

"You said Phillipa forgave her." He searched in his own heart for forgiveness and found none. He wanted Bennington strung up by his toes and whipped until the muscles dropped off his bones. He wanted Daphne fed to the wolves. "Why?" he asked.

"I felt it." She raised her shoulders in a small, wondering shrug. "I didn't think about it. I felt the words come out of my mouth." She wouldn't go so far as to claim she *had* made contact with the spirit world, but she believed it. He saw the mistiness in her eyes and the delicacy with which she now touched her throat, as though it were the site of a miracle.

She believed Phillipa had spoken through her.

"You didn't know her," he said bluntly. "She would not forgive."

"Maybe death changed her." Ella dropped her hand from her throat. "I don't mean that facetiously. Maybe things look different from the other side."

"Adultery? Murder?" He shook his head. "If they do, they shouldn't."

She took his hand, and he felt the shock of her cool fingers. "Be careful, Isidore." She stroked his skin. There was something ancient in her voice, a wisdom that was far older than she. Wisdom and woe—they came into the world together.

"When you deal with them, be careful. Not for their sakes, but for yours." Her face was wan, her voice fading, but her eyes glowed.

"You know what happens to things that do not bend," she said.

• • •

He opened the door, planning to ask Penn to send for a warming pan, but saw that the doctor had anticipated this and half a dozen other necessities. Two maids stood at his side with stone hot-water bottles, a basin and compresses, a tea tray, and brandy. The women entered the room at once. Penn paused to look at him questioningly.

"She's lucid," he said. "But tired. Penn … Thank you."

Penn made a dismissive gesture. "St. Aubyn came looking for you," he said.

"I have to find him," said Isidore. He furrowed his brow. How to begin? Deterioration. Madness. Where did her ideas come from? What was fact and what was fiction? Was there a course they could navigate between false hope and fatalism?

"Penn … "

"We'll talk," said Penn, touching his arm. "After I've spoken with her, we three will talk."

• • •

Clement had done an adequate job dispersing the guests, or else the unsettling conclusion of the séance combined with the want of refreshments had sped them on their way. Only a few people lingered, drifting in small groups through the halls. Maybe they couldn't find their way out. It was terribly dark.

"Have the gaslights turned back on," Isidore said to Brinkley, who was still stationed outside the dining room. He passed into the room. Louisa was standing in front of the rows of empty chairs, standing in the spot where Ella had fallen. The candelabrum flickered on the floor by her feet. She was looking down into the flames but raised her head when he entered. He didn't know what to tell her. About Ella. About Phillipa. About Daphne. He let her speak first.

"How is she?" she asked as he walked toward her.

"Recovering," he said. Gaslights flared as Brinkley set the servants to work. The rug tent looked silly again: a three-dimensional carpet collage of Rococo foliage, acorn and peony medallions, and Gothic diaper. In the darkness, the shadowy hulk had looked sepulchral enough.

"Mr. Penn went with you." Louisa exhaled. "It's good that he did. I should have had a doctor see to her the first time. She *is* sick, isn't she? The poor girl."

He made a noncommittal gesture. He scorned to hide Ella's sickness. Let anyone who so much as looked askance at her answer to *him*. But she felt differently, and he wouldn't speak of what caused her so much shame. Not until he'd made that shame go away.

"And yet ... " Louisa's eyes seemed illuminated from within. She looked younger. She looked almost as she used to look chasing the rabbits from the kitchen garden at Trombly House. She looked happy. "That doesn't explain what happened. Before she fell down." Louisa broke off, overcome. "When she said *Mama*," she continued, voice low. "I heard Phillipa. It was she. She wanted to tell me she loved me. To tell me goodbye. You heard her too."

It would be kind to nod. Ella had told him there could never be too much kindness.

He nodded and was rewarded with Louisa's smile, radiant as the sunlight after a winter's worth of rain. And maybe he wasn't lying. Maybe he *had* heard her, a different Phillipa, changed by death, speaking of love and forgiveness through the lips of the woman he was going to marry. Blessing him.

"She's not in shadow anymore." Still smiling, Louisa reached out her hands. He took them.

"I think she can leave us now. I whispered to her that she should." Her smile didn't falter, but her eyes brimmed. "It's all right, my sweet child," she said, gazing up around the room at the dim arches of the ceiling that the light could not reach. "You can go."

They stood, hand in hand, he and this woman he had never called mother himself but who had been a mother to him. The peace she had found was worth bending for. He wouldn't imperil it. He squeezed her hands and released them.

"I'll call on you soon," he said.

"Miss Reed will continue on tonight at Blackwood Mansion?" Louisa's voice was bland.

"Yes," he said. *She will be with me. This night. Every night.*

"And then," he said, "as soon as she feels better, I mean to take her to Castle Blackwood."

Louisa tore her gaze from the ceiling and looked into his eyes, searching, he knew, for the terrified little boy who had marched home to those towers like a damned soul returning to the depths of hell. She didn't see him, that terrified boy whose anguished face used to break her heart. He knew because she brushed his cheek with her finger, and her eyes grew even brighter.

"That's good, Isidore," she said. "It's time."

He found Clement pacing outside the third-floor sitting room. He stopped instantly, face tense, and folded his arms across his chest.

"She's in there," he said. "She hasn't said a word to me. I'm afraid something's come loose in her head. She's just staring. I waved my hand in front of her face, and she didn't even blink." A muscle in his jaw flexed. "Sid, you don't think that *Daphne* … "

"You read Blake now." He looked away from Clement to study the heavy oaken door. What if he could turn a key, shut her up in that room, and walk away, never looking back? What if he could avoid this confrontation? He didn't trust himself.

"Blake?" Clement unfolded his arms, cracking his knuckles. He was vibrating with suppressed emotion.

Isidore quoted softly, "Cruelty has a Human Heart. And Jealousy a Human Face." He paused with his hand on the doorknob. "Where's Bennington?"

"Gone. Slipped out. I didn't see him." Clement leaned his shoulder on the door. "Tell me what you know. You owe it to me, Sid."

He withdrew his hand and stepped back. Clement straightened, and they stood toe to toe, looking into each other's eyes. There was nothing abstract, nothing placid in Clement's green gaze. He was prepared for the worst. His fine-boned face looked hard. The set of his jaw was merciless. These five years had blooded the white knight. Isidore knew that if he asked Clement to help him cut Bennington's heart out he would do it. He didn't want to ask. He wanted to end it.

"I owe it to you," he said. "Believe me, I know that. For now, though, I ask you … stay on this side of the door."

• • •

A few hours ago, Ella had sat in the very chair Daphne now occupied. Isidore crossed the room and stood in front of the fireplace, looking at her. Her face was swollen, tear-tracked. Her round blue eyes, reduced to slits, stared dully into space. Suddenly, kindness deserted him. In this house, with the Blackwood wolves watching, he could not bend. He knew it like he knew his name. He would crush the life from her body. He reached out to seize her throat, slowly, with the calmness of a man enacting the inevitable, and she shrank back in the chair, her sobs choking her so that she could not scream.

If she did scream, would Clement charge in to save her? He thought not.

"Please," she whimpered. "I'm afraid to die." Her fists were pressed to her mouth, arms guarding her torso. "Even if she forgives me, God does not."

That almost amused him. The idea that Phillipa might be more magnanimous than God. He could imagine Phillipa's perverse laughter. The shadows seemed to move in his peripheral vision, rippling, like a girl's unbound black hair. He pried Daphne's hands from her face and forced them to her lap. He held her wrists with one hand and, with the other hand, gripped her throat, forcing her head back. She gasped and jerked against him. He leaned close to her, pushing with his weight. She smelled floral, a meadow's worth of French scent drenching her. She rattled. Her tongue protruded. His hand was wet; her tears had run down her face and dripped from her chin, dripped over him. He could feel her pulse against his hand, faster than a rabbit's. Yes, he would kill this soft, small creature. He would twist the head from the body. He pushed, and the Blackwood wolves pushed with him, a savage pack, and her pain and her panic as she squirmed and choked in his grasp made him feel something like pleasure. She should suffer as he had suffered, as all things must suffer.

You know what happens to things that do not bend.

He heard Ella's voice. And all at once, he broke. He threw himself back from Daphne, and he wept with his forehead pressed to the thin carpet. He could hear her gurgling, sucking in air, and his own hoarse sobs mingled with the sounds of her life flowing back into her. He rose to his knees, dashing at his face with fists that glistened with both their tears. She didn't shrink from him. She fell from the chair and huddled before him, hugging his legs, shaking, and he dropped his hands to her back, bewildered, the tears coming faster and faster. He had never wept. Not once that he could remember. This flood—it was a kind of deliverance.

"I love him," she moaned. "She knew it. She didn't care."

"So you broke her skull." His head throbbed, the pain so intense he wondered if the moisture on his face was blood, if blood was pouring from his eyes, from his nose.

"She was going to run away with him." Daphne lifted her face, all the prettiness distorted, the dimple a gouge in the heavy cheek. Once upon a time they were friends, all of them, laughing, dancing, drinking, lying, cheating, playing at hero and villain by turns. Phillipa wasn't blameless in this. They'd all been so young, so stupid, so brutal in their appetites. "I followed her to the balcony. I was going to try to talk to her, but there was a candlestick on the table, and as soon as I had it in my hands … "

He knew. The rage took over.

He had almost killed Daphne. He lifted his hands and looked at them, fingers spread. They trembled.

"Sid." Daphne clung to his shirt, her face against his shoulder. "Sid, I am cursed."

He made no move to comfort her. But he didn't push her away.

"She was pregnant," he said, and he felt her body jolt. Her fingers dug into him, but he didn't flinch.

"With his child?" She flailed at him, struck his chest, but he was motionless, a rock. "Oh God," she said. "Oh God, oh God."

She crept backwards, until she hit the chair. She leaned against it, hands pressed to her middle. Then she doubled over, trying to close the emptiness inside her.

"Tell him," he said and stood. "Tell him everything."

He would leave them to their hell.

He'd nearly remained there with them. But he stumbled from the room, from that realm of infernal desolation, still weeping, but free.

303

Chapter Twenty-One

Ella slept through the night without waking. Isidore kept vigil at the bedside through the long hours. Every now and then he touched his cheek, surprised that the tears still flowed. He wondered if they would ever stop. By dawn they'd slowed, and when the scent of ham reached him from the kitchen, they stopped completely. His mouth watered instead. A hopeful sign.

Mrs. Potts brought the breakfast tray into the bedchamber without so much as a sniff. He had righted himself in her eyes. The other night, she had recognized the emotion in his face for what it was. But he hadn't done right yet. Ella had not agreed to be his wife. Now he was going to have to get another man to convince her. In other circumstances, he thought it would rather have wounded his pride.

Penn heard her out, sitting on a chair by the bed, his slender legs crossed, chin propped on his hand. Isidore tried not to pace, finally installing himself at the foot of the bed so he could see both Ella and the doctor.

"Degeneracy is a theory," said Penn slowly, weighing his words. "It may hold true in some cases that the irritability of the nervous system increases over time. But it's not certain. Sometimes fits cease completely."

"Because the symptoms have become masked," Ella whispered. "And the disease finds other outlets." She was sitting up in bed, toying with the coverlet.

"Such as?" Penn raised his eyebrows.

"Murder," said Ella with an oblique glance at Isidore.

Much to Isidore's chagrin, Penn nodded gravely.

"Some crimes are committed by people in maniacal and delirious states. Those crimes might be considered epileptic manifestations." Penn paused. Isidore looked daggers in his direction, but he was oblivious, musing.

"Moments of inspiration might also be considered epileptic manifestations. The convulsive shock that attends the creative experience." He smiled. "Murder isn't the likeliest outcome. You might just as well compose a symphony."

"But the taint in my blood … " Ella began, and at this, Penn's face darkened.

"There's nothing wrong with your blood. Occasionally gray matter discharges rapidly in your brain. That's what causes the attacks. Bromide of potassium has proven remarkably effective in suppressing fits. Your doctor never gave you bromide as a remedy?"

"He gave me tincture of henbane," said Ella softly. For the first time, Penn looked startled.

"He bled you as well, I imagine," he murmured. Ella didn't deny it, and Penn gave a slight grimace, almost tsking his disapproval.

"Mr. Norton was our family physician," said Ella sharply. "He attended all of us. He still cares for half the county. My father had great faith in him."

"He said you were destined for violence and depravity because your bad blood made an irremediable stain on your character," Isidore broke in. "Penn, tell her the man's an absolute quack."

Penn only said, mildly, "He may be a competent physician in certain areas. However, I must say, Miss Reed, many of his ideas are outdated."

"He *was* born in the eighteenth century," said Ella, and suddenly, a brightness came over her, and she giggled. "The earlier part of that century, I'd guess."

Giggling. She did this even more rarely than she laughed. Isidore stared at her, at the curve of her lips, at the sudden flush that highlighted her cheekbones. More of *this* was definitely in order. Tickling would help.

"But Mr. Penn … " She was somber again. "It is inheritable?" She looked down fiercely at the bed. "If I were to have children, they too … "

Isidore gritted his teeth. Penn was a prince among men, but sometimes a month of Sundays went by between a question and an answer. *Spit it out, damn it.*

"They might be epileptic, yes," said Penn. Another pause. During which Isidore's thoughts were not charitable.

"Then again," Penn said. "They might not be."

"What would you do?" Ella looked at him intently. "If you suffered from this condition, knowing the risks, what would you do?"

This was the moment Isidore had imagined. He longed more than anything to ventriloquize the good doctor. If only he could cast his voice.

Why, I would marry Viscount Blackwood!

Penn took a measured breath. And let it out. He took another breath.

"I would live my life," he said. "I would remember that I am a person and not a pathology." He glanced from Ella to Isidore and back at Ella. "And that every life has risks."

"Phillipa was incandescent with health." Isidore spoke quietly. He wondered—now that the seals were broken—if every time he spoke of Phillipa the tears would come. But he didn't embarrass himself. His eyes were dry. "Her life was a white-hot flame, and it snuffed out, just like that. None of us can predict the future. Even the brilliant Mr. Penn is not an oracle."

"I *can* give you bromide," said Penn. "And recommend you try to put yourself in situations conducive to calmness rather than irritation."

"Live your life," said Isidore, circling round the bed to stand beside Penn's chair. Ella was holding the coverlet tightly now, gripping it with both hands. Her eyes were glowing brighter and brighter. Marriage. Children. He could see the ideas taking hold. *Yes, you can have that. We can take the risk together. We can try.*

"Don't fear what comes next. Live *now*." He smiled slightly. "Or, as the poet once said … " He leaned closer to the bed. "Gather ye rosebuds while ye may." Her eyes opened *wide*. Now his smile was wicked. "Old Time is still a-flying."

Did Penn wonder why Ella had turned red as a beet? He shot her a brief, curious look and raised his eyebrows. It *was* an alarming shade. Luckily, he decided against a professional intervention. Instead, he turned to Isidore. "That's a verse with a familiar ring."

"And this same flower that smiles today," said Isidore, nodding. "Tomorrow will be dying."

"Who wrote it?" asked Penn.

"It's on the tip of my tongue," said Isidore, staring at Ella.

"Herrick," she said in a strangled voice. "Robert Herrick."

"Of course." Isidore slapped his forehead. "Herrick. Wonderful poet. Doesn't he also have one called 'The Vine?'"

Ella's face turned even redder, a feat, which, a moment ago, he would have declared impossible. She looked as though she might pass out. He didn't want Penn to be the one to resuscitate her.

Thirty thousand years later, when the doctor finally left them, he fell onto his knees beside the bed.

"Marry me, Ella," he said. She let him take her hand in his. She looked down at him from the bed. Her face was lovely with that waxing brightness. She was so fully *everything*. He was already reaching up to take her face in his hands when she spoke.

"No," she said.

He stuttered, fell back, the world closing in on him. Still dark. Still *no*. Then he noticed her lips twitching. There was a sparkle in her dark eyes. That mischievous gleam that appeared when he least expected it.

"Won't it be fun," she asked, "to try to convince me?"

With a moan that was anything but sweet, he threw himself onto the bed and kissed her until they were both breathless, and then they were laughing between kisses, which made the breathlessness worse, and they clung to each other, not kissing, not laughing, just trying to breathe, dying like all mortals, but living, really living, while they died.

• • •

The sky was a deep blue, light pouring between clouds that cast moving shadows on the meadow. Ella and Isidore walked on the dirt road to the market town. They visited the graveyard by the little stone church. On the way back to Castle Blackwood, Isidore tugged her hand and led her into the beech wood. She couldn't look down from the canopy of leaves, their green so bright and new and tender, warming the light, exhaling the very scent of sunshine.

"You'll trip," warned Isidore at the moment her foot hit a root and she stumbled.

"I'm not a very good fairy," she said, somewhat crossly. *Clumsy, Ella. Always so clumsy.* Toes could hurt overmuch for what they were worth.

"You're the best fairy," said Isidore, tucking her arm more firmly in his. "Crashing about to let all your sylvan friends know you're coming."

She laughed, leaning into him. For all his solidity and warmth, she still couldn't believe he was there, by her side, that he would be there, day after day, night after night. When her mourning was over, they would be married. She would be the mistress of Castle Blackwood, a building so vast and gloomy she had quailed when they arrived by coach last evening and she first saw its towers rising above her. There were ghosts in the castle. It wasn't the Scotch woman she sensed, but something amorphous. The loneliness, the sadness, of the generations of women who had lived there. Blackwood brides. The spell of sorrow wouldn't be dispelled in an instant. She and Isidore would have to work their own magic, charm by charm, until the moldering house became a home to them. There was much to be done, to the manor and to its lands. They would do it together.

"Do you miss your sylvan friends?" Isidore asked as they walked on, weaving between the smooth trunks of the trees. "The ones you left behind in Exmoor forest?"

He was still teasing, but the intensity of his expression belied his tone.

"I will go with you to Somerset," he said, very low. The wood held a kind of hush that made whispers seem natural. "You don't have anything to fear from Alfred."

It was true. She had nothing to fear. Except perhaps her hatred. She could still feel it, leaping in her blood. She wouldn't call it a taint. She was done with Mr. Norton's vocabulary. But it was something to be wary of.

"If I can't persuade him to make you a gift of your harpsichord and your mother's sheet music and your father's books …" His voice told her that he found this *very* doubtful. She knew he would relish the confrontation. "Then I'll buy them," he said. "I'll buy the whole estate."

The green-gold light played across his bold features. The tenderness she saw in his face made her heart catch.

"Someday," she said, "we'll go there. Not yet." Someday she would walk with him in the forests of Somerset and even along the beaches, so austere and terrible in their beauty. For now, though, she wanted to grow into her new life, her new self. She didn't think it would be possible in Somerset or, for that matter, London. Following the séance, she'd been bombarded by written invitations from spiritualist organizations, society ladies, even a duchess; it seemed that half the city was trying to engage her services. Dozens of mediums were claiming close acquaintanceship, supplying sensational details of mystical Miss Reed's mediumistic biography to gossipmongers and paper-sellers. She'd weathered the worst of the storm indoors, with Mrs. Trombly on Mount Street, refusing to go out or receive visitors, hoping that the fervor would die down and Miss Reed would be forgotten. She wanted to shed "Miss Reed," *had* shed her, with Isidore, with Mrs. Trombly and Lord St. Aubyn, but to step out of that identity with the *ton* more generally, to meet people again as Mrs. Eleanor Blackwood, that would take courage. She would have to figure out what to explain to whom, how to make her way in the open, after so many deceptions, without secrecy or lies.

It would be good to spend time away, good for her, and good for Isidore, too. Mrs. Bennington had left London—"to visit a cousin in Newport for the summer" was what St. Aubyn had heard—but Bennington himself remained. He had tried to speak with Isidore and St. Aubyn both, showed up at each of their houses, in broad daylight and at night, but they'd refused to see him. Ella knew they still considered beating him bloody. On evenings they'd spent together, she, Isidore, and St. Aubyn, in St. Aubyn's library or in Isidore's warm, cluttered study in Pimlico, the two old friends had spoken frankly in front of her, admitting her into their friendship with a naturalness that made her heart swell. Isidore loved her, and that was enough for St. Aubyn. She liked to watch the two men deep in conversation, animated, easy with each other, so different in appearance and bearing, yet so clearly aligned. They didn't only speak of the past, recalling faults and failures, weighing revenge against forgiveness; they spoke of painting and poetry, and of the future, and Ella joined her voice to theirs, debating, sharing, teasing, reveling in the little circle of intimacy they created. Before the end of the month, St. Aubyn was to visit Castle Blackwood with his easel to do some landscape scenes.

"Clouds and trees and maybe a gorse mill," he'd said. "That sort of thing."

"Sounds dull," Isidore had responded. "What would Goya say?"

"Exactly," said St. Aubyn, and both men had laughed.

She heard a rustle and glanced at the tree branches overhead, and in that moment, she tripped again. Isidore let her arm go, and she tumbled onto her knees. Stunned, she looked up at him. He grinned and stubbed his toe into the earth, pitching over, his arms windmilling in an exaggeratedly graceless display. He caught himself, of course, with his hands, when his face was a few inches from the ground, lowering himself soundlessly to the damp ground. The man couldn't even playact clumsy.

"We fell down," he whispered, crawling over to her. He rose to his knees and pressed against her, his mouth moving over hers, hot and slow. Ah, this kiss, with the scent of the woods all around them, newborn shoots, decaying leaves, rich and dark with life and death, this kiss was everything.

"Fall down then," she whispered against his mouth and pushed him, hard, on the chest. He obliged her by tipping over, landing flat on his back in the moss. She sat astride him, skirts bunching, staring down at his broad body pinned beneath her. *Mine,* she thought. And then, as he wiggled suggestively beneath her, situating himself more firmly between her thighs, so that the heat flickered between them: *Ours.* She leaned over to devour him, but he devoured *her,* sucking in her tongue, taking her lips between his teeth, until she gasped and rocked on his lean hips. The wind blew lightly through the trees, and the whole world seemed to stir. She had to straighten, to stretch into it, the shifting light, the cool air growing even more fragrant. His hips were still between her thighs, but he lifted his torso, curled himself up so he could unbutton the bodice of her black day dress, pushing it down from her shoulders, sliding the laces from her linens beneath, baring her. His roughened hands closed on her breasts, making her arch, making her want to roll backwards and pull him on top of her, opening her legs so he could plunge between them, driving her into the ground. But there was something so delicious about the idea of remaining upright, as though she sprouted from him and from the earth beneath him. She slapped his hands away.

"Fall. Down," she said and threw her weight against him, driving *him* into the ground, dragging her breasts up his chest, the buttons on his shirt catching at her nipples. Oh God, she loved the way it stung, the half notes of pain that made the pleasure sing. She reached for his face, but he caught her wrists and pulled her forward, so her breasts hung above his mouth. She shuddered, twisting her spine as his tongue laved her, gravity and his suckling working together to torture her. The pulling ache was beyond her capacity for endurance. She had to press her breasts against his mouth. She jerked her wrists free and worked herself down his body, ripping the buttons from his shirt.

"Ella," he said, lifting his head. She kept prowling down and down. She yanked the shirt from the waistband of his trousers and reached for the buttons of his trousers. She could feel him straining beneath the fabric, his cock hard and thick, humped like a tree root, and she tugged at the buttons, reaching through the flap. She pulled it out, roughly, with her hand. His eyes were glazed, stunned. She moved her hand along the length of him, looking at his face, her lip caught between her teeth. His chin jerked up; his throat tensed. The crown of his head pressed into the leaves. She leaned to kiss the flat of his lower belly, felt the muscles clenching against her lips. His cock stood up from his trousers, and she brushed it with her lips, licking the salty skin, and he bucked with his hips, groaning, and then his hands were fumbling in her skirts, pushing them up her legs. He tore at the ribbons that laced the slit in her undergarment, his fingers finding her slick flesh, sliding into her, pressing deep up inside her, and now she groaned, pulsing around him, and her need condensed, became the hot, wet energy that bursts the green shoot through the seed. A germinating violence. She reared, lifting herself, and he slid his fingers free and took himself in his hand, guiding his cock into her folds as she worked her hips down. She gasped as she sank onto him, lowering until he filled her completely, a hot, hard core around which she shivered, quaked.

"Look at me," he demanded, the cords in his neck standing out as he held himself up to watch her, the muscles bunching in his arms as his hands gripped her, jerking her hips, forcing her to roll her pelvis against him.

"Moan," he said, the musculature in his abdomen gleaming, each tiny muscle standing out, limned with shadow. He thrust upward, and she moaned, the moan issuing from the plucked center of her being, vibrating out of her throat and into the wind that surged again through the trees, stroking against her fevered skin. Her head fell forward, torso curving over him, until her lips were on his, their moans mingling, tongues twined together, and the heat at the base of her belly flowed up through her, filling her everywhere. The fullness expanded until she was *too* full, and as he pushed up from the forest floor, she went rigid over him, fused with him, stock-still and then shuddering, a thousand tendrils tickling through her, flickering into her fingers, her toes, lifting through the top her skull. He surged a final time, the flats of his hands pushing the moss as he lifted his buttocks off the ground, crying aloud as he dropped back, arms closing around her shoulders, pulling her down with him.

She lay against his chest, breathing into his neck, and finally, she unfitted her body from his, sliding off to curl up against him on her side. Her dress was twisted around her waist; her bare upper body absorbed the soft, prickling damp of the earth. She slid her arm across his chest, and he pulled up her leg so it rested on his thighs.

She heard a rustle again, above them, and gazed sleepily into the treetops.

"It's an eagle," she whispered. "Do you think? An eagle flying to the pharaoh to tell him that his love is waiting by the river."

His voice was deep, rumbling with a note of suppressed laughter. "I kept your boots," he said, almost guiltily. A sheepish confession. "I made sure they weren't thrown away."

"The ones with the laces you cut?" She pressed her face into his shoulder to keep her smile from flying off into the clouds. "The ruined boots?"

Dark, whimsical Isidore. *Her* Isidore.

"Wouldn't one suffice?" She laughed, imagining it, Isidore stowing her fouled, stinking leather boots in his study among his carvings and violins. As though they were precious. Fairy slippers. Her smile was too big. Her cheeks hurt.

"I didn't want to take any chances," he whispered. "What if you disappeared one midnight and I needed to find you?"

It was ridiculous, and she laughed again, rolling onto her knees and standing. The light fell all around, and she tipped her head up and lifted her arms, relishing her nakedness in the hidden glade. Then she sighed, buttoning her dress. It would be teatime soon, and Isidore had meetings with tenants and farm specialists, and she had promised Mrs. Trombly that she would write and tell her if the woodbine was flowering and if the graveyard wanted roses and whether the brook beneath the stone bridge was full or dry. She would tell her too how Castle Blackwood struck her and what songs Isidore had played their first night, standing on the terrace under the moon with the violin pressed to his shoulder. She would tell her that she'd heard eerie sounds in the dead of night but that she'd fallen back asleep and dreamed the sweetest dreams.

She looked down at herself. One of the buttons on her dress had popped off. The skirt was stained and wrinkled about the knees. It would take considerable imagination to suppose that she *hadn't* just tumbled Isidore in the moss.

"Oh dear," she said. "Does Castle Blackwood have a secret entrance?" Mrs. Potts had come with them from London to oversee the newly hired staff. There wouldn't be much dignity in scurrying past them all holding together her gaping bodice.

"If you wait in the trees, I'll dig a tunnel." Isidore grinned his crooked grin as he offered his arm. She supposed then that dignity was a small price to pay for delight. They meandered on, their footfalls swallowed by the forgiving ground.

Suddenly a flutter of black and white broke from the green canopy and settled before them. Hopped. A black eye fixed them with a beady stare.

"A magpie," said Ella. She tried to smile. "Not an eagle after all." She glanced at Isidore, disheveled as a satyr, twigs in his hair. "You know the nursery rhyme about magpies."

Silly superstition. Silly to let it bother her. But her heart knocked queerly against her ribs.

"One for sorrow," she whispered.

Isidore lifted an eyebrow, glancing at the magpie, unperturbed. "I do know the nursery rhyme," he said. There was a light in his eye. "But you're not looking hard enough," he added, bending so his cheek pressed hers. He turned her head and pointed.

"There's two," he said, his lips making the words a kiss against her ear, and she saw the other, the two birds together flapping back into the trees. "Two for joy."

A Sneak Peek from Crimson Romance

Once Upon a Scandal
Julie LeMense

London, England
June 16, 1813

One young lady, going astray, will subject her relations to such discredit and distress as the united good conduct of all her brothers and sisters.

—Fordyce's Sermons to Young Women

It was a miserable day by anyone's measure, unseasonably cold, with rain just beginning to fall and thunder rolling across a darkening sky. As Jane burrowed deeper into her black, woolen cloak, a sigh escaping the tight line of her lips, she decided the weather was well-suited to the occasion. That was her father, after all, boxed up in a casket and being lowered into the ground. At least her veil hid the fact that she wasn't crying.

Not that anyone was there to notice. Despite having passed only two days ago, Lord Reginald Fitzsimmons had been dead to the world these past nine months, an outcast in Society, a scandal. The wages of sin and all of that. When you maligned a war hero and tried to compromise the girl he loved in the process, you were not well-liked. And his passing had made him all the more shameful. He'd died in a pool of his own blood outside London's most hardened gaming hell, either murdered for his winnings or set upon for sport. The Bow Street Runners hadn't even mounted an investigation. As if she'd needed a reminder he would not be missed.

Nor would she be, if some unfortunate accident happened to befall her. She was all but invisible now, just like her father, a pariah in the Society that had once prized her. Such a paragon she'd been, no less than the founding patron of The Ladies Auxiliary to Improve Manners and Morals. How amusing to remember a time when friends did not cross to the opposite side of a street as she neared.

She shook her head to clear it. She was not only being maudlin, but also unfair. Not all of them crossed the street. Nor was she entirely alone. Sir Aldus Rempley, Father's only remaining friend, was here at the graveyard too, a small act of kindness, even if he was a good distance away. Beside another grave entirely, as a matter of fact. Far enough away that no one would see him offering his last respects to a rogue.

Just yesterday, he'd sent a note promising to call, along with a bank draft to settle the burial's expenses. She should have refused it, of course, but she could no longer afford her pride. The reading of Father's will had made that abundantly clear. He'd gambled away almost everything in the long, final months of his disgrace.

A cough sounded, recalling her attention to the two men waiting with shovels nearby, the grave diggers, clearly restless. Waiting for the minister to finish, so they too could finish, covering Father's casket with the dirt piled beside it. Returning him to the earth, and ultimately to dust.

She wished the cleric would get on with it. What was the point of praying for absolution when there was none to be had? Besides, the rain was starting to come down in earnest now, pooling in the dirt, sending streams of muddy water into the pit where Father lay. She could feel it seeping into her cloak and through the leather of her serviceable boots. How she envied the enclosed carriage that had just stopped at the edge of the graveyard. The walk home would be interminable. Perhaps the loneliest she'd ever undertaken.

With a dull sense of detachment, she watched as a postilion jumped down, umbrella in hand, to open the carriage door. A man with a multi-tiered greatcoat stepped out, though she couldn't make out his features at this distance. He took the umbrella and turned towards her, coming forward with long strides, moving like a shadow through the descending darkness.

Was he here for someone else? She looked behind her, but even Sir Aldus had departed now. Turning back, she lifted her veil, the better to see the stranger's approach, and her breath caught. How quickly he had come upon her. Benjamin Alden, the Viscount Marworth. It made no sense he was here.

"I am sorry I did not arrive for the start, Miss Fitzsimmons," he said, his voice hushed. "Please accept my sympathies for your loss."

For a moment, she didn't know what to say. He had come here, in the pouring rain, to pay his respects when they were only acquaintances. She ought to be touched—moved even—but instead, she was suspicious. Because Marworth was one of those other people, the kind who'd been born under a perfect alignment of the stars. Parties in Society weren't counted a success until his arrival. When he wore a new style of waistcoat, men raced to their tailors for the same. And he was almost painfully handsome—blond, with the bluest of eyes and classically sculpted, symmetrical features. The man moved seamlessly through life, encased in a nimbus of perfection. Even the minister had stopped his droning, struck no doubt by the appearance of a seemingly celestial being.

"Thank you for coming, Lord Marworth, and for the protection of your umbrella. A moment later, and I would have turned my back on this whole sorry affair and swum my way home."

And what incredibly poor taste she had, to jest at a funeral, to disrespect the dead. She felt so far away now from the woman she'd been just nine months ago. Was that why he'd come? For a moment's amusement, to see a lesser being laid low? To marvel at the depths to which mere mortals could plummet? Didn't he have a party to attend or an innocent to seduce? According to rumor, he excelled at that, too.

But he merely gave her a sad smile and said, "I am sure it is the rain that has kept others away."

"I am sure it is not, but how polite you are to say so."

The minister cleared his throat then, apparently freed from his Marworth-induced bemusement. "May he rest in peace," he said, before ducking away and heading for cover. Determined to move quickly, the gravediggers punched their shovels into the dirt—thick mud now—slopping it into the pit, her father's final resting place, where she doubted there was any peace to be had. Marworth clasped her gently by the elbow, perhaps to move her from the sad scene and towards the carriage.

"You needn't witness this."

But she would not move till it was done. She stood firm until he released his hold. Then she reached down and took a fistful of the mud, and then another, throwing them onto the simple pine casket, which was rapidly vanishing beneath the muck. "My father left me alone to clean up the mess he made of things," she said, hearing the bitterness in her voice. "This is as good a place as any to start."

• • •

Much later, Jane was once more in the home that was no longer to be hers. Gerard, her cousin and Father's heir, had sent a note that his family would be moving into the house on Curzon Street by the month's end. Supposedly, little Violet, his daughter, loved the view from Jane's bedroom window, with its small, enclosed garden filled with roses. So, quite simply, she would have it, along with the bedroom Jane had slept in since she was a child. They would tolerate her as a guest, but not for long. It was the way of things. No matter how unfair.

The house felt so empty now. When they'd been consigned here together, Father had at least been company, despite his misery. She was eternally grateful to Thompson, their longstanding butler, for staying on despite the fact that his wages were overdue. And also to his wife, Bess, who served as cook and housekeeper. Jane was struck again by the irony of it. She was gently bred, of course, but as poor now—if not poorer—than the pair of them. If anything, she should be the one cooking and cleaning. But it was not the way of things, so they would not hear of it.

Really, there was so little she was suited for now. She was more than well-enough educated to be a governess, but who in Society would hire her? And while she could probably give a lecture on Britain's parliamentary system, having learned it at her father's knee, she had no other discernible talents. She painted watercolors insipidly, desecrated any tune, and couldn't stitch a straight line, despite her best efforts. She'd never be hired at a dressmaker's, that much was certain. The one thing she excelled at was being a lady in the strictest sense. But that did not feed you. And how she loathed her self-pity, even though she couldn't seem to suppress it.

All of a sudden, however, a solution presented itself. Thompson entered Father's study and announced a visitor. Sir Aldus Rempley.

Willing away the indigestion the announcement prompted, she took several calming breaths. Because there could only be one reason he was here. She'd turned down his previous proposals of marriage, but she no longer had the luxury of choice. And really, she should be thankful for his offer. He'd come to rescue her from a fate unknown—and likely terrifying.

She ran quickly to her bedroom via the backstairs and rinsed her mouth out with a brush and powder. After a glance in her bedside mirror, where she smoothed her hair and pinched her cheeks, she descended the front stairs with as much dignity as she could muster, to find him waiting, hat in hand, in the drawing room. With a smile at Thompson, indicating they would be fine alone, she sat upon Mother's favorite settee and waited for her future to unfold.

"May we speak privately, Miss Fitzsimmons, or if I may call you so, Jane?"

"Of course," she said, even though her smile was forced. Didn't he realize they were already alone? Their union would be truly tedious if he hadn't wits enough to discern that. It was unkind to think it, but he was grey-haired and paunchy, when she'd once hoped for so much more. This would likely be the man to bestow her first kiss. To introduce her to the intimacies of the marriage bed. A remarkably depressing thought.

"You are looking unwell, my dear. Understandably so, given the shock you have suffered, but you owe it to your looks to take better care."

"Burying one's father in a storm does make appearances difficult to maintain. Wouldn't you agree, Sir Aldus?" Dear Lord, had she really voiced it aloud? When had she become so flippant? Surely, he expected better manners in a would-be wife. Even in the face of a comment bordering on the obnoxious.

He flushed an unbecoming shade, embarrassed perhaps. "One does not wish to speak ill of the dead," he continued, "but your father has left you in a vulnerable position. Alone and without the funds to support yourself."

Really, had it been necessary to remind her? Did an intelligent person ever have to state the obvious? According to Father, Sir Aldus was a man entrusted with state secrets, for goodness' sake. A bit of subtlety should come naturally. But she held her tongue. The one that suddenly wanted to run away with her mouth, contravening their longstanding peace. "May I thank you for your help with his funeral and for your attendance? It was an affirmation of the friendship the two of you shared, and I am sincerely grateful."

"It was but a small thing, the first of many I hope to do for you, Jane," he replied, his gaze disconcerting. "Can you guess why I am here?

"I think so," she said, with what she hoped was becoming modesty, even as her stomach roiled. She could do this. She knew she could. She had no other choice.

"I have a very personal question to ask, an offer to make," he said, smiling intently, looking quite old and oily. Old, she'd reconciled herself to, but oily was another matter. She decided to be bold, though, because the quicker this was settled, the better.

"My answer is yes, Sir Aldus."

She'd expected a smile and a small expression of affection. That dreaded kiss, perhaps. Instead, there was only a look that struck her as sly, lascivious even.

"Do you know what you are saying yes to?"

"I was foolish to refuse your proposals of marriage before. I can see that now," she said, as discomfort settled upon her. "However, I know we will deal well together. Our lives intertwined will be happy ones."

"Jane, you do understand I no longer offer marriage? Your reduced circumstances and reputation don't support that possibility."

Over on the mantel, the clock struck, its clang a dull thud echoing in the room. "I'm sorry," she said. "Could you please repeat yourself? I'm afraid I don't understand." Even though she suspected she did.

"If only you'd not spurned my last proposal, when I was still willing to protect you from all this." His eyes were harder now. "But I can offer carte blanche. A small home of your own, a carriage at your disposal, a lady's maid, a butler, and a modest clothing allowance. I'd prefer a bit more color on your person, however, and necklines that showcase your assets."

She was dizzy with mortification, and for the briefest of moments, she wondered what the members of The Ladies Auxiliary to Improve Manners and Morals would do in this situation. Politely decline? Offer tea and a tract on the unfortunate diseases associated with indiscriminate sexual congress? If only she could be Shakespeare's Ophelia in this moment and get herself to a nunnery, sidestepping the need to reply at all. Although, wasn't a nunnery actually a brothel in the Elizabethan era? She'd read that somewhere. Perhaps a brothel was more appropriate after all.

All the while, he sat watching her, that sly smile on his face, hat in hand, oozing expectancy. He had a bulbous lower lip. If she pulled on it hard enough, could it be swept up over his face and secured at the back of his head with a spike? How tempted she was to try. "Is this how you repay my father's friendship to you, Sir Aldus?" she asked, ice in her veins and voice. "By shaming his daughter?"

"I should think you'd be honored by my willingness to see you set up in a house of your own. I understand you won't long be welcomed in this one."

"You do me no honor. When have I led you to believe such an offer would be welcome? I've been raised as a lady, and despite my reduced circumstances, a lady I will remain."

"Always so proud, Jane. On the contrary, I do you a great honor. You have your mother's beauty, which I greatly admired, but none of her zest. It's unfortunate she died so young. She might have loosened you up a bit."

This was all so hideous it couldn't possibly be happening. And how dare he mention her mother, who'd died when she was only twelve.

"I insist that you leave."

"There are things I can show you, Jane, and pleasures to be had. Better me than a stranger on the street."

"You are a disgusting individual." It would serve the man right if she vomited upon him, for she was distinctly nauseous now. He'd donned his hat and eyed her up and down in the most outrageously insulting fashion.

"I will give you a week to understand just how desperate your situation has become, and then I will return. I sincerely hope we can come to the point that very day, so to speak, because it's better for you to know how it will go on between us, don't you think?"

"Nothing will go on between us," she seethed. "Of that, you may rest assured." But dear God, he was right. Her situation was far worse than she'd allowed herself to believe. And he knew it. He'd discarded all pretenses of gentlemanly behavior.

"If you choose the streets over me, Jane, your fine manners and lofty pretensions will hardly protect you." He turned to the door but stopped before opening it, looking back at her. "Then again, it might be exciting to see you brought low and not quite so proud."

And with that, he departed, as her horrified gasp echoed in the room.

• • •

After the frightening encounter with Rempley, Jane returned to the library, her feet unsteady. Everything in the room was several degrees off center, as if distorted in a poorly crafted looking glass. Or was she the one off center? She'd always been so proud of her place in Society, confident her breeding would protect her. She'd just learned otherwise. None of her etiquette books would offer a way out of this fix.

She sat behind Father's desk, withdrawing a piece of parchment and a quill to write out a list of her options. She was very fond of lists, which were so orderly and concise, after all. Once she'd mapped everything out, things would seem far less bleak.

Option One: Submit to Sir Aldus.

Which she refused to do. Better to take up holy orders, even though she wasn't much in charity with the Lord right now. And given her behavior this morning, He'd probably spear her with a lightning bolt if she dared to try.

Option Two: Throw myself upon the mercy of my few remaining friends.

When the scope of Father's misdeeds had become public, Alec and Annabelle, the Earl and Countess of Dorset, had invited her to stay at Arbury Hall in Nuneaton, away from the palpable disaffection that followed her in the City. But, any day now, Annabelle would give birth to their first child. And besides, one could only tolerate so much marital bliss. When she was feeling less than charitable, their love bordered on the nauseating.

There was also Sophia Middleton, the Countess of Marchmain. An eccentric with a spotted reputation of her own, Lady Marchmain was planning a European tour and had claimed she'd be lonely without Jane's accompaniment. A bold lie, of course, though an appreciated one. But the countess was in Nuneaton, as well. Annabelle was her niece, and while it was difficult to imagine her bearing witness to the birth, Lady Marchmain would certainly be the first to toast it with a glass of brandy. Not that she would stop at one.

Option Three:

She chewed on her lower lip, because that small bite of pain sometimes sparked inspiration. So did drumming her fingertips on the surface of the desk. She also stroked the quill against her cheek and moved the inkwell precisely two inches to the left, because it looked better there.

Unfortunately, Option Three was not making itself readily apparent. Perhaps answers lay elsewhere? Her eyes swept the room, falling to the sideboard not far from the fireplace. Upon it sat the last bottle of Father's prized French cognac, a short glass beside it.

She promptly looked away. She'd never indulged in spirits, and now was no time to start. The very idea!

Then again, Father had always claimed it made a bad day brighter. She'd need a vat of the stuff to improve this one. Setting aside her list, she walked over and uncorked the bottle, pouring a small measure and lifting it to her mouth. Its wafting smell was enough to make her eyes sting. Best to get it down all at once then. Offering a silent apology to *A Lady of Distinction's Guide*—which glowered from the bookshelves in condemnation—she closed her eyes and swallowed. The cognac burned, nearly curdling the contents of her stomach, but she'd not let weakness defeat her. She was far too determined.

Luckily, the second glass descended more easily.

And the third? Well, it was very nearly bliss. No wonder Father had liked it so much. Ladies of Distinction did not know what they were missing!

She'd read that the excessive consumption of spirits led to very bad things … bilious features and fevers, degenerative illness, and atrophied body parts. But none of that seemed consequential at the moment. She was so glad she hadn't saved the cognac for her cousin, Gerard. He was a bit of a bastard and hardly deserved it.

Dear Lord, just a few small tipples and she was swearing like a docker. Not that anyone could hear her. And wasn't that a marvelous thing to realize? She could think all sorts of shocking, scandalous thoughts. She just couldn't say them aloud. The rule to which she'd always adhered—be ladylike in thoughts as well as deeds—had just been shattered by the lovely haze of her insobriety.

She wished she'd discovered cognac sooner. She was close to crying because she hadn't. Why must men keep all the best things for themselves? Like strong spirits, and boxing clubs where one could purge one's frustrations, and ancestral homes. God save the King and all that, but Britain's inheritance laws were horribly unfair. And very possibly, they encouraged insanity. After all, old King George had been given any number of titles, estates, and countries upon his birth, and he babbled incessantly now, talking to dead people. Or so Father had said.

She wished she could talk to dead people. She'd ask Father why he'd mucked up so many things.

Why she was being forced to leave their home.

If little Violet, too, would sit in the window seat of Jane's bedroom, dreaming of a handsome husband and the blessings of children ...

This would not do, this depressing turn in her thoughts. Perhaps another glass—just a tiny one—would return her to the heady state of her initial euphoria. She poured a draught, although the mouth of her glass had shrunk in size, causing some of the cognac to slosh over its sides. Such a loss! But she swallowed its contents nonetheless.

Really, it was marvelous stuff. Perhaps Thompson and Bess would like some? She reached for the bell pull, but they'd be too shocked by her drunkenness to join in. With whom should she share the pleasures of this sin, now that she'd abandoned all propriety? Because one ought to be generous. She'd not forget that dictate.

Someone known for enjoying sin. Someone who'd already proven he had little else worth doing today. Someone well acquainted with the intimacies the wretched Sir Aldus had hinted at.

It took her a moment to find a piece of stationery and yet another to still her hand enough to write the thing. Even if her usually impeccable penmanship had deserted her, she was quite happy with the note when she was done and rang for Thompson. She had an invitation that needed delivering this very instant.

In the mood for more Crimson Romance?
Check out *Honor Among Thieves by Elizabeth Boyce* at
CrimsonRomance.com.

Printed in the United States
By Bookmasters